MW00528242

Sign up for our newsletter to hear
about new and upcoming releases.

www.ylva-publishing.com

Other Books by Lee Winter

LEE WINTER

Hotel
Queens

Dedication

This one's for my mum. She spent many years in the Middle East for work, with most of her time spent in Saudi Arabia in particular. I heard a lot of stories about the warm, welcoming people and far-flung places that she loved so much. I think she'd have greatly enjoyed my elusive businessman Nedal getting such an important role in this book. In fact, Nedal and his sister, Mariam, remind me of several of her close Saudi friends.

Thanks for the inspiration, Mum.

Acknowledgments

Hotel Queens is a book in two parts. I started it in early 2018 but had to put it to one side when the complex plot did my tired head in and I needed a break. At the time I wasn't sure I'd return to it, and I'm so glad I did. I've adored falling back in love with Amelia and Kai.

The most interesting thing I discovered in researching my book was how much incredible history there is in New York's buildings. Quite a few early New York hotels were built by Jewish family businesses.

Before long, I realized that even though the Duxton and Stein hotels didn't go back as far as New York's earliest days, it would be a nice nod to history to make at least one of the rival hotel families Jewish. Eventually I opted for both since the two warring patriarchs had such similar backgrounds.

That did mean I had to learn all things about the New York Jewish experience, and that's where I had some wonderful help. Thanks greatly to novelist Ann Aptaker for her insights into food and cultural experiences— as well as supplying a Hebrew curse word or two—back in 2018 when I started research.

Thanks also to beta readers Sandy, who added in the flavor of religious teachings and holidays, too, and to Kristen for her hotel expertise and excavation of plot holes.

A huge and grateful nod goes to my girlfriend for her amusing, brutally blunt feedback that at times probably entertained my Facebook readers more than me whenever I posted snippets.

Astrid, my Ylva publisher, was incredible and stepped up to beta read the book at the last gasp. Fantastic support.

Thanks, finally, to my wonderful editors who make my words look far better than I deserve and my readers who make it all worthwhile. You keep me inspired.

Chapter 1

Playing with Fire

Kai Fisher drew in a deep gulp of coffee to shed another layer of *too damned early.*

She headed toward the beautiful Grand Millennium Hotel, a gracefully aging building in the heart of Manhattan that had existed for longer than all the surrounding monstrosities of towering glass put together.

As tired as Kai was, the sight of the building never failed to nudge her spirits higher, reminding her of how her life might have turned out if she hadn't stepped through its regal doors.

Today, though, like every other day before dawn, her destination was not the hotel itself but its elite ground-floor gym, which drew to it like moths those with excess wealth, influence, and power.

"Hey, Vince," Kai said, trying to sound awake as she reached the main doors.

"Mornin', Ms. Fisher." The doorman sprang to attention.

"Lovely weather," she suggested, wondering if she could produce it by sheer force of will.

They both glanced up at the gloomy sky, barely holding back rain. Dawn light was slowly creeping across the horizon.

Vince's snort was soft and skeptical.

She chuckled in agreement.

"Do you know what day it is, Ms. Fisher?" Vince asked.

Kai frowned. "Um...Friday?"

"Anniversary of you joining Grand Millennium. Fifteen years today."

"What…" *No.* She did her math. *Actually, yes.* "How do you know that off the top of your head?"

"Oh, I recall the day real well. Your first day on the job, you took one look at me and asked Mr. Stein, completely straight-faced, mind, whether freezing the door staff was company policy. And before the boss could answer, you said he should either give me a thicker coat with my uniform or a raise to buy one."

"How bold of me. Did you get your new coat?"

Vince smiled. "Well, Ms. Fisher, I ended up getting a new coat *and* a raise. And I remember that day well because when I got home, Aliyah told me she was pregnant."

"That's—"

A blur of fluorescent green shot past her. Kai slammed herself into the side of the building to avoid being hit. The bicycle courier didn't even slow.

Him!

It was the same jackass who'd been terrorizing pedestrians along West 35th St. for months. He'd caused an elderly news vendor to fall and fracture a hip.

"Watch it, asshole!" she shouted, peeling herself off the glass.

The cyclist flipped her the bird over his shoulder and laughed.

"You okay, Ms. Fisher?" Vince asked.

Kai took stock of herself. "Son of a bitch!" Coffee coated her wrist and had drenched her watch. Her *designer* watch, which had cracked upon impact with the wall.

A beat later, she registered the scalding burn. *Goddamnit!* She hurled her coffee cup away. Adrenalin spiked her throw, and the cup slammed into the back of the cyclist, who'd just braked hard for a wayward pedestrian. Brown liquid spattered up his ass, legs, and bicycle.

Kai blinked.

"Ouch." Vince murmured, sounding impressed.

The cyclist shrieked, did a little wobble, then hit the ground in a tangle of man and machine that Kai probably shouldn't have found quite so satisfying.

She strode over to assess the situation. The man scrambled to his feet, pulling his bicycle up with him. "You fucked up my bike!"

"Your *bike*?" Kai's burnt arm throbbed, her watch looked ruined, and tales of all the pedestrians this asshole had half-flattened filled her head. "You're worried about your damned *bike*?"

He stared at her, finally registering her fury.

"You could have killed me, the speed you were going!"

"Shoulda got out of the way then. *Shit.* I think the handlebars are bent."

"You shouldn't have *been* on the sidewalk in the first place. What the hell's wrong with you?"

"Whatever." His gaze raked his machine. "Thanks for screwing up my bike."

"*My bike, my bike!*" she mocked as rage flooded her. Kai snatched the clip-on bell from his handlebars and shoved it under his nose, where she dinged it obnoxiously three times.

He gaped at her stupidly, then tried to grab it.

Kai snatched her hand away and hurled the bell out into the road.

A second later, a delivery truck rumbled by and crunched it flat with a sad ding.

"The fuck, lady? I needed that!"

"All evidence to the contrary. If you'd used it, we wouldn't be here."

He straightened to full height. "You itchin' to get hurt for real?"

She lifted an eyebrow. The man was lean, with a hipster neck beard, earrings, and mean brown eyes. "Oh, for God's... Threats of violence? Must we?" Kai huffed out an indignant breath. "Don't bother. I have a black belt."

"So do I." He offered an ugly smile.

Oh shit. Kai wondered if her temper had finally written some checks she couldn't cash.

Plan B. She glanced at the logo on his shirt, then whipped out her phone and snapped a photo of him.

"The hell you do that for?"

"I will be notifying your company that mine..." Kai poked a thumb over her shoulder at the doors behind her, "...will no longer be using Couriers Direct USA for any deliveries, and that you are the reason."

He glanced to where she'd gestured and laughed. "You think anyone'll give a shit that some gym doesn't want to use us?"

Kai leaned in close and said silkily, "Look. Higher."

3

His gaze shifted to the sign above the gym. In towering letters, it read *Grand Millennium Hotel*.

"There are sixty-seven Grand Millenniums across the US," Kai said. "None of which will ever use your company again. Well, unless you apologize and agree to stay off the sidewalk in the future."

"You expect me to believe *you* have the power to blacklist a company?" He took in her dark-brown, shoulder-length hair and gym outfit of black tights, ethically sourced sneakers, and a padded jacket over her tank top. "Yeah, right. What are you really? Receptionist? Housekeeping? Some entitled Karen who goes around saying 'I'll call the manager?'"

Kai regarded him. "Test me. I dare you."

His eyes hardened.

From somewhere behind them came a guffaw. "She doesn't have to *call the manager* for anything, son," Vince called to him. "She *is* the manager."

The courier's eyes widened. Then came the flash of panic. "Uh…"

Finally. Kai gave him a withering look, turned on her heel, and strode away.

"No, look," he called after her, voice tight. "Wait up, lady, there's no need to get hysterical. If you could just calm down, we can talk about this and…"

Calm down? Hysterical? Oh, she would crush him.

"Wait!" His voice was now an annoying, high-pitched whine.

Kai left him to his meltdown. She had better things to do. As she was about to pass Vince, she murmured, "You know I'm not actually the manager, right?"

"Close enough," he replied with a grin. "Hey, Ms. Fisher? You really got a black belt?"

"Sure." She smirked. "Lovely Donna Karan number. Goes with my heels."

Amelia Duxton studied the morally diseased employee seated in her visitor's chair, her lip curling in distaste.

She snapped her gray jacket sleeve back to perfection and waited for Douglas to cease his witless blather, his streams of denial falling like the rain sleeting down her London office window.

She glanced at her Yellowspotted Scorpionfish in its bowl on the edge of her glass desk. Privately, Amelia thought it was pretty cute for a voracious predator, with its sweet, round face, orange-and-yellow spotted skin, and huge eyes. Publicly, she enjoyed stressing its more lethal attributes to visitors. It sent a certain message.

Quinn, her second-in-command, had been trying to convince her to name it for a year. That always seemed a bit ridiculous. The fish wouldn't know any different. What was the point?

Amelia straightened the name plate on her desk with one poke of her finger. It read *Amelia Duxton, Vice President — Hotel Duxton International: Europe.*

One would think such a title would prevent her having to listen to this.

Apparently not.

She regarded the man opposite. Chaos in devolved, fleshy form. Amelia hated chaos about as much as she loathed imbeciles who thought they could put one past her.

Douglas paused for a breath, his face flushed despite Amelia's precise room temperature of 66F. Too cold for some, she supposed. She ran comfortably on ice—a fact her detractors loved to point out.

"So, obviously," the man declared with a flourish of hands, "it couldn't be me."

Uh-huh. Amelia was only hearing Douglas out in the first place because of who his father was. And because Quinn said people were less likely to create legal problems when you gave them a fair hearing before pointing out they were a waste of skin and oxygen.

She peered at Douglas so hard that, for a moment, he looked as if he'd slither right out of his rumpled suit in an anxious puddle of sweat. Guilt choked his expression.

"Oh, very convincing," she drawled.

Looking startled, Douglas launched into round three. "Look, I know the suppliers screwed up. Don't worry, I'll fix it. I'll find us new suppliers."

Seriously? He was delusional if he thought she believed a word of this. "You're fired."

There now. Order restored. Universe realigned.

As much as Amelia hated chaos, she loved discovering an order within things that seemed disordered. She had a keen eye for puzzle solving. That's what had led her to this moment, leaning back in her tall, Herman Miller graphite chair, terminating her Head of Purchasing.

Several months ago, she'd noticed a pattern in the invoices sent to her Accounts Department from technology suppliers. Suddenly the details on new computers and accessories her company had bought were all far too short, barely even stating what the product was. What did it mean? Multiple suppliers had all suddenly decided brevity was the new black?

Most people would have shrugged and moved on. Not Amelia. She'd read the fine print on all one hundred eighty-two IT invoices, all ordered by Douglas over the past four months.

Silence fell. And fell some more. It yawned out between them, but Amelia had no interest in obliging Douglas by easing his discomfort.

"How did you know?" he asked finally.

"An asterisk." She shuffled her papers. "Every computer part you ordered contained an asterisk. You were supposed to be buying *new* computers for our European concierge desks. Instead you bought refurbished goods and told suppliers to hide that within the terms. Our suppliers have confirmed to me that you instructed them to do this. You pocketed the difference in cost."

"A fucking asterisk." The shock was all over his face.

"Attention to detail," she corrected. "And no need for profanities. Pack your things." She swiveled her chair to face the window, unwilling to endure the sight of a man who had offended her so deeply.

It wasn't the lying, although that had been predictable. Nor even the embezzlement. She'd make sure she wrung him out until she got every penny back. No, it was that he knew who he was dealing with, better than most, and yet he assumed she wouldn't figure out his criminal endeavors.

Why did people do that? Underestimate her? So many people assumed she'd just inherited her job title. Well, she supposed that was somewhat true, even though she had a CV worthy of her position, too.

Amelia heard no movement. "Still here?" she asked the window in front of her. The view of London's streets far, far below was always absorbing, even through the shimmer of rain. The city was a geometric puzzle to solve. Sudoku in human form. Which way would the little dots flow to achieve the most efficient route around each other? Mathematics in nature. Pure wonder.

Douglas's chair creaked.

Amelia calculated the odds of the man's next move. More denials? No, she'd already laid out the proof.

Was he working out a face-saving retreat? Possibly.

Blaming it on an underling, perhaps? Hmm.

"My secretary—" he began.

Bingo. "—is innocent," Amelia said. "I investigated her first. And it's not Betty who has the six-figure gambling problem."

Amelia spun her chair back to face the man who had just thrown her schedule out by half an hour. *Unacceptable.*

"Look at you, Douglas, thirty-three years old and *this* is all you're good for? Embezzlement? Your father is going to be so disappointed. You only got this job because he begged me."

Douglas shot her a sour look. "You don't have to tell Dad," he mumbled, with little conviction.

"I think he'll notice when you miss Hanukkah for the next seven to ten years."

He paled. "You'd call the cops on me? I'm your *cousin!*"

"Yes, you are. Regrettably." She toyed with a silver pen on her desk, a gift from Hotel Duxton's Chief Financial Officer, Joe Duxton. He was Amelia's favorite uncle—although that was setting the bar low given the choices on offer—and he was also Douglas's father.

She gave a weary huff. "You embezzled from the family business. By my estimates, you stole £127,553 but had planned to take much more." For conciseness, Amelia left out the pence, although it made her itch not to be strictly accurate.

"But that's chicken feed to you! Come on, we can sort something out. Something that won't be embarrassing all round. Think of the family name even if you don't give a shit about me."

"I *am* thinking of the family name. That's the point. Security will escort you out." She punched a button on her desk to summon them. "They'll detain you downstairs until the Fraud Squad arrives. And don't mention our family to me again. You're a disgrace to the Duxtons."

"You little cunt." Douglas's soft white hands formed fists.

Amelia narrowed her eyes. "Eloquent as ever."

"Stuck-up bitch, aren't you? Always lording it over us. About as approachable as a dog's snout in winter. No wonder you've been exiled here."

"At least I'm not going to prison." Her words were soft and goading, delivered with a mocking smile. She refused to show how close he'd come to hitting a nerve.

Fear flashed into his eyes, but apparently he wasn't done yet.

"You act like you're better than everyone else but you're just bitter. Because your brother got America instead of you, and you were sent packing." Douglas's eyes glittered in triumph.

She arched an eyebrow. "That was years ago. I'm content running the European division." Amelia folded her arms. "And the main thing is that our company's prospering. I'm sure Oliver has everything under control at Duxton USA." Like hell she'd admit anything else.

Douglas's laugh was explosive. "You think Oliver has things under *control?* Haven't you seen the headlines today? Very entertaining."

Worry snaked through her. What the hell had her little brother gotten himself into now? She hoped it was just another of his ridiculous publicity stunts gone wrong, nothing worse.

"I have no time for what passes as 'news,' unless it's in the financial pages," Amelia said. "I have thirty-four hotels to oversee. All I care about right now is the fact that you're making me late for my Mayfair Palace final negotiations. If we don't get this deal signed because of you, I'll point that out to your father, too."

Douglas's mouth instantly clanged shut, proving he wasn't completely stupid. Everyone at Hotel Duxton knew how huge Mayfair Palace was to them. Uncle Joe had been especially anxious for her to finalize the blue-chip hotel deal that had been so long in the making.

His constant phone calls about it were a little insulting. When had she messed up even once? Amelia's operations were run efficiently, with carefully managed risk and little room for budgetary fat. And there were none of the showy flights of fancy that her brother indulged in back home. To be fair, Oliver's manic marketing campaigns seemed to play well in North America. No accounting for taste.

Amelia's cell phone rang, a distinctive ring tone that could only belong to one person.

Douglas's eyebrows flew up, but she wasn't about to explain to him Taylor Swift's "Shake It Off"...or anything else.

"Darling," she answered warmly, then gave Douglas a slow, taunting smile as she replied, "No, nothing important." Amelia spun her chair back around to face the window and listened to her nine-year-old cousin, Imogen, in full flight. After a minute, she got a word in.

"No, I don't *think* owls have knees, but that's an excellent question. We should research it together." Amelia did her math from Sydney to London time, then paused. "Why are you calling me at midnight?"

Amelia listened patiently as a stream of exuberance filled her ears. "Well, I understand that a new Taylor Swift album is 'too exciting to possibly sleep after hearing,' but you should at least try. Make a list of your questions and we'll go through it soon."

There was an almost audible pout down the line before Imogen asked, "What sort of soon? One that isn't really?"

"It's soon—like a promise from *me*."

"That's soon." Imogen sounded cheerful now. "Okay."

"Night, darling." Amelia swiveled her chair back to face Douglas as she ended the call.

He was wearing a bemused expression. "Either you have weird taste in girlfriends, or my niece is up to her usual nonsense. Why not tell the brat to Google shit like everyone else?"

"A thirst for knowledge is never a bad thing." Amelia eyed him coolly. "A shame *you* never had a similar inclination for self-growth, or we might not be sitting here right now."

His expression darkened, but before he could answer, security arrived in a thunder of boots.

Amelia nodded toward Douglas. Meaty hands clapped her cousin's elbow and shoulder, assisting him to the door.

The sight of the back of his bespoke suit—no doubt paid for with his illicit gains—grated on her. She scowled until he left, then slumped a little.

Douglas had been right about one thing. This would be damned embarrassing for the company.

Amelia exhaled and pressed a button on her desk phone. "Quinn? A moment."

Her second-in-command, a dark-skinned, charming East Londoner, flung herself into the room with her usual boyish exuberance. At thirty-six, Quinn Hartman was almost ten years younger than Amelia, but some days it felt like twenty. Quinn was all pent-up energy contained in a sharp, chic, quixotic plum suit.

Amelia had always appreciated fierce, independent women. Spare her the simpering waifs with weak handshakes and insincere laughs, hiding their clever minds from the world. Women should be upfront and honest about who they were.

Of course, that bold approach had not gone down well in her own family, had it? Still, Amelia could no more change her own bluntness than Quinn could present as a dowdy pushover.

"Bad?" Quinn asked, folding her arms, gaze flicking to the now vacated visitor's seat.

"No. Just tedious."

Quinn nodded.

"I need to call Joe." Amelia sighed. "I'll have to tell my dear uncle what his offspring's been up to at work these past four months. Not only hasn't Douglas kept his job, but this time he's off to prison."

"Crap." Quinn dropped into the visitor's chair. "Why would he do that?"

"Douglas has a gambling habit big enough to have blown through his trust fund. My greater concern is why he chose to harm the family."

"I think he's still butt-hurt about Simon getting that job in Sydney that he always wanted. Must be frustrating as hell when your younger, stupider brother gets the job you always thought you'd be better at. Or, in your case, *would* be far, far better at." Quinn looked pointedly at Amelia.

Not this again. "Don't you have work to do?" Amelia muttered, shooting her an evil look.

Quinn smirked, apparently unintimidated.

"Well?" Amelia tapped her desk. "Could we not be lounging around speculating about my dysfunctional family? I need to talk to Joe before Douglas spins his firing as some innocent misunderstanding."

Quinn hesitated. "Sooo, about your uncle... Joe's called already."

"How could he know so soon? Douglas will still be sitting under guard downstairs."

"It's Oliver he called about. And check your email. It's...well, it's really bad this time."

"How bad? Worse than that hot-air balloon stunt?" Amelia pulled her laptop closer. "What could my brother possibly have done now?"

Quinn winced. "A better question is, what hasn't he done?"

Chapter 2

The Thrill of the Chase

KAI'S FEET FLEW ALONG THE treadmill, fueled by the adrenalin of her encounter with the courier. She was so damned close today; that personal best that had been eluding her for months was hers for the taking.

Heat was swallowing her whole, flaring outward from inside her muscles, encasing her thighs like tendrils of fire. She loved this: the delicious, heady burn, the power, the feeling of victory.

Her eyes darted to the numbers flying on her machine. It'd be good to have a win—something she needed badly after the past week.

Kai's boss, Benjamin Stein, CEO of Grand Millennium Hotels, had asked her to acquire an overseas hotel for him.

Mayfair Palace in London was nearing completion and would soon be coming on the market. Mr. Stein had decided this would be the one: A hotel so beyond compare that it would be worth his company dipping a toe in the foreign market for the first time.

The hotel dripped with opulence and elegance, boasting everything from pillow menus and a pool suspended over the atrium, to upside-down trees dangling artfully in the foyer. Architects, travel writers, and designers swooned over it.

Kai was more curious about how it all worked than anything else. What was the deal with the upside-down trees? Why didn't the dirt fall out?

Maybe she should get her assistant to see if inverted trees would be doable in Kai's executive office. It might be worth it just for the look on everyone's faces. Unsettle them. That was always a good business tactic.

"Please have a seat," she'd say earnestly. "Mind your heads on the ficus, gentlemen. It's just been watered."

She snorted, before remembering the rest of that meeting with Mr. Stein. Her seventy-four-year-old boss had given her a look of such faith that any thought of not pulling off the Mayfair Palace deal made her slightly nauseous.

Worse had been the revelation that Mr. Stein had his pride on the line.

"I need this one, Kaida." He'd drawn out her full name in a plea, so it sounded like *Kayyy-da*. Mr. Stein had then leaned over his antique desk and puffed out his ruddy cheeks until he looked like a ventriloquist's dummy. "Last month when I was in London, I met Mayfair Palace's developer to express our interest in buying it. And this Nedal al-Hamadani just smirked at me."

He'd growled. "*Smirked.* Like Grand Millennium was chicken feed to him! How dare he? Sixty-seven luxury hotels all over the US and the seller doesn't see us as a credible buyer!"

His eyes had become slits. "You *know* why. More lies from the *mamzerim*!" He wagged a pudgy finger at her. "Mark my words."

Whipping out the Hebrew for "bastards" meant he was truly furious at the snub. Of course, every time a deal went sour, her already slightly paranoid boss was convinced that his arch-rival of the past fifty years, Hotel Duxton International, had torpedoed it somehow.

This time, though, his suspicions might actually be well founded. Hotel Duxton would have to be after Mayfair Palace, too. It was exactly the sort of monument to decadence loved by the pretentious hotelier family.

Mr. Stein had finished his rant with a rueful smile. "I know I'm not the best with the making nice and the *talk, talk, talk*. That's why I hired you, Kaida, my dear. You are The Closer for a reason. Your networking and charm are unmatched, and you've got a golden touch with people. Well, the people who don't want you twitching in a gutter." He chuckled.

Hilarious. It'd be nicer if he'd been kidding.

"Nail this for me so I can laugh in the Duxtons' smug faces. If you do, I'll give you an end-of-year bonus that'll make last year's look like a stale bagel."

Well, hell. No pressure. Besides, weren't all bagels stale? Kai had never developed a taste for them despite being a New Yorker.

13

She applied a new burst of speed at the reminder of what she was up against. Her muscles protested, but she pushed harder. Pain meant nothing compared to winning.

Kai hissed in a breath as she recalled the rest of her week. Having renowned negotiation skills were of no use when someone refused to take your calls. Why would this Mayfair Palace seller duck her? Didn't he want the best deal for his project? Competition only drove up prices.

She'd scoured social media, hoping to find an event Nedal al-Hamadani might be attending that she could corner him at, even if she had to fly to London, only to discover he wasn't online. *Anywhere.*

Kai had pulled apart the internet like a possessed woman, hunting for photos of him, LinkedIn accounts, business interviews, places he socialized, people he partied with. She'd scored big fat goose eggs all around.

How unusual. Oh, plenty was written about the elusive businessman, but not one single article had been written with his input. And no photos existed of him at all.

When she'd finally made phone contact with Hamadani's officious personal assistant, he'd told her his boss wasn't interested and would be leaving England shortly anyway, so she should "give up" her efforts to see him.

She should just *give up*? Did the dismissive little toadie not realize her reputation? Kai wasn't called The Closer because she sold zippers.

The assistant's information was disturbing. If Hamadani was readying to leave the country, it meant he already had a buyer lined up for Mayfair Palace. *Three guesses as to who.*

Mr. Stein would not be happy.

It *was* puzzling, though. Surely Hotel Duxton's offer couldn't be so generous as to completely shut out any rival bids?

Which negotiator could have possibly pulled off that coup? Duxton's in-house lawyers had all the ingenuity and charisma of dung beetles, while Oliver Duxton, who was known to occasionally attempt a deal himself, made "useless" at least look pretty.

Kai slid that question—*Duxton's Mayfair Palace negotiator*—to the top of her mental list for her assistant to research, just ahead of figuring out inverted trees. With a smile, she pictured Milly's pained expression at the request.

Seriously, the woman was far too tightly wound. Kai's eternally harried assistant needed more fun in her life. Maybe the frizzy-haired redhead, with her pale skin and huge green eyes, forever swamped in cream cardigans and sensible dresses, needed a hot new lover to put a spring in her step. Or any lover, come to think of it.

Hmm. Did Milly even have a life outside work? She'd never mentioned it. Well now, that didn't sound terribly well-rounded, did it? Even Kai found time to keep her engine purring fairly regularly.

She flicked a glance to the treadmill's screen. Sixty seconds left. Kai distracted herself from her shaky legs by trying to picture who Milly Valentine's type was.

Complete blank.

Thirty seconds. Kai went all out. Her mind shifted back to her impending failure to deliver Mr. Stein's dream hotel. Kai's ability to ferret out information, figure out what mattered to people, and charm the socks off them meant she'd rarely lost a business deal in a face-to-face meeting. Except it was impossible to charm thin air.

Her treadmill beeped. Through sweat-filled eyes, she made out the red flashing numbers. *Damn it.* She'd missed her target by two seconds.

Kai hit Recovery mode and cooled her pace, eventually slowing to a walk.

Perspiration gleamed on her arms, and she grabbed the bottom of her tank top and wiped her face with it.

An athletic, blonde, ponytailed woman powering along on the spin bike opposite shot her a long, appreciative look.

Well, well. That's flattering. Still attracting the college girls?

Kai glanced around. It was still early, so they were alone except for an intense-looking muscle man on the far side of the room, lost in his own world, doing bicep curls in front of a mirror.

Gaze fixed back on the woman, Kai's imagination meandered to entirely pleasant places and possibilities. Oh yes. Speaking of keeping her engine purring...

She scolded herself. *Not today.* She had two hotel deals to assess and a missing Mayfair Palace seller to track down. There was no time for passing distractions, even if they looked like they'd tumbled straight out of a Nike ad.

Her machine beeped again and stopped. Kai stepped off the treadmill and languidly stretched. Okay, so it was closer to preening than stretching, but her audience seemed to enjoy Kai's gleaming biceps and clinging tank top.

Kai's gaze flitted to the large TV screen on the wall, which had been running the financial news. A breaking news headline began to scroll the crawl feed. She froze.

Oh. No way. No fucking way.

She stalked across the room. Ponytail's smile widened as she neared, dipping when Kai strode straight past.

Finding the remote control, she cranked up the volume.

Oliver Duxton, Vice President of US Operations for Hotel Duxton, has been arrested.

Just after three in the morning today, six police cars followed the hotel boss in his Porsche convertible across Manhattan in a slow-moving police chase. Duxton was reportedly driving erratically, side-swiping parked vehicles and throwing cans of beer at passing cars, buses, and pedestrians.

Police cornered Duxton, arresting him for driving under the influence, leaving the scene of an accident, reckless endangerment of another person, and multiple traffic offenses.

His companion, porn star Scarlet Lay-Dee, was released without charge. Police seized bags containing a suspicious white substance from the car. Further charges are expected.

Oliver Duxton is best known for his wild parties, famous girlfriends, and publicity stunts for the American arm of the international hotel chain he manages.

Bystanders' phone footage showed Duxton face-down on the road as he was cuffed, shouting at police that he'd have their badges.

Insulting arresting officers? They loved that.

Kai stared at the mug shot that flashed up on screen. Well, well. So Duxton's Chosen One was going down? Couldn't happen to a nicer asshole.

Reaching into the discreet pocket at the back of her leggings, Kai withdrew her cell phone and fired off a quick text to alert her boss, keeping one eye on the TV.

A reporter had moved on to backgrounding the Duxton hotel business and how Oliver was supposed to be inheriting the entire kingdom when his CEO father retired next month. Shareholders would be stampeding away when markets opened.

Oh, to be a fly on the wall when conservative Conrad caught up with his cokehead son today. The man had been training his wayward offspring since Oliver was fifteen. That was a lot of time and investment to just throw away, but surely Conrad would have to consider it now? Although, who could replace Oliver? The rest of his family were too old, too useless, too inexperienced, or... *Wait.*

Kai stabbed her phone, eyes sharp on the TV.

"Milly?" She waited a beat for her assistant to wake up a little before plowing on. "Yes, I know the time. Stop yawning and pay attention." Scrabbling-for-a-pen noises filled her ear. "Okay, I want you to pull together a file on Amelia Duxton, Oliver's sister. She's based in London, I think."

Kai tapped her lip and tried to picture the woman. Being over in Europe, Amelia had been of no strategic interest, so Kai had mostly ignored her.

Milly mumbled a question.

Kai's attention snapped back to her cell. "Don't you watch the news? Yes, even at..." she glanced at her phone's clock, "five fifty-three I expect my doting and impressive assistant to be abreast of breaking news affecting our industry. Oliver's just been arrested. And if his sister replaces him, we need to be ready with a strategy. This could change our negotiation approach when we're up against Duxton bids. Have a full work-up on her on my desk in two hours."

"Yes, Ms. Fisher."

"And while you're at it, get our mailroom to blacklist a courier company. Couriers Direct USA." She paused. "Yes, yes, *another* company boycott. So sue me if I don't like organizations with reckless bullies. I'll text you a photo of the reason for the boycott. Make sure the company knows he's been nearly killing pedestrians for weeks. Hell, maybe we'll save a life."

"Right. Photo." Milly yawned again.

She smiled at Milly's struggle to sound coherent. Kai did like to keep the woman on her toes. But she also paid Milly twice what most senior executive personal assistants earned to put up with her.

"Sorry, Ms. Fisher."

"How many more times will I have to ask you to call me Kai? Especially this early."

"At least once more," Milly said, a smile in her voice. It was an old debate, one Kai always lost.

Kai said goodbye, then contemplated her next move. Mr. Stein would love it if she stirred the pot a little on his worst enemy. Obviously, there was mileage to be had with the Duxtons' heir-apparent imploding so spectacularly. It would be so easy to make Oliver's shit go from bad to apocalyptic, and she knew how to work the news cycle to her advantage.

"You know that guy?"

Kai jumped.

The spin-bike behind her had stopped whirring. Ponytail now stood beside her, staring up at Oliver's face on the screen.

"I've heard of him," Kai hedged. You never knew who the Duxtons' friends were. They had tentacles everywhere. "Do *you* know him?"

"Not personally. He's a spoiled brat."

Kai relaxed a little. "He does have that face."

"Nasty boss, too. You should see all the stuff Scorched Earth's dug up on him."

"Scorched Earth?" Kai gave her a blank look.

"It's this name-and-shame citizen-journalism outfit that goes after bosses who mistreat employees. It used to have this whole big website, but now it's just a Twitter page. Either way, that Duxton guy's who they hit most. They've named him New York's Worst Boss five years in a row." She pointed at Oliver's mug shot, with his blood-shot eyes and unshaven jaw.

"I could believe it." Kai nodded. "Why are you so interested?"

"I think it's good to stay in the loop. Information is power." The woman smiled, and a pair of adorable dimples appeared like matching lawn divots. "I'm Tracy. Tracy Fox."

Information was *not* power, connections were power, but Kai didn't correct her. *Tracy Fox...* The name skittered around Kaida's head. "You're the fitness blogger."

"I prefer 'fitspo guru.' You know...fitness inspiration?"

Ah yes. Kai had seen her posts on occasion. Fitness tips and aspirational photos of Tracy—and her delightful, lean muscles—filled social media. She was wildly popular, forever posting motivational quotes about girl power. *Women can do it. Don't bow to the patriarchy.*

"So, how many followers?"

Tracy puffed up a little. "Two-hundred forty-three thousand."

The number mattered to her. Kai filed that away and smiled. "Impressive." The spark of pride in Tracy's eyes told her she'd said exactly the right thing.

"You should talk. When I was on the elliptical before..." Tracy waved at the equipment facing the large tinted windows, "I saw your run-in with that courier. I laughed my head off when you threw his bell under a truck."

"What can I say? My blood was up. And I'm a sucker for justice."

"Well, *that* and he'd ruined your coffee," Tracy said. "If my cappuccino had gone to God, I'd totally understand the impulse to throttle something."

"Cappuccino girl, huh?" Kai grinned.

"My secret weakness."

"That's not a bad weakness to have. It's not like you sit up at night eating double-chocolate-chip ice cream from the carton and shouting at the judges on *Dancing with the Stars* for kicking out the wrong person." Kai coughed. "Not that that has ever happened to me."

Tracy laughed. "So you're not even slightly cool? Is that what you're trying to tell me?"

"I thought we agreed this *didn't* happen." Kai feigned innocence. "If anyone asks, I was not throwing things at my screen when Paige VanZant, supreme goddess of salsa, lost."

"That UFC fighter? And wasn't that years ago?"

"Time has no meaning when injustice occurs." Kai's lips twitched.

"At least you had your ice cream to console you. Tell me the truth—did you like her just because she's really hot?"

"Who, me? Have my head turned by a woman's breathtaking beauty?" Kai's eyes fell to Tracy's shapely form. "That doesn't sound like me at all."

"That's quite a come-on." Tracy's amused expression said she'd heard every pick-up line going.

"Well, in my defense, you're really attractive and my brain reached for the flirt button by reflex. Does it bother you?"

"I didn't say that. It's just, you don't even know me."

That wasn't a no to the flirting. Kai beamed. "You're right, so let me fix that. Hi, I'm Kaida Fisher. Kai, for short."

"Unusual name."

"It means *little dragon* in Japanese."

"Why a Japanese name?"

"Well," Kai leaned in, warming to the subject, "my mom's an artist who was going through her *shikki* phase—that's lacquerware—and decided to learn from the best in Wajima, Japan. While she was there, she had a fling with a European backpacker. Mom can't remember exactly where he was from anymore. She has a hopeless memory and it was decades ago." Kai shrugged.

"Oh." Tracy blinked at her, mouth slightly open at that revelation. "Right."

"I might do one of those DNA tests one day," Kai said with a casual wave, trying not to laugh at Tracy's baffled expression. "To find out."

"DNA..."

"But I digress. So when I was a baby, Mom's Japanese neighbor dubbed me Kaida, because I roared like a dragon. Mom liked it so much it stuck. My 'real' name's Annabelle." She winced at the reminder. "What else? I'm a hotel executive, a Leo, briefly a Buddhist, and probably a fair bit older than you. Just being up front about that one." Her smile turned impish.

An answering smile tugged at Tracy's lips. "Are you always this sure of yourself?"

"It depends on who I'm with."

"So you're not the same person with everyone?"

"Is anyone?"

"I like to think I'm always myself."

Kai smiled. "Well, among other things, I negotiate hotel purchases for a living. Want to know the secret to my success?" Her voice lowered to conspiratorial. "It's giving a negotiating party their *optimal interaction*. They think they're funny? I feed them some straight-man lines to allow them to be hilarious. Sometimes they want 'uptight lawyer' me, reeling off facts and figures to make them feel safe, or 'charm-offensive' me, telling them how sharp their tie is, to make them feel like they still *have it*. Whatever they want, I supply, whether they're aware of what that is or not."

"You're a chameleon."

"I prefer 'covert fulfiller of unspoken needs.' Well, more or less—I don't fulfill *all* needs. The sharp-tie guys get compliments; nothing else."

"And they don't realize you're just changing who you are to suit who *they* are?"

"No. It doesn't work if they know what I'm doing."

"Yet you've just told *me* what you get up to." Tracy's eyes danced. "You realize you've ruined your superpower with me."

"I wonder what that means?" Kai drawled. "Blurting out all my secrets? I must like you."

Tracy chuckled. "Very smooth. I bet you're great at your job."

"My boss hasn't fired me yet."

"I'll bet he hasn't." Tracy studied her. "Would I be right in thinking you're one of the best in your field?"

A smile curled Kai's lips. Yes, she was the best. She'd won ten times more deals than she'd lost. She could read people effortlessly, which helped enormously.

Tracy Fox, for instance, was fairly easy to work out. Social-media influencers responded well to people over-sharing personal tidbits. So Kai had supplied a personal story about her origins—admittedly one she didn't care if anyone knew.

Next, she'd tossed in a business secret. People felt special when given insider information. And because Tracy then felt she was inside Kai's personal bubble, she hadn't noticed she'd just been gifted an "optimal interaction" of her own.

Maybe all of this made Kai calculating or something, but it seemed hard-wired in her to charm people using every skill at her disposal. Half the time she wasn't aware she was doing it.

But all the charm offensives and games aside, Kai had to admit Tracy was very much her type: smart, beautiful, and interested in the wider world. A pity Kai was such a train wreck at relationships.

"So you are the best, huh?" Tracy's look became considering.

"I didn't actually say that," Kai pointed out.

"Your eyes did." Tracy pivoted and walked back to a small towel that was slung over the spin-bike's handlebars. She ran it over her bare arms, then tossed it over a shoulder. With a playful look, she added, "I can believe it. And are you always so…passionate…about everything?" Tracy's eyes danced. "From closing deals and shouting at TV judges to avenging your spilled coffee?"

"Always. Life's meant to be lived, loved, swallowed whole. Otherwise, what's the point?

An intrigued look flitted across Tracy's face. "Interesting." Her gaze lingered. "Well, time for me to hit the showers." She wiggled her shoulders. "You know, I might need a hand washing my back. Someone with skills like yours might be useful."

Kai raised her eyebrows. "You never know." A thrill skittered through her, but she hesitated. The woman's blue eyes glowed a little too brightly to be safe. "I'd really love for us to have some fun together. Just putting this on the record, though… I don't do relationships. Is that okay with you?"

"Never?" Tracy studied her curiously. "Bad breakup?"

"No, nothing like that. It's just, I'm barely able to keep a goldfish alive, let alone a relationship," she admitted. "Work is my whole, sole focus. I live for it. Love it. Even dream about it. And it's not fair to expect someone else to put up with me, always off hunting the next deal."

"I see. Thanks for explaining." Tracy studied her for a moment, then walked away, leaving Kai watching the pleasant rear view.

Well, that was that then. It was best to be up front, though—fewer broken hearts all around. Kai had been there, done that, and piled up plenty of regrets. She never again wanted to be the cause of another woman's tears.

Besides, as delicious as Tracy was, as impressive as the sway in those sashaying hips, Kai had a lot of work to do.

When Tracy reached the exit, she glanced back, a playful smile on her full lips. "Coming?" There was no mistaking the wicked innuendo.

Kai swallowed thickly and smiled. "Only if I'm not the only one."

Tracy chuckled.

Okay, so maybe Kai's disastrous week was looking up after all.

Amelia locked her office door and set a small dish of paper clips in front of herself. She considered her options. Okay. Her brother first.

"Calling to gloat?" Oliver's tired voice was its usual snarky self, but instead of cockiness, there was defeat.

Amelia's eyebrows lifted as she reached for a paper clip. "Ollie, I'm worried about you."

"Well, save it. I'm fine. As I've told Mom and Dad, plus my lawyers, the court-appointed psych evaluator, the judge, and Isabella. Fuck." His tone turned dark. "She's dumped me! So much for 'stand by your man.' What a bitch."

"I see." So Isabella had some self-respect after all.

Oliver huffed. "I suppose you're circling now? Especially since I can't get to the emergency board meeting. My lawyers have me stuck at the penthouse on house arrest as a bail condition."

Amelia's twisting fingers stopped. "What board meeting?"

"Uncle Joe's calling everyone in. Didn't he tell you?"

She relaxed. "I'm returning his call next."

"Well, you'll be told to attend. Everyone who's anyone at Duxton is being brought in." His voice became indignant. "Apparently the *future* of the company's being discussed."

She froze. "Is that so?"

Oliver grunted. "I asked if I could Skype in. They said no. Don't have to guess why."

There'd be no Oliver? They'd be discussing replacing him then. And if Joe wanted her there, could it mean she was being considered as a serious contender at last?

Hope slithered through her before she could stop it. *No.* She'd been down this path twice before, thinking she might have a chance at one of Hotel Duxton's highest jobs. Although...that was before Oliver had committed public career suicide.

"...and then the judge said I'm banned from even crossing the state line! Bastard."

What?

"I'm on *all* the fuckin' news broadcasts. Like no one else in history has screwed up before! What's that about?" He sounded mystified.

"You really can't see it? It's about a rich, famous, showy executive acting like a drug-addled frat boy. People love it when people like you implode. Makes them feel better when someone who has it all gets taken down a peg or two."

"People like *us*, you mean. You're also rich."

"But not showy or famous. And I'm not the heir-apparent to Hotel Duxton International."

"Not yet," he muttered. "So...does it make you feel better, too, Lia? Seeing me taken down a peg or two?"

"No." She sighed. "It doesn't. Shocked?"

"I guess. Although it's you, so not really. But I believe all's fair in love and war."

She was well aware that if it'd been her who'd humiliated herself all over the news, Oliver would have ordered the party starters and left mocking messages.

"S'pose you finally got what you wanted?" Oliver continued, his breath shaky. "My job running Duxton USA? And you'll be given CEO instead of me? You'll get all of it?"

That just didn't seem real. "Oliver, come on, you're more slippery than Teflon."

"Not this time."

If succession plans were changing, she'd have heard from their father. She hadn't. Amelia deflated. How delusional she was even entertaining the idea. "You know Dad will never see me as an option. Especially not when he's been grooming you since birth."

The pause was long. "Yeah," he said. "Hell, yeah, you're right!"

Great. Amelia snapped her paper clip in half and reached for another.

"Hey, sorry. That was a bit shit of me, I guess."

Just a bit?

"I'm not oblivious, you know. I know you hate me."

"For what?" she asked, curious.

"That you're way better qualified than I am. I know you pulled some clever shit during the financial crisis to save all your hotels. Honestly? I wouldn't have had a fuckin' clue what to do. So I get why you're pissed at me being in line for the company, not you."

Amelia wondered where this rare bout of self-reflection was coming from. He was dead wrong, though. She didn't respect her brother, but she wasn't about to be angry at Oliver for a decision he hadn't made. Resentment was wasted energy. Amelia's sole aim in life was to be the best manager at Hotel Duxton, so even her father couldn't miss it.

"Shit, I need something for this headache." The sound of liquid pouring came down the phone. A clink of ice. Then gulping. "Where was I? Oh, right. You're better than me at hotels. Blah-blah-blah. But it doesn't matter, does it?" He sounded positively cheerful now. "It's not like Dad's gonna evolve any time soon about your…*tendencies.* Sucks to be you." He sounded anything but sorry.

She sighed. Her fingers twisted hard. "I don't know why I bothered to call."

"Me, either." Oliver snickered.

Amelia tossed the warped paper clip down. She was a fool to hope anything might have changed for her in the fallout. "I wasn't calling to gloat," she muttered. "Just for the record."

"I'm getting that now." He laughed. "I'm glad you did, though. I'm feeling so much better."

Of course he was. "Think you can stay out of the headlines for the rest of the month?"

"Sure. I have an ankle bracelet and random drug tests to guarantee that. Mom's staying with me, too. Says she wants to keep me on the straight and narrow until my next court date."

Naturally. Her do-no-wrong son would need much pampering and feeding. For their eternal peacemaker mother, the natural order was fulfilling the ambitions of whatever the men in her life needed.

"Oh, and thanks," Oliver said, more seriously. "For agreeing to do my shit while I'm out of action."

"Your what?"

"Ask Joe to fill you in."

"Why don't you tell me?"

"Ask him." He sounded cagey. "I'm bailing. Need more sleep. But hey, thanks for the pick-me-up." He hung up without waiting for her reply.

She stared at the phone. What the hell had Oliver gotten her into now? And how badly would it screw up her life this time?

Chapter 3

That Way There Be Dragons

Kai settled into the chair behind her desk and reached for her steaming coffee.

"Perfect timing. Thanks, Milly," she murmured, drawing in a deep gulp. The caffeine hit went some way toward rejuvenating her after the morning's strenuous workout. Not to mention all the non-gym muscles she'd put through their paces. "Did you get my email about upside-down trees?"

"I did," Milly said, only her eyes betraying her incredulity. "I'll get right on it. In the meantime—the information you requested on Oliver's sister." She slid a folder across the desk.

It was suspiciously thin. Kai lowered the coffee to her desk. "Is this everything?"

"There's not a lot on her. She's just turned forty-six. Never married. No kids. No hobbies beyond work that I can see."

"How dull."

Milly's expression morphed into a polite version of "you should talk."

Touché.

"Like Oliver, she was born in New York," Milly continued. "She's based in London and oversees three dozen Duxton hotels across Europe. Apparently she made a play to run Duxton USA in '95 when there was a management reshuffle. One of the business magazines ran a small piece on the rumors when it happened. She'd have made her pitch just after she finished college." Milly tapped a paragraph to draw Kai's eye.

Kai whistled. "She did a Bachelor of Science in International Hospitality Management at École Hôtelière de Lausanne? That's the best hotel management course in the world."

"She did."

"Most CEOs would kill to have an École Hôtelière graduate in charge of their hotels."

"Conrad Duxton isn't most CEOs. And he didn't just say no to his daughter once. She made another attempt to be VP of Duxton USA in 2002, which was just before Oliver was due to take over the job."

"Two goes? She must have really wanted it."

"Or she thought her younger brother was a poor choice. After that, she dropped off the radar. She's kept a low profile in Europe. No social media, scandals, or much of anything else I can find."

"How can anyone raise a hotel's profile without *any* social media?" Kai frowned. "Her marketing manager should be shot. Even Mr. Stein does the occasional tweet for Grand Millennium, and he's seventy-four!"

"Only because you make him," Milly reminded her. "She might just be a really private person."

"Or maybe she simply has more humility than her brother."

"Oh, she's *nothing* like her brother." Milly pushed a few pages at Kai. "Look at the rest of her background. One year she was profiled in a Hotel Duxton annual report."

Well, well. So Amelia Duxton had followed her École Hôtelière BSc by doing an Executive MBA in Hospitality Administration. Superb credentials that could see her running any hotel in the world. By contrast, Oliver had no formal qualifications. He'd dropped out of high school and been mentored by his father ever since. "I see what you mean about being nothing like him."

"It gets better." Milly slid over a printout of a news story. "During the European economic crisis in the late 2000s, hers was one of the few hotel operations across Spain, Portugal, Greece, and Italy that didn't get into financial trouble. She even managed to snap up a couple of quality bankrupt hotels at bargain prices."

"How on earth did she manage a profit during that mess? A lot of excellent hotels went to the wall."

"She ran this huge international promotion that gave away free conference rooms for any convention with over two hundred people."

"Ah. Conventions bring guests. Guests pay for rooms... Smart," Kai conceded. "Typical of the Duxtons, though, isn't it?"

"Ms. Fisher?" Milly asked.

"They have some underrated business genius on their hands, so they've parked her over in Europe, out of sight, out of mind, while the idiot son runs the main company and is set to inherit it all."

"Um... except Ms. Duxton's not exactly underrated."

"How so?"

"*New Economy* named her its Businessperson of the Year in 2010 for how she thrived during the economic crisis."

"That just makes it worse. There really is no excuse for her not being given a greater position in the company."

"I guess they just really like Oliver."

"That could be about to change. All right, so what does our Duxton business wunderkind look like?"

"I don't know." Milly sighed. "They never include her in family photos or in the AGM reports."

"Never? Is she self-conscious about her looks or something? Hit every branch of the ugly tree on the way down?"

Milly frowned and made a tiny tsk.

"Just a question." Kai lifted her hands in surrender. "Would you prefer 'genetically unblessed?'"

Milly sighed.

"No, you're right. Anyway, it's unlikely. The Duxtons might be bastards, but they're all beautiful bastards. Okay, are there no photos of her *anywhere*?" Kai tapped her lip in thought. "What about whenever she's done press? Or when she won that business award? She'd have been interviewed then."

Milly pointed to the folder. "Look at the last page."

Kai flipped to it and stared. A lengthy news feature on Amelia Duxton in a British finance magazine. It contained a photo of the businesswoman staring out a window, taken from behind her chair. All that was visible was the sleek line of a charcoal-suited arm and the top of light-brown hair. "So she's media shy?" Kai's gaze fell to Amelia's quotes within the story:

The best thing about hotels for me is they're about tradition, offering guests a sense of belonging. They're somewhere comfortable, reliable, and wonderful to escape to when you need a break. They'll always be there. At Duxton Europe, we try to establish a connection with our guests so they feel like they're part of our family, no matter how far away from home they are. That is one of the core values our hotels stand behind.

"Oh hell!" Kai laughed. "That's priceless. I have to use that."

Milly's expression shifted to unsettled. "But she seems so nice." She paused. "Well, not *nice*. I mean people call her colder than the polar caps, but she seems better than the other Duxtons."

"That isn't saying much." Kai whipped out her phone and called up the Scorched Earth Twitter page. With a small smile at the tiny dragon logo next to the feed's name, she logged in. "Family, core values, and Duxtons in the same sentence?" She snorted. "Sure, okay." She cracked her knuckles. "Time for The Dragon to have some fun."

The Scorched Earth website might have been semi-retired well over a decade ago when Kai had moved into hotel management from law, but her Twitter feed and its two million loyal followers remained. Right now, Kai didn't feel even slightly retired, and the familiar thrill of the hunt came roaring back as she slipped into her anonymous alter ego.

Drugs, booze, porn stars, hit and runs, and all before sun-up. Good luck bribing your way out of this one, Oliver Duxton.

Kai added a link to a juicy news story about his arrest before posting it. A second tweet followed, this one including his mug shot.

New York's worst boss, shittiest human, and greatest ad for toxic entitlement behind bars. Not even an Insta filter will save this sorry look.

And in case people didn't know what he'd been up to all these years, she dropped in a third tweet.

Full list of 100s of complaints of wage theft made against hotel
heir Oliver Duxton over the years. A Dragon never forgets.

Kai dug up a story outlining the worst of Oliver's misdeeds and added that link to her tweet, posting it with a gleeful stab.

Already her followers had begun retweeting Scorched Earth's first tweet with comments along the lines of "Good to see you back, holding the bastards accountable."

Hmm. She wondered if she could get #OliverTwisted trending. His downfall was long overdue, and this time, his wealth and connections wouldn't get him off the hook so easily.

Now then, something for the sister and her ridiculous comments. Kai typed in her name, then contemplated what to say.

Milly murmured, "Aren't you just going to make the Duxtons angrier stirring this all up? And you're targeting the only Duxton who's never hurt anyone. She has no employee complaints against her."

Kai glanced up, having forgotten her assistant was still there. "That we know of." She resumed tapping out the tweet.

Milly and Mr. Stein were among a tiny handful of people who knew her secret cause. The anonymity had been necessary given how many deep-pocketed, vindictive, bad bosses would have loved to see The Dragon permanently silenced.

"Look, we know how bad Oliver is, underpaying his staff and treating them like automatons," Kai said. "So if *we* know, Amelia does, too. And you sure as hell can't be talking about family values when your brother has his mug shot on the news. That makes you a hypocrite."

"Ms. Duxton talked about family *and* hotel core values, not family values. You know there's a big difference," Milly said with the world's tiniest tut. "Besides, she said it over ten years ago."

"And her brother was an asshole then, too. That's not a secret." Kai finished her post. "But I'm not just stirring up this hornet's nest for fun. I'm trying to draw out this mysterious Amelia Duxton. If she comes out swinging, we learn something about her. It's tactical. Besides, if she doesn't want her earnestness used against her, she shouldn't make it so easy."

Kai posted her tweet, suppressing the tiniest twinge of guilt for dragging the sister. Still, for a tweet from The Dragon, it was tame. Kai had only quoted Amelia's words next to Oliver's mug shot, and added, "Some core values."

"By the way," Milly said, "I think I've found your businessman. The one you've been trying to track down in London?"

Kai sat up straight and dropped her phone to her desk. "If the next words out of your mouth are 'And I know exactly where he is,' I'll double your Christmas bonus. And find you a hot date. Someone juicy." She leaned forward. "I do know everyone."

Milly looked at her skeptically. "No thanks. Last time, you tried to hook me up with a weird guy who kept looking at his reflection in the fork."

"Well, he was a model."

"I keep telling you, Ms. Fisher, I can find my own dates. And I'd rather not have to threaten them with a butter knife again."

"Wait, you did?" That seemed awfully proactive for Milly.

She sighed. "Remember? He tried to steal my iPhone? *While* I was using it?"

"Oh. That. Right, yes." It was all coming back. The brazen robbery attempt. Milly's valiant tackle as he fled the restaurant, despite being a third his size. "Well, I'll do much better next time."

"Oh God." Milly groaned softly. "Ms. Fisher, you're impossible."

"Not *entirely* untrue," Kai agreed. "So can we get to my businessman? Where is Nedal al-Hamadani?"

"I don't know where he is now, but I know where he will be. And it'd be an easy thing for you to be there, too, to mix, mingle, network, and… negotiate."

"Yes! Milly Valentine, you are a gem." Kai leaned in. "Okay, tell me everything."

"The big international hotel conference in Las Vegas next week. I've heard he'll be there."

"*Vegas?*" Kai blinked. "Seriously? This mysterious, international hotel developer, who few ever get an audience with, has decided to go hang out in… *Vegas?*"

"It seems Mr. Hamadani's always had an interest in the future of our industry. He wrote a paper on it once, how technology is transforming hotels. And 'The Future of Hotels and Hospitality' is the conference topic. That'd be why he's attending."

Ah. That did make sense. "All right, send me the paper he wrote." Kai rubbed her hands. "I need to know what gets him excited. Get inside his head. Then I need our corporate jet booked, along with a room at the hotel where the conference is and…"

Milly slid some paperwork across the desk. "I've already emailed you what he wrote, made the accommodation arrangements, and notified Mr. Stein you'll be gone for a week."

"Book everything for two." Kai eyed her. "I'll need you there."

Milly didn't bat an eye. "Done. The jet's ready when you are."

How did I cope before Milly Valentine? "Good," was all she said.

"By the way," Milly said, "I heard the Duxtons are making a play for Mayfair Palace, too."

Aha! "I thought they would. Who's negotiating for it?"

"Since Mr. Hamadani is based in London, the Duxtons chose someone on the ground there." Milly tapped Amelia's folder.

Now it all made sense. Of course the usual Duxton negotiators felt inadequate to the task—because *they* weren't the ones doing the deal. So this Amelia Duxton was Kai's competition? Bring it on.

"But we might be too late." Milly winced. "I hear Ms. Duxton's been in talks with Mr. Hamadani for months. A deal is close to being signed."

Damn it. Still… "Close is not final, and Hamadani hasn't met me yet."

"Okay." Milly hesitated. "So about the conference? The hotel it's at?"

"Hmm?" Kai gaze drifted back to the magazine article in front of her, trying to get a bead on this mysterious Duxton VP with her back to the camera. That arm was long and shapely. Elegant outfit. What sort of negotiator was she? A good one, obviously, if she was close to nailing the hotel world's deal of the decade.

"It's about where we'll be staying in Vegas. *You* have to tell Mr. Stein," Milly said in a rush. "I'm not going to break the news. And I won't just slide it in on expenses, either. He'll notice, and you know he'll go crazy." Her head tilted toward the hotel booking confirmation. "He won't be happy about paying his enemies one dime."

What? Kai's gaze dropped to the booking confirmation in Vegas—for *Hotel Duxton*. "Oh."

Amelia inhaled deeply, then reached for her phone again. No putting it off.

"Really, Amelia? You had to do that?" Joe snapped before she could greet him.

Yes, well. She had just fired his eldest son and called the cops on him. With a sigh, she pulled the dish of paper clips over and selected a red one. "It was my corporate responsibility. Failure to deal appropriately and promptly with criminal behavior would have led to all sorts of—"

"We could have dealt with him in-house."

"And have Douglas repeat his embezzlement at someone else's company? A company where they won't find it as quickly as I did?"

"Damn it, you're always so…black and white. Rigid. Did you even ask Douglas why he took the money?"

"His gambling debts said it all."

A startled noise came down the phone. Wait, Joe hadn't known?

"Did it occur to you to find a way for it to be paid back, and our family name kept out of it?" he demanded.

"I have a fiduciary responsibility to…"

"Yes, yes, and I am Duxton's Chief Financial Officer. You think *I* don't know what our responsibility is, Amelia?"

His anger startled her. Joe had always been the moderate uncle, the foil to her father's aloofness and hostility. Did he really not understand why she'd been forced to do this?

"Look," Joe exhaled, "I know Douglas has had issues with keeping jobs. It just bothers me you didn't even consider any other options before you got the authorities involved."

"But if anyone found out that we'd done a cover-up, we'd be liable for—"

"Amelia," he cut her off. "I know. I was hoping you understood on a *human* level why what you've done is so difficult. This is more nuanced to me as a father than simple corporate embezzlement."

"There *is* no nuance, though." Couldn't he see that? "I'm protecting us. I'm putting Hotel Duxton first."

"We're going in circles. I like to believe that deep down, somewhere, you know why I'm frustrated, even though you didn't hesitate at being the cause of it."

The cause? She wasn't the cause! "I—"

"No. Don't bother. You are who you are. Let's…shelve it. I rang to tell you an emergency board meeting's been called. It's to brief everyone involved given the…recent events."

"When do I need to be there?" She clicked on her computer's online diary.

"Amelia…" he cleared his throat. "You aren't invited."

She froze. "What?"

"Neither's Oliver. Because we want to talk about you both."

"Oh?" She didn't dare hope. He couldn't mean…

"There'll be a full board meeting after Oliver's court case next month, which will result in a vote on who should be named CEO. But this emergency meeting next week will consider our options. The contenders will be debated."

"And…am I on that list?" She stilled, heart pounding.

"Yes, Amelia. You're being mentioned as a serious option. You've impressed a lot of people by keeping Europe on an even keel in the worst circumstances. Me included."

Amelia drew in a breath. "Is it just me being considered?"

"No." Joe sounded dissatisfied. "A couple of other less well-known contenders are on the table, but they're miles behind you in credibility, qualifications, and experience. You're by far the frontrunner."

"But Dad would never—"

"I know. Conrad wouldn't. He wants to stick with Oliver. But this is too important. You'd be an excellent choice to lead Duxton when your father retires. If I'd had my way, the US division would have been yours in 2002. Hell, maybe even '95."

"Oh." That was astonishing to hear. Joe had been on her side all this time? He'd never said.

"Even if Conrad won't budge, while his views might carry a lot of weight, that isn't enough, not now with the shareholders in an uproar and the share price sliding. I think I might be able to swing the other votes to you."

"Thank you," she said, shocked.

"It's time for a change. Even if Oliver skates away with a rap over the knuckles in court, we can't keep being held to his erratic whims."

"No. Chaos is not sound business," she said firmly.

He chuckled. "Yes, Amelia, your views on chaos are well known. Anyway, so while we're waiting for Oliver's case to get heard and for the board to deliberate on the contenders, I need you to take over a couple of Oliver's responsibilities stateside. I've emailed you the details. I'm assuming you're up for it?" The challenge in his tone was unmistakable.

"Of course," she said smartly, opening her email. She skimmed. *Right. Yes.* She could evaluate a staff-turnover problem at one poorly performing Duxton USA hotel. Evaluating efficiencies was a point of pride for her.

"It's probably another bad run of troublemaker employees causing a fuss, then everyone starts leaving. Oliver assures me we do everything by the book there, despite the lies from Scorched Earth."

Was that toxic whistleblower feed still targeting their business? "Okay. I'll look into what's happening and send a report. Is that all?" She could do this in her sleep. Why had Oliver been so cagey?

"Amelia, didn't you see which hotel it is?" Joe asked, sounding amused. "Las Vegas."

Oh lovely. The sweaty delights of Sin City with its wall-to-wall gambling and sleaziness? Just great.

"No. Problem," she said through gritted teeth.

"There's one other thing. Oliver was supposed to give a keynote address at the hotel conference being held there. Unfortunately, the judge won't let him leave the state."

Her heart sank. "I don't do speeches, Joe, you know that. Well, nothing beyond annual meetings and maybe briefing financial journalists."

"The CEO of Hotel Duxton International does, and if you want that to be you, then you'd better start learning to. For all his faults, Oliver has no problem with the public side of things."

Amelia winced at his pointed message. And, of course, Oliver had agreed to give the keynote—because it was all about him being in the spotlight. And, most likely, he wanted to gamble, drink, and bed a pretty showgirl or three.

"It requires courage to put yourself out there," Joe continued. "To be the face of a company… To be watched by the industry's movers and shakers at a big event like this is important for our corporate image. Oliver understands that. You need to as well. The media will be there for the speech, so make it good."

Distaste filled her. Being in the public eye was akin to a cavity search. People prodding you as if they had the right to.

"And in case you're working out how to say no," Joe continued, "consider something else: Oliver is seen by board members as bold, a risk taker, unafraid of grabbing a chance. And sorry, Amelia, but you aren't. You need to shake off that academic, ivory-tower image. You need to seem adaptable, confident, and ballsy. I can only talk you up so much; you have to show them I'm right. Treat Vegas as a CEO audition."

"I see," she said stiffly.

"You can do this. You have to. Anyone with half a brain knows you're Hotel Duxton's best hope—even if Conrad's too stubborn to see it."

"Then I'll make sure I don't screw it up."

"Good. I've just sent you Oliver's speech. You'll have to rewrite it to tailor it to you, but for God's sake, keep it interesting. Do not do some statistical monologue that sends everyone to sleep. Make it exciting. Fight your natural instincts and be engaging."

Engaging? And who didn't love statistics?

"We'll need you over there ASAP. A week's barely enough time to do a thorough evaluation on the staff turnover mess. Make the efficiency report a good one, too. Give us something powerful to show the board you can root out issues as needed."

Powerful? For an efficiency report?

"Before I go, what's the status on Mayfair Palace?"

"I'm meeting Nedal at three. I anticipate a deal signed by COB today." Amelia's fingers tingled at the prospect.

"Good." He paused. "You know, if you pull this off, it'll be a massive tick in your column."

"Of course."

"And a huge cross if you don't."

"I hardly think Nedal's going to pull out now. We've been negotiating this for months."

"Right. When you finalize it, we want to make an official announcement from HQ in New York. Don't put anything out from London. Understood?"

"Yes."

"All right, that's everything. Bye, Amelia." He hung up.

Fine. New York could take the credit. The real prize was winning the most beautiful hotel ever conceived. And that reality was so close she could taste it.

Quinn peeked in on Amelia after she'd finished with Joe and slid a steaming tea on her desk. "Courtesy of Tamara."

Amelia took a sip. *Lovely.*

She eyed Quinn, wondering why she was playing messenger for the office assistant…and lingering. "What?" Amelia grumbled.

"What did your uncle want?"

"They're having an emergency board meeting in New York next week about Duxton's next CEO. Oliver is no longer the automatic pick."

"Yes!" Quinn punched the air.

"Premature."

"You getting the top job isn't out of the question, though?" Quinn sounded so hopeful.

"No, not out of the question."

This time, Quinn double punched the air. "And? Why does your face look like that?" She made a circular motion around Amelia's head.

"I'm not invited to the meeting."

"I don't understand."

"I have to go to Vegas straight after Nedal's signing to do some of Oliver's work." She glanced at her watch. "Can you order our closest corporate jet to be fueled up ASAP?"

"Why Vegas? *You* in *Vegas* is different." She tapped out a text on her phone as she spoke.

"I have to give a keynote speech at a conference and work out some efficiency issues at Duxton Vegas while Oliver's sidelined. It's a test of my suitability, apparently."

"You're giving a speech?" Astonishment lit Quinn's expression.

"Mmm. I'll email you Oliver's draft. Maybe you can come up with ideas that don't start with a joke about showgirls' cleavages."

"Ouch." Quinn rocked back on her heels. "Okay, boss." Her phone pinged. "Good news. The jet's already fueled up. Bad news is, it's been booked to pick up Simon in Sydney and get him to New York."

Amelia drew in a sharp breath. Douglas's lightweight younger brother, a man as dim as a broken light bulb, was invited to the board meeting? Well, she supposed as the head of Duxton Australasia he'd get a vote, too, on who ran the empire. Amelia wondered if he'd back Oliver over her. About the only thing they had in common was a shared love for Simon's daughter, Imogen.

"What about our other jets?"

"Both busy stateside, getting everyone to HQ for the board meeting."

"Can I jump ahead of Simon?" Amelia asked. "Vegas needs me on the ground today. It's only a ten-hour flight. If I wait for the pilot to do a return trip to Sydney, I'll have lost..." She did a quick mental tally of the pilot's route, adding in refueling time. "Forty-six hours. I cannot waste two days."

Quinn tapped away at her phone for a few minutes. "Okay, the pilot says he *can* get you to Vegas first, but he'll need to have wheels up today at Farnborough by fifteen-thirty if he's to also get Simon to the meeting on time. Can you be ready by then?"

Amelia frowned. "But I'm supposed to finalize Mayfair Palace at three." She paused. "Can you see if Nedal will agree to ride with me on the way to the airport? We only have one clause left to sort out and it's not a tricky one. Then our driver can turn around and run him straight back to our office. You can meet Nedal here and ensure all the paperwork is signed, stamped, and approved by our in-house lawyers."

"Should be no problem. Especially since Nedal loves our limo."

"He does? Why? He has his own. Several in fact." Amelia gave her a perplexed look.

"Ours comes with Zane, who's as crazy about the Al Wasl football team as he is. Makes sense since they're both from Dubai."

Amelia blinked in surprise.

"You really didn't know, even though Zane's driven you for thirteen years?"

"Why would I know where he's from, or that he loves some boring game involving melodramatic men clutching their legs at random intervals?"

Quinn laughed. "Oh, shit. Don't ever say that in public around here. Wait, you can calculate every variable of world-hopping flights but don't know even the basics about your driver?"

"It hasn't come up. Our discussions involve only where he has to drive me."

"I can see we'll have our work cut out for us on your speech. Connecting with people really isn't your strength."

"Well, I can't be expected to know everything. I focus on important things. Like keeping my forty-five thousand staff paid and my 3.942 million guests across Europe happy each year."

Quinn chuckled. "Love the three decimal points, boss." Her phone pinged again. "Nedal's agreed. Pretty fast, actually. Something to do with Al Wasl *crushing* Hatta at the weekend." A few more taps. "I've let the pilot know to expect you by 3:20. So you can go home and pack while I finish up things here if you like."

"Good." Her second-in-command's efficiency was matched only by her occasional cheekiness. Still, Amelia had never met a smarter or more hard-working employee. The trade-off was worth it. She made to rise.

"Oh, by the way, just a head's up," Quinn said, "there's some bad stuff on Twitter about the Duxtons. Social media's not a fun place for the company today."

"I've avoided social media so far. Why would I change a habit of a lifetime? Twitter's just verbal effluent from the lowest rungs of society."

"I mention it because Scorched Earth's been attacking Oliver since his arrest."

"Juvenile and predictable, but hardly a concern. Really, Oliver should expect—"

"Actually, they just named you."

"Me?" Amelia snatched up her phone and poked around the nightmare that was Twitter until she found a series of tweets that made her scowl.

Will NY's worst boss Oliver Duxton need big sis Amelia to clean up his sordid mess? #DuncetonHotels

Dunceton? Hardly high wit at work. Her eye fell to another post. Amelia's quote from years ago about family and core values at Duxton was staring back at her. Mockery dripped from the tweet.

"How mature." Amelia snapped. "Who did this?"

"No one knows who Scorched Earth is. Plenty have tried to find out, especially Oliver. Repeatedly."

"I see." Apparently her brother was useless on multiple levels.

"This is killing Duxton on the PR front," Quinn said. "It might be time to fight back. Fight fire with *ice*." She gave Amelia a pointed look, leaving no doubt as to who she thought the ice was.

"No." Amelia narrowed her eyes. "Absolutely not. It's beneath us."

Quinn looked unsurprised. "Your call, boss."

"Okay, while I'm in Vegas, hold the fort here until Mayfair Palace is set in stone, then meet me out there in time for the conference next Saturday."

"Sure thing."

"And Quinn?"

"Yeah?" She glanced up.

"You stay off social media, too."

"You don't even want to hear my best comebacks for The Dragon?"

"I'll just have to imagine. Besides, you can't spell to save your life."

Quinn laughed. "True. Right, let me brief our lawyers, and you can go get ready for Vegas." Her brown eyes brightened. "You know, I've never been to Vegas. That place could actually be fun."

At the reminder of her destination, Amelia's lips thinned. "Unlikely. All right, I'm going home to pack for the most un-fun place on planet Earth."

Chapter 4

Winners and Losers

KAI PAUSED IN FRONT OF the brushed gold doors of Hotel Duxton Vegas and drew in a breath. This was it. The biggest deal of her life lay inside.

Milly joined her as a porter busied himself with their bags.

"Not like other Duxton hotels, is it?" Kai murmured.

"No." Milly's neck craned up. "Not like other hotels, period."

The hotel cast an enormous shadow, with its gleaming walls of curved glass that shot up fifty floors. Kai had checked the stats on the way over. At 600 feet, it was the eighth-highest hotel in Vegas. The gaming floor alone was 150,000 square feet. It was an ode to ostentatiousness—which meant it fit the Las Vegas vibe perfectly. She had to admire the showmanship.

"However, none of Las Vegas's hotels seem exactly normal," Milly continued. "Did you see the one shaped like a pyramid?"

"The Luxor. At night they turn on their Sky Beam and shoot a light into the heavens from the top."

"Seriously?" Milly's mouth parted a little. "Can we see that?"

Kai smiled at her hopefulness. "Your first time in Sin City? Gird your loins."

"I'm ready," Milly said quickly. "Although, there's nothing this crazy back home in Delaware."

"I'll bet."

A doorman swung open the double doors for them.

"All right, let me give you some pointers," Kai said. "Rule number one: Only gamble what you can afford to lose. Set a timer on your phone, and when it goes off, leave, no questions—"

"I'm not going to gamble, Ms. Fisher. I'm here to work."

"We're in *Vegas*. Of course you're going to gamble at least once. Do it, get it out of your system until the allure is gone."

"But…" Milly shook her head. "I don't even like—"

"On that note, scammers are everywhere. So, rule two: If some charming, handsome gentleman suddenly wants to be your best friend, there *will* be a catch. And I'm not just talking assorted venereal diseases."

Milly's eyes widened. "Ms. Fisher, I'd *never*…"

"Oh, that's right. You're still claiming you don't have time to date anyone, ever." She squinted at her assistant, trying to assess whether she was genuine or just saying what she thought her boss wanted to hear. "Look, I don't care if you indulge in fun after hours, as long as you're on the clock when needed."

Milly's cheeks went scarlet, and she shook her head again.

Kai snorted. *Lord, how did I find this one?* Well, she knew exactly how. Milly had seemed so impossibly innocent in the interview that she'd hired her on the spot. Kai had wanted to find out if that adorable earnestness was an act or not. Astonishingly, Milly was exactly what she claimed. To this day, Kai couldn't shake the woman's perfectly polite veneer or insistence on calling her "Ms. Fisher." And she never showed any hint of even having a personal life.

"Ms. Fisher, I promise I'm not interested in any random strangers."

Kai considered that, then adopted her most reassuring tone. "You know, if you're someone who prefers a nice bowl of ice cream to shaking the plasterwork off a bedroom ceiling, that's perfectly fine, too."

"I'm not asexual," Milly said in exasperation. "I'm just so busy! And I have a demanding boss."

"Ah, *her*." Kai tossed her an amused glance. "If I can manage a private life, so can you. What are you? Twenty-seven? Twenty-eight? That's far too young to give up. You need to savor everything. Eat the world."

"Eat the…" Milly shook her head, making her red curls bounce. "I barely have time to eat lunch, Ms. Fisher, let alone the world."

Kai smiled. "At the risk of adding to your burden, can you check us in, then meet me back here? I want to get a feel for things."

Her assistant nodded and scurried off.

Kai's gaze drifted around the lobby. Some of the floor art, like the floral-themed, three-tiered fountain in front of her, was as over the top as the bling on a millionaire's second wife. But that was just Vegas.

It was so easy to drown in sensory overload. This bright, showy city divided opinions like no other, but Kai was firmly in the love-it camp because Vegas never pretended to be anything other than what it was: glitzy, greedy, unashamed, and entertaining.

There was something to be said for offering wish fulfilment 24-7. Kai especially appreciated that. All she ever did was sell people their dreams—dressed up as hotel deals—one optimal interaction at a time. Here was a whole city dedicated to the same idea.

But Vegas also had something else going for it: that prickle of anticipation. It was in the eyes and energy of tourists, the expectation that something thrilling was about to happen, be it winning at the tables or getting laid or seeing a show they'd saved all year for.

Kai drew in a deep breath. Jasmine, lily of the valley, and vanilla notes immediately tickled her nostrils. *Florasian*, they called this scent. Every hotel on The Strip had a unique smell, thanks to the essential oils they diffused through the vents along with fresh oxygen to keep gamblers awake.

The Mirage, for example, smelled like coconut. Nobu, lemon ginger. And the Silverton, hot apple pie. It hid the stench of smoke and spilled booze. More than that, it tapped into guests' senses in a subconscious way, luring them in, and then drawing them back to the familiar, visit after visit.

Kai's four-inch black heels clacked over the polished floor as she made her way past the lobby, with its V-shaped bronze scaffolding erupting from floor to ceiling. Metallic was clearly the theme of this hotel. She eyed the historic signage and smart staff uniforms... Okay, metallic with a dose of Roaring Twenties.

Her eyes lit on several employees gathered near a staff entrance, a supervisor talking to them in low tones.

Kai dropped to a padded bench seat, wondering who would be the best person to approach for her special project.

When Milly joined her fifteen minutes later, Kai rose, having identified their first target. "Come along, Milly," she murmured, choosing the most exhausted looking of the employees. *Probably worked a double shift or has two jobs.* "There's fuckery to be had."

The key to cracking this deal would be the same as always: alliances and contacts. Her mind darted back to delicious Tracy Fox and her conviction that information was power.

Information was power only if you already had it. To acquire information, one needed connections. Her pulse kicked up. Kai always loved this part—the chase.

She applied her most charming smile as the staff member she'd chosen peeled away from the others.

Game on.

Two hours later, she and Milly were back in Kai's room. Kai was finishing up her garden salad dinner while perched on the edge of her bed, notes surrounding her.

Milly was hunched over a small table by the window, writing up notes on what they'd learned and from whom.

Greasing palms and a lot of expert schmoozing had yielded the usual results. One universal constant was how underpaid hotel employees were.

Nedal al-Hamadani hadn't checked in yet, but the staff she'd forged contacts with had agreed to keep an eye out for his arrival and text her his movements when he did.

She'd also initiated a side project unrelated to her main mission. It involved putting out feelers to learn who on staff most needed a hand. Kai liked to privately employ the hardest-luck cases to do some personal work for her.

Disgust had burned in her for years since discovering how many service-industry staff worked full-time yet lived in cars or on the street because their employers were too greedy to pay a living wage.

Her extra tasks were all nonsensical and lavishly overpaid—such as getting someone to track down a dozen bottles of basic lemon-infused water and paying a hundred dollars a bottle. It prevented the employees feeling like charity cases even if it meant they looked at her like some eccentric, crazy rich idiot.

Kai did this quietly, without Milly's knowledge. She much preferred her assistant's fearful respect to any soft looks if she found out. *God forbid.*

So far today, Kai had unearthed two employees deserving attention: Maria in housekeeping—she worked two jobs to help put her gifted daughter through college. And on the roulette table, elderly Darius had bad hips and heart, costly medication, and no insurance. Both would now have no trouble paying rent for the next few months.

"Who is Maria?" Milly suddenly asked. "She stopped me to thank me profusely for your help. I know how much we tip our informants, so it shouldn't have caused *that* much gratitude."

Ah hell. "She's the head housekeeper. I gave her a little more than the others. But her valuable intel will be worth it," Kai lied smoothly.

"Valuable intel? From someone in housekeeping?" Milly studied her. "You know, this reminds me of when we were in Chicago. You spent a lot of time with that war-veteran busboy. He told me later you'd asked him to find you a green tea that was 'not the weak nonsense on the hotel menu.' But Ms. Fisher, you don't even drink green tea."

"Oh." *Shit, shit, shit.* "I'd read about a green tea cleanse and wanted to try it but the product I wanted was impossible to find. Then I changed my mind." She waved the topic away. "Besides, James was a good networker for us."

"Ms. Fisher, I submitted no networking expenses for him."

"I must have forgotten to include him. It was a busy week."

Milly's expression was one she'd never seen before: skepticism.

Oh, for God's sake. Kai's little benefits scheme was no one's business. "What *are* you suggesting?" Her eyes narrowed.

"Well, a person might think you were helping out some struggling employees a little to be nice. And a person might think it's hardly the first time. Or even the tenth."

"Now that doesn't sound like me, does it?" Kai glared.

Milly paused long enough for her reply to sound like a punchline. "Of course not, Ms. Fisher."

"I'm The Closer for a reason. I *crush* rivals on deals. I have a reputation as driven and impossible to beat. So I certainly do not do altruistic or soft or *nice.*"

A longer pause followed. "I understand, Ms. Fisher." Milly's tone was placid enough, although her eyes seemed amused. "And Scorched Earth isn't about helping people, either."

Damn it. "Bad employers should be held to account. Scorched Earth is purely about vengeance. Naming names. Harming those who do harm." Kai attempted her fiercest look to sell her BS even if it was a lost cause.

Milly's expression had turned...*fond.*

Kai sighed. This was exactly what she'd been afraid of.

"Purely vengeance," Milly repeated. "Of course it is, Ms. Fisher. You're all fire and fury and dragony. Got it." She might as well have thrown in playful *grrr* noises while she was at it.

"You know, I much preferred you when you were afraid of me," Kai muttered.

"Oh, I was never afraid of you," Milly said pleasantly, clasping her hands in her lap.

"*What?*"

"Um...well, okay, you can be a bit imposing sometimes. Maybe... um...a little exasperating. Especially before your coffee. Super scary then. *I'm* intimidated."

Great. She was being humored by a woman so dark that she kept a kitten calendar on her desk.

Kai straightened, well and truly over this dumpster fire of a conversation. "That's settled," she said with a hand flap. "We'll never speak of this again."

"No, Ms. Fisher."

"Now let's focus on what's important. Any new intel on Hamadani?"

"Graham at the concierge desk just texted that Mr. Hamadani is booked to arrive in two days."

"Excellent." *Interesting.* Although the conference wasn't until next week, often attendees arrived early to network. Of course, some guests turned up days ahead just to have fun. Having read her target's file on the flight over, not to mention Hamadani's bone-dry academic paper on hotels, she had little doubt that the businessman would not be among the chandelier-swinging crowd.

Kai made a mental note to approach Hamadani accordingly. She'd be all business, facts, spreadsheets, and profit to nail down this deal.

Oh, how she'd love this conquest. Winning had always given her comfort when the rest of her life was falling apart, but Mayfair Palace would be no ordinary win. If she achieved this—a hotel so damned perfect that even risk-averse, US-centric Benjamin Stein wanted it—Kai doubted she'd ever come down off that high.

She paced, visualizing "bumping into" Hamadani, and exactly how she'd play it. Finally, she gave up. She needed to burn off her excess adrenaline in more space and calm her overflowing brain.

"I'm just going to do another lap of the hotel," Kai told Milly. "Get the lay of the land."

Her assistant rose. "I'll come down with you. I need to use the fax machine at the front desk. Martin Keys, the owner of St. Louis Heritage Hotel in Missouri, wants to review some of the confidential clauses before signing."

"Right." Kai led the way to the door.

The elevator was empty and whisked them down to the lobby with a low hum.

Kai stepped out first, and Milly matched her step.

"When you fax Martin, tell him that's our best offer," Kai said. "The best we've ever made."

"Is it?"

"Of course not, but he's a man who needs to feel unique. Make him feel everything's custom-made for him. He wants to feel..." She faded out, distracted by a new sight. "...*Special*."

An arresting woman in her mid-forties had just swept through the hotel doors on her way to the check-in counter, trailed by a porter and Louis Vuitton luggage. Her pale features were angular, almost sharp, with pronounced cheekbones, an aquiline nose that suited her slightly longer face, and full lips. Any slight imperfections worked together and balanced the effect—somehow only enhancing her power, refinement, and beauty.

The arrogant tilt of her chin made Kai come to a stop. The woman looked so sure, as if she owned the whole damned world.

Kai's gaze roamed her. Glossy, light-brown hair reached the top of the woman's starched white collar, which coordinated perfectly with a tailored navy pantsuit. She seemed imperious. She didn't walk so much as stalk. The whole effect was...

"Stunning," she whispered.

"Ms. Fisher?"

She turned, having forgotten Milly was beside her. "What?"

"I said, I'm going to send the fax now. I'll leave you to your, er…" Her eyes flitted to the woman and back. "Sightseeing."

Kai lifted an eyebrow, refusing to be embarrassed at being caught staring at magnificence. "Careful, Milly. One day you'll be in love, too, and I will gleefully torment you about it."

"I expect that's true." Milly's lips ticked up the faintest amount, and she headed over to the front desk.

In love? Kai snorted at the ill-chosen words. *Lust* was what she'd meant, obviously. Although, judging by the woman's fine, tight ass as she bent slightly over the counter, Kai couldn't dispute there was at least *some* love.

Who was this woman? A high-stakes gambler? A business leader? A hotel VP, perhaps? Here for the conference? Ah, the last one made sense. Kai didn't recognize her, though. She was sure she'd remember *her* if they'd crossed paths before.

Disdain crossed the woman's face as she turned abruptly from the check-in desk. Kai was too far away to make out the words, but she would dearly love to know what had prompted that uncensored reaction.

Interesting that the woman didn't seem to care what anyone thought of her. Whatever her world entailed, she was most likely used to being in charge.

Kai was tempted to make a few discreet inquiries, learn who the woman was and determine a way to meet her, but any distractions or a loss of focus right now were completely unacceptable.

She had a job to do. Not just any job…THE job. Kai was closing in on a deal so momentous that if she nailed it, she'd be one of the few people to leave Las Vegas as that rarest of things: a winner.

ONE HOUR EARLIER

Amelia gazed out at the tarmac as the pilot taxied into McCarran International Airport. Suppressing a yawn, she glanced at her watch. Just before one in the morning her time. She'd caught a nap on the way over, but it wasn't nearly long enough.

Nevada's gradually setting sun poured through the windows. Amelia adjusted her watch to Vegas time, then turned her phone on. It sprang to life with missed-call alerts.

A message from Joe, who'd be expecting an update on the deal by now. And four calls from Quinn?

Four?

With a frown, she called her second-in-command. "Quinn? I've just landed. What's so urgent?"

"Did he call you? Did he explain?" Gone was her usual confidence.

Amelia's stomach tightened. "Who?"

"Nedal."

An awful moment of silence stretched out between them.

"No," Amelia said slowly. "No calls. Why? Didn't he return to the office and sign?"

"He never showed," Quinn said quietly. "His phone's off and he hasn't returned my calls. So we had a room full of bored lawyers and no deal."

Nedal was *gone*? Mayfair Palace was unsigned? "What happened?" Amelia demanded in disbelief.

"I was hoping you knew. How did you two leave things?"

"We finalized terms in the back of the limo. No issues at all. He seemed fine. We made dinner plans to celebrate on my return. He was also a proud uncle and showed me a photo of his sister's new baby and her doting husband. That was fun, let me tell you." She ground her jaw at the reminder. "I wondered if he'd forgotten Mariam and I were once…" She exhaled. "Involved. It has been eight years."

Quinn made a wincing noise. "Awkward."

Only for me. She thought back. "Then he took a call and…" Amelia stopped and rewound. The call had changed the mood in the car. Worry and stress had crept into the edges of Nedal's normally genial features.

"Everything okay?" Amelia had asked him, concerned, after he ended the short call.

"Just my father's assistant in Dubai." He had smoothed down his impeccable pants and given her a strained look. "It is requested that I call my father immediately. You know how he loves to share his wisdom in business."

A polite way of saying the man was a control freak who meddled in his son's affairs.

"Does he have concerns about our deal?" Amelia had replied carefully.

"This deal is mutually beneficial." He had drawn in a breath. "I hoped he'd find it satisfactory. For whatever reason, my father has demanded a conversation immediately and does not like to be kept waiting." He'd met her eye. "Would your associates mind if I delayed meeting them for an hour while I sort out this…family business?"

"Of course not." Amelia had immediately texted Quinn his request. A reply had pinged back quickly. "All set for four-fifteen at the Duxton offices, and Quinn will meet you and take you up." She'd glanced at Nedal. "All right?"

"Yes." He had smiled then, as if to draw a line under the serious conversation. "What of you? What has you traveling to the United States this fine day?"

"Just family business." She'd repeated his words with the same vagueness he'd supplied, offering the ghost of a smile.

His eyes had crinkled, and he'd given a knowing nod. "Mm. Where would we be without our relatives making our lives more interesting, hmm?"

Ah. He'd definitely heard about Oliver's indiscretions then. "Indeed."

With a small laugh, he had changed the topic to something bland.

Amelia shook herself out of the memory and told Quinn, "He had a call from his father. Urgent family business. That was what prompted the meeting time change."

"Some family matter was more pressing than signing a huge deal?"

"You know how powerful his father is. He owns half the hotels in the United Arab Emirates. That power extends to his family. Nedal had no choice but to obey. Everyone jumps to his orders."

A sour reminder rose as to how true that was. Nedal's warm, smart, funny sister, Mariam, swam into her mind. They'd met at a charity fundraiser. The beautiful languages teacher had teased that she should teach Amelia Arabic to make her a "more well-rounded hotel manager" and capitalize on the boom in wealthy Middle Eastern vacationers.

For six glorious months, somewhere between learning Arabic and Mariam's intoxicating body, Amelia had gained an unforgettable education.

When Mariam's father had learned of their relationship and that his daughter was bisexual, he'd blamed Amelia and ordered Mariam to cut off all contact with her. And...Mariam had. Just like that.

It was ancient history now. And if Amelia had any doubts about that, today she'd seen proof that Mariam had moved on.

Was that why Nedal had shown her the photo of Mariam looking so happy with her husband and baby? He wanted her to see, to *really* see, that despite Amelia's worst fears, she'd found happiness?

Amelia hated the faint curl of jealousy she couldn't entirely force back down. She *was* happy for Mariam. It had all ended well—for Mariam, at least—even if Amelia's heart still contained the hairline fractures.

"You're worried Nedal's father demanded our deal be shut down?" Quinn asked.

"He's the only one with the power and motive to pull it."

"Think he's still mad you defiled his darling daughter?"

"I defiled no one," Amelia snapped.

"Sorry." Quinn sounded contrite. "His words, not mine."

That Amelia had "defiled" Mariam was the most unfair charge of all the insults the man had leveled at her. Mariam had been the pursuer, for God's sake. She'd been so confident and self-assured—until it had all become too real.

Quinn's theory looped around her head, though. *Surely Mariam's father isn't still furious with me?*

No. This was business. The man was too much of a pragmatist to let a personal grudge get in the way of that. He'd never stopped Nedal making any other deals with Amelia, so why balk at this one?

But...maybe he knew what failing to secure Mayfair Palace would mean to her? Had someone filled him in on the leadership tussle? Had he been waiting all this time to punish her? She'd somehow stolen his dream of a perfect daughter, so now he'd stolen her dream of the perfect hotel?

"Too soon to tell," Amelia finally answered. "What happened after you couldn't reach Nedal?"

"I spoke to that asshole assistant of his."

She grimaced. The man acted more like a bodyguard than a PA, which seemed fair since that was his former occupation back home in Dubai. Nedal's PA held the singular distinction of being the only person in Amelia's circles who had less of an interest in cultivating people skills than she had.

"The man had his usual stonewalling-on-steroids going on," Quinn continued. "He wouldn't tell me anything except that Nedal was okay, but no longer available to do business with us now. He seemed to enjoy telling me that a whole lot."

"No longer available to… What does that mean?"

"He emphasized the *us*. As though Nedal was taking his deal elsewhere and we can kindly go fuck ourselves. He sounded happy about it."

Amelia stared out at the runway as little carts buzzed around, carrying supplies to the various private jets. What *was* going on? She'd saved Nedal's ass once when he'd been desperately trying to offload a massive Greek hotel resort during Europe's financial crisis. She'd taken it off his hands at a fair price and prevented him having to skirt bankruptcy and, worse, his father. Nedal owed her. In fact, when Mayfair Palace had come up, he'd called her first. So this made zero sense.

"Do you think…" Quinn paused. "I mean, we have to consider all possibilities, right? Do you think he was maybe dealing with a second buyer all along? And in the end their deal was better, so he's ghosted us?"

"Not his style."

"Is it his style to just skip a signing meeting? Who does that? Not to mention the fact that he's torpedoed a deal we spent months negotiating."

"Nothing's torpedoed. I don't accept that. Keep digging and get to the bottom of this."

Quinn exhaled. "Leave it with me."

The door to the cockpit opened and the co-pilot appeared. He took in the fact that Amelia hadn't budged since landing and pointedly looked at his watch. "Ma'am, we have to get underway again ASAP. We cannot miss our slot."

She nodded, said goodbye to Quinn, and unbuckled from her seat.

If Nedal had changed his mind—or been forced to change his mind—or been up to some other game all along, there was nothing she could do now. All she could control was what lay ahead of her. Quinn was exceptional. She would get answers. And then they'd deal with whatever this was.

Convincing herself to take the Zen approach was easier said than done. And Amelia definitely did not want to return Joe's call and explain how she'd failed to get Hotel Duxton's new jewel in the crown.

The limo came to a halt in front of Duxton Vegas as Amelia closed her phone, frustrated she'd been as unable to reach Nedal as Quinn had been. She studied her brother's hotel. It was suitably obnoxious, exactly as she'd expected given its environs.

The packet Joe had sent her said the hotel boasted a fluorescent-pink nightclub and a sports-viewing room tricked out with sofas that had a "Booze Button" built into armrests, to place orders. She hated it already—although her view was irrelevant. The only question that mattered was: What do the guests think?

She strode to the check-in desk and waited impatiently as an older woman behind the counter found her reservation at a turtle's pace, between discreet dabs at her red nose with a tissue.

"Sorry," the woman mumbled. "The flu's going around. Our manager's off sick and so are half the team. I'm actually the assistant manager."

That explained her speed, but still. Assistant managers should be cross trained on every aspect of hotel operations. Amelia could check in a guest in her sleep, for God's sake. She was half tempted to lean over the desk, rattle a few keys, and do it herself.

Amelia sighed. It was now approaching two a.m. for her, even if it was only six in the evening here. This incompetence just made her long day even longer. "Do you have no one who can replace your ill check-in person?" she asked briskly.

"They both quit a few days ago."

Both? Apparently turnover was as bad as Joe had indicated.

A room key card was slid over the counter and the porter summoned with the crook of the assistant manager's finger. "Thank you, Ms. Hanson."

The woman gave Amelia's credit card, which bore the name *Lia Hanson*, back to her. The name was courtesy of Quinn, years ago, when Amelia had asked for a way to be incognito when checking into hotels. It was hard to assess a place when everyone instantly knew she was the boss. Amelia wasn't entirely sure how Quinn had pulled off obtaining a fake name on a credit card. Her deputy would only say that Amelia's obsequious bank manager had "wanted to make their most-valued customer *very* happy" and that he trusted Amelia would continue banking with them for many years to come.

"*Enboy* your stay," the assistant manager finished. Well, that was how it sounded. Then she sneezed.

Amelia recoiled. This was unacceptable—she could infect all the guests. *Including me.* Amelia shuddered and headed for the elevators.

The moment she was safely inside, she extracted anti-bacterial gel and liberally coated her hands with it, along with the door key card and her credit card.

"What?" she asked acidly as the porter side-eyed her. "Did you not see the disease-incubus at the front desk?"

He cleared his throat and looked away.

Once ensconced in her suite, she was grateful to be alone again. Amelia took a moment to examine the view. She stared down at the garish mess of blinking marquees and neon signs, feeling her life force draining from her body.

Look at me! the lights shouted.

Must I? she wanted to shout back.

Stepping back, she pulled the curtains closed and shed her business suit. She hung it and snapped the sleeves straight before meticulously unpacking the rest of her garments.

Satisfied all was in order, she stepped into the shower and let the water sluice over her.

It hit her then. The exhaustion and stress. She leaned into the fogging glass and allowed the warmth of the water to soothe her.

By the time she stepped out, pink and pruned, twenty minutes had passed. That counted as practically hedonistic for her. She caught sight of herself in the brightly lit mirror and stared. Had she aged five years on the way here?

"Thanks for that, Ollie."

Although, really, Nedal was equally responsible. The problem was, unlike her brother, she actually liked Nedal, so assigning him blame was painful.

She dried off and dressed in pale blue cotton pajamas as she weighed up her options for the rest of the evening. She could figure out her plan of attack for tomorrow: visiting the various section managers, having a discreet word about what they saw as being the hotel's key issues affecting staff retention.

Or she could tackle her conference-speech rewrites. Quinn had been too busy hunting Nedal to make any suggestions, though, so it was all on her.

Amelia yawned. *Right. Too hard tonight.*

She tried checking in with Quinn again, but all she got was voicemail. Then she remembered it was almost three in the morning in London. She hit play on a message from Imogen.

> *Auntie Lia? I'm borrrred. I have more questions: Do fish know they're in a tank? And if they don't know, how does anyone? I mean what if WE'RE in a tank? And don't just say we aren't, because how would you know-know? We could be like fish! Can you call me soon? Love you. And remember, don't worry about what the mean people say about you... know why?*

Her voice broke into song... something about *haters gonna hate.* Amelia recognized it after a few moments from the ringtone Imogen had put into Amelia's phone last Hanukkah and assigned to herself—"So you'll always know it's me when I call," she'd explained earnestly.

The message ended.

Warmth filled her. Although Imogen was technically Amelia's first cousin once removed, she'd always called her Auntie Lia. Amelia had asked her why, and the reply would stay with her forever. "Duh! Cos I'm the only one who gets to. I get a special name for you that's just for me." Imogen had rolled her eyes as if that was *so* obvious.

Imogen's father, Simon, might have limited talent, and be of dubious parental worth since he kept forgetting to pay attention to Imogen in favor of his romantic distractions, but he'd done something spectacularly right the day he'd fathered that inquisitive little girl with his late wife.

Thumbing to the next message, Amelia sighed as she saw the sender. Joe.

Just touching base with you, Amelia. Is Hamadani signed and sealed? We'll make the announcement in... rustling papers sounded... *ten days. This'll play well with the board. You'll be a star. Let me know.*

Worry surged. Ten days until the announcement? Amelia could stall Joe a few days until Quinn had answers—but there was no guarantee this was even fixable.

Where on earth was Nedal? And if family was the reason for his disappearance, why leave a message that he was no longer doing any business with her?

That sounded too final for her liking.

Amelia rolled over and distracted herself with the news feeds, disturbed to see how often Oliver had been named and shamed. That reminded her of Scorched Earth's dig at her. Unable to resist, she flicked over to Twitter and hunted through the feed. Just to see if The Dragon had mentioned her again. For research, of course. Knowing thine enemy.

Amelia snorted at her own nonsense.

Q: How do you know you work for a Duxton hotel? A: Your bank can't tell when it's payday.

Lies! She'd never underpaid an employee in her life. In fact, in some cases, she'd paid well above market rate to retain staff in critical roles. Her teeth ground at all the comebacks she was itching to say. Typical of Scorched Earth. It was always easy to snipe from the sidelines.

Tiredness and annoyance were clearly affecting her because before she knew it, she'd started hitting buttons, looking for a way to reply to one of these things. Eventually she found herself directed to a sign-up page. Moments later she created her Twitter name: @AEDuxton.

Well. Now what?

She hesitated. She'd told Quinn to stay off social media for a reason. It was a bad idea to engage one's critics when emotional. But perhaps she could just leave one little message, explaining Duxton's side of things? Would that be so bad? Everyone should get a right of reply. So, she should just...

A link. That's what she'd do. There had been a business story a year ago that had ranked hotels across Europe based on staff satisfaction. Hotel Duxton had come second. Personally, it still annoyed her a little she hadn't come first, but who could compete against The Radford's free vacations for staff on their CEO's private island? She tweeted:

> *Facts are just as free as ignorance. Choose wisely. FYI: Employees voted Hotel Duxton No. 2 in Europe.*

Amelia dug up the link to the story and included it before tweeting. There. That wasn't too combative. Just the facts, laid out for the discerning readers of Twitter to objectively examine. People could make up their own minds now.

She waited a minute or two, noting with consternation that she had not received any "likes." Perhaps people were still reading the article? It was quite wordy.

Users soon began replying with comments that ran the gamut from "@ aeduxton's a bot account, ignore!" to "You're brothers an asshole" and "Isn't Duxton the biggest advertiser at that newspaper? Hardly an unbiased poll. More like advertorial crap. #fake news."

What? People were deliberately misinterpreting the article's data, and some users, she was quite sure, had not read her story at all before commenting. Also—the word was *your* not *you're*. Infidels.

A new tweet appeared from Scorched Earth itself, quoting Amelia's tweet.

> *We always knew Hotel Duxton was second best, but thanks for the proof. :) Oh, and welcome to the Thunderdome, Amelia Duxton.*

Welcome to the... What did that mean? Scorched Earth then dropped another tweet showing the Titanic sinking.

Amelia was supposed to believe she'd sunk her case somehow and had been...Amelia peered at the screen at the word that kept appearing... "owned"? And coming second in an international poll was not the same as second best! Against her better judgment, she tapped out a new tweet.

When you twist data to your own ends to create propaganda, you're no better than Gobbles.

Amelia hit *Post* before realizing her phone had auto-corrected Hitler's propagandist Goebbels to "Gobbles." She looked around for an edit button. Nothing. What caveman had produced this backward atrocity?

A cartoon turkey suddenly stared back from her feed, saying, "gobble, gobble." Then Scorched Earth tweeted again.

Wow, you really suck at this. You sure you want to take over Duxton if you can't even handle Twitter?

Amelia's eyes narrowed. She did not "suck" at anything. Well, all right, people skills, perhaps, but nothing important. She cracked her knuckles. This two-bit, basement-dwelling troll who probably had yet to liberate himself from his mother's teat would never "own" her.

Her phone rang just as she started typing. *Not now!* It kept ringing. She reluctantly answered, still weighing up whether to post another comment.

"Boss?" came a tired voice. "What happened to 'stay off Twitter?'"

"Quinn? Is there a problem?"

"Um, yeah. I never realized you don't know how social media works."

"I don't follow."

"There's an art to being clever and not letting crap get to you, and working out who's trolling, and knowing when and when not to bite...and *most especially* to noticing when you're being set up. Look, it's too late here for me to explain it now. Can you just trust me and walk away?"

"Excuse me? I'm behaving with decorum!" Amelia glared at her phone.

"You are. But I've been getting messages from Duxton managers worldwide asking if I'm seeing what's going down on Twitter. They woke me up, in fact."

"I'm sorry you're not getting your beauty sleep, Quinn, but that's hardly—"

"Boss, *please*. You're getting *roasted*."

"Nonsense. I'm simply laying out facts in order for Scorched Earth's followers to understand my position."

"They're not interested in facts. They want to make you look bad, and you keep engaging with them. So, come on, kill the Twitter account, okay? If you're still interested in social media tomorrow, I'll give you the skinny on how to work it to your own ends."

Amelia paused at the thought she might have been embarrassing herself enough for people to alert Quinn. *Goddamnit.* "Fine."

"Hey, I'm sorry people are shit. We'll talk tomorrow. Night, boss." She hung up.

Amelia hit a few buttons until she found an account deletion option, then flung the phone away.

Wonderful. She'd apparently humiliated herself. There was a reason she'd always distrusted social media. And The Dragon was clearly uninterested in the truth and merely enjoyed belittling others.

What a lovely end to an already dreadful evening. At the reminder of why it had started off so badly, Amelia groaned, closed her eyes, and tried to sleep.

It was a battle, despite her exhaustion. The faint glow of Vegas's light display brightened her room even through the thick, ugly, bronze-brown curtains.

Christ.

Chapter 5

Prohibition Bar

Kai stared at the photograph on her phone, obsessing over every detail. It might be breakfast rush hour in the hotel's ground-floor restaurant, with distracting smells of bacon and fresh-baked pastries, but the place could have been on fire for all Kai cared. Because while it had taken two days, the staff at Hotel Duxton had managed to do one thing the entire internet had failed at: cough up a photo of Nedal al-Hamadani.

The blurry camera-phone photo revealed a swarthy-looking man at a bar with a cleavage-enhanced blonde on his arm—the sort of woman who could smell extreme wealth a mile off and charged by the hour. He'd checked in late the previous night and, by the looks of things, was making up for lost time.

So *this* was Nedal? She had imagined a clever, measured, serious entrepreneur to go with his Master's degree in law and finance at an elite London college, not some rich party boy.

Kai slid her phone over the linen tablecloth to Milly. "Tell me who you see."

"Nedal al-Hamadani," Milly replied with a glance before tucking into her fruit salad.

"Not his name, tell me *who* you see."

Milly studied the photo again. "He likes to play."

"Mmm. And?"

"And what, Ms. Fisher?"

Kai sighed. "Dig deeper."

"Well, he's not what I expected, I guess. I thought he'd be more… restrained. Although a lot of people let down their hair in Vegas, especially when they're away from anyone who knows them."

"Very true. What else do you see?"

"Um…I didn't think Muslims drank alcohol." Milly pointed to the beer on the bar beside his elbow. "Although we don't know for sure about his religion—however, statistically speaking, the odds are good."

"Other conclusions?"

"It might be her drink, not his." Milly eyed Blondey McBoobsy.

"Yes. Any other theories?"

"Maybe it's not him? Is the waitress who sent you this sure he's our target?"

"An excellent question," Kai said, pleased. "And I asked. The room number on the bar tab matched Hamadani's."

"Perhaps the man is Mr. Hamadani's associate?" Milly suggested. "Staying with him and using the same room number?"

That was something Kai hadn't considered. "One way to find out." With an approving look at Milly, she emailed the phone photo to Mr. Stein. Her boss had met with the man in Hamadani's London headquarters, so he'd know if they were dealing with the right target.

Mr. Stein's reply landed by the time Kai had finished her toast and was deciding on whether a fourth cup of coffee was overkill before nine.

Yes, that is him. Good. Now seal this deal.

"Identity confirmed." Kai dropped her phone back to the table. "Just goes to show you can't judge a book by its cover. Then again, he might be quite conservative back home."

"He'd have to be. A party boy wouldn't have the focus to pull off all the hotel developments Mr. Hamadani's spearheaded in the past decade."

"No." Kai eyed her cup. Probably best to skip that fourth coffee. "Right, phase two: we track down our businessman, today preferably, and pray we're not too late to make a counter-offer."

"How? He was at that bar hours ago. He could be anywhere now."

"We memorize his appearance." Kai stared hard at the photo, willing the focus to magically sharpen. "And we wait for our other little birds to report in. Hamadani will have to surface again sooner or later, even if it's only for the conference. Then?" She glanced up at Milly and offered her most lethal smile. "We pounce."

Hey Ur guy's in here now. Prohibition Bar

Kai blinked. It was eight in the evening by now and, after no sightings all day, Kai had resigned herself to the fact that her target might be hibernating for the duration until the conference. Possibly with that busty new friend.

Rising swiftly, Kai hurried to the adjoining room's door and knocked, her mind already filling with plans. "Milly?"

Her assistant poked her head through the gap. "Yes, Ms. Fisher?"

"I was texted a tip on Hamadani. He's back at that same bar."

"Do you need me to come with you?"

"No. A solo approach is best."

"Okay, I'll keep working on answering Mr. Keys's email."

"Excellent. Don't wait up for me. I have no idea if our businessman's still there, but if he's not, I'll hang around for a while in case he returns."

"Good luck."

"Oh, I don't need luck." Kai hoped her attempt at confidence would go from her lips to God's ears. "I'll just be my usual fabulous self."

"Of course, Ms. Fisher. What *was* I thinking?"

Kai laughed at Milly's dry retort and headed off to the bar.

This was it.

As she entered Prohibition Bar, Kai's head whipped around the tables, seeking her quarry. The room comprised Roaring Twenties-themed paintings, a barman in suspenders and a pin-striped shirt, and a few assorted customers sitting around.

Damn it. Would it be too much for Nedal al-Hamadani to sit in one place for longer than ten minutes? With a disappointed sigh, Kai slid onto a bar stool, summoned the bartender, and ordered a Negroni.

An hour later, she was debating whether to call it a night when a woman entered. Kai stilled as she recognized her immediately.

It was *her*. The commanding, "I own the whole damned universe" guest from the lobby.

With an appraising eye, the woman slowly took in her surroundings, as if she were cataloging the room. There was such a stillness to her.

Kai's breath caught.

The woman slid onto a bar stool two down from Kai, somehow making that graceful despite how high the seats were.

With a long index finger, the woman tapped the counter once. Her pronounced tap was sharp, and the flick of her wrist allowed Kai a glimpse of her watch. A vintage Gallet.

A *Gallet*. She drew in an impressed breath. Kai's weakness was luxury watches, and this one was as divine as it was rare.

When she ordered, the woman's clipped, cool voice was the polar opposite of what Kai's insides were doing.

Then she registered what the woman had ordered.

Kai leaned across the vacant stool between them, smiling at this beautiful stranger, suddenly knowing exactly what to say.

Even after two days, jetlag was still kicking Amelia around. Sleep beyond an hour here or there had proved fruitless. She couldn't face turnover issues while barely awake, so instead she'd spent her time working on her speech. Joe's insistence she make it entertaining was giving her a migraine that was not helped by Quinn's latest text message.

> *Went to Hamadani's HQ and found out he's left the UK. No staff will spill on where he went. FYI half of Duxton now have screencaps circulating of a certain @AEDuxton trying to take on Scorched Earth. I told everyone who asked that it wasn't you. Not sure if they believed me but that's our story. Sorry about Hamadani. - Q*

Amelia's jaw clenched, and she pushed her late-night shame from her mind.

She glanced at her watch. Too early for bed, but still time to see the hotel at peak hour. At least the day wouldn't be a total waste.

The place was much as she'd expected. Adequately busy restaurants and a jam-packed casino. However, while the venues were crowded, they were also short-staffed. Far too many gaming tables were shut down.

How many employees *had* the flu knocked out? Or was this all part of the turnover crisis?

Prohibition Bar, the largest bar at Duxton Vegas and the one supplying drinks to the adjacent gaming-room floor, was her final stop. She was curious as to how efficient it was. Keep gamblers waiting too long, and they tended to choose a different casino.

Sliding onto a bar stool, Amelia ordered a Negroni. Not her preferred beverage, but the gin, vermouth, and bitters drink was a basic test of drink-making skills. Measures had to be precise, and it should be stirred, never shaken.

"Brave woman," came a warm voice from a seat down. "Ordering that."

She turned to find an attractive brunette regarding her. The woman's legs were impossible to miss—tapered and toned, under a maroon thigh-length dress. She pivoted a little, angling toward Amelia, her dress riding up an inch higher.

Stunning.

Amelia squelched that errant thought—she was on the clock. Business was her sole focus, not seriously perfect legs like these.

The woman's sculpted eyebrow lifted in amusement at the direction of Amelia's gaze.

It was like a dash of cold water. Amelia detested cockiness. "Oh? Why's a Negroni brave?" Her tone could have frozen the Sahara, with enough ice left over for every drink in the room.

"I tried one earlier and I'm still trying to peel my tongue off the roof of my mouth. I'm guessing that Tim's new."

Amelia glanced at the bartender, who was *shaking* her Negroni. "I see," she replied noncommittally.

The woman fell silent, apparently content to watch with interested eyes so dark they were almost black.

Tim placed the drink in front of Amelia, and she examined it with a critical eye. The color was a garish red—a sure sign of excess bitters. With a soft sigh, already knowing where this was going, she reached for it.

"Your funeral," the woman said lightly, and her lips curled.

Amelia hesitated, then sipped.

Oh God. Her taste buds shrieked in protest and her eyes watered at the overdose of bitters in it. She slapped the glass back on its coaster. "I see you were not joking," she ground out.

"No." The woman's lips quirked wider. "I'd never joke about something as important as alcohol. The bourbon and Coke's passable, at least."

"High praise." Amelia's mouth felt as if she'd licked lemon off sandpaper. "So have you just been sitting here all evening, testing Tim's drinks?"

"I'm not *quite* the sad drunk you're making me out to be."

"I apologize for impugning your reputation." Amelia smiled. "I'm quite sure you're a sensible drinker with no lush-like tendencies."

The woman moved one seat over to sit beside Amelia. "Actually, I'm here filling in time. I think I'm being stood up." She sounded unbothered.

"They're not worth it," Amelia said archly. "Time is valuable. Why is your time worth less than your companion's?"

"You'd be right, normally. But my information on my associate's whereabouts is a bit hit and miss. It's not his fault. I thought I'd wait in case he came back."

"I...see." What sort of meeting involved unspecified times and locations? Amelia finally caught the eye of the bartender and signaled for his return, then shifted her attention back to the woman. "So what is it that you do that involves tracking down elusive associates in bars at nine at night?"

"I'm here to do a deal."

"With the man standing you up."

"Yes. Sometimes I acquire new hotels for my company. I go where the deals are. Right now, that's Vegas."

Buying a *Vegas* hotel? Amelia's business brain kicked in, fascinated. Idly, she wondered whether showgirls and other stage acts would be automatically included as assets or not. She was about to ask when Tim reappeared. Amelia pushed the Negroni his way and glared.

"Was the drink not to your satisfaction, ma'am?"

"No." She regarded him coolly. "What quantity of bitters did you put in there?"

"What the recipe called for. Ten ounces of Campari."

"Why don't you bring that recipe over here? So we can both see where you went wrong?"

The man frowned but headed down the counter to fetch the chart.

"I must say I'm curious as to what it says, too," the other woman whispered.

"It says *one* ounce," Amelia said with absolute certainty. She'd read the Hotel Duxton drinks chart six years ago, and she never forgot a number. Recipes were standard across all their hotel bars.

The red-cheeked bartender returned and slid the laminated page on the counter. "Um, I think I see the problem."

"I'm sure you do." Amelia said sharply, not even bothering to glance down to confirm she was right. "How long have you worked here?"

"Just over two weeks."

"I suggest you brush up on the recipes more closely if you expect to stay. Campari is expensive. I doubt your company would appreciate you using ten times the required amount in every drink."

"No, ma'am. Sorry, ma'am. I'll get you a new drink."

"Yes you will. And this time, stir it, don't shake it, as the recipe also stipulates."

He scuttled away, looking thoroughly chastened.

"I'm Kai," the other woman said in an admiring voice. "And that was something else."

Amelia peered at her. "I don't see why. All I asked was for him to do his job."

"Yes. But it was *how*."

"What other way is there to request precision?"

Kai laughed. "Oh boy. So you work for Hotel Duxton?"

"Who says I do?" she asked curiously.

"You knew how many ounces of Campari were in the recipe. Every recipe is different, but they're standard throughout hotels in the same chain. So, conclusion, you work for Duxton. Middle management? Possibly here for the conference? Your lovely suit screams hotel executive, by the way. But like I should talk." She tugged the sleeve of her own dress.

"I'm afraid your reasoning is flawed. Sorry to disappoint."

"I'm so rarely wrong about these things," Kai murmured, eyes teasing. "But please, *educate* me."

How did she manage to make that sound sexy, especially since that awful cockiness was back? Amelia refocused on her earlier train of thought. "Fine. While there is some variation in Negroni recipes, the amount of bitters used is almost constant across the world: one ounce. Knowing that hardly makes me middle management at this hotel."

"Ah, I stand corrected." Kai patted Amelia's arm, then left her hand there.

Amelia eyed it in surprise. Had she forgotten to remove it? Or was this deliberate?

"What's your name?" Kai asked. "And if you're not a Duxton employee, what do you do? Because, I can't help saying—you really do come across as a hotel executive."

Warmth burned through her sleeve from Kai's fingers. Amelia should extract herself from that hand. She hated when people touched her without permission; it was so rude. And yet, Kai's grip didn't feel territorial, as though Amelia was some conquest. Instead, it felt like a plea for Amelia to not leave. That thought alone made Kai's fingers feel softer.

How...curious. Amelia was well aware she had an unapproachable energy, so much so that people tended to avoid her when they could. That suited her fine. Minimizing time spent dealing with those she couldn't relate to, or vice versa, was preferable.

Kai, on the other hand, was someone people would find desirable. She exuded openness, warmth, and seductiveness, and was the sort of woman who could choose any companion she wanted. And yet it was Amelia's arm that Kai's fingers had clasped. Why?

Suddenly Amelia didn't want to tell this stranger her name. She pictured Kai's teasing, sensual smile dissolving as she did that inevitable calculation. Upon learning Amelia was part of a billion-dollar hotel empire, everyone immediately stopped to consider her value, financially or professionally.

Maybe Kai wouldn't do that, although history suggested otherwise. It felt nice just sitting here for five minutes with a beautiful stranger who treated Amelia like anyone else. A stranger whose soft hand had yet to leave her arm.

"You do *know* your name?" Kai teased. "And your job?"

Amelia tensed, not wanting to lie outright.

"Woman of mystery, hmm?" Kai suggested. "Okay, let's see then... If I'm right and you are in hotels, then you've been sent here for the con. That means you wouldn't be upper management—no offense, but bosses at the top of the heap rarely have time to swan around Vegas conferences— especially not a whole week before they're due to start. So I don't think it'd be a state secret to ask for a humble, middle-management hotel executive's name?" Her eyes crinkled.

Amelia regarded her for a beat, deciding whether she wanted to be drawn farther into this odd conversation at all. "I'm Lia."

"Lia." Kai drew the word out as if tasting it. Under her drawled New York accent, it sounded like *leee-ahh*. "Lovely to meet you, Lia. And I promise I'm not judging you for being a middle manager. I just like to figure things out."

"You're so sure I'm in hotels," Amelia replied. "I could be CIA. Or in town for an illicit liaison with my gambling-addicted lover."

"No, you're not CIA." The hand on Amelia's sleeve clenched for a moment at the idea. "You see, Lia, you don't like to lie. And you wouldn't tolerate a gambling-addicted person in your circle, either."

"What makes you think I don't like to lie?"

"The way you handled the bartender. So blunt and forthright—almost insulted by his mistake. I think you mainly hated the imperfection of his error, which offended you more than the bad drink itself. So I see someone who loves accuracy and precision. Therefore, small logic leap, dating a gambler would make your brain explode. So much imperfection, you'd barely last an hour."

"I...see."

Kai chuckled. "Bullseye, huh?" The hand on her arm squeezed gently. "Can I buy your next drink, Lia?" Her voice was low and mesmerizing.

Amelia considered that. "That depends. Are you flirting with me, Kai?"

"If I'm doing it right." She paused. "Unless I'm barking up the wrong tree? Please tell me if I am."

Well, it was definitely the right tree, but did she want this complication? Amelia could stop this right now if she said something else: *Sorry, I'm not interested.* They'd finish up their drinks and conversation, go their separate ways, and Amelia's brief brush with the hedonistic delights of Vegas would be buried before she'd even left the bar.

It was the smart move, actually. She wasn't here to play, even if Kai was entertaining enough beneath all that cockiness. So, that settled it. Amelia would draw a line under things right now.

Her heart sank at the decision…then sank even farther. She stared at her drink.

Or…not. She lifted her head again.

Amelia's gaze drank in Kai. Laughing, intelligent eyes drew her in, as did the sensual mouth, so ready with a smile. Kai seemed so sure of herself, and while overconfidence was a huge turn-off in general, what if it was just well-placed confidence? Amelia had to admit she was interested enough to find out which it was. Not to mention, there were those amazing legs to consider.

Legs, mouth, and eyes versus cockiness? Three against one.

"A drink," Amelia murmured, the edges of her mouth turning up. "I will accept one drink."

"What's your preference?" Kai's eyes sparkled. "In *drinks*."

"Anything that doesn't taste like battery acid this time." Amelia offered a small smile in return. "Why don't I have what you're having?"

Pleasure lit Kai's face. "Absolutely." She exhaled so deeply that it sounded like she meant every syllable. "Let's do that."

Her sheer delight startled Amelia. It had been a long time—years—since anyone apart from Imogen had been this enthusiastic about spending time with her. How novel. Amelia was only too aware of how out of character it was for her to say yes to a drink with a woman she'd just met. But it was all harmless fun, right?

After all, what was the worst that could happen, having a drink with an attractive stranger in a bar in Vegas?

Chapter 6

Flirting

Hour one—Efficiency

"So," Kai said once their drinks had arrived, her confidence sky high, "what *do* you do? I mean assuming you aren't CIA after all? And I know you don't work in Vegas."

"I don't, hmm?"

"I saw you check in. Two days ago, same dashing suit as tonight. I couldn't help but notice you." Her admiring eyes flitted all over Lia's outfit. "You wear it so well."

"Your repertoire needs work. If you were a steak, I'd send it back as overdone."

"I'll try not to over-do my sirloin in the future." Kai smiled.

Lia eyed her over her glass. "Do you do this a lot? Hang out at bars and flirt with women?"

"Why not? I find women exquisite in general, and you remarkable in particular."

"You barely even know me. How do I count as remarkable?"

"I'm great at reading people. I just know."

"That's like saying 'Because I said so.' Prove you're good at this and I might actually believe this isn't a line you use on every woman you flirt with."

"All right," Kai said, "I'll start with that you've spent a lot of time in Europe."

"I have an accent?"

"Sometimes you use English turns of phrase. And you have a rare watch that isn't American."

"You know watches." She didn't wait for an answer. "Maybe I do mail-orders."

"You don't. You go into some high-level jewelry store, assess every piece, and then make your selection. Carefully. After weighing up every facet of the item for imperfections."

"Perhaps." Lia's expression was neutral.

"Your bearing is formal, as is your speech. You went to a private school. A fancy one. Boarding school abroad, perhaps? One of the snooty ones?"

"No. Tutors." Amelia looked faintly amused. "Although several of them were definitely snooty."

"I was close."

"Not close enough."

Kai laughed. "All right...you love precision and control and everything in its place. It's why that bad Negroni bugged you so much."

"Or I prefer to get what I order. And I did not order toxic swill."

Kai lifted her hands in surrender at that point. "What else... You're used to giving orders. You're a manager at your company."

"In a sense."

"How can someone be a manager in a sense?"

"An intriguing question." Lia did not elaborate.

Kai waited expectantly, but silence fell.

"I can hear your cogs turning," Lia finally said. "What have you concluded from all this?"

"I wonder if maybe you like to take charge in *all* things." Kai taunted. "From boardrooms to bedrooms."

"Awful line. The absolute worst." Lia tutted. "Consider that steak a charcoaled ember now."

"Too much, huh?" Kai asked lightly. "I was hoping you'd be in the mood to try something a little *un*predictable. Vegas rules apply."

"Vegas rules aren't real. And you've crossed the line so far beyond charming that you've somehow lapped yourself. Sorry to disappoint you, but it was self-inflicted."

"That's a shame. So I'm not even slightly charming?" Kai's eyebrows lifted.

"Hmm." Lia ran a slow finger down the condensation on her glass. "I suspect 'well practiced' is a better description. You are far too good at this."

"I'm taking that as a compliment."

"You would. But I hate cockiness."

"And yet you're here with me."

"I am, aren't I?" Lia regarded her. "Should I reconsider?"

"I hope you won't. How else will you learn all my insights into which of Tim's drinks are safe for consumption?"

"There is that." Lia almost threatened a smile. "Far be it for me to turn down such valuable intel."

Kai chuckled. "Okay, all games aside, I notice you dodged my question earlier. What *do* you do? Are you here for the conference?"

"Partly. Yes, I'm attending, but right now my interest is in hotel performance."

"Performance?" Kai considered that. "Are you a bean counter of some sort? An…accountant?" She couldn't picture it.

"More…" Lia paused. "An efficiency expert."

Kai pieced together what she wasn't saying. Comprehension dawned. "Ah. The turnover problem. You must be someone the Duxtons have brought in to find the cause of the staff exodus."

"Something along those lines."

"Okay, I have to scrap my 'middle management' theory now and suggest you're the boss at this efficiency-expert firm. You'll have your work cut out for you here. Duxton Vegas finds it impossible to retain staff."

"Who told you about its turnover issues?"

"Everyone knows Hotel Duxton is the worst place to work in Vegas—and that's saying something."

"The worst?" Lia eyed her skeptically. "Well, I'm sure *that's* based on entirely legitimate information."

"You think it's a lie?" Kai asked curiously.

"Of course." Lia sounded so sure. "It's most likely gossip spread by this establishment's rivals to stir up trouble. Grand Millennium comes to mind—they're always smearing the Duxtons." Her voice hardened. "It's simple: if you can't beat them, wage a whispering campaign against them, and get social media to help, including attack websites, such as Scorched Earth."

Kai blinked. "You really don't believe any of the anti-Duxton stories have a factual basis?" How could Scorched Earth's posts be dismissed so easily? When Kai's whistleblowing site had been at its peak, she'd been fastidious to back up allegations with statistics or fact-checked quotes from her sources. "I mean, Scorched Earth has a reputation as—"

"Gutter amateurs. Trolls and bullies making up silly hashtags and smearing people. Oliver *Dunce*-ton comes to mind. That was only a few days ago."

Kai suddenly realized her most recent posts could be perceived as juvenile trolling if someone didn't know the history of how long Scorched Earth had pursued Oliver over his terrible work practices. Maybe Lia was defending him because Oliver was the one to hire her to appraise Duxton Vegas. She switched tack. "If it's all a smear campaign, then why are you even here?"

"The high turnover issues are real." Lia's lips pressed together in obvious dissatisfaction. "But that could be caused by entirely benign reasons, not whatever gossip flies around passing for fact."

"Okay," Kai said gently, "how do you intend to investigate the facts?"

Lia looked more certain now. "Speak to the section managers, examine the books." She waved her hand. "Dig deep through the numbers. That's my skill; numbers. I'll investigate it all quietly, though, as much as possible. I don't wish for the floor staff to be aware. Errors occur when people feel watched."

"Oh, Lia." Kai couldn't believe she was serious.

"What?" Her clipped voice became defensive.

"How can you hope to get any company's true picture without talking to people?"

"I *am* talking to the people. I just said! Managers and…"

"Not managers. Come on, they won't know why people are leaving. They'll tell you it's natural attrition, that no one stays for long, it's just Vegas being Vegas. And it's all bull." Kai drew in a breath. "Or if they do know the truth, they'll lie because it makes them look bad. You need to ask the people on the front lines." She waved for Tim. "I'll prove it. I bet I can learn more in one minute than you could find out in a week of going over the books and talking to the suits."

"Another drink, ma'am?" Tim asked. His expression was cagey after Lia's dressing down.

"I have a question," Kai began with an encouraging smile. "We're having a little debate about Duxton Vegas's infamous staff turnover. Is it averaging one employee quitting every month? Or two?"

Confusion darted onto his face. "Ma'am?"

"Ballpark figure." Kai leaned over and jammed a twenty in his tip jar. "Please?"

"I really couldn't say," he said diplomatically. "And I am new."

"New people hear things, too," Kai pressed on. "Staffrooms are hotbeds of gossip. I'll tell you what: Loan me that water jug and tall glass for a sec." She pointed to a jug on the counter.

He passed them over.

"I'm going to start pouring," Kai said. "Every inch is how many people leave Duxton in a month. Tell me when to stop pouring."

Tim's eyes darted around, then he looked back at her. He didn't agree, but his gaze was fixed on the glass.

Kai began to pour. And pour. She was starting to wonder if he'd misunderstood when the bartender suddenly said in a low voice, "Stop."

The water was near the rim.

Kai stared. This was unsustainable, and it was clear from Lia's face that she thought the same. "So…seven staff a month?"

"Actually, the glass wasn't tall enough," he muttered. "It's more than five a week."

A week? Kai choked. "Why are they leaving? Is it the points scheme?"

Lia looked puzzled.

Had she not heard of it? She really should read Scorched Earth more often.

Tim's eyes darted nervously around the room.

Another bill landed in his tips jar courtesy of Kai. "Please?"

"That's a big reason, ma'am. It doesn't affect me so much as I don't have a family so I can afford to lose a little money without it being too bad." Tim stiffened as the assistant manager passed through the bar area on her way to the gaming rooms. He said loudly, "Care for another drink?"

"No, no, that's fine." Kai smiled. "Thanks for your time. Don't worry. This is our little secret."

His shoulders relaxed a little, and he returned the jug to his side of the bar and left, taking the overflowing glass with him.

"See?" Kai said. "The working stiffs in the trenches know what's going on."

"What is this points system?"

"How can a workplace efficiency expert not know that?"

Lia's eyes narrowed. "It's not in place anywhere I've ever been."

"I suppose that's a fair point. I think this is the only hotel using it. So: Each employee starts with a hundred points a week. For every infraction, no matter how minor, no matter if it's an employee's fault or not, points get deducted. Such as being five minutes late due to road construction. Or having a missing button on a shirt. Or having a complaint made against you by a guest. Even if it's a stupid complaint."

Lia's mouth fell slightly open in disbelief.

"At the end of the week if you've fallen under sixty points you get a small wages deduction. Fall under thirty points, it's a big cut—they barely pay you anything. It's so bad I've heard stories of staff sleeping in cars and others stealing food from the kitchens. The points system contributes heavily to that."

"That is ridiculous," Lia said. "How can people function like this? And the turnover alone would eat into the profits. Staff would forever be needed to train new employees instead of being focused on their own workload."

"Exactly." Kai nodded. "It's ineffective and cruel."

"So how can it exist?"

"Ask Oliver Duxton. He's the mastermind."

Lia's expression turned suspicious. "How do you know any of this? Are you really a reporter?"

"Can't write to save my life. No, I promise I'm in hotel marketing and management, and sometimes I negotiate a hotel deal."

"Then how?"

"I listen. If you talk to the little guy, you hear all sorts of things. You should too if you want to be good at your job." She regarded Lia for a long moment. "Actually, you want the truth about what goes on around here? I dare you to find it, Ms. Efficiency Expert."

"You…dare me?"

"Yes. Go undercover for a day each in room service, housekeeping, waitressing in a gaming room, and at the front desk. Those four sections would provide the answer to every question you ever had about working here. It'll make for a mind-blowing report. If you're brave enough."

Astonishment lit Lia's face. "Except that's not how I—"

"Logistically it'd be no problem, either," Kai barreled on, warming to the idea. "Since you've been contracted to get to the bottom of things, the manager wouldn't dare say no to your request. It'd look like he was hiding something otherwise. You have all this power, Lia. So use it."

Lia frowned.

Silence fell.

"You're really thinking about it, aren't you?" Kai said slowly.

"Possibly."

Kai lifted her drink. "Kudos to you then." She clinked her glass against Lia's. "I'm curious as to what you'll dig up. A hundred metaphoric roaches hiding in dark corners, no doubt. Or maybe real ones." Kai laughed.

"Or maybe nothing. Those rumors could be just a nasty whispering campaign from a bitter rival."

"So did we just imagine what Tim told us then?"

Instead of answering, Lia took a deep swallow from her drink.

Got her. Kai hid her smile.

"Well," Lia said after a moment, "enough about my work, let's hear about yours. Which hotel has sent their occasional deal-maker to this abyss?"

Kai hesitated, leery of admitting the truth. Lia seemed to hate Grand Millennium a great deal. "You know, I don't think we should ruin our first date talking shop. Let's just say that the hotel I work for is not one you're interested in. Okay?"

"You're…embarrassed?" Lia guessed. "It's perfectly acceptable to be with a small hotel. There's no shame in that."

"No argument from me."

Lia suddenly froze. "Wait, ruin a first date? You believe this is a date?"

"Sure it is." Kai supplied her most charming smile. "So let's forget work and find out more about each other. I think you're fascinating. I love that you say what's on your mind without fear. That's far too uncommon, especially among women."

"Is it?" Lia's tone was challenging.

"You know perfectly well it is. So," Kai lifted her glass, "to kick-ass women."

Lia lifted her glass, too, and that proud, perfect chin lifted again. "A worthy toast. To kick-ass women."

Hour 2—Manipulations

Amelia could not get Kai's startling idea out of her head. This could be a way to get noticed by the board. A way to show she wasn't stuck in an ivory tower, but someone brave, bold, and ingenious. The question was, could she do it?

She toyed with the cardboard coaster in front of her—an image of a stack of poker chips, with the words *Duxton Vegas: Play Big, Win Big.*

Play big, win big. Easier said than done. Much as she hated to admit it, Joe was right about her quirks. Amelia struggled to schmooze, lie, or be diplomatic. And Oliver was the brash one. She wasn't.

Oh, Amelia was fine at running her eye down a prospectus and instantly knowing a hotel's potential. That was simple math combined with experience. But out-of-the-box thinking? That required flair and imagination.

So...what if she did this silly dare? Amelia pictured sweeping into a board meeting with the most thorough report in Hotel Duxton history, slapping it on the desk, saying, "You wanted answers? Here they are, gentlemen." She imagined the shocked looks. She could also bury Oliver as a CEO prospect if this points system could be proven, because there was no way Duxton's top management had approved such an unsound, risky concept.

"Lia?"

Amelia dropped the coaster and glanced up. "Yes?"

"I asked if you wanted another drink. I've been meaning to try a Vieux Carré."

"And let Timothy loose with more bitters?" Amelia pursed her lips. "No thanks. I'm switching to water. I prefer to be clear-headed by morning." She glanced around for Tim, only to find him at the far end of the bar testing how slowly he could load a waitress's tray while talking to her cleavage.

"Good idea." Kai leaned over the counter, snaring the water jug plus a pair of fresh glasses from a stack.

Amelia stared. Casual rule breaking. Another thing she was not adept at.

Kai poured them both a glass. "Water sounds sensible. Then again, you do strike me as a sensible type."

"So what are you, if I'm sensible?" Amelia asked, reaching for the glass.

"I'm…hmm. Creative and spontaneous. A little chaotic." Kai smiled.

Amelia winced. "How does anyone live like that? Not knowing how their day will play out? Sounds like hell."

With a laugh, Kai said, "Do you always say exactly what you think?"

"Why not? Directness is far less complicated than lies."

"Sometimes complicated is fun. Half my life is working out what people are thinking and how to use that to my benefit in deals. Read someone well enough, and half my job is done. If you make them think your suggestions are their idea, even better."

"You…manipulate." Amelia frowned.

"I observe closely, read cues," Kai corrected. "Then I adjust how I come across to people accordingly." At Amelia's skeptical look, she added, "Fine, yes, I manipulate, too. Only a little. Occupational hazard." She smiled. "But I'm good at it. It's why I'm so effective at work."

"Not just at work."

"Pardon?"

"Aren't you manipulating me now?"

"What makes you say that?"

"You've been aware since I sent my drink back that I prefer directness. You just told me you love games, but for the past hour you've been nothing but direct with me. It's a sales technique, isn't it? Being what the customer wants in order to be more liked? You're playing me. Well, trying to."

Kai's eyes widened in surprise.

"Just because I don't play games, Kai, doesn't mean I can't recognize them."

Kai regarded her for a long beat. "What if I told you I wasn't consciously copying you? Half the time I forget I'm doing it."

"Do you really believe that?"

"You think all I do is manipulate people twenty-four-seven? Seriously? How many friends would I have if I did that?"

"That's not really the right question," Amelia replied. "Isn't it: Do your friends know how clever you are at mind games? Have you ever shown them exactly who you are without any manipulations?"

Kai rolled her eyes. "You make me sound like I'm one mustache twirl away from a life of villainy."

"Hmm. I suppose I'm being unfair. Why single you out when practically everyone fakes who they are and hides what they really think?" Amelia asked thoughtfully. "Although you do have one distinction: You freely admit your games. Most people pretend, even to themselves, that they aren't faking things. You own it. I almost admire your honesty about your dishonesty."

Kai contemplated her for a moment. "It must be *so* frustrating for you," she said, her tone bone dry, "being aware of everyone else's self-deceptions while having none of your own."

Amelia frowned. "I didn't say that."

"Didn't you?" She lifted a hand to stop Amelia replying. "Never mind; it's fine. As far as I'm concerned, there's no crime in being good at making deals and getting people to like me. I never hurt anyone. You might look down on it as dishonest, but all I do is use my persuasive skills to win. But now you have me curious: Do you truly never lie? Even to yourself? What about to your family?"

"My family knows never to ask me something if they don't want an honest opinion." Amelia gave her a rueful look. "And I have learned to be... creative...at work when being truthful and blunt is not ideal."

"I'll bet." Kai chuckled. "So do you piss off a lot of people by not sugar-coating things?"

"Irrelevant." Amelia shrugged. "How does an underling thinking I'm a rude, uptight 'ice bitch' have any bearing on my life? Although watching ego-puffed middle managers squirm because I refuse to tell them they're God's gift to something occasionally has its moments."

"That sounds like fun. Of course, the downside for me of catching more flies with honey than vinegar is that I spend my days being underestimated by those ego-puffed asses."

"Because you pretend to be less than you are to make them feel like more," Amelia deduced.

"Exactly."

"I couldn't do that," Amelia said with distaste. "I don't care what it costs me."

"I think we've already established that." Kai looked intrigued. "You never answered the other half of my question: do you ever lie to yourself?"

"No one can avoid that. I *am* human, despite some of my employees' beliefs to the contrary." She smiled.

Kai laughed. "How impressive you must be to them to have attained mythical status."

"Actually, I suspect they're just bored and it's diverting to invent tales about their cold and heartless overlord."

"Overlord? Ha, I knew you were a boss."

Amelia's lips twitched. "I did not deny it."

"Are you a good one?"

"I have low staff turnover. That's a sign."

"A very good sign. I think we can safely say you're better than a Duxton."

Amelia clamped down her first reply. "What the Duxtons do or don't do around here remains to be seen. That's premature."

Kai's eyebrows slid up in surprise at the acid in her voice.

"I don't like to prejudge situations." Amelia tried not to sound quite so sharp, well aware that Kai hadn't intended to insult her whole family. Still, the comment stung. "I prefer to be facts-based and transparent in all things."

"*All* things?" Kai asked. "How is that possible?"

"Everyone in my life knows exactly who I am." She paused. "Can you say the same?"

Kai's expression cooled. "You know, I don't manipulate all the time, despite your theory I do. Even if I wanted to, it'd be exhausting."

"It would be." Amelia considered that. "But why do it at all if you don't have to? Is the direct approach really that unpalatable?"

"More like unsuccessful. My way is like having a superpower, and it works nine times out of ten. Although, yes, I admit there are times I wish I could just say what I'm thinking. A lot of times, if you must know."

"A very honest answer." Amelia regarded her with interest. "So, Kai, are you yet again saying what you think I want to hear? Are you still playing me?"

"Jesus Christ, Lia." Draining her glass, Kai then pushed it away from herself and stood. "Excuse me."

Hour 3—Playing with Ice

Kai headed to the restroom while she picked over their conversation. She had never been so thoroughly analyzed and dissected by someone in the same way she did to others. Lia's bullshit detector was clearly unmatched, too. It was unsettling to consider, for the first time in her life, that *just maybe* her schmoozing button had been fused to the 'on' position—even in her downtime.

When had that happened? Kai stared into the mirror, regarding her reflection.

Who am I when I'm not on the clock? Who really knows me, all of me, under my harmless little games?

Milly, certainly. Definitely not her mom. Maybe…Remi? She thought harder. So was that it? Just her assistant and one former school friend?

How depressing she'd been out of her own skin for so long. Kai didn't like the sound of that.

As for Lia's final question, was she right about that, too? *Was I playing her just now by being so honest?*

Kai frowned, uncertain of the answer. She hadn't *thought* she'd been up to her old tricks, but now she was doubting her every gesture and syllable.

Okay, this was insane! Why was she questioning anything? Kai studied her mulish expression in the glass. She didn't need some midlife crisis in a bar in Vegas. How clichéd could you get? Why had she let that woman get under her skin, anyway? Although, to be fair, Lia did ask annoyingly good questions.

Not the point!

Kai shifted her focus to what mattered. The most mesmerizing woman she'd ever met had agreed to a drinks date with her, and they hadn't even come close to discussing more earthly delights. Time for that to change.

She swept from the bathroom and headed back to the bar. Her gaze sought out Lia, who was now debating with Tim the optimum way to 'muddle' fresh mint for a Mojito. *Poor man.* Lia did have firm opinions on so many things.

As Kai slid back on the stool, she wondered for a moment how far Lia's need for control and being in charge extended. Was she demanding in bed? Or did she retract her claws and become a kitten?

It was tempting to cut to the chase and find out. Except, if she propositioned Lia now, then one way or another their intriguing conversation would be over.

Disappointment swept through her at the thought. Perhaps she wasn't ready to let go just yet.

"So, Lia," Kai said when Tim left again, looking defeated, "big question: what are your views on TV dance shows?"

Half an hour later, Kai stared into her drink—she'd finally tried Tim's Vieux Carré (not too awful)—and readied herself to ask what she'd wanted to know all evening.

"What's on your mind?" Amelia prodded when the silence dragged on.

"I'm a little torn. There's something I want to ask."

Lia nodded, as if expecting it. But hadn't they been flirting all evening, more or less? Lia had to suspect a romantic proposition was next.

"Ask."

"Now, see, that's the problem. My dilemma is, if I ask, and you say no, our evening's over. And I don't want it to be over yet. That would pain me greatly. But if you say yes, our evening could go from wonderful to spectacular."

"Ah," Lia murmured. "Maybe...you shouldn't ask then."

Well, that confirmed that. It was nice of Lia to tactfully decline in a way that allowed Kai to save face and avoid asking. Except...

"That's not me, though, *not* asking what's on my mind. I always like to roll the dice, come what may."

"So roll the dice." Lia's gaze was as direct as ever, but this time, Kai felt like she was being filleted. And screw it, she loved being the complete and utter focus of this riveting woman.

"I think I know what your answer will be," Kai began. "I might have mentioned I read people well."

"Once or twice." Lia sounded amused now.

"I can actually see how this whole conversation will go. See, I'll ask, 'Are you single, Lia? No cute Mr. or Mrs. at home waiting for you?'"

Lia tilted her head as if confused by the question.

"And now you're thinking, 'I wouldn't be here otherwise.' Because cheating is like lying to you. Right?"

Lia gave a tight nod. "Definitely."

"Then *you'd* have to ask if I'm single, because suddenly you'd be wondering if I'm the cheating kind, if the question's occurred to me to ask you."

"You wouldn't be wrong." Lia's jaw clenched.

"And I'd explain I'm single and fancy free."

Lia's shoulders relaxed.

"At which point you'd probably roll your eyes and ask if I'm attempting to seduce you," Kai said. "I'd probably make a joke about how if I'm *attempting* it, I'm not doing a very good job."

With a soft laugh, Lia said, "Do continue. I'm enjoying my witty commentary."

"Okay, so then I think you'd ask, 'Why me?'" Kai said. "As if you really can't see how sexy someone might find your cool, take-charge, 'I run the world' vibe. I'd point out how your uncompromising attitude is so hot."

"I thought you just said I was cold?" Lia's tone was droll.

"Oh, that, too. Of the two of us, you're more ice; I'm the fiery one."

"I see." Lia made a 'go on' gesture. "Tell me how this ends."

"Well, you'd give me a haughty look and say, 'I suppose you have designs to *melt* me.'"

"Accurate." Lia's lips twitched.

Kai grinned. "And I'd say, 'Haven't you ever wondered what happens when fire meets ice?'"

Lia moaned softly. "Nooo."

"I know, I know. You'll say my line needs major work or I've turned my steak into a cinder or something. And then I'd say I thought you'd appreciate a straightforward approach, instead of some artful subterfuge where you aren't quite sure whether I'm hitting on you."

"So your dubious lines would have been for *my* benefit?" Lia's eyes sparkled. "I'm so glad you cleared that up."

"Right?" Kai chuckled. "And then I'd tell you which room I'm in. After we've laughed hilariously at my awesome wit, of course."

"Or mocked it for ten minutes."

"Or that." Kai met her eyes, now suddenly earnest. "I'm in room four-eleven." She bit her lip.

Silence fell, and the amusement washed from Lia's face, replaced with something charged and interested. But when she spoke, her words were stripped of emotion. "How exciting for you."

"It could be exciting for you, too." Kai braved dancing her fingertip along Lia's jacket sleeve. "You would have deduced by now I'm not after a relationship. And you strike me as someone as busy as I am. Who has time? But we could have a lot of fun answering that 'fire meets ice' question." Her finger daringly darted over to tap a button at the vee of Lia's shirt, before dropping back to her wrist.

Lia's expression was impossible to read.

"Would you like that?" Kai asked, and this time, there was nothing teasing in her tone. "Would you like to let down your hair, break out of your nice, safe mold, be a bit…unpredictable?" Her finger trailed Lia's wrist, brushing against pale skin. Lia's pulse thudded against Kai's fingertips. It was fast. "With me?"

There. She'd rolled her dice. Breath caught, Kai waited.

"No," Lia said quietly. "I don't want to be with anyone who wants to melt me for a challenge." Her cool eyes held Kai's gaze. "That's not me."

Kai knew that by now. Intellectually, she knew and understood. But still, the answer in that thick air between them felt painfully harsh.

"I'm worth a lot more than what you're offering tonight," Lia continued. "Your proposal is lacking." She leaned in until her lips were almost touching Kai's, as if she were about to kiss her.

Kai's heart began to pound.

"But just so you know?" Lia's soft breath warmed Kai's lips. "It was tempting. You are amusing. You play your games so very well. But *this* is the closest you're going to get to me." She plucked Kai's wandering hand off her wrist and placed it back on the bar.

Kai was frozen. Her desire to be with Lia wasn't some shallow game. In that split second, Kai wanted her even more than Mayfair Palace.

For the first time in years, Kai wondered if she should suggest more than one night together. Maybe...several nights.

She stiffened. *No.* She absolutely didn't do relationships. She'd broken enough hearts to know she didn't want to toy with anyone again.

Kai knew what she was like: She'd start out strong, then become distracted by work, becoming less and less emotionally available until she may as well have not been there at all. Relationship death by a thousand indifferent cuts. So offering something more to Lia was off the table. She sagged. That only left a fling, and Lia had just shut that suggestion down cold.

Smoothing her expression to unruffled, Kai said, "That's a shame. Can't blame a girl for trying." She forced a smile.

"I'm sure you'll bounce back. Especially around here."

Around here? She thought Kai would be fine picking up just anyone after an evening spent with Lia's sharp, interesting edges and world view? That casual dismissal of Kai's interest burned.

Lia brushed her lips against Kai's ear in a goodbye kiss that had an air of finality. Then she followed it up with a tiny nip of her earlobe. Lia tugged the flesh with her teeth long enough for it to be painful—a warning almost—and then let go.

Oh my God! What was that? Tingles shot from her ear straight to Kai's core.

Lia pulled back, and her lips curled up into a half smile. "How's that for unpredictable?" The smile widened into wicked.

"Oh," Kai gasped, hand lifting to touch her throbbing earlobe.

Lia's tone became cool and professional, as if she hadn't just wrapped taunting lips and teeth around Kai's earlobe. "Good evening. I *do* hope you enjoy the rest of your stay in Las Vegas." She slid elegantly off the stool, then sauntered to the end of the bar to settle her tab.

Briefly, her gaze caught Kai's in the mirror behind the bar, between neon-bright cocktail bottles. Kai's astonishment and arousal were clear in the glass. Lia's expression was serene and smug.

With a rueful smile, Kai watched her go. *Smart, beautiful, and knows her own worth?* Kai missed her already. When was the last time she'd felt challenged like this? Her ear still tingled from that teasing nip.

"Crash and burn, huh?" Tim returned to collect Lia's glass, an amused glint in his eyes.

"No. That was just the opening salvo," Kai retorted with a grin. She wondered if that were true. Her throbbing ear said one thing, although she wasn't entirely sure how to interpret the message. But even if she never saw Lia again...

What a woman.

Chapter 7

Croissants and Charm

Two days later, Kai lay in bed, tired and grumpy, having tossed and turned for hours yet again. She was still keyed up, as she had been all day yesterday and the night before, after meeting a certain imperious efficiency expert. She could still hear Lia's voice.

I'm worth a whole lot more than you're offering tonight. Your proposal is lacking.

The sheer disappointment Kai felt was the most surprising thing. This wasn't her. She was more a make her play, move on, no regrets kind of gal.

For Lia, though, Kai was sorely tempted to sweeten her offer. She'd love to spend a lot more time with her, but then they'd be straying perilously close to dangerous territory. No woman deserved to be put through the Kai Fisher Bad Dating Experience.

Besides, Lia had said she was rarely in New York after Kai mentioned that was her home. So what more could there be?

Even knowing all of this, desire rippled through Kai at the reminder of those beautiful, watchful eyes. Her ear no longer burned from that cheeky nip, but she swore it still tingled whenever she touched it. The sexy way Lia had stalked off, her beautiful ass doing that haughty swish? Kai thought she'd die happy if that was the last sight she ever saw.

Her phone beeped. Kai sighed and rolled over in bed, reaching for it. One of her little birds had texted.

Ur hammerdanni guy is in East grnd floor dining room rite now 4 breakfast

Kai gasped and flung back her sheets, a victorious thrill coursing through her. Good news at last.

Nedal al-Hamadani was tall, bearded, and in his mid-forties. He didn't look much like that roguish playboy photo from the bar. Perhaps he'd gotten his just-landed-in-Vegas fun out of his system already.

Kai hung back at the restaurant entrance, studying him as he tapped on his phone between bites of toast. Her eye slid to the obnoxious gold watch flashing on his wrist and several fat rings on his fingers. Hamadani ran a hand absent-mindedly through his manicured beard.

She drew in a deep breath, plastered on her most charming smile, walked up to him, and said, "I hope you don't mind the intrusion. Is this seat taken?" She rested her hands on the smooth wooden back of the chair opposite him.

The businessman put down his phone, and his gaze swept the room, pointedly assessing all the empty tables. Then he smiled and politely said, "Apparently not, madam." He waved at her to sit.

"I'm Kai Fisher," she said as she did so. Then, in case her intentions might be misunderstood, she added quickly, "VP at Grand Millennium Hotels. I think we have a proposal you might be interested in."

He regarded her. "I believe I know what you might be inquiring about. A certain about-to-be-launched five-star hotel in London? Yes?"

Kai's lips curled. "That would be the one."

"I'm afraid you're too late, madam. I have received an offer so exceptional, I'm not even bothering with the competition."

"If it's so exceptional, why hasn't a deal been announced?" Kai smiled warmly to take away any hint of accusation. "And no offer is so good that an alternative one can't be considered. *Yes?*" She cocked an eyebrow.

"I'm not so sure about that."

He hadn't denied it, though. Hope surged. "Mr. Hamadani, I have an offer that will have them talking about this deal for decades. Your father will want to build statues in your honor by the time we're done."

It was a gamble, but Kai would never go broke underestimating any man's need to impress his father, especially when said man came from a culture centered on family. There was a reason so many Arabic surnames included family-focused honorifics such as *ibn* (son of), *abu* (father of), and *al* (of).

"Statues. Is that so?" He did not sound remotely enthused.

Had she overplayed her hand? Too much BS before her coffee? Kai gave him an unrepentant grin that she hoped he'd find at least a little charming.

He regarded her for a long moment, as if weighing her up. Maybe he just liked watching her squirm. "Join me for breakfast, Ms. Fisher?" His expression was curious now. And he still hadn't shot her down outright on negotiating for Mayfair Palace.

"Absolutely." And that was the moment she felt it—the feeling she always had when she knew she'd close a deal. She had him.

Two hours later, Kai left the man to a business call, wearing a smile as wide as Texas. They'd arranged a second meeting for later in the day.

Discussions had gone well. After the first hour, he'd even stopped mentioning that he'd made a commitment to another party and started actively listening to her proposal. Progress.

She texted Mr. Stein an update—*He's interested and talking*—and beamed when the old man's reply landed minutes later.

I knew you could do this. Great work

His faith in her always kept Kai going. Mr. Stein's paternal affection and fierce loyalty to her were what made working for Grand Millennium worthwhile. When threats against Scorched Earth had virtually ended her career, he'd offered her a lifeline. A new start in hotels.

She wasn't naive enough to believe he'd done it out of the goodness of his heart. His motives had been clear: Benjamin Stein despised the Duxtons. And Scorched Earth had been slamming Hotel Duxton for years. But whatever his reasons, he'd provided a soft landing when she'd needed him the most. That included a fresh career, top executive salary, and financial protection from any lawsuits that might threaten.

Mr. Stein might be a hardnosed businessman prone to bouts of paranoia about his rivals, but no one could say a bad word about him to Kai. She'd always love him for what he'd done for her.

I knew you could do this.

Did she dare believe it, too? Her fingers were still tingling at the thought of the deal when she turned into the lobby. And then she saw her. Lia, standing behind the front desk, poised and elegant.

So, she'd actually done it. Taken Kai's bold suggestion and run with it.

Lia clattered the keyboard keys in front of her like she'd done the job forever. A stern older woman was supervising her. Kai fished about in her head for the other woman's name. Ah, yes. Mrs. Menzies: loyal to her company, cranky, and not to be approached for bribes.

She was standing far too close to Lia to be polite, issuing snappish commands although Kai couldn't make out the actual words.

Trying to intimidate her new, temporary employee? *Good luck with that.*

Sure enough, after a moment, Lia swiveled to face her supervisor, eyed her, and then arched an eyebrow while shooting her a look that said, *I have this. Back off.*

Mrs. Menzies scooted backward, despite Lia not uttering a single word.

Kai resisted the urge to cheer. *That's my girl!*

She frowned at the absurd thought. *The hell?*

Resuming course to the elevators, Kai forced her mind back to the paperwork she needed for her afternoon meeting with Hamadani.

As the elevator doors began to close, a wicked smile crossed her lips as a new thought hit: *Surely, I must need the front desk for something today?*

Chapter 8

Front Desk

MANNING THE FRONT DESK WAS something Amelia had done years ago when she'd been learning the hotel ropes, and few of the basics had changed since.

Yesterday Quinn had arranged through Duxton HQ for "Lia Hanson" to intern around various departments, starting today.

"You'll have to be careful to maintain your cover," Quinn had told her. "Won't Duxton staff think it's weird one of their own is staying at the hotel?"

"Who'd know that? The assistant manager was barely with it when she checked me in, so I doubt she could pick me out of a line-up today."

"Okay. Anyway, it's a good thing you checked into a regular room and not the penthouse suite or that might have made someone on staff notice you."

"Of course. When I'm assessing a hotel, I need the average guest's experience."

"True. But even so, be careful or you'll stick out like dog's ears."

"Your faith in me fills me with confidence. Do you really think me incapable of doing a day each in four different departments without setting off klaxons that I'm not a regular employee? I *can* fly under the radar."

"No, boss, you can't."

"Oh?" Amelia's tone cooled. "Why not?"

"Honestly? You give off this vibe that's impossible to hide. You ooze 'elite, powerful human,' with a dash of imperious."

"I do not!" What elite lifestyle did she have? She owned a luxury one-bedroom apartment overlooking the Thames that suited her to perfection. Everything in its place, everything minimalist. Anything more than she needed would have been wasteful, after all. How was that in any way elite?

"You do—not that there's anything wrong with that. But I think your cover will be blown in an hour."

"Ridiculous. I can be incognito. I'll simply copy those around me."

"You'll leak. You'll order someone to do something without thinking, or correct someone."

Amelia frowned. "I do know how to let things slide if necessary. I can… fake it."

Could she? Amelia wasn't entirely convinced by her words even as she said them.

Kai could do this in her sleep.

Amelia cursed the woman for popping back into her brain. *Focus.* "Anyway, I've been in the service industry my whole life. I will adapt."

"Your idea of the service industry and mine are a little different. You know Mum worked thirty years as a hotel maid. She'd come home exhausted, with everything aching, while having heard every kind of sexist and racist crap going despite being as British as pork pies. That's *working in the service industry.*"

Quinn was right, of course. Amelia's view was too simplistic. "Well, now's my chance to learn a few things of which I'm apparently unaware. I'll become a better hotel manager if nothing else."

There was a silence. Then: "Mad respect to you, boss. Okay? I mean it."

"It's not going to be *that* bad, is it?"

This time, the silence was even longer. "Just don't quit, okay?" Quinn said quietly. "Stick it out even when everything hurts. Just remember why you're doing it."

Of course. "To become CEO."

A strangled moan followed. "Um, isn't it to understand what your employees go through and why they're quitting?"

"Well, that, too." Obviously. She sighed.

"Right, so you're all set." There was a definite smile in Quinn's voice as she added, "Just remember not to correct the guests on their maths, even if they don't carry the two."

"That was *one* time," Amelia muttered.

"Bye, boss." Laughter sounded. "The supervisor will expect you at the front desk at ten tomorrow. You'll be doing a mix of check-ins and concierge work."

And now here she was. Dressed for success, hair in a fist-tight bun, being condescended to by one Mrs. Menzies, who seemed constantly annoyed. The officious woman was probably put out at having some blow-in land in her lap for a day, upsetting her routine. Amelia understood. Routine was important.

"This button brings up the customer names on the upper floors," Mrs. Menzies was saying. "Floors forty to fifty are the VIP suites. You will be extra polite with those guests."

Extra polite? All guests should be treated as VIPs. It was one of the most basic rules Amelia drummed into her own employees. Still, she kept her tongue.

"And if they ask for a discount or have a special card, call me over. Some of our regular guests get extras because they're here so often. All right?"

"Yes," Amelia said, before remembering she was in the US. "Ma'am," she tacked on.

Mrs. Menzies' eyes narrowed, as if she was unsure whether the delay had been deliberate.

"Sorry. Jet lag."

"Where did you come in from?"

"London."

Mrs. Menzies' eyes narrowed even further. "No excuses around here," she snapped. "Even if you're from some fancy part of the world, you're here now. This is America. The customer is always right. No insolence or uppity nonsense will be tolerated."

Insolence? Uppity nonsense? She gave Mrs. Menzies a withering look.

The supervisor took a step back and looked uncertain. Then she regathered her composure and went in for a new attack. "I'll be needing you to work overtime tonight. We're down a staff member due to the flu going around."

Or them quitting.

Mrs. Menzies' expression dared her to say no. Amelia nodded.

The phone started ringing.

"Take that call, Ms. Hanson. Let's see your customer-handling skills."

The phone was flashing with the internal-call light, and *Room 612* appeared in the LED display. Amelia leaned forward and answered. "Concierge desk, Lia speaking, how may I help you?"

"KY Jelly," came a sultry voice. "Please. I've run out and I can't get it myself. And I simply cannot manage without it."

KY Jelly. As in… Amelia blinked.

"Also, a whip."

"A…whip?"

"A flicker whip, to be precise. Mine just met an unfortunate accident."

"It…did." She dreaded to think.

There was a muffled sexual moan in the background.

"Can you be quick? The pot is on the boil, if you follow."

"I don't believe that's a service we provide, ma'am." Amelia called up the Yellow Pages on her screen. "I can direct you to local establishments that could assist with your, er, special requests—"

"You're new, aren't you?" The woman purred. "Well, darling, Mrs. Menzies *always* ensures my needs are catered to because I'm a VIP. Well, I don't stay in one of the VIP suites—Goddess, what a waste of money—but she treats me as one because I'm such an *exceptional,* long-term guest." She drawled out the word exceptional. "So talk to her if you have any questions. Then put my purchases on my account. There's a dear. I'll be waiting." Her voice turned even more sexual. "Monique Carson, six-twelve."

The phone went dead before Amelia could argue they were in the accommodation business, not a supplier of sex toys.

Mrs. Menzies eyed Amelia's expression and rising heat. "Room six-twelve, by any chance?"

"Yes."

"Ms. Carson's been staying here full-time for over two years. She's a most valued guest. We're in the business of fulfilling people's needs, Ms. Hanson. Guests of certain means or status deserve to have their special requests met if they stay in a high-caliber hotel." Mrs. Menzies reached under the counter and withdrew a business card with a lurid pink silhouette of a nude woman on it and the name *Pleasure Chest.* "Ask for Aaron. He knows the drill. His company delivers within the hour."

"Is this...a common occurrence?" In all Amelia's years, she couldn't recall being informed of such requests. Perhaps her staff had never told her?

"One must learn to be adaptable around here." Mrs. Menzies gave Amelia an arch look before relenting a little. "Although, honestly? It is surprising what happens in Vegas. Besides, Ms. Carson is discreet and has only upmarket clientele, although her particular enterprise does tend to go through supplies somewhat quickly."

"What is this enterprise?"

Mrs. Menzies' lips pressed together. "You'll understand when you deliver them. Make the call."

Amelia phoned through an order for a flicker whip and KY Jelly to a blasé Pleasure Chest employee named Aaron who promised prompt service.

After she put the phone down and refiled the card under the counter, Mrs. Menzies waved toward an approaching guest. "You're up."

Kai was sauntering toward the desk. It was hypnotic watching her, and Amelia realized she wasn't the only one who thought so. Many guests were swiveling their necks to follow her.

Amelia pondered what she could possibly want. Would Kai blow Amelia's cover to stir the pot a little? Play games? It wouldn't surprise her.

As Kai reached the counter, she offered a cocky, slow smile.

I hate cockiness, Amelia reminded herself.

"Good morning, ma'am," Amelia said. "Can I be of assistance?"

"I don't know, *can* you?" Kai replied, eyes dancing. "What *is* your skill set?"

Amelia sighed. Games it was.

Mrs. Menzies slid an impatient glance at them, then turned to some paperwork.

"I have a wide range of skills. Just ask."

"I'll bet." Kai smirked. She cleared her throat. "I need a new suite. Phone reception in my room is terrible and I'm trying to conduct business. I think it's in a blind spot."

"I'm sorry to hear that," Amelia said. "Which room number is it?" She knew exactly what room Kai was in, of course, but Mrs. Menzies was standing right there.

Kai's eyes met hers with considerable amusement. "Four-oh-seven."

Amelia frowned. Kai had told her four-eleven two days ago. "Are you *quite* certain, ma'am?" Turning to her keyboard, she tapped in "411," and sure enough, the name "Kai Fisher" came up.

"Oh, silly me. It might be four-eleven." Kai smirked.

Amelia gave her a cool, unimpressed look.

Slapping her room key card on the counter, Kai said, "How could I forget?"

With great difficulty, since the number was on the damned key card.

Was she trying to see whether Amelia had memorized her room number? What Kai didn't seem to grasp was that Amelia couldn't forget any number if she tried. Kai was hardly special in that regard.

Amelia rattled the computer keys, bringing up the vacant rooms directory. "Room three-oh-three is free and has an adjoining suite which is in your original booking."

"Yes, I have an assistant."

"Right." Amelia plucked the "303" key card off the wall and lay it between them. "This is a corner suite so should be clear of interference."

"*Allegedly* clear." Kai made no move to touch it. "I'd hate to relocate all my things only to find the same problem. Why don't you take me up there now so we can assess its suitability before I commit?"

Mrs. Menzies glanced at Kai. "I'm due to head over to that side of the hotel now. I could take you there myself, ma'am." She straightened. "If you'll step this way." She reached for the plastic pass.

Kai's expression lost all amusement, and her hand snatched up the key card first. "I'd prefer it if *this* employee took me." She waved at Amelia.

"Why?" Mrs. Menzies asked. Then she seemed to realize she'd forgotten her number-one rule of customer service and said, "Of course, ma'am. Ms. Hanson will assist you." She waved Amelia away.

Amelia didn't speak as she led Kai to the elevators.

"Ms. Hanson, huh?" Kai said conversationally.

Amelia chose not to comment.

The crowded elevators prevented any further conversation, which suited Amelia fine. As they stepped out on level three, Amelia took off fast enough to avoid small talk on the way to the room.

She unlocked Room 303 and waited for Kai to catch up and enter.

"I had no idea," Kai huffed when she reached her.

"About?" Amelia flattened her back to the door to hold it open as Kai entered.

"That you trained under Usain Bolt. Full of surprises there, Ms. Hanson." Kai brushed past her and their breasts briefly touched as she entered.

Amelia shivered. An unwelcome awareness spread through her. Closing the door, Amelia launched into a tour of the room's minimal facilities.

"So?" Amelia finally said when she ran out of commentary. "Does this meet requirements?"

Kai sat on the bed, bounced once, leaned back on one arm, and regarded Amelia with interest. "So far so good. Now tell me, Ms. Hanson, how's your first day as an undercover grunt working out? You know, I wasn't sure you'd do it."

"Do you really have a poor reception issue? Or is toying with me your new game because I turned you down?"

"I recall. My ear's still ringing." Kai's smile was wide. "I wouldn't object if you turned me down again."

Amelia rolled her eyes. "I'm here in a professional capacity, Ms. Fisher."

"Yes, of course. And you do look so uptight and professional right now. Not like the other night. You flirted, too, you know."

Amelia stiffened, unimpressed at Kai for turning this into an ill-timed autopsy of an evening she was trying to forget. She waited for an answer.

Kai sighed. "I really do have a phone problem. I've been putting up with it, but now it's just annoying me too much." She waved her cell about, directing it at various points in the room. "Three-bar signal. That'll do. Thanks."

"Good."

Kai tilted her head. "You really do give off a powerful management vibe. I'll bet Mrs. Menzies has you worked out by the end of shift. Faking it isn't really you, is it?"

"Are we done?" Amelia ignored the innuendo and headed for the door.

"Sure." Kai followed. "I do declare there's a career in reception work in your future."

"I'm honored to have your approval," Amelia said with faint sarcasm. "*So* honored."

Kai laughed. "*There* you are." She headed for the door. "I wondered where that sassy woman I met had gone. *She* was amusing as hell."

"*She* is on the clock." Amelia closed up behind them. "And I'm the consummate professional."

"Sure you are." Kai smiled. "Although your tone might need a little work." They headed toward the elevators. "But I'm sure Mrs. Menzies will beat that right out of you."

"She's welcome to try." Amelia stabbed the *Up* button on the elevator for Kai and the *Down* one for herself. "I'll book you and your assistant into the new rooms, then send a porter up to assist you with relocating your luggage and supply you with the three-oh-four key as well." The Down doors opened. "Have a *lovely* day."

"You, too." Kai waved goodbye as Amelia stepped inside, her fingers brushing Amelia's sleeve. Kai's sensual laughter, rich as an exotic liqueur, lingered.

When she got back to the lobby, Amelia straightened her jacket, wishing she could smooth away any remnants of her encounter with Kai Fisher.

It would be easier if her arm wasn't still burning from her brief touch.

Upon arrival back at the desk, Amelia was promptly sent upstairs again, clutching a lurid-pink bag from the Pleasure Chest.

All Mrs. Menzies had said as she'd passed over the delivery was: "Be careful with her. She amuses herself in most direct ways."

"Most direct?"

"You'll see. If she wasn't such a good guest, I'd have shown her the door years ago. When you're done with her, there's an executive's child in forty-nine-oh-two demanding attention. So don't let Ms. Carson talk your ear off. She will try and detain you for her own amusement."

Amelia knocked on Room 612.

The door flung open, and Amelia was greeted with a woman about her own age in a short black skirt suit, heels, and a green silk blouse unbuttoned to her waist, revealing a sliver of tomato-red bra. On her face sat bookish black glasses and an amused expression.

Amelia found the effect somewhat confusing. Business attire shouldn't be exciting, and yet Monique Carson somehow made it tantalizing. How had she achieved this?

"Come in, darling. Package on the counter, please." Monique disappeared back into her suite, apparently assuming Amelia would follow.

The room was decorated in shades of red. Amelia's nose wrinkled at the smell of sex, her gaze darting around uncertainly.

A shower was running in the bathroom, where steam escaped from a gap in the ajar door.

Amelia slid the package onto the counter and turned to go, only to find herself caught in a calculating gaze.

With long fingers drumming against her hips, Monique regarded Amelia. She stood near a rumpled king-sized bed, its sheets looking as if they'd lost an argument with a category-five hurricane. "What's your name?"

"Lia Hanson."

"I'm not what you expected, am I?" She looked amused.

"No." Amelia agreed.

"And you like what you see?" Monique smiled.

Amelia hesitated. Well, there was *something* alluring about her, an awareness, but Amelia was damned if she'd admit it.

"No need to be embarrassed. It's my job to make people want me. Didn't Mrs. Menzies tell you what I do? Women come to me for the CEO fantasy experience."

Women? Her clients were all women?

Monique's smile was knowing and seductive. "I boss them around, take them over...or under...the desk if that's their desire. Rub myself *all* over them while I reel off my orders for the day, such as how I want my coffee."

Amelia tried to block the highly specific visions flooding her brain. "I...see."

Monique smirked. "You're new, aren't you? Come closer. I want to see what June Menzies is up to with her latest hire." Despite her command, Monique was the one to move, her hips sensual as she sauntered closer. She sized up Amelia again, then frowned. "All right, who are you really?"

"Excuse me?"

"You have Fifth Avenue attitude."

"Fifth Avenue attitude?" What the hell was that?

"It's in the body language and the air about you." Monique's eyes sharpened. "That fancy watch rules out you being a reporter or an undercover cop. Neither gets paid that well unless they're on the take."

"You think I'm undercover?" Amelia asked, alarm shooting through her.

"Aren't you?" Monique cocked an eyebrow. "Do you know what all Hotel Duxton employees have in common? The floor staff? Desperation. They'd have to be desperate to work here and risk having their pay slashed for any minor nonsense."

She knew about the points scheme? Did everyone?

"They reek of fear. They are all tightly wound, stressed, and nervous. Even a minute wasted talking to me would have them inching to the door in panic. Not you. You saunter in here like you're on a catwalk. You look at me as though I'm a puzzle that you have all the time in the world to figure out. And you don't seem to know fear."

Great. So I really do leak? Quinn would be impossible after this. "That's quite a theory."

"Oh, please. We both know you're no underling." Monique eyed her thoughtfully. "Are you an undercover boss, checking up on things? Not before time, I must say."

Amelia stared, astonished.

"You should never play poker, darling. Are you a Duxton then? If I looked that family up, would I find your photo all over social media?"

"I don't do social media." A flash of regret filled her—what a pit of hate, shallowness, and mockery that foray into Twitter had been. "Brain-dead waste of time."

"Oh, I *like* you. Forthright, aren't you? And no denial you're a Duxton. So, why *are* you here, Lia Duxton?" Her red lips curved. "Looking for some pointers on how to diversify careers? Because I have to say, with your vibe, you could do my job. You're exactly what my clients love: commanding women with charisma and power. You know, you can't teach that. Lord, you'd be a star and I'd be rich." Monique's eyes crinkled. "So, Lia, are you looking for work with a difference? You can keep your tips."

Her expression said she wasn't serious in the least, but still Amelia couldn't prevent her irritated reply. "Absolutely not. I'm happy with my job."

"You know, if you want to convince people you *do* work here, never say you're happy with your job." She snorted. "You really aren't very good at this, are you?"

"What do you want from me?" Amelia asked with a sigh.

"Oh yes, I could blackmail you, couldn't I?" Monique laughed. "Don't worry, that's not my style. Instead, just answer me one thing: aside from dating women—"

Amelia's eyes widened. "Excuse me?"

Monique waved her hand, "Don't look so stunned, it's clear from your appreciation of me that you have a certain preference. Aside from dating women, have you ever done anything wild? Something inappropriate? A little...reckless?"

"Never." That was her brother's idiotic domain, not hers.

"Hmm. A pity." Monique's admiring eyes ran over her. "You are *so* tasty. I'd give quite a lot to turn you a little wild. I'd love to have you under my expert fingers, chipping that ice off you. Your imperious routine is irresistible, and it takes quite a lot to turn my head."

"No thanks." Amelia's jaw tightened.

"Well, the offer stands if you ever change your mind. Personally, I think doing the occasional inappropriate thing keeps us young," she said confidentially. "Look, darling, I only say this because you seem so uptight on the topic: Try to remember at some point while you're so focused on your career, that it's okay to let your hair down every now and then. Sex is just sex. No one dies if you get your rocks off with another consenting adult. Humans do tie themselves up in knots over these things. One day I'll write a book about it."

"A...book." How had she even gotten into this conversation?

"I'm just suggesting you might remember to live a little. If not with sex, just have fun—run around your house naked, go skinny dipping, scream at the top of your lungs for the hell of it."

"Sounds cold and loud."

"Lord, I do love you." Monique snorted. "Stubborn as a tomcat, thicker walls than Fort Knox, and stunning to boot." She leaned in, close enough for Amelia to feel the warmth of her, and bopped her nose with a finger. "Lighten up."

Amelia reared back. This woman was dangerous. A familiar sensation hit her as she processed Monique's seductiveness, confidence, and faint mocking undertone. *Oh.* She reminded Amelia of Kai.

The shower in the other room stopped running. "My cue." Monique kept her mischievous eyes squarely on Amelia when she called out, "Darling, are you wet for me?"

Amelia glared at Monique—*so damned inappropriate*—and strode from the room.

Outside, she leaned against the wall. How disconcerting. The longer she was in Vegas, the more she found herself distracted by hormonal irrelevancies. Now she'd started seeing Kai everywhere, including in the seductive energy of random guests.

This was not acceptable. Her employees called her an ice bitch for a reason. She was focused, clear-eyed, and didn't get weak-kneed at the thought of…of…certain annoying people.

Oh no, you just bite their ear instead.

Amelia strode down the hall, frustration fueling her pace. Why was *that woman* still on her mind? Kai was nothing to her. The matter had been settled two days ago. It was *done.*

Her brain snickered as Amelia stabbed—repeatedly—the elevator's call button.

Oh sure.

Chapter 9

Fax and Figures

IT HAD BEEN A LONG day. Kai picked over her room-service dinner, trying to make sense of her lunch meeting five hours earlier. Between the many courses Hamadani had insisted on, Milly had been excellent at remembering the smaller issues, leaving Kai to read the man before her.

The developer seemed amenable to a deal, if not too interested at such an early stage in drilling down on the specifics, saying that was for his lawyers, later. The main thing was he was actively engaging. Something seemed to have clicked in him, and now he was on board with Grand Millennium.

The only tension had come when she'd asked why his photo wasn't anywhere online. Was he shy, she'd asked, smiling.

His eyes became slits. "You cannot understand why the son of a billionaire might keep his face hidden from the wider world? All my life, kidnap threats have been made against me and my family. If any photo of me appears online, I pay people a lot of money to find ways to get it taken down. This is no joke to us."

Hamadani waved an index finger around the room. "I have security everywhere. Be grateful you didn't come too close to me when you first introduced yourself." His eyes hardened.

Kai's eyes darted around the room, wondering who his undercover security detail were. Before she could form any conclusions, her phone rang with an urgent call about a time-sensitive deal.

She excused herself to take it, and when she returned, Hamadani was gone and Milly was gathering up their paperwork, looking pale. Something felt off. Kai's stomach knotted into worry.

"He received a text and said something had come up," Milly said, not meeting her eye. "We'll get his terms tonight from his lawyers."

Terms? So the deal was still on?

Kai had been checking her emails constantly ever since, and now she caught an odd expression on Milly's face. "What's wrong?"

"Nothing."

It didn't sound like nothing. Kai realized Milly hadn't been herself since lunch. "Did Hamadani say something when I left to take that call?"

"No."

"Did he...Was he inappropriate with you?"

"God no." A pinkish tinge began to rise up Milly's cheeks. "Definitely not possible."

Kai frowned. "What does that mean?"

"Nothing."

"Tell your face that."

Milly shook her head. "You'll make a big deal out of it. It's fine."

"Now you're really scaring me." Kai gently placed her hand over Milly's to stop her writing. "Tell me?"

"It really isn't much. When you left to deal with that call, I pressed him on a few points, small things I was afraid he might forget to include in the terms."

"Okay, and...?"

"He asked where I'd studied management. Or finance. Or law." Hurt flashed in Milly's eyes, along with embarrassment. "I said I hadn't studied any of those things. That I was an assistant.

"And he said, *exactly*." Milly sucked in a breath. "He wasn't obnoxious or rude. But he stared at me hard and told me that The Closer has a reputation for a reason. You're a dealmaker and he highly respects you. *Only* you." She swallowed. "He said I had to understand that he only deals with his equals, not juniors pretending they're important, and therefore we had nothing to discuss. Then he got up and left."

"Asshole." Kai muttered. "You're my right hand for a reason. You're brilliant, Milly."

"Thank you. He is right, though. I was sort of negotiating with him when it wasn't my place."

"In my absence you have every right to speak for me on a deal."

"Mr. Hamadani doesn't see it that way."

"What he said is not acceptable—he belittled you. Why are you defending him?"

"I'm not. I just don't want to be the cause of problems. It's fine, Ms. Fisher."

"It's not fine. If I'd been there, I'd have…" *What?*

"What could you have done?" Milly asked curiously. "You wouldn't jeopardize Mayfair Palace. Or shouldn't."

"You're worth it—don't doubt that."

"I appreciate you saying that, but I think you're beating yourself up for something that bothers you more than me. Why does it upset you so much?"

Because I'm supposed to fight for the underdogs, not side with the powerbrokers screwing them over!

It was so unsettling, this truth. It wasn't the first time she'd dealt with a businessman whose attitude or morals were borderline. It *was* the first time one had attacked one of her own.

"I should tell him to screw his deal. Let the Duxtons have this one. I could tell Mr. Stein he wouldn't be budged. The Duxtons and Hamadani deserve each other."

"Ms. Fisher?" Milly gaped in shock. "You can't throw this deal away over nothing."

"You. Are. Not. Nothing. People who treat others as beneath them make me sick."

"I know. That's what Scorched Earth is all about: justice for the vulnerable."

Kai opened her mouth to refute that. She'd been telling Milly for years it was only about vengeance, but she had no energy to lie today. "Hamadani had no right to treat you like dirt."

"Thank you," Milly said quietly. "I love that you care."

"Well." She rolled her eyes. "Of course I do. Just don't make a big deal of it. I have a reputation."

"Absolutely." Milly said earnestly, her eyes sparkling. "But Ms. Fisher, even if he does this again, please don't end this deal over something I consider so minor. In the future, I'd be proud to be able to say I was on the team that won Mayfair Palace."

Kai hadn't considered that. From Milly's point of view, this would look extremely good on her CV. "All right. But I'm never leaving you alone with him again."

"Okay." The word was quiet and understated, but the relief in Milly's eyes was clear.

The room phone rang. Milly reached for it. "It's Reception," she mouthed.

Kai's heart skipped. Was Lia still on duty?

Milly put the phone down. "That was Graham. They've received a fax from Mr. Hamadani's lawyers for us. It'll be our terms."

"Why fax us? His people could email me direct."

"Security? Emails can be hacked, but it's nearly impossible to crack a fax."

"Well, that's lovely, but it's not very confidential if it then lands on a hotel front desk! What were they thinking?"

"That no one at some random hotel in Vegas can read Arabic?"

"What?"

"The fax is in Arabic, Graham said."

Kai went cold. "That's even worse. We have to negotiate these terms tomorrow. How can we do that if we can't read them?" Kai grabbed her phone and stabbed a button. "Mr. Hamadani? Kai Fisher. I'm sorry to call so late... Yes, yes. Thank you. I did receive the terms. But there's a problem: why are they in Arabic?" She paused, listening. "All right." She ended the call.

"What did he say?"

"That it's probably some simple error and he'll call us back."

"Okay."

Kai stared at the blank wall, zoning out as she waited for the return call. Finally, her phone rang. "Mr. Hamadani." Her mood darkened as she listened to him. "Wouldn't he still be there now if the fax has just come through fifteen minutes ago? Can't he do it again now?" She frowned. "All right. Tomorrow." Kai hung up and sighed.

"What was his explanation?"

"That it's some silly mistake. He has a junior law clerk in the London office who switched faxes and accidentally sent the English version to Hamadani's father to review and the Arabic to us. The young man had apparently been working all night on translating it into Arabic and is exhausted because it's now five in the morning in London."

"Ah."

"He was on the Tube, heading home, when Hamadani got a hold of him. He didn't want to send the man back to the office just for this. He promised to get the first person who arrives at his office to send us the English copy first thing in the morning, our time."

"That's frustrating."

"More than that. We're forced into a negotiation, on the back foot, with little prep time tomorrow. We're still digesting the contents, working out the ramifications, trying to negotiate clauses on the spot, while Hamadani's on top of all of them. Huge advantage for him. I'm sure if it was a huge *dis*advantage for him, he'd have ordered the kid to turn around and fix his screw up."

"We could ask for time to study the terms after we get them tomorrow," Milly suggested. "Another day?"

"He's leaving just after the conference, off to Dubai for a few months. If we take a whole day off to digest this and plan our counteroffer, we'll run out of time to settle the main terms before he's gone. Hamadani said repeatedly he wants our agreement done before he takes off so he can leave it in the hands of his lawyers to finalize with us."

"So we're stuck losing a day?"

"I don't accept that. We just need to find a translator now, even though it's late."

Milly glanced at the clock. "A more common translation might be doable, but I don't imagine there's much call for twenty-four-seven Arabic translators in Vegas."

"We need to try. I'll fetch the fax; you find us a translator. I don't care the cost." Kai made to rise.

"Um…Ms. Fisher? Any reason that you don't want *me* to pick up the fax?" Milly asked. "I can ask them about translation services while I'm down there. Concierge staff know way more about local services than any phone book."

Kai inhaled. It's not like she could confess to Milly that the real reason she had a burning desire to play fetch was because she had the hots for a certain temp employee. With a sigh, she waved Milly away. "No, fine. You're right. Go."

It was better this way anyway. How would she be able to concentrate on outwitting Hamadani if all she had in her mind was Lia Hanson's popped-collar shirt porn?

Amelia glanced up as a short, freckled, frazzled woman appeared in front of her desk. Her large green eyes were fixed on the night desk supervisor, Graham.

"I'm here to pick up a fax," she told him. "You just rang me?"

"Ah, Ms. Valentine, yes." Graham disappeared into the office and returned with paperwork. "Here you are."

"I don't suppose you know anyone at this hour who can do translations?" Ms. Valentine asked him.

"We offer our own service during business hours, but that's not something we can handle this late, especially given the language involved. And I'm afraid there are no twenty-four-hour translation services in Vegas. But I could leave a note for Mrs. Menzies to follow up for you in the morning."

"Oh. I see." Her shoulders sank as she nodded and thanked him.

Amelia's feet were aching, her back was worse, and she'd not been allowed a dinner break yet. All she wanted was to sink into her bed and sleep for a week. Even so, in the face of the young woman's desperation, she couldn't stop herself asking: "Which language? I know a few."

Ms. Valentine turned in surprise. Before she could reply, Graham gave a soft snort and said, "Arabic."

Amelia simply nodded and came around the counter. "You're in luck. I can handle this."

The woman gasped. "You can?"

"You know Arabic?" Graham asked with equal incredulity.

"Yes. Do you want me to do it here?" Amelia asked the woman.

"Oh my goodness. Yes, no, I mean, please, come up to my boss's room. We need confidentiality."

"Lead the way."

She glanced back at her supervisor, who stared after her, astonishment rendering him mute.

"Thank God," Ms. Valentine was saying as they walked. "I can't believe you know Arabic. Thank you." Her brow wrinkled for a moment. "Do I know you from somewhere?"

"Not that I'm aware of." As she said it, the name Valentine did ring a faint bell. "Did I check you in today?"

"No, ma'am. We've been here four days already."

"Then no."

Ms. Valentine accepted that answer and wordlessly led them to her suite.

Amelia followed, barely taking in her surroundings. She was exhausted, but it felt good to help a guest who seemed so grateful.

The woman opened her door and pointed Amelia to a desk by the window. "This way, Ms...?"

"Call me Lia."

"Sure. I'm Milly. So we received a legal document, but we got an Arabic version instead of English by mistake, and we're supposed to negotiate the contents tomorrow."

We? Amelia looked around but saw no one else.

"How can my boss be prepped tonight and know what the seller wants if we can't understand it? And online translations are unreliable."

"I understand." Amelia eyed a half-eaten plate of food on the desk as she slid into the chair. "And you are quite correct about the internet's quality control."

"Oh, sorry." Milly snatched up the plate. "My boss was too worked up to eat... I'll just..." She scampered off with it.

Moments later, a thick sheaf of documents were placed in front of Amelia, and with them came a scent she'd recognize anywhere. Her head snapped up to find Kai had entered from the adjacent suite's doors.

Oh. That's how she knew the name Valentine. She'd reassigned her to a new room today, along with Kai.

"Why, the multi-talented Lia Hanson," Kai drawled as she slid into the chair opposite. "I had no idea Arabic was in your box of tricks. I suppose it makes sense. It's a numbers thing."

"A numbers thing?"

"People good with numbers are good with languages. Music, too."

"If you say so." No need to prove Kai right by admitting she played a pretty decent piano. Amelia pulled the first page of the fax closer to give herself something to focus on.

"Would you like a drink?" Milly asked.

"No thanks," Amelia replied.

She scanned the words and frowned. Several confidential aspects of the contract were missing, namely the price and buyer, which made sense since this was clearly an early draft from the vendor. But one thing she could see all-too clearly was the vendor's name…and exactly what he was offering.

Nedal al-Hamadani was selling Mayfair Palace. To someone else.

Amelia's heart stopped. *How could he?*

Who was the buyer—who did Kai work for? She scanned the contract a second time, but those details had been left blank, waiting to be filled in.

Why was the contract in Arabic? Thanks to his university education in London, Nedal had a superb command of English. His legal and business background meant he could write a pretty decent first-draft contract when he wanted to.

How could he?

The shock started wearing off and a worse thought hit. It was wildly inappropriate for her to even be reading this. Theoretically, Duxton Vegas could be sued for providing a compromised translator to handle sensitive documents. But it was already too late. She'd seen the contents and knew Nedal was selling, even if the buyer's name wasn't listed. What good could excusing herself do now?

"What is it?" Kai asked, concern darting across her face. "You look like you've seen a ghost. Or a whole haunted house worth of them."

Amelia drew in a breath and considered her options. All she could do was her job. She stared in dismay at the words, still unable to believe her friend would take away her dream hotel.

"Seriously, Lia, are you okay?" Kai asked, and this time, the concern was clear.

"I'm sorry. I was not expecting such a long translation. It's late, I haven't eaten dinner, and perhaps my blood sugar levels are low." Not even a lie.

Kai frowned. "We'll get you food. Anything. What would you like?"

To rewind this evening? To unknow what she did?

Milly's voice came, muffled, from the inside the mini-bar fridge. "There's chocolate. Would that help your condition?"

"I…" Well, for all Amelia knew, she *did* have low blood sugar. "Thank you."

A moment later, Milly placed a chocolate bar beside her. "I could order you a meal, too? So you can eat and translate?"

"No, this will be fine." Amelia undid the wrapper and slowly bit in. She swallowed, forcing the small mouthful down her throat.

"Well?" Kai asked. "Feeling better?"

After one bite? Amelia looked at her incredulously.

"Sorry," Kai murmured. "I'm too damned focused on this contract."

"I understand."

"Can you tell me what the main points are?"

"Um…" Amelia mentally shook herself. "You've been sent a Heads of Terms agreement, that's a Letter of Intent in the US. It contains a list of pre-conditions to negotiate between two parties before the sale."

Kai nodded. "So what are these terms?"

"This hotel developer, Nedal al-Hamadani…" she pushed back the rise of bile at his name, "…wants the Mayfair Palace buyer to…" Amelia trailed off, eying a batch of errors. This had clearly been slapped together quickly. And the deal had to be completed by February the…*thirtieth*?

Had time been so short that Nedal had flung this to some office junior and they'd dashed it off too fast, filled with errors? That might also explain why it was in Arabic to start with.

"Let me write down the main terms he wants to negotiate." Amelia scribbled down the key points, warts and all.

Kai leaned forward to read upside-down as Amelia wrote. "That can't be right," she said, tapping one point. "Are you sure the word isn't meant to be 'vendor' there? Why would a seller tie a buyer to exclusivity? Sellers don't care how many other hotels a buyer purchases at the same time as theirs."

No kidding. Amelia looked up. "I promise that is exactly what it says. On that note, I'd recommend a thorough appraisal of this document by an expert."

It was the closest she could come to screaming that the whole thing was a hastily written mess. Her warning was the most ethical thing she could think to do without editorializing, which was absolutely not a translator's job. And she had to be painfully neutral given how compromised she was. Any hint she was trying to influence this deal or deliberately mistranslate the fax could end badly. Hell, the ethics of the entire situation made her stomach churn.

"Thanks so much again for helping us," Milly said. "We don't have much experience with foreign deals. This is our first. There's bound to be a learning curve all round."

A learning curve? Amelia really hoped these two weren't just winging it on their first international deal because Nedal might present as easygoing, but he was also a shrewd negotiator who could pick his teeth with their bones if they weren't on the ball. She and Nedal had always had a wary respect for each other when it came to doing deals.

At the reminder that Nedal was behind all this, her stomach clenched again. *How could he?* He'd been such a strong ally to her and Mariam when their relationship had come out. He'd been loyal and steadfast, despite his father's anger. And now this?

Milly clasped her hands in front of herself. "We got so lucky you were on duty tonight." Her sweet, unguarded gratitude warmed Amelia.

"Yes," Kai said, her voice a sultry murmur that made Amelia tingle. "You do have *so many* skills. You're a life saver."

Amelia pushed her bullet points over to Kai. "Will this summary be sufficient? Or do you want it translated line by line?"

"That seems to be enough to start our negotiations. We don't have a lot of time to be on top of it all." Kai studied the list. "Seriously?" She pointed to the February 30 error.

Amelia sighed. "Yes. Seriously."

For once, the woman seemed robbed of words. Her eyes narrowed as though contemplating the implications of such a glaring mistake. Kai's gaze settled on Amelia. "Thanks again, Ms. Hanson." The warm timbre of her voice was unsettling.

"You're welcome, Ms. Fisher. I do aim to please our guests." The words came out sounding like a challenge. She honestly hadn't meant it that way, but the way Kai's eyes widened told Amelia she'd liked it very much.

They stared at each other until Milly, eyes darting between them in confusion, cleared her throat.

Kai glanced back at the paperwork. "Milly, please get me a coffee. I can see it's going to be a long night." Her eyes flicked back up to Amelia's as Milly left the room.

For a moment, they studied each other. Finally Amelia realized she had far better things to be doing, and guest-gawping was certainly not an approved job activity.

She rose to her feet, which protested, nodded at Kai, and left. As she closed the door, she couldn't hold back the start of a smile at the thought of the distracting Kai Fisher. Until she remembered what she'd just read.

Nedal al-Hamadani was selling her out.

Amelia stretched out her aching legs, relieved her twelve-hour shift had ended, and stared at the ceiling above her bed.

How had she misjudged Nedal so badly? She'd never seen him double-cross anyone, but that didn't mean he wasn't capable. Throw his powerful father into the mix, a man who'd been micromanaging his son more and more lately, and who knew what was going on?

What if it wasn't too late, though? A deal that had been countered by a better offer could be countered again…as long as this wasn't about Mariam. If it was, well, this was game over.

Her thoughts spun chaotically until she finally gave up. She needed Quinn. It might be only six in the morning for her second-in-command, but this definitely counted as a disaster.

"Amelia?" came a sleep-fogged voice.

"Did you find out where Nedal went?"

"Not…exactly."

"Well, we need him *exactly*. We need him more urgently than ever."

"What's happened?" Quinn asked, sounding more alert.

"It seems he's selling Mayfair Palace to someone else."

"How do you know?" Quinn gasped.

"An unfortunate series of events I'd rather not go into at the moment, but it looks very bad. Just tell me: Are you making progress?"

"Nedal's phone goes straight to voicemail. I still try it every hour."

"Damn."

"Yeah. So I, um, may have also gotten a little desperate."

"Oh?"

"I called Mariam. Her number's still in your contacts list."

Amelia's heart did a painful clench at her ex's name. She steeled her tone to even. "And?"

"I'll let you know what she says when she returns my call. But at least she'll know where her brother went, right?"

"I suppose." Amelia closed her eyes, too exhausted to think about this properly. "Yes, she'd know."

"Are you okay?"

"I was better until I found out Nedal betrayed us."

"We don't know for sure yet, do we? It's just a tip-off, right?"

A lot more than that. "I really can't talk about it."

"Okay, then tell me how your first day went undercover? Front desk, wasn't it?"

"Mmm. A lot of standing about and fixing people's minor issues that could be easily solved themselves. Plus dealing with a good child with a bad temper and an AWOL nanny."

"You had to deal with a kid?"

"Why so surprised? Kids love me."

"I've noticed. I think it's because you treat them all like short adults, you don't lie to them, and you answer all their annoying questions without complaining."

"I have no idea why people always find questions that expand one's knowledge annoying instead of a sign of intelligence. That reminds me: I owe Imogen a chat. God forbid we don't get to the bottom of her pressing owl-knee conundrum."

"I won't ask." Quinn chuckled. "So, fess up—did anyone pick up that you weren't who you claimed?"

"One guest figured out I was a fake in, oh, two minutes flat." Amelia sighed. "Worse, she deduced I was a Duxton, too."

"Holy shit. So you *did* leak all over the place?"

"You make me sound like an incontinence ad." Amelia huffed. "That particular guest was just unusually perceptive. No one else suspected a thing." Amelia rubbed her eyes and remembered her other task for Quinn. "Can you look someone up for me as soon as possible? A Kai Fisher?" She remembered the unusual spelling she'd seen in the check-in computer. "That's K-A-I. She works in hotel marketing and acquisitions. I also gather her company's based solely stateside."

"Why the look-up? Is she involved in Mayfair? Or is this more personal? Someone you...like?"

Amelia grimaced. "She is *far* too cocky to like."

"So she's attractive? Since you're avoiding an outright denial?"

Amelia was too tired for this. "Just find her for me, will you? I need to know exactly who I'm dealing with."

"Hmm." Quinn sounded entirely unbothered by the sudden bite to Amelia's tone. "Sure thing. Get some rest. You'll need it. Tomorrow's room service, right? At least I got you a late start."

"Yes. I'm sure I'll manage. Anyone can survive one day ferrying food from the kitchen to guests and returning plates. How hard can it be?"

"Right." Quinn's laugh was soft. "That's the spirit."

Amelia's eyelids were fluttering closed as she faintly heard Quinn say, "You're falling asleep. Hanging up now!"

Mmmph. "Find me Kai," were the last words she could remember mumbling before surrendering to unconsciousness.

Chapter 10

Room Service

AMELIA'S ROOM-SERVICE SHIFT THE NEXT evening was so busy that if she were the superstitious kind, she'd blame herself for overconfidence. Telling Quinn how hard could it be? Foolish.

Staff were allocated seven minutes to arrive at a room, get food laid out and signed off, and then return to the kitchens. Being late back was a one-point deduction. Slow elevators chewed up a lot of time, which meant every meal run so far had resulted in lost points.

Amelia's stomach rumbled, and she wished she'd thought to pack a granola bar. The irony of being surrounded by food but not allowed to eat until ten-thirty? Absurd. She controlled her irritation by mentally drafting a scathing report on the staff conditions.

"Hanson! Service!" the chef barked. "Room three-oh-four."

The aroma of pasta tortellini drove her mad all the way up in the service elevator. It was only when she'd lifted a hand to knock on the door of 304 that she realized whose room this was. Milly Valentine's.

As in, assistant of Kai...who might be inside, too.

A mix of conflicted and intrigued emotions rose up before she reminded herself that she didn't care either way. Amelia rapped sharply and called out, "Room service!"

Milly let her in and then blinked. "Oh hey! It's our translator." Her smile was wide and welcoming. "You do dinners, too? Your hotel sure moves you around."

"It does." Amelia pushed the trolley inside. "I'm versatile."

Milly laughed. "You sure are."

Amelia glanced to the desk where she'd normally unpack food, but it was strewn with paperwork. "Pasta tortellini, salad, and champagne."

"Ugh. Too early for champagne." Milly sighed, clearing a space on the desk. "Just dump it all here."

"Too early? It's rather late, I'd have thought."

"No, I mean premature. Our deal's not as simple as we thought." Milly grimaced. "A lot less simple, actually."

"Okay." Amelia kept her voice light.

"Some of the clauses our seller wants are apparently not…logical. Some are not even legal in the US, for that matter. And one's just plain wrong."

No kidding. "Ah," Amelia said neutrally. At least they'd had the paperwork checked over then.

As Amelia laid out the dishes, she suddenly wondered why she was rooting for a rival.

As an abstract concept, she sided with the underdog and didn't want Kai tripped up by some badly translated draft or Nedal's clever clauses. His highly paid team of lawyers were the most impressive she'd ever tangled with. Once they got their hands on a deal's agreed terms and began pulling the details apart, Amelia's own lawyers tended to go down with migraines. Even so—underdog or not, Kai was trying to muscle in on Amelia's territory.

Mayfair Palace is mine.

Amelia straightened. "Would you like me to bring you a different refreshment? Wine, perhaps, if you're not in the mood for champagne? Or something else?"

"God, I wish you could get me a new brain. Is that on the menu?" She rolled her eyes.

The woman was impossibly adorable. "I'm afraid not." Amelia smiled faintly.

"That's a shame." Milly blew out a frustrated breath. "I can't figure out this marketing report for my boss, and she wants it summarized within the hour. Honestly, I just don't understand it. It says one thing and concludes the opposite. It's really frustrating, but my boss is so tied up in knots about our deal that I don't want to bother her."

"Your boss?" Amelia prodded, curious as to the assistant's take on Kai.

Milly glanced over her shoulder at the adjoining door to Kai's suite. The door was ajar, but there was no sign of movement. She lowered her voice. "Sometimes I think she forgets we're not all as smart as her. Like she'd immediately know why celebrities endorsing our hotels is seen as such a terrible idea even if the report also says it's fantastic when famous people give a shout out about our hotels. I don't get it."

"Hey." Amelia took pity on her. "The report's discussing brand leakage. That's when a spokesman, such as a top actor or rap star, is so closely linked to the brand they're endorsing that the two brands become interconnected."

She interlocked her fingers. "So if the chosen celebrity gets into trouble, the brand does, too. If they become a huge success, the brand is seen as an extension of them and can take off as well."

"Okay." Milly nodded. "I have heard of that, but not related to hotels."

"That's because it's seen as too risky for the hotel industry. You see, hotels are about stability and longevity, not flashes in the pan. Hotels like to avoid brand leakage at all costs, although they never mind if a random, unaligned celebrity shouts all over social media that they liked where they stayed. I can see why it would be confusing if your report didn't say they were addressing brand leakage."

Milly stared at her. "How on earth do you know that? I mean yes, that explains *everything*, but how could you possibly know all that?"

"A very good question," came a seductive voice from behind them. "Isn't it, Ms. Hanson?"

Amelia turned to find Kai leaning against the doorframe of the now fully open adjoining doors, scrutinizing her. Her arms were folded, and her eyes raked Amelia.

"I multi-task." Amelia decided she didn't appreciate that knowingness in Kai's tone.

"She really does," Milly agreed. "I mean with the Arabic translation and all."

"Yes, about that...how many efficiency experts know Arabic and brand leakage, I wonder? Not to mention you're apparently a whiz at food delivery. Quite the Renaissance woman. Can I expect deconstructing ancient Egyptian glyphs next, along with fluffing my pillow?"

Milly glanced between the two and frowned. "Is everything okay?"

"I don't know," Kai's sharp gaze was fixed on Amelia. "Is it? Because every time I turn around, Lia Hanson is pulling off some casual brilliance one would not expect from someone who is what she says she is."

Amelia's expression cooled. She would not be goaded. "Dinner is served."

"Mm, I'm sure you're losing points by the minute. Tell me, have you fallen below sixty yet? Will your pay get docked after only two days?"

Amelia was ten points away from a pay deduction. Just then her phone pinged softly. A reminder her seven minutes allocated for this job were already up. Another deduction.

"So they *are* cutting into your pay already?" Kai prodded as she neared. "Is Duxton's staff turnover less of a mystery? Or is there some innocent explanation, in the same way there is for your varied CV?"

"Why are you doing this?" Amelia eyed her. What had Milly said? Kai was stressed because negotiations weren't going well? That was no reason to give an innocent party the third degree. "I have no wish to discuss my life with you right now."

"Well, forget your life, let's discuss your accent," Kai said, leaning in. "There's another fascinating topic. It's got a bit of everything, hasn't it? A bit of English, American, possibly…New York?"

"I'm well-traveled."

Kai's eyes became half-lidded, "Hmm." She took the hotel's leather room-service folio, scribbled, then signed off. "Don't worry, I've left you a generous tip for looking after us so well and educating my lovely assistant on topics that usually only marketing and hotel-management graduates are well versed in." Her sarcasm was thick. She handed the folio to Amelia.

Milly's eyes darted back and forth between the two women.

"Thank you," Amelia muttered. "Good evening, Ms. Fisher. Ms. Valentine." She shoved her trolley out of the room with force.

How arrogant was Kai to think she was owed Amelia's story simply because it didn't add up neatly for her? Her jaw ground. The infuriating woman would do better focusing on her apparently tanking deal. Nedal was probably eating her alive on the fine print, and by now she knew it.

Amelia rolled the trolley back to the kitchen, still annoyed. She didn't owe Kai any explanations.

"About time," the chef groused. "You're burning through points." He scribbled a note. "Okay, five-seventeen is first…" he slid a tray onto the bottom shelf with a perfunctory clang, "then five-oh-five, top shelf." He added a dish.

Twenty minutes later, Amelia returned from the fifth floor to the sight of a pair of steaks sliding onto plates. Her stomach grumbled in earnest.

"For three-oh-four," the chef said. "Guest said they under-ordered last time. They asked for you specifically."

Under-ordered? Sure they had. She scowled. Gritting her teeth, Amelia retraced her steps to the now-familiar door.

Milly answered, an embarrassed blush on her cheeks. "Still hungry," she murmured unconvincingly. "Please come through."

The pasta they'd ordered earlier sat, barely eaten, on top of the counter, with crumpled napkins around it. The desk had been cleaned off and was set for two.

"Just place it down there, please, Ms. Hanson," Kai said, wandering in from her own room.

Amelia laid out the meals then returned the cloches to her trolley. "Two steaks and salads."

"Sit for a moment?" Kai waved at the chair in front of the meals. "Have some food."

What on earth? "I don't think so. As you pointed out earlier, I'm on the clock."

"I'm also aware they don't feed the staff properly or allow them proper breaks. You can't perform at peak efficiency if you collapse…and I know you're all about efficiency." Her eyes crinkled. "I won't tell. And my assistant here is sworn to secrecy. Aren't you, Milly?"

A mop of red curls bobbed up and down once, although Milly didn't look up from her phone.

It was tempting, Amelia had to admit. But… "It's unprofessional."

"Suit yourself." Kai settled into a chair and proceeded to cut her steak. The delicious aroma of seasoning and perfectly seared meat filled the room.

Kai glanced up. "Why do you do what you do? Streamlining other people's businesses? Someone with your vast talents could do anything."

"I enjoy my work." Amelia placed the pasta debris on her trolley. She handed a leather folder to Milly to sign for the bill and waited until the young woman handed it back. "I like taking something that's poorly run and turning it into a model of good business." All true. A point of pride was how all the hotels she'd bought—including the rundown ones snapped up during the financial crisis—were now profitable and humming along smoothly.

"Is that so?" Kai cut an exacting slice of meat, eyed it, and slid it into her mouth. She chewed slowly, swallowed, and looked up again. "So tell me, Ms. Hanson, how is it that you don't exist?"

Amelia froze.

"My excellent assistant knows everything about everyone working in and around hotels." Kai waved at Milly. "And those she doesn't know, she is superb at researching. Milly looked you up between courses. Imagine my surprise at discovering 'Lia Hanson' isn't real. No efficiency experts exist with that name in business or on social media."

"Not everyone likes social media," Amelia said coolly.

"Now why do I find it so hard to believe that someone who has a thorough understanding of brand leakage and hotel marketing could possibly have no presence in the online world?" Kai asked casually. "Out of interest, where did you learn about brand leakage? Was it at college? Doing which degree?"

Amelia was in no mood for this. "I trust that's all?" she asked with finality, just as her stomach grumbled, spoiling her steely exit.

"Oh hell, you poor thing." Concern instantly filled Kai's tone. "For God's sake, just sit and have a bite. We'll only throw it out otherwise. Milly's a vegetarian."

Amelia hesitated. It *was* tempting. The scent was overwhelming. Her stomach churned again.

"Please?" Kai's expression turned gentle. "I'd be horrified if you keeled over because I dared you into this undercover scheme."

Milly blinked. "Scheme? So you two *do* know each other? How?"

"It's a long story." Kai's gaze remained fixed on Amelia. "Honestly, Lia, I'm sorry if I was pushing. I'd like you fed and not fainting. Besides, you should look after yourself before anything else. It's only logical, right?"

Amelia paused.

"I'll even stop being annoying," Kai promised. "Well, for now." She smiled.

"I'm sure," Amelia muttered. Still, she suddenly found herself sitting opposite Kai, the woman's argument impossible to resist right now.

"I heard that." Kai laughed. "Don't worry, I'm sure your view on how annoying I am is shared. Shall we poll my assistant?"

"Please don't," Milly said. "I'd like to be excused from this conversation. You two can tease, argue, or kill each other without me." She resumed tapping on her phone with great concentration.

Kai looked amused. "Ah, we've finally found Milly Valentine's breaking point."

"I think killing is far closer to the mark than the other two options." Amelia carved off a neat piece of steak and bit in. *Phenomenal.*

"So, Lia, is your second-in-command as brilliant as you are? As diverse in their skills?" Kai asked as she watched Amelia eat.

"She's excellent, yes." Amelia sliced off a second piece of steak.

"If you have a second-in-command, you are running a department at the very least. Maybe more?"

Amelia looked up. "I'm sorry?"

"But it's not efficiency work, is it? So what do you actually do?"

Pushing her plate away, Amelia stood. "If you'll excuse me." Clearly hunger had allowed her to lower her guard. Annoyance filled her. "I see you're not good at keeping promises."

"You're right, that was cheeky of me. I'm sorry. It was a reflex to ask."

"Your excuses are worthless." Amelia stalked back to her trolley.

Real regret filled Kai's expression. "Now I'm afraid my nosy streak has robbed you of food. I can promise you I do this everywhere I stay: make sure the staff are fed and, while I'm at it, I often like to learn who they are." She glanced over to her assistant. "Am I lying, Milly?"

"No, Ms. Fisher," she replied, without looking away from her phone. "You like to feed employees at every hotel we stay in."

"There, see? I'm not singling you out," Kai said. "Please stay. Eat some more."

"I can't." The small piece of meat she'd already ingested felt like cement. "If you'll excuse me."

She pushed the trolley out of the room, irritation rising. Amelia had given Kai a chance to not be intrusive, to let it go, and she'd instead doubled down.

Anyway, Amelia reminded herself as she viciously punched the elevator button, the woman was irrelevant. She might have some minor charms, but they were offset by how dangerous, nosy, and infuriating she was. From now on, Amelia would completely ignore her. No excuses, no exceptions.

"Something to say?" Kai asked Milly who was silently eying her from the other side of the room like a disgruntled kitten.

They'd both watched Lia scurry out like her ass was on fire. *Her hungry ass.* It was criminal how Hotel Duxton never allowed its staff proper breaks. The Dragon should probably tweet about it again.

"She was *really* hungry," Milly said reproachfully.

"I know." Regret filled Kai. She'd screwed this up.

Milly bit her lip.

"Okay, out with it."

"You scared her off! Usually you just feed the room-service staff, not grill them, too."

"Didn't it bother you she's been lying to us?" Kai demanded.

"Lying to *you*, you mean," Milly said tactfully. "I think you took it personally. Her reasons for having a false identity would have nothing to do with you."

"Not the point. I don't like being lied to to my face. Or my back."

"Mm," Milly murmured.

Kai regarded her assistant's admonishing look. "And why do you care so much?"

"I liked her. She was helpful. Efficient. Graceful under fire," she added pointedly.

"And at times colder than a winter drift," Kai said. "She bothers me." *Unsettles me, more like.* "Have we had any response from Hamadani's lawyers about our revised terms?"

"Not yet." Milly paused. "What if they come back in Arabic? Who will we get to translate them?"

"Ms. Hanson, of course."

"I saw her face when she left. She's annoyed and hurt. I think we've burned our bridges."

"Fine," Kai conceded, feeling more regret than she cared to admit. "I'll get her back and apologize."

Milly gave her a skeptical look.

"What? I can do 'nice.' And humble."

Milly didn't say a word. But the "we're screwed" was loud and clear.

As it turned out, Milly was right. A different room-service attendant arrived with their next unnecessary food order, despite Kai asking for Lia.

For some reason, knowing she'd annoyed Lia that much was more depressing than she could imagine.

Chapter 11

Housekeeping

AMELIA TUGGED AT HER BORROWED housekeeping uniform, willing it to conform to her shape, not the other way around. The gray dress with a white apron and white cuffs on the short sleeves was as unflattering as it was itchy.

Her name tag said "Dora." Amelia had no idea who that was, but given how the dress reached only to mid-thigh, she gathered Dora was much shorter.

Housekeeping's team leader was an intimidating, dark-eyed, fifty-something woman called Mrs. Espinosa. The name fit. Amelia's passable Latin told her that *spinosa* meant thorny.

Mrs. Espinosa was brutally efficient and ruthless. She reminded her staff constantly of the time limits: twenty minutes on small rooms; forty minutes on larger suites. Failure to adhere to these limits would result in point losses. *Of course it would.*

Last night, when Amelia had refused to deliver to rooms 303 or 304 again, even when she'd been specifically asked for by the guests, she'd been deducted so many points it was useless keeping track.

Amelia wondered if she'd be presented with a bill at the end of her working week instead of a wage.

Mrs. Espinosa sounded exhausted, which might explain her snappish tongue. She did, however, offer an approving grunt when Amelia finally got a bed's corners exactly right. "Yes. This is it. Repeat, all rooms. Now you handle this alone. I will return each twenty minutes to approve the rooms. Go."

Unsupervised work? High praise.

Amelia worked quietly for most of the morning, stripping and making beds and scrubbing floors, benches, and toilets until they gleamed. It was the fiddly work that required concentration, such as remembering that paper coasters on upturned glasses should be turned so the hotel logo faced the user.

Her back twinged as Amelia rose from a shower stall and rinsed out her brush. Done a few minutes early, she pulled out her phone and texted Quinn.

Any Nedal updates?

Can I call? Quinn replied instantly.

The sound of a distant vacuum cleaner started up in the next room, telling her where her supervisor was. She texted back.

Quick call

Her phone rang, and she thumbed the answer button one-handed as she packed away her supplies.

"Hey, boss. How goes your back and knees?"

"Still bending—for now. I don't know how your mother did it for decades. My back is screaming after three hours. I'm too old for this."

"You poor thing." Quinn chuckled unsympathetically.

"What did Mariam say?" Amelia was proud of herself for how even her voice sounded.

"Don't know. I missed her call because she rang really late, then I couldn't reach her when I returned it. In her message, she said she'd call back."

Amelia ground her jaw. *Great.* "Any other leads?"

"I tracked down Nedal's home address and went to visit. No answer. His neighbor asked who I was. After I explained, she said she saw him leaving with his driver and luggage in a limo days ago. She doesn't know where he went." Quinn paused. "This makes no sense. I just think…"

"Could you repeat that? The other maid's vacuuming."

Quinn laughed. "Funny hearing you call yourself a maid. You know, if it's seriously getting too much, I'll have Corporate call and say they're 'transitioning' Lia Hanson elsewhere."

She sounded far too smug.

"No," Amelia said briskly, refusing to be goaded.

"Okay…hey, have you had a chance to enjoy the bright lights of Vegas yet? Seen any sights? Had fun?"

An image of Kai filled her mind…teasing and distracting. Not what she'd call fun exactly, but not *not* fun, either. Besides, Kai Fisher was also a manipulator, and her inquisition last night had been beyond the pale.

"I am here to work," Amelia said firmly.

A movement outside the bathroom alerted her that she was no longer alone. She quickly ended the call as the bathroom door began to open.

Mrs. Espinosa cleared her throat. "Are you done?"

Was that a trick question? Had she heard her on the phone?

Amelia checked the bathroom and couldn't see anything she could improve on. "Yes."

"Good." Mrs. Espinosa beckoned. "You have three more rooms on this floor before we go to the next one."

With a nod, Amelia exited, already exhausted. And she only had six hours left.

She definitely felt done in every sense.

Kai eyed Hamadani across the restaurant breakfast table. This was it. If she could just sell this last point, she'd have this nailed, she was sure of it.

"Clause 12.1c would effectively shift the deal's payment terms into the following quarter, which would act as a pseudo tax break for you with the new write-off rules coming in," Kai said. "In exchange, I'd like your new room-allocation system included at no extra charge. The benefits from the date change would offset the cost." She held her breath.

Mayfair Palace's state-of-the-art booking system was a thing of beauty. Customers could look at the hotel's rooms virtually online, taking a 360-

degree tour of each of them, room by room, examining the view, bed, cupboards, everything, to determine if the room was what they wanted, and then select it at booking.

That was only the start of it. Cutting-edge tech was embedded into every part of the hotel, running through every club, bar, and restaurant—all interlinked, all user-friendly. Any area could be called up by a manager to assess how busy a hotspot was and what the financial turnover was in real time.

While it cost Kai absolutely nothing to push the settlement date into a new financial year, Mayfair Palace's technology added close to one percent to the value of the hotel. Kai was essentially asking for something for nothing.

Assuming her most relaxed expression, although her heart was pounding, she waited.

Hamadani let his pen drop and looked up. "Yes."

Yes? Yes! Honestly, she'd thought he'd put up more of a fight. She did the mental sums on how much she'd saved her boss with 12.1c. *Hmm. Over seven figures. You're welcome, Mr. Stein.*

"Tomorrow we'll put our verbal agreement into writing." Hamadani sounded uninterested. "Then everything's sent to our lawyers to finalize. But I really must get this off my plate tomorrow, yes?"

Why did he look bored? Maybe he had a new iron in the fire. Another development? That could be it. He might be one of those people who found the challenge in the chase, not the catching.

"Yes," she agreed. "Let's do that."

With that settled, Hamadani bade her farewell and left her to stare at the remains of her half-eaten toast.

It was odd how flat she suddenly felt. Kai should be on a high and calling her boss. *The Closer wins again!* Except something niggled, stopping her from reaching for her phone. What was it? Nothing came to mind, so she headed back to her room, suddenly in desperate need of a cleansing shower.

The shower didn't help shake her out of her odd mood. Perhaps she was tired? Sleep had not come easily the previous night thanks to Lia's words circling her head.

Lia had said she had no wish to discuss her life right now. Kai hung up her towel. The "right now" was killing her. It sounded as though Lia hadn't been opposed to discussing her life with Kai at some point, and she'd ruined that.

Enough.

Dragging a brush through her hair, Kai forced her mind back to Hamadani. So, the deal didn't excite her as it once did, but her reputation would be cemented for years after this. That felt good at least. She knotted her robe's belt and left the bathroom in search of clothes.

Two sharp raps sounded on the suite's door, followed by a call of "Housekeeping."

She stopped dead and tried to process why the voice sounded familiar. Kai was still trying to unclog her brain when the door opened.

Lia Hanson, in a housekeeping uniform, pushed a trolley inside. She started at the sight of Kai frozen in the middle of the room.

Even in the plain maid's uniform, Lia had a regal bearing and poise. How could anyone look at her and think for a second she was a maid? The woman might not run an efficiency company, but she ran something.

Kai eyed her, curious as to what she'd do next.

"Ms. Fisher." Lia's words were cold and polite.

"Lia. It's good to see you again."

"The feeling is not mutual."

"I know." Kai offered a smile. "I'm surprised you're here."

"I didn't notice this was your room. Would you like me to send in my supervisor instead? She's attending to your assistant's suite. Or I could come back later?"

"And have you lose points for not following orders? I can't have that. Besides, I owe you."

"You...owe me?"

"For being a little out of line last night."

"A *little*?" Lia's tone was razor sharp.

"No, you're quite right. That's why I tried to get you back again—to apologize for my behavior."

Lia did not look impressed as she began unpacking cleaning supplies.

"I was totally out of line," Kai continued. "Your business is your business. I promise I won't push again. If you choose to share, I'd be delighted, but I get that I was an ass."

"On that we agree."

Kai's lips quirked. "Am I forgiven then? For my ass-like qualities?"

"How optimistic." Lia straightened a pile of towels.

"Okay, yes. I'm an optimist. That's accurate." Kai smiled wider. "I mean, pessimism never really sat well with me. And I doubt I'll ever be a clear-eyed realist like you."

Lia gave her a long look. "Don't do that—the empty flattery. It doesn't impress me."

Empty flattery? It was a fact. *Whatever.* Kai raised her hands in surrender. "Let's stick to the truth then."

"If you can manage it."

Ouch. Also a little hypocritical.

Before Kai could reply, Lia's gaze darted down Kai's body, then flicked away. Her cheeks suddenly stained red.

Kai glanced down at herself. *Oh.* Her gaping robe was showing considerable cleavage. She wrenched it closed. "Sorry," she muttered.

"I apologize for having interrupted you." Lia's voice was even cooler.

"Not interrupted. Just needed a shower after a meeting about my hotel deal."

"That bad?" Lia asked, a flicker of interest in her eyes.

"Just weird. Thank God it's done. Well, virtually."

Lia's face fell. "Congratulations."

"Thanks. I couldn't have done it without you. Your translations came right when I needed them."

"Great," Lia muttered, and for a second it looked as if she wanted to ask something else. Then her eyes did a slow, deliberate scan of Kai, pausing on her cleavage. The inspection wasn't sexual in the least, more...clinical.

Kai shifted uncertainly. "Something on your mind?"

"Did you conspire for me to find you like this? Because if so, it's disrespectful, even more than last night's interrogation. Not to mention I'm on duty. At least respect my work if you refuse to respect me."

"You think this is a set-up?" Kai gaped at her. "How was I supposed to know that you were on housekeeping duty today, and were going to do my room right at the moment I sprung from my shower?"

"I don't know, Ms. Fisher. You're resourceful. You tell me."

"I'm good at a lot of things, but even I can't predict staff schedules." Kai's eyes narrowed. "But, hey, I love your faith in my powers of bending the whole universe to my will."

"You're saying it *would* be your will to meet me exactly like this then, if you could?" Lia's eyebrow arched.

"I..." Kai's lips curled a little. "That depends on your reaction to that specific scenario."

"I have no interest in finding you in this manner."

Well...Lia had spat that answer out pretty fast. Still, Kai hadn't imagined that blush when Lia had first noticed her robe's disarray. "Is this one of those times when you're lying to yourself, Lia?"

"You're so damned presumptuous." Her look was dark and warning. "Always a player, it seems."

Whoa. That snappish tone was way over the top. The memory of Lia nipping her ear came to mind—the scent of her perfume, the teasing lips. How could the same woman she'd met in the bar, who'd slid Kai's earlobe into her mouth and tugged it playfully, be so indifferent and frozen now?

Kai's heart stuttered as she realized the answer. *She isn't.*

Drawing in a deep breath, wondering how badly she was about to crash and burn, Kai stepped closer. "Yes, I'm presumptuous. I'm sorry about that. It's a character flaw." Achingly slowly, she lifted her hand to Lia's face, waiting for it to be slapped away.

Instead, Lia's lips parted, but whatever protest she had planned died when Kai's fingers made contact with her jaw. Strong and proud. Her skin was so warm. Why had Kai ever thought Lia would feel cool?

"So now what happens?" Kai whispered. She trailed her index finger along Lia's jaw. "Do you want to keep glaring at me? Or do you want to touch me, too? You can, you know." Her voice was sincere.

"Did you miss the part where I'm on duty? You expect me to indulge in some fast and furious liaison right *now*? Or was it just some fumbling foreplay you had in mind?" Her eyes blazed.

Kai ignored everything except the fact that Lia hadn't immediately slapped her hand away. "I'm up for whatever you're offering—now or later," she said evenly, dropping her hand. "And for the record, I'm hardly some player." Honestly, she only had a lover every other month, and even then it was only a one-time thing. Hardly crazy bed-hopping antics.

"You give the impression you're quite...active," Amelia said.

"Lia, I happen to be scrupulous with my sexual health, I'm choosy, and I make no apologies for enjoying the company of women. But is that really what's bugging you? It sounds like you're trying to find excuses for not wanting me, instead of just admitting you do. Because, I should point out, you didn't say no."

"I apologize for my imprecision. *No.*" Lia's mouth curled in disdain. "Was that any clearer?"

Crystal. Except...it was funny how she'd swayed in a little to make her point.

Did Lia want more? It was a fine time for Kai's legendary people-reading skills to go on the fritz.

Suddenly Lia's gaze collided with Kai's, and the turmoil in her stormy eyes was laid bare. *Oh.* She was thinking about it all right—and she wasn't happy in the least.

"Perhaps you want me to be the one to start something, to give you deniability?" Kai suggested. "Is that what you need? A way to have me where it won't be your fault?"

Lia's eyes widened. "What gives you the idea I want this *at all?*" Her tone was incredulous.

"Your hand, Lia."

They both looked down to where Lia's hand now rested against the lapel of Kai's robe. The fingers were curled slightly, ensuring a good grip on the white toweling, as if subconsciously clenching Kai closer.

Gasping, Lia stepped away. Her eyes flitted around the room as if deciding what to do next. Was she about to bolt? Say something vicious? Her gaze finally came back to rest on Kai, her nostrils flaring. "Damn it." Lia suddenly grabbed fistfuls of Kai's lapels, dragged her against herself... and kissed her. *Hard.*

Lia's lips were impatient and arousing, and she kissed with delightful precision.

Of course she does.

Kissing her back desperately, messily—precision be damned—Kai tried to get enough of those demanding lips. She tangled a hand in Lia's tight bun, wrenching it loose, feeling all the more wanton for the brazen act.

That only seemed to spur Lia on. She wrapped her arms fiercely around Kai, as if trying to pull her inside herself, while her lips sought out more.

Desire coursed through Kai. She was ready to tear off Lia's uniform and demand they finish this—on the floor if they had to. Then Lia groaned softly—a needy sound that made Kai soaking wet and curled her toes—and drew away.

Kai sagged, already missing that possessive, exacting mouth.

Lia wiped her fingers across her lips and drew in a ragged breath. "Damn." Her cheeks were burning, her eyes far too bright. Her hands came to rest flat against Kai's chest as if about to push her away. "I should not have done that."

Before Kai could offer an opinion either way, Lia pulled Kai in and kissed her again. Heat swirled through Kai, firing up all her nerve endings.

This time, the kiss was even more powerful, because Kai could feel Lia trying to will herself to stop...and failing miserably.

When it was over, and they stared at each other slack-jawed, drawing in deep, shaky breaths, Kai was aware of only one thing: that had been the most arousing fucking kiss of her life.

Lia stepped backward. She stared at Kai as if unable to believe what had transpired. *Twice.*

"Um." Kai seemed to be unable to form words. She had obviously pegged Lia Hanson all wrong. Not so rigid, after all. She ran a quivering hand down her robe, checking she wasn't as bare as she felt. "Well, you seem to have overcome your objections to me."

"And you seem to have found your tongue again." Lia's tone was dry, but her eyes were as wild as her hair.

"In more ways than one." Kai chuckled. There had definitely been plenty of tongue in that second kiss. The reminder sent a small, excited shudder through her. She teasingly tapped Lia's nametag. "So, is Dora an explorer after all?"

Lia grumbled. "Must you?"

Okay then. So apparently they weren't talking about how expertly—and thoroughly—Lia Hanson could kiss. "Do I want to know why you kissed me?"

Lia pressed her lips into a thin line. "You had it coming. You and your teasing, smart mouth and that...poor excuse for a robe." She waved vaguely at it.

Kai glanced down. Her robe had splayed apart even more, offering liberal glimpses of the sides of her breasts and her stomach. But at least the essentials were covered, so she wasn't entirely sure what Lia's problem was.

Lia's eyes were dark as she roamed Kai's skin. Suddenly her fists curled into tight balls.

"You really hate yourself for doing that, don't you?" Kai asked quietly. Lia was such a paradox. Haughty derision one moment, plundering Kai's mouth with abandon the next.

The other woman gave her a mutinous glare. "This is all you do, isn't it? Hold up people's weaknesses for your own amusement?"

"Wanting me is a weakness? Why? Because I affect you? But, Lia, you affect me, too. I'm melting over your kisses."

For the briefest moment, Lia's walls came crashing down. Kai was shocked at the naked need in her eyes. It was gone so fast that she wondered if she'd imagined it.

"My condolences," Lia drawled.

"You want me to believe you wouldn't love to have your wicked way with me after you kissed me like *that*?" Kai coaxed her. Because they had to discuss this crackling energy between them.

Lia's look turned lethal. *Lord.* That probably worked well on staff.

"No need to plan my murder." Kai held up her hands. "I'm the first to admit the laws of attraction are illogical and, despite what your awestruck employees think, we both know you're human."

Lia scowled. "Mocking me now?"

"Whoa, tiger. That's some death-ray glare you have there. And no, I promise I'm not making fun of you."

"I'm supposed to believe that?" Lia's jaw clenched.

"Look," Kai tried again, even more gently, "I see now that this is really messing with your equilibrium and you hate it. You like control, and this isn't it. Right?"

Lia's eyes became steely. "Don't presume to know me."

"I won't. But there *is* something between us. I'm just saying, what if we addressed that?"

"How?"

"Well option one, we could just go with it. You could kiss me senseless again." Kai's voice dropped to a daring register. "Or...we could get it entirely out of our systems—not necessarily now, but soon. You could strip me naked, fling me down, make me understand who's in charge. That'd sure show me." Kai's smile was teasing. "I won't even fight. Much."

"What's option two?" Lia's voice was chilly.

Kai's tone went from teasing to curious. "Not even going to consider it? You and your love of control, huh? Would it be scandalizing for you to consider breaking your own rules?"

"Reverse psychology now? You say that so I'll have to prove you wrong? Let me be clear: anything more than what just occurred is *never* happening, so stop looking at me like I'm some...tasty treat."

Kai put her hands on her hips, which inadvertently widened the gap in her robe.

It drew Lia's eye instantly, and she drank in Kai.

Does she even realize how much she gives away?

"That's a real shame," Kai said genuinely. "If you'd let me, I'd worship you."

"My body, you mean."

"Yes."

Lia's glare was withering.

Kai frowned. Did the woman really think that her body was all she was to Kai?

Have I given her any reason to believe otherwise?

"I remember the day I saw you check in," Kai said earnestly, willing her to see the truth. "You strolled through the lobby and looked like you owned the world. I could barely breathe. That was about your energy not your body. I appreciated all of you that day, and I have every time we've met. You never stop surprising me. Honestly, I think it'd be amazing spending more time with you."

"I'm not one of your conquests."

"I don't see you as a conquest." Kai drew in a sharp breath, shocked by her words and the stark truth of them. She gave Lia a rueful look. "Yes, I've been known to seek out one-night stands with beautiful women. I don't shy away from that, but that's not what this is. I want to know you better, Lia.

I don't know what it is about you that's so different, but you make me want to break all my rules."

She couldn't say it more plainly. It had been many years since she'd opened herself up to something more. Something deeper.

A skeptical look greeted her. "You really are very good at games. I almost believed you that time."

Fuck. Kai's head dropped.

"Why so surprised?" Lia asked. "So far you've hit on me at a bar, confessed all the ways you scheme, told me you don't do relationships, interrogated me like the KGB, and hit on me again. What part of all that was supposed to engender trust? How am I supposed to believe anything you say?"

"I don't know." Kai truly didn't. "I'm sorry you don't believe me, but...I hear you. You don't want to go any farther." Disappointment flooded her. A tactical retreat was in order.

As if reading her mind, Lia glanced at the clock and said, "I haven't cleaned your room and my supervisor will be here in a few minutes to inspect. I'll put a 'Do Not Disturb' sign on your door and say you didn't wish to be serviced today." Lia paused at the double meaning. "I mean..."

"A pity. I would enjoy being serviced by you," Kai said with a half-smile.

Lia moaned softly, but her eyes crinkled. "Why are your lines always so bad? Now I'm definitely going."

Kai laughed. "I know, I know. It was a reflex, I swear. I'll let you go."

With a nod, Lia reached for the trolley, but her gaze remained on Kai. For a moment, neither woman moved.

And then Lia's roaming gaze dropped to Kai's lips. *Jesus!* The hunger was back as if it had never left.

Kai was startled when the woman took a deliberate step closer. "Lia? Were you after...a goodbye kiss?"

"Of course not," Lia said tartly even as her scorching gaze met Kai's. "Haven't you been listening? I'm not your conquest."

Right. Of course. I've misinterpret—

Suddenly Lia's lips were no longer pressed together but against Kai's mouth.

Her brain fritzed, and the ache of desire was back between her legs.

"Why," Lia muttered when she came up for air with a soft, strangled sigh, "would I want to kiss someone as frustrating as you?"

Kai snorted. "And why would I want to kiss someone as uptight as you?" She pointedly kissed the edge of Lia's now quirking mouth. "And yet here we are."

"I'm not uptight," Lia protested as her gaze dropped to Kai's mouth again. "I just believe in order and everything in its place." She leaned in again.

Their next kiss was like their first ones—overwhelming, intoxicating, thorough, and so damned arousing. This time, the want on Lia's face wasn't hidden at all.

"Mmm. Yes, you like everything in its place," Kai said, looking down. "I guess that explains your hand."

Lia's gaze snapped down to see her hand was now inside Kai's robe, perilously close to cupping Kai's bare breast. "Oh!" Her eyes widened as she attempted to snatch her hand back.

"Don't you dare." Kai covered Lia's fingers, shifting them and pressing them to cover her breast fully. "Now kiss me again," she ordered. "Do it harder this time, so we know how much you hate all this." She smirked.

Lia's next kiss was the best of all of them. Her tongue tangled with Kai's, stroking her in such an intense, deliberate way that all Kai could think of was what it might do to some lower part of her anatomy.

She slid her hands around to Lia's ass, squeezing the tight swells as she got lost in their deepening kisses.

The noise of a door opening from Milly's adjoining suite sounded behind Kai. A clipped voice spoke. "Ms. Hanson, are you fin…"

Lia snatched her hand out of Kai's robe and leaped backward. Simultaneously, Kai grabbed her lapels, pressing them together to protect her dignity, and jumped back a foot herself.

Mrs. Espinosa, mouth parted in shock, backed abruptly out of the door again, murmuring an apologetic, "*Perdóname,* Ms. Fisher." She snapped the doors closed behind her.

"Damn it. I'll talk to her," Lia looked disturbed. "I'll try and say something convincing. Not that it'll help. Mrs. Espinosa does have functioning eyeballs."

"She can't fire you," Kai reminded her. "You don't work here."

"No, but she will put in a Serious Incident Employee Report to the duty manager, explaining what she saw. Those reports go to Duxton headquarters. My unprofessionalism will have done the rounds everywhere within the hour."

Kai frowned. "Um, you know Hotel Duxton's boss doesn't have the high moral ground. Oliver Duxton just got caught driving while drunk and high. And his entire company is a dumpster fire of assholes just like him."

Something dark passed across Lia's eyes.

Kai wondered why.

"His situation is irrelevant," Lia snapped. "*I* will be judged. This will be the ammunition that some powerful people in my particular organization have been looking for. It's leverage. You're naive if you think this won't get around. Gossip in hotels spreads at the speed of light; before long the whole industry has heard."

"Your bosses would be idiots if they threw away someone like you for something so minor."

"Minor? My supervisor just caught me groping and kissing a guest." Lia's neck turned pink, and the arrogant tilt of her chin couldn't disguise the embarrassment radiating from her eyes.

Lia pulled her cleaning trolley closer with a hard jerk. "And for all you know, my company's upper management would be happy to see me gone."

"Why on earth?"

"Politics are at play." Her expression became pinched. "Kai, I know you're trying to make me feel better, but it won't work. Because while this was all just a bit of fun for you—melting me or some such challenge—I'm allowed to be annoyed that this will cost me dearly."

"Wait, this again?" Kai's eyes widened. "This wasn't a game for me. You're still talking like I orchestrated this whole thing."

"Didn't you?" Lia arched an eyebrow, but Kai could clearly see panic setting in.

"Have you forgotten that *you* kissed *me*? You started this, not me," Kai retorted. "And it was your hand that went boob grabbing."

"I'm aware." The color in Lia's cheeks darkened. "But you're claiming you didn't manipulate anything? So all your flirting was in my head? Tell me I didn't stick to the script you wrote the moment you saw me today and decided to *have* me? I suppose I should say well done. The master tactician wins again." Lia gave an exaggerated bow.

Kai felt her mouth hang slightly open, but she was too shocked to care. "I'm going to excuse what you just said as panic because I sure as hell didn't deserve any of that. And you might want to look more closely at your actions not mine."

"What does that mean?" Lia snapped.

"Come on—you want to pretend that you were maneuvered into this so you don't have to face the fact that you liked it. That's bullshit, Lia. It takes two. We both wanted what happened." She gave a tiny snort. "Christ, just admit you're human for once and deal with it."

Lia bit her lip and glanced away. Finally, she nodded. "All right." Her tone was flat when she added, "Obviously I'm weaker than I thought." She returned a cool gaze to Kai. "Did you like making me admit that?"

Kai heard the pain behind the question, and it made her own heart clench. "Don't hate yourself for this. I mean, why do you?"

Stony eyes met hers. "You don't understand."

"Explain it?"

"No."

Kai exhaled. The finality in the word sounded harsh. "Lia? Would it have really been so bad? Us?"

Lia stared at her, startled, as if she couldn't even understand the question. As if the answer was so self-evident.

Jesus. That look hurt worse than a slap. "So that's it then," Kai said, forcing a neutral tone to hide the rejection.

"It has to be." Lia gave Kai one last, long look, then began to push the trolley out of the room.

Kai watched every deliberate step, giving away no emotion, even though it stung like hell. She'd put herself out there, and this happened. That was always the risk, though.

She straightened and realized she was being ridiculous. It wouldn't have worked anyway. She didn't even know where Lia worked or lived, but she'd already said it wasn't New York. Funny how that didn't make the rejection hurt less.

Before opening the door, Lia stopped and stared at it. "Whatever else you are, Kai, you are chaos to me," she said voice flat. "I'm the opposite. I cannot survive chaos any more than I can survive controversy. So, yes, that's it."

Chapter 12

Disarray

Amelia found her supervisor in Milly's room, waiting for her with a grim, cold expression that screamed, *You're a disgrace!*

And she was. She'd let Kai get under her skin with those heated gazes and that beautiful body that had been barely hidden. How arousing she'd been. Those long, muscled legs. Soft skin. The swells of her breasts. Tension had crackled and arced between. All Amelia had wanted was to close the gap. To touch. To taste.

So…she'd done both. She'd devoured those cocky, beautiful lips. She'd enjoyed that tongue, that mouth, that skin. Her hand had cupped Kai's breast, feeling its heat and the excited, taut press of nipple against her palm. And it had felt magnificent.

Until…it hadn't.

Until she'd realized the impact of what being caught would mean. Mrs. Espinosa was required by company policy to report her. Amelia would be written up for her conduct, the report cc'd everywhere. Soon Oliver would ensure everyone knew. He'd paint her as someone lacking judgment and unfit to be CEO. Knowing him, he'd offer some vague, tawdry suggestion that she was a repeat offender. Something for their imaginations to fill in.

Of course, if Oliver had been caught in a similar position, the board might have found a way to shrug it off—after a brief reprimand—as "Oliver being Oliver." That wouldn't work for her. Her homophobic father and his hand-picked conservative board would never see this as a harmless indiscretion, even if Joe took her side. It would be seen as proof they'd been right all along about her.

All her hard work and determination at winning them over with her management skills was for nothing.

The supervisor's jaw was set hard as they faced each other. Amelia waited for the inevitable.

"That was wrong, Ms. Hanson." Disappointment laced her tone. "Very bad."

"Yes, I am aware. I'm sorry." Amelia cleared her throat. "Ms. Fisher and I have known each other before today." She suddenly hated the idea that the supervisor thought Amelia went about groping random guests. "Obviously I don't usually…" She inhaled, not sure how to categorize their encounters. "It's a complicated matter."

"*Si*, I can see that you know each other. Ms. Fisher doesn't usually look *that* happy."

Amelia's head snapped up.

"Understand me, Ms. Hanson, I want only the best things for Ms. Fisher. So if you are what makes her happy, I will not be in the way of that. We will not speak a word further of this."

Amelia stared at her. "Why?"

"That is my business. Just know that she is good."

"Good?" She shook her head. "She's always after something, though. That's who she is."

Anger flared in the older woman's face. "Then you do not know her at all."

Now confused beyond words, Amelia dipped her head, unwilling to argue. Nothing made much sense.

"Ms. Hanson," Mrs. Espinosa concluded with finality, "you will take fifteen minutes to…" She patted her own hair to demonstrate. "Fix this. You are in much disarray." Her eyes flitted to Amelia's mouth and she clucked. "Return here after this is done."

Disarray? Was her lipstick smeared? And she vaguely remembered Kai attacking her hair, too.

Could the day get any worse? When had Amelia ever, in her whole perfectly ordered adult life, succumbed to being in *disarray*?

Amelia waited for the elevator to arrive, praying it was empty. She obsessed over what had happened. Great trifecta: weakness, unprofessionalism, and now disarray. And, the worst part, it was self-inflicted.

The doors opened with a ding, and she stepped inside to find she was not alone.

The curious eyes of Monique Carson, sex mistress, stared back at her. She was arranged artfully against the wall in a stylish executive suit. Her stockings were sheer, her cleavage deep. And her expression was as knowing as ever as it raked Amelia.

Amelia felt stripped naked under that gaze as she jabbed the button for the eighth floor.

Would silence be too much to hope for?

"We meet again, Lia Duxton."

Apparently it was.

"Ms. Carson," Amelia said stiffly. She willed the elevator to move faster.

"You took my advice then?" Monique sounded amused. "Let down those fortress walls?"

Amelia ignored her and glared up at the numbers. Now passing the fourth floor...

"Your lipstick, darling, is smeared like honey down a woman's thighs. Someone's been having fun, and in a maid's outfit no less? A bit clichéd, and I'd know. Trust me, I've done them all. Is *that* your thing? Dress up?"

"It's not a thing." Amelia glared at the lumbering elevator impatiently. "There is no thing."

"Oh, sweetie..." Monique leaned in to straighten Amelia's collar. "There is *definitely* a thing. Still in denial? Shall we talk about your hair? Oh, that's been tugged on by hands that badly want to do much more. Or have they done so already?"

"So imaginative," Amelia said with a scowl.

Monique's eyebrow shot up. "Why so gloomy, darling? You know," she said confidentially, "you might want to reassess your bedroom technique if this is how you are after sex. It's *supposed* to be fun."

"It isn't just fun though, is it?" Amelia turned to face her. "And, for the last time, I didn't have sex with anyone! I'm on duty!"

Monique regarded her with surprise. "I...see. Are you one of those women who sees pleasure as weakness or vulnerability? Perhaps some guilty, regretful secret?"

Amelia ignored her.

"You know, my dear, I might have gilded the lily last time we met," Monique said. "Boasting that all my clients float out of my room satisfied. Some don't, I'm afraid."

That got Amelia's attention. She glanced at Monique in surprise.

"They don't because they weren't ready for the CEO fantasy experience. They weren't prepared for the strong emotions. It's a lot to process when you don't know what it can be like, especially if you've led a more...sedate... life. All those overwhelming sensations kicking in? Some women crawl out of my room looking more thunderstruck than satisfied."

That made sense. Strong, unexpected emotions could derail anyone. Another good reason to keep a firm lid on them.

"But do you know what's interesting about those clients?"

"What?" Amelia asked in spite of herself.

"They all come back."

Amelia blinked.

"Every single one. And the next time, they *are* ready. More than ready. Once they understand how their bodies will react and feel, they want more."

Well, that won't be me. Mistakes had been made with Kai. Certain... lapses. But she had no interest in re-creating those events. It had scared the life out of her knowing how close she'd come to losing everything. She shuddered at the thought. Amelia was incredibly lucky to have had a stay of execution.

The bell dinged, and the doors opened on the sixth floor. However, Monique made no move to exit.

"Your floor," Amelia murmured.

Monique stepped forward and raised her milky white hand between the doors to keep them open, eyes never leaving Amelia's. "Tell me something: Do you regret your lovely *not*-sex romp because it was bad? Or do you regret it because it was good?"

"Excuse me?" The audacity!

"If I'm right—that you enjoyed it even though you didn't want to, that's not regret. It's *opportunity*. And if you're smart, you'll go back for more. Life's too short. Trust me." She strode out of the elevator without looking back.

Amelia stared at the closing metal doors, aghast to have been so easily read by a stranger. A sex-fantasies expert, at that.

Slumping, she admitted the worst to herself. Yes, she'd enjoyed those kisses. They'd set her on fire. Kai's heated lips had burned. And Amelia had almost come apart over how Kai's beautiful breast had felt under her fingers. She wasn't made of stone.

And…being honest…she might crave a great deal more from Kai. But that wasn't the point, no matter what Monique or Kai seemed to think.

Because one thing she knew for a fact: Kai Fisher was far too dangerous. She'd be Amelia's undoing if Amelia let her—and that was completely unacceptable.

Chapter 13

Distractions

KAI POKED AT HER CAESAR salad with little interest. It was hard to concentrate on lunch when she remembered the alarm on Amelia's face as she'd flown out of Kai's room a few hours earlier.

What would have happened if Maria hadn't interrupted them?

As soon as Kai had dressed, she'd sought out Maria, requesting her discretion, and asking there be no reports. The woman had seemed offended to even be asked.

"It is already handled, Ms. Fisher," she'd replied. "Do not worry."

Thank God. It was frustrating everything had ended the way it had, but Lia had been pretty clear about where this wasn't going. Kai would respect those boundaries.

Milly coughed and side-eyed her.

Kai shifted her full focus to her lunch companion. "Milly Valentine, do I want to know what's giving you *that* look? Have you met someone dashing who's diverting your attention?"

Milly's pale eyebrows lifted. "I was wondering the same about you, Ms. Fisher."

"I wasn't swinging from the rafters with anyone, before you ask," Kai said dryly as she lifted a wine to her lips and eyed Milly over it.

"I wasn't going to ask. I was more interested in knowing if you made up with our translator?"

Warmth heated Kai's cheeks. She returned her glass to the table and rotated it slowly, watching it bunch up the linen tablecloth slightly. Lia's warm hand fondling her bare breast flooded her mind. "No. I anticipate Ms. Hanson will be avoiding me for the rest of our stay. We had a disagreement about going forward."

"What if we need her again?"

"I doubt we will. My breakfast meeting with Hamadani was…" *Odd. Confusing. Fast.* "Satisfactory. We're signing the agreed terms tomorrow and then it's off my plate and for Grand Millennium's lawyers to worry about. I assume Mr. Stein will be doing cartwheels all over Twitter as soon as I tell him. Didn't you get my email on all this?"

"Yes, but—"

"So you know I don't expect any more Arabic this late in the game. And if we get more, we'll find someone else." Kai took a quick gulp of wine.

"Yes, Ms. Fisher." Milly paused. "I remember her, by the way. I mean, it threw me off, her doing all those different jobs, but isn't Ms. Hanson the same woman we saw checking in?"

Milly's powers of observation could be mighty inconvenient at times. "Possibly." Kai studied the tablecloth.

"Why is someone who can afford Louis Vuitton playing hotel concierge? And doing room service?" Milly became thoughtful. "Or maybe the bags were knock-offs?"

Louis Vuitton bags. Lia *did* have those, didn't she? As well as that gorgeous Gallet watch. She was rich then? "Lia Hanson is a mystery. That's all we know for certain."

Milly merely nodded. Kai took in the tiredness around her eyes. Her assistant had been working long hours, ensuring their New York office was operating smoothly as well as running around after Kai here.

"I trust you will remember my advice at some point and have some time for yourself?" Kai said. "Maybe find someone fun to amuse yourself with? That'd be a good pick-me-up."

"I will remember your advice," Milly said lightly.

Laughing, Kai said, "And not take it. Nice dodge."

Milly gave a long-suffering sigh. "Anyway, I meant to say, I bumped into Mr. Hamadani near the gaming room earlier."

"Did he behave himself?" Kai would throttle him if she had to—even if it'd be damned inconvenient.

"He did. He didn't apologize for what he said before, but he wouldn't meet my eye, either."

"Self-awareness from an asshole? I don't think my heart can take the shock."

Milly smiled.

"So he'd been in the gaming room?" Kai asked.

"Maybe?"

Hmm. Hamadani's risk-averse profile didn't fit a gambler, but then you never *really* knew anyone, did you? Like icy Lia Hanson, who kissed with so much heat she could start a wildfire.

"Mr. Hamadani asked for the signing location to be the Prohibition Bar at two tomorrow."

"A bar? Of all the odd places to do business."

"Maybe he wants to watch the big poker tournament going on next door afterwards?"

A half-a-billion-dollar deal was being signed off on and the man wanted one eye on gaming screens? Christ, Vegas made people a little crazy.

"Email and confirm." Kai shook her head. "I'll be glad when this is done. I don't like this deal one bit."

Milly gave her a surprised look.

"I know. Weird, isn't it, since it's the deal everyone wants."

"Well, maybe just focus on the finish line."

Now that was excellent advice.

Amelia fell on her bed, every muscle aching. Even after a long, long shower she was sure she could still smell cleaning chemicals from her day in Housekeeping. Her mind kept looping over Mrs. Espinosa deciding not to report her, the keynote speech that still lay half-written, and…Kai.

Kai Fisher. Her teasing lips had awakened things in Amelia she'd rather not dwell on.

Dangerous. Amelia couldn't work out whether she was being played by Kai from one moment to the next. Thank God she'd finally put an end to whatever was going on between them.

Although it was late and she was exhausted, her brain refused to relax, so Amelia began flicking through work emails.

The man who had replaced Douglas as Head of Purchasing was not making a good first impression. He'd been besieging her inbox, seeking approval on every little thing. She shunted that mess over to Quinn to resolve, with a terse email.

> *Get it through his pea brain that he can't email me every five minutes when he gets the jitters about whether to choose Cat 6 or 6a Ethernet cables. Either fix him or I'll fire him.*

New uniform designs for her hotels in Italy had landed. She gave them a thorough once-over and wrote back.

> *Lose the cleavage. Four open buttons sends a message that our staff will definitely not be delivering on. Otherwise, approved.*

She clicked the next email. Marketing wanted to query the CMPs on her Spanish hotels. She tossed off a snide reply.

> *It's called a Complete Meeting Package because it's complete, Ms. González. No, we're NOT lowering the price we advertise and then sneakily asking people to pay more for conference center access later. It wouldn't be a complete price then, would it? Find another way to beat our rivals on CMPs that doesn't involving lying about price.*

Incompetence. If she knew Gabriella, that'd be the last she'd hear from her on that. Amelia's word was final. That was definitely a benefit of being the boss.

For a moment, she stared at her ceiling and tried to imagine this not being her life.

How did everyone else do it? How did they go about their long, tiring jobs, often having children and so many bills…and then turn around and do it all again the next day? And how did they do it without having any locus of control—that knowledge *you* held the power of your own destiny, a knowledge that, studies showed, removed a lot of stress.

Amelia didn't think she'd like it very much. As taxing as her career could be, at the end of the day, she got to call the shots. She had the control. Amelia was well aware of how lucky she was. Well, she had more than luck, didn't she? She had entitlement, too. As annoying as her family was, they had given her an enviable start to life.

At the reminder of her family, she switched to her personal email. Something from her mother, reminding her about a distant cousin's birthday party that coincided with Amelia being in the US. She had no intention of attending, because there, at the bottom, was why:

> *Just a reminder, Amelia, please don't bring any special friends as your plus one. You know how your father is.*

Every single invite included that reminder—as had been the case since she'd come out at nineteen—as if Amelia had forgotten from every other prior invitation. Did her mother truly think Amelia was that forgetful? It didn't matter that Amelia hadn't dated anyone seriously since Mariam. No, come birthdays to bar mitzvahs, *don't bring any special friends* was practically in her mother's email signature.

Amelia sighed and thought about what she wished she could reply but never would: *Don't worry, Mom, you're quite safe from me sprinkling any big ole lesbian fairy dust all over your traditional family affairs.*

For a brief, subversive moment, she had a wicked thought of bringing Kai Fisher along. Bright, clever, scheming Kai Fisher, who hated the Duxtons and would almost certainly argue circles around her parents. They wouldn't know what hit them. *Hilarious!* But…no. As maddening as Kai could often be, inflicting Amelia's judgmental family on her would be cruel.

She clicked the next email. It was a picture of an owl with someone's hand lifting its feathers up to show surprisingly long legs.

> *I don't see any knees, Auntie Lia! But I know that doesn't mean it's totally proven. Cos science!*

Amelia beamed proudly, then dashed off a reply.

It's excellent, darling, that you remember observation alone isn't enough to answer a question scientifically. I have to agree, though, those are some very long legs! I promise we'll Skype properly soon, Imogen. Love, Lia.

Next, an email from Joe. He was like a dog with a bone.

Have we sealed Mayfair Palace? Don't forget we want to announce it soon.

As if she could forget. On that topic, things were getting stranger. It had dawned on Amelia, while up to one armpit in a hotel toilet, wielding a brush, that she had all the pieces of the puzzle. She just hadn't put them together.

The mystery man Kai had planned to meet at the bar who hadn't showed? She'd been lying in wait for him, hoping for a chance meeting. The man Kai had had a breakfast meeting with today for her deal? Only one person could sell Mayfair Palace. That meant Nedal al-Hamadani was in Vegas, too. He'd been under her nose the whole time!

As soon as her shift ended, she'd hurried down to the front desk and asked Graham to see whether a Nedal al-Hamadani was checked in. He'd given her the oddest look, muttered "popular guy," then confirmed it.

Minutes later, she was at Nedal's door, but received no answer to her knocks. Phoning his room a moment later had yielded the same result.

Was he out or hiding?

Her cell phone jangled to life, throwing Amelia back into the present— in bed, with everything aching. *Quinn* flashed on the screen.

Finally! She'd been waiting an hour for her assistant to wake and find Amelia's text to call her ASAP.

"Quinn," she said. "Good morning."

"Hey, boss." Quinn yawned. "I have news."

"As do I. But you go first."

"Right. We've found that woman you asked about. Full name Annabelle Janis Fisher, goes by Kaida, or Kai for short."

Amelia sifted through her tired brain. "Never heard of her."

"That's because most people know her by her nickname. Ever heard of The Closer?"

Something pinged in the back of her head, a memory of Oliver ranting over a deal he'd lost to The Closer a few years back.

"She's a VP of marketing who sometimes does deals for her hotel company—hence the nickname," Quinn finished.

Wait... Amelia dredged up the rest of Oliver's rant. "Doesn't The Closer work for Grand Millennium?"

"Yep. She's Stein's deal maker..."

Quinn's words faded out as Amelia digested what that meant. She'd *kissed* the deal maker at *Grand Millennium*. A company that spent all its spare time smearing Hotel Duxton. No wonder Kai Fisher knew so much about Duxton business that she could reel off all the lies against them. She was one of them. Hell, maybe she was the one spreading the sordid tales around Vegas in the first place.

I kissed her. Not just that. Amelia's fingers tingled in reminder of what else she'd done.

"...known as a killer in hotel buying," Quinn was saying. "She can read a room like no one else and absolutely fuck over her competition. Eat 'em for lunch."

Based on what she'd seen, Amelia didn't doubt it. "What else did you find out?" Her voice was tight.

"She was a lawyer...well, she's still registered, but she's not practicing. She left some prestigious Manhattan law firm—no one knows why—and reappeared months later at Stein's side." There came the soft pings of a phone being tapped. "On the personal side: age, forty-three. Never married, no kids. Rumors that she likes the ladies. But main gossip is on how hard to beat she is. When she sees what she wants, she gets it most of the time."

That was definitely the woman she'd met. So...what had Kaida Fisher offered Nedal that was so good he'd betray Amelia? Or had the woman identified some weakness in Nedal and exploited it so he couldn't say no? Was that it? After all, Kai was so *very* good at homing in on weaknesses.

"You okay, boss? You've gone quiet."

151

Amelia cleared her throat. "Your news relates to mine. Fisher is here, and today, while I was cleaning her room, she revealed she's virtually sealed her latest deal."

"Okayyy," Quinn sounded puzzled. "And her latest deal is...?"

"I'll give you one guess."

A silence then. "*She's* who's stealing Mayfair? But why's she doing that in Vegas of all places?"

Amelia pursed her lips. "Who loves talking about the future of hotels and would fly halfway across the world to attend a conference about it?"

"Shit! *That's* where Nedal's been hiding?" Quinn's intake of breath was sharp. "But The Closer's with Grand Millennium—aren't their hotels exclusively USA based?"

"They were. Fisher's assistant told me a few days ago that their current deal is their first overseas one."

"We are so screwed," Quinn muttered. "The Closer's crushed Oliver's bids on at least a dozen US hotel deals in the past ten years. She's that good."

A *dozen*? No wonder Oliver hated her. "I need you here ASAP," Amelia rubbed her temple. "Christ. I'm so disappointed in Nedal."

"What're you are going to do?"

"Well, I'm not giving up. If Nedal's double-crossed a buyer once, we have to see if he'll do it twice. I'll try to get him to renegotiate with us."

"Right."

"I am not letting this deal slip through our fingers again. I don't care how good this Closer thinks she is."

"I'll fly out today and we'll figure out a strategy. Tamara will handle things here. She's even promised to feed your fish, even though it scares the living crap out of her."

Amelia rolled her eyes. "My Scorpionfish doesn't feed on human flesh."

"Unlike you," Quinn teased. "Those rumors are circulating again. Hey, good luck for the waitressing shift tomorrow."

"Why is luck required?"

"The casino customers: Drunk ones on a high from wins, and frustrated ones on a low from betting the farm. They get handsy or mouthy." More tapping noises sounded. "Okay, our pilot can take me in three hours. I should go. Bye, boss."

Amelia ended the call, her mind still circling on just how very good The Closer was. Of course, Amelia was very good as well, and she had the element of surprise. The Closer was about to suffer her first major loss. A determined smile curled her lips as Amelia flicked to Google.

But first, a promise was a promise. She needed to research owl knees.

Chapter 14

Games People Play

"Hanson!" Antonio, Prohibition Bar's day-shift manager, snapped his fingers.

Amelia looked up from her drinks tray and glared. Finger snapping now? She wasn't a dog.

He pointed out to the gaming floor. "Move it."

Move. It? She decided it would not be professional to share her view that he resembled a chest-beating primate.

Amelia headed out to the gaming room floor and dispensed her drinks, then looked for new orders. Poker machines dinged and churned, their customers stabbing buttons, pausing only to rummage around their coin cups. Most ignored her queries as to whether they wanted a drink, some bothering only with a half grunt.

She moved on to the packed crowds near the gaming tables, courtesy of a poker tournament. Observers watched the action unfolding on a series of big screens. The crowd seemed transfixed by the pro players. Score one for Oliver.

Her feet hurt, but nothing like yesterday's agony that had seen every muscle in an uproar for hours afterward. Maybe that's why she'd enjoyed kissing Kai so much? Her body had been crying out for a blissful endorphin rush?

She brightened at the idea. That made more sense than being attracted to a professional schemer like Kai Fisher. The woman was merely an ill-considered, pleasing distraction.

Well, it was irrelevant now. Kai could scheme and lie and whatever else she'd been up to, and that was of no interest to Amelia. None at all.

Returning to the bar, Amelia slid her tray on it. "Four Buds, two scotches, one on the rocks, LLB, and a Diet Coke, extra ice."

While Antonio filled the order, her phone vibrated. Pulling it out, Amelia smiled at the text.

> *Auntie Lia, why do toenails exist? And why's it called a near miss? Shouldn't it be a near hit?*

Excellent questions.

> *If I went to New York, could I take my fish with me?*

Amelia quickly texted back.

> *Why New York? Wouldn't that freeze my favorite beach-mad cousin? How about Fiji?*

Before she received a reply, a familiar voice made her turn. Was she now imagining Kaida Fisher everywhere? Her gaze scoured the room.

At the far end of the bar, tucked around the small corner of its L-shape, almost out of sight, sat Kai. She was bent over paperwork, talking to a tall man in a navy suit whose back was to Amelia.

A shiver ran through her at the reminder of what she and Kai had done yesterday.

She is also the enemy. Stealing my deal.

There was that. Edging closer, Amelia picked up a few key words. "Asset value," "due diligence," "hold period." Were they discussing Mayfair Palace?

"Yes, Mr. Hamadani, I agree—"

Hamadani!

"Hanson!" Antonio barked. Amelia spun back to the bar.

He waved at her tray, now full of drinks.

Right. She collected it and made her way back to the gaming room.

What's my next move? Amelia thought furiously as she handed out the drinks, returned change, and eyeballed one weasel who had the temerity to argue she'd short-changed him. *Liar.* He backed down when she pointed out the security cameras and asked "just how sure" he was he'd given her a twenty.

She finished and focused on what most mattered: clawing her deal back. What should she do? Confront Kai right now? Demand to know what Nedal was doing, going behind her back? She had time. It wasn't as if they'd sign anything in a bar. No one did that.

Should she wait till the meeting was over and confront Nedal privately? That might be a better prospect. Humiliating the man wouldn't make him more eager to deal with her.

Amelia headed back to the bar, her mind whirring. Out of the corner of her eye she saw a pen being slid across the bar to Nedal. Amelia stopped cold. *A pen? As in…sign here? No, surely not.*

Next, paperwork was pushed over.

Amelia's blood chilled. The paperwork could be anything, right? Anything that someone *signs…*

Nedal picked up the pen and reached for the document. Then signed.

"Hanson! What are your new orders?"

Antonio's annoyed call cut through the background noise and caused heads to swivel. Among them were Kai's and her companion's. She locked eyes with the man.

What. The. Hell?

That man was *not* Nedal al-Hamadani.

Kai took back her paperwork and also signed with a flourish.

Amelia edged close enough to hear them.

"I'll send a copy to Grand Millennium's lawyers immediately, Mr. Hamadani, and I trust we will have a formal deal to announce soon."

"Excellent, Ms. Fisher. It's been a pleasure negotiating with you."

Amelia was rooted to the spot. Kai…no, The Closer…was being scammed.

She backed away. *I shouldn't care. It's none of my business.*

Grand Millennium's lawyers would figure out pretty soon what was up, and if they didn't, they should be fired. Maybe The Closer would be fired, too. But that was none of her concern, either.

On the other hand, it *was* her concern in one sense: Nedal wasn't swanning around Vegas selling his hotel to Amelia's rival. Her friend had someone impersonating him, and wasn't it her place to intervene? Wouldn't she want him to speak up if he encountered a fake using her name? Besides, fraud was being committed. Shouldn't she report a crime happening under her nose?

A crime against a woman who works for your enemy.

How many times had Grand Millennium shredded the Duxtons? Amelia's father would be incensed if it came out that she'd helped his hated competitor escape public humiliation. So maybe Amelia should let this go. Let Grand Millennium self-immolate and just walk away.

But how was that *right?*

"Hanson!" Antonio barked again. "Orders! Wake up!" He snapped his fingers.

Amelia drew herself up to full height, and said through gritted teeth, "Water, one glass, urgent."

"That's it?" He stared at her.

She provided him with her most imperious glare.

He blinked. After a moment, he thunked a glass on her tray and said, "One water."

Amelia plucked the glass off it and walked to the end of the bar. She'd seen this in movies—people tripping on purpose, pouring water over someone. She wasn't so derivative. Amelia loomed over the pair, and slowly, with great care, poured the water all across the paperwork. It splashed everywhere.

She kept going, despite Kai's startled yelp and the impostor's string of curses, until she saw the bleed of ballpoint ink across the waterlogged page.

Kai and the man shot to their feet in unison, sweeping water off their clothes.

Shock and outrage filled Kai's face, her eyes narrowing at the sight of Amelia. "You did that on purpose!"

"What was your first clue?" Amelia turned to the man and offered a half-hearted apology in Arabic.

"Um…" He glanced away, but she'd already caught the fear in his eye.

So whoever had planned this sting couldn't even find someone who spoke Nedal's language? Her annoyance rose. Fully irritated now, she rattled off a few choice insults in Arabic about him being a horse's ass, while also asking if he spoke any Arabic at all, was even from the Middle East or

157

Muslim, and if he could actually find Dubai on a map if his life depended on it.

The man growled. "I must get changed. And *you!*" he pointed at Amelia, "should be fired."

"Yes." Kai gave her a matching, furious glare. "You damn well should."

Horror filled Kai as she stared at the pulpy mess that had been the Heads of Terms agreement. She'd have to get a new printout, go through the signing process again, and what if Nedal changed his mind in between?

She glanced into the determined eyes of Lia Hanson. No remorse.

Why would she do this? No, irrelevant. She'd deal with that later. Salvaging this was the most important thing now. Kai turned. "Mr. Hamadani, it won't take me a moment to get a new agreement printed off."

He slapped at his wet pants. "Fuck," he muttered.

Lia grabbed Kai's arm in a death grip. "I need a word."

Of all the rude… Kai glowered at her before turning back to Hamadani. "Could you please give me a few moments? I'll get a new agreement printed off. Stay here, have some drinks on me?" Kai suggested. "I won't be long."

"No." Hamadani shook his head hard. "I will go."

"But—"

"Ms. Fisher, I understand your need is to finalize terms. *My* need is to be dry. I will not conduct business in this condition." He exited swiftly, leaving Kai staring daggers at Lia.

"The hell?" Kai said, fuming. "You could have just cost me a half-a-billion-dollar deal. Why would you—"

"Not here. Come with me." Lia tugged her arm.

Despite her outrage, Kai followed and was led into an empty staff bathroom.

Rounding on Lia the moment the door slapped closed, Kai snapped, "What were you thinking?"

"That the deal should be ruined."

Shock filled Kai, tinged with dismay. "Do you hate me that much? That was unhinged."

"No, that was necessary. Who did you think you were signing with?"

"Nedal al-Hamadani. Why? Is this some sort of petty revenge for me calling you out as a fake? You're spiking my deal to hurt me?"

"For God's sake, stop talking!" Lia gave her an impatient glare. "I *know* Nedal personally. We've done multiple deals. I don't know who you think you're negotiating with, but that man is *not* Nedal al-Hamadani."

"Bullshit." Kai recoiled from Lia, even as fear shot through her. It was a ridiculous accusation.

Suddenly the unsettling moments of the past week slithered into her head: How the man never matched the profile she had of him and had never seemed very well-versed on the deal's finer details. How he'd approved clause 12.1c without a murmur. And then there was the error-riddled Arabic paperwork.

She hissed in a breath. *No!* The next stage of the deal would see their lawyers poring over the details, so pulling a scam like this was pointless.

Lia fiddled with her phone, then held it up to Kai. "*This* is Nedal al-Hamadani."

The photo showed a bearded Middle Eastern man, graying at the ears, gazing at two smaller children and a sweet-faced woman in a hijab with amused eyes. His expression was soft as he smiled at his family.

This had to be a mistake! Lia was wrong. Except…Lia didn't strike her as the sort of person who'd make mistakes like this. Which just left one option: She was lying.

"Okay, enough BS. Who are you really?" Kai demanded.

The woman met her eye with a directness that felt as powerful as a shove. "Amelia Duxton. I run the European division of—"

"Hotel Duxton," Kai finished flatly.

"Yes."

God. Lia was short for Amelia. *This* was the media-shy, over-qualified, economic fucking genius who ruled Europe's hotels and had the awards to prove it. It explained so much about her bearing, attitude, knowledge of hotels, languages, and brand leakage, and every other goddamned thing, right down to those expensive Louis Vuitton bags.

Kai sagged against the sink as all the ramifications hit her. Amelia's brother was Oliver. He'd been Kai's whipping boy for years on Scorched Earth—which he'd richly deserved. It also meant that Lia was one of *them*. "You're a *Duxton*."

"Yes." Amelia's expression was cautious now.

And then all the other pieces fell into place. Hadn't Amelia spent many months negotiating for Mayfair Palace? She was based in England, so that meant the only reason she'd be in Vegas would be to win the deal back. So was the con still going? Amelia was pretending Hamadani was fake to scare Kai away from him? God, that was clever.

She pulled that thread. Amelia's little game wouldn't work if Kai didn't trust her. Their brief, intimate moments had been an act. A way to get close, to make Kai believe Amelia the moment she declared Hamadani was an impostor.

Oh shit! Amelia had seen Kai's terms when she'd translated! She knew all the key points in Grand Millennium's deal. Amelia had certainly found a way to insert herself into every part of Kai's business.

Of course this was just supposition, but which scenario was more likely? A Duxton conning Kai to win back a prized hotel? Or a man faking being a developer to do a deal that would fall apart the moment Kai's lawyers dug deeper?

Mr. Stein's email declaring that the photo she'd sent to him was Hamadani flashed to mind. He'd expressed no doubts, and he'd met Hamadani. First-hand intel over a stranger's tall tales? That clinched it. Lia was a liar and a fraud.

"A 'thank you' would be appropriate." Amelia folded her arms.

The fucking gall of her! "The seduction thing was a bit over the top, don't you think?"

"Excuse me?"

"Did you profile me? Did Conrad and Oliver decide you were the best choice to stop me, or did you volunteer?" Kai asked acidly.

Amelia's face became pinched. "Are you seriously suggesting I prostituted myself for a business deal?"

"Wow, your innocent face is magnificent. But you expect me to believe you lost a huge deal, then just happened to be in Vegas and randomly met the woman who stole your deal, a woman who works for Grand Millennium—a company you detest?"

Amelia showed no surprise.

"You knew who I worked for, didn't you?"

"I only found out last night." Amelia looked exasperated. "You think I'd kiss you to gain your trust over a *deal*?"

"You did more than kiss me. Or was the boob fondle an added bonus? Lucky me. By the way? I'll be suing Duxton Vegas over the breach of confidentiality with that translation. There is no innocent spin you can put on that."

Amelia's eyes narrowed. "This is absurd! If I wanted to renegotiate for Mayfair, I'd simply approach Nedal directly and do so. Why would I do what you suggest? You see game-playing everywhere because that's all *you* do."

"Oh, really," Kai said sarcastically. "What easier way to win a deal than to eliminate the only rival bidder? Were you expecting me to say, *Oh, thank you, Amelia, for exposing a fraud*, and then just walk away, leaving you a clear run at Mayfair Palace? How gullible do you think I am?"

"Gullible enough to get sucked in by a conman. The fake you were dealing with doesn't know enough Arabic to realize I just called him a horse's ass. He thinks nothing of signing deals in *bars* adjacent to *gaming* rooms, despite being a devout Muslim. He's a man who supplies legal terms in Arabic that were so amateur even you commented on them. But, no, *I'm* the one pulling a con." Amelia shook her head. "To think I bothered to help you."

"Help me?" Kai exploded. "Scheming and finding angles is what your family *does*. Look around you! This hotel? The way staff are treated? Or was playing an employee just a way to snoop on what I was up to and you had no interest in learning the truth at all?"

"Not just gullible but delusional. Believe me or not, I don't care. It's your funeral."

"Okay, if Hamadani isn't who he says, then how come my boss identified him?"

"What do you mean?"

"I sent his picture to Mr. Stein. He's met him. He confirmed I'm negotiating with the right man."

"Then your boss is mistaken." Amelia's gaze was cool.

Kai studied her. She was a good actress, but Mr. Stein would never make a mistake like this. "You're as bad as Oliver—and your brother is despicable."

Amelia's face closed off like a sheet of ice. "Sign, then, if you believe that. It'll make the 'Conman hoaxes The Closer' headlines worth it, because you'll know I warned you." She gave Kai an appalled look. "And do not *ever* compare me to my brother. I'm nothing like him."

"Nice try." Kai slow clapped her.

Amelia's expression hardened. "I don't say this very often, so please consider this heartfelt: *Fuck you!*"

"No thanks." Kai gave a chilly smile. "I have standards. That ship has sailed."

Amelia's eyes turned mutinous. She turned on her heel, slamming the bathroom door behind her.

The moment she was gone, Kai sagged. *What the hell just happened?*

Hauling out her phone, she emailed her boss. It was only prudent, she told herself, even if she was sure Amelia was no better than the rest of her slimy family.

> *Mr. Stein, how sure are you the man in the photo I sent was Hamadani?*

A few minutes later, her phone pinged.

> *It's Rebecca. He's in a meeting. His phone's off but I get copies of his emails. Is this urgent? Need me to interrupt?*

Was it urgent? Kai studied the assistant's message. Oh, for God's sake, she'd let Amelia get into her head. The woman was a Duxton: cunning, clever, scheming. Her boss had expressed no doubts about the photo. None. She replied.

> *No. I'll call him later.*

Now all she had to do was calm down a furious property developer and hope he'd accept her apologies for that drenching interruption.

Chapter 15

Chain Reaction

AMELIA QUIT HER "JOB," SNEERED as a wide-eyed Antonio threatened to deduct points, and stalked back to her room.

No good deed went unpunished, apparently.

I could have let her hang, and this is the thanks I get.

Amelia kicked off her shoes, wrenched her hair out of its bun, and sank onto her bed.

"Hey, boss."

She started, head whipping around. Shock immediately turned to relief. Quinn was sitting in the armchair by the window, tapping away at a laptop.

"Hope you don't mind me letting myself in. Your room has better phone reception and nice light. Benefit of adjoining rooms." She waved at the open doors between their two rooms.

"Not at all. I'm glad you're here." Amelia exhaled.

Quinn frowned. "Not a moment too soon by the looks of things. Is this about our deal?"

"Yes." Kai's furious expression marched a huffy little circuit around her head. "Well, not entirely."

"Okay...does this have anything to do with the woman you had me look up? Fisher?"

Amelia balled her hands. "I need a drink." She headed to the minibar and rummaged through it. "Three types of vodka, four types of whiskey, and only one gin? Would it kill them to have Plymouth?" She brought out a mini gin bottle and squinted at the unfamiliar label. "Fisher's a menace.

I did her a favor today, a huge one, and instead of thanking me, all she did was insult my family name."

"And?" Quinn waited.

"And what?"

"Boss, plenty of people insult your family name. Especially right now, thanks to Oliver. Why do you care what some stranger working for the opposition thinks?"

I don't. Amelia decided the gin would have to do and dug out a soda water.

Quinn eyed the items with interest. "Things must be dire if you're making a Gin Rickey. Don't you need limes?"

Amelia cursed. *Damn.* Before she could answer, Quinn's phone rang.

Quinn's eyebrows lifted. "It's Mariam."

"Wait." Amelia walked over to her, hand out. "May I?"

"You sure?"

"Mmm." She wasn't. Mariam hadn't spoken to her since that day eight years ago when she'd tearfully explained she was choosing family over love.

Quinn handed over her phone. "I'll be in my room. Come get me when you're done."

Amelia nodded and hit Answer.

"Quinn?" came a voice so achingly familiar that Amelia's knees felt weak.

She sank into a chair. "No, it's Amelia."

"Lia!"

The warm surprise in Mariam's voice brought up so many memories, like the gentle way her lover used to make fun of her "ice bitch" persona.

From day one, Mariam had always known who Amelia was at her core. "It's just us here," she'd often murmur, taking Amelia's hands in hers. "Flatten your prickles, sweet Lia."

Amelia had never felt so seen and understood. How she'd missed that feeling as the years had passed. Everyone else she'd dated seemed to be with her *because* of her persona—seeking some larger-than-life character—not in spite of it.

"Sorry it's not Quinn," Amelia said quietly. "I don't mean to spring myself on you, but there have been some developments I should discuss."

"Oh." Mariam hesitated. "Is everything well?"

"That depends. First, where is your brother?"

"Nedal's with me in Dubai."

"Why's he gone home?"

"Didn't Hanif explain?"

As if Nedal's stonewalling assistant would ever volunteer a thing. Amelia snorted. "No, he did not."

"Our mother fell very ill. We were told she might not have long so Nedal rushed home. He has not left her side at the hospital."

"I'm sorry to hear that. He hasn't been taking our calls. I wondered—"

"He hasn't been taking anyone's. He turned his phone off and said now was no time for work. I mentioned to him you'd called, by the way. He apologized for leaving so abruptly and said to tell you he'll sign your deal the moment he returns."

"His assistant led us to believe he was canceling it. That he no longer wanted to deal with me at all."

There was a silence. "You do remember Hanif used to be my father's bodyguard? He was there when everyone found out about us. He's made no secret of the fact he blamed you for our relationship. It sounds as if he's been trying to drive a wedge between you and Nedal. He's always taken his loyalty to our family somewhat too far. He does not speak for us. I will see to it that he is reminded yet again of his place."

"I see." Amelia rose and headed back to the kitchen, suddenly desperate for a drink. The rush of relief was strong, but her guilt was stronger.

"I'm sorry if you thought the worst about my brother," Mariam said, "but you know Nedal would never stop being your friend? He doesn't answer to Hanif, even though he had no say in hiring him."

Amelia felt like the worst human for doubting his loyalty. "Will you tell him I'm thinking of him? And if there's anything I can do, either of you, please just ask."

"I will tell him, thank you."

"Will your mother be all right?"

"The worst has passed. She's rallying now. We are praying for a full recovery."

Silence fell. Amelia wondered how to ask the thing she most wanted to know. "How have you been? I heard you had a child." *And a husband!* "Are you happy?"

Mariam hesitated. "I am, Lia, very. I know what you're thinking: was I pressured into marrying because my father found out about us? No, sweet Lia. Oh, I don't deny many suitors were trotted past my nose for a few years. I said no to them all. They weren't you."

"Oh." Amelia bit her lip.

"For the longest time, no one came close. But then one day I met a new teacher on our staff. I never expected to fall in love again, but then, love is unexpected, isn't it?" Her voice filled with warmth.

Amelia's heart clenched. "It is, yes."

"He's a good and kind man, Lia, and he's a wonderful father. He's talking of moving to London so we can have more opportunities. I want to do more study, perhaps get into academia. He wants to give me the moon... the way you did."

"I..." Tears welled up at the reminder of her old, naive promises. "That's...that's good. I only want you happy."

"And I only want the same for you. Please tell me you've found someone, too? You haven't just thrown yourself into work and been busy empire building? It'd be a terrible waste if you decided to embrace a vow of chastity."

Amelia could almost see her ex-girlfriend's eyes crinkling at that. Mariam had often teased Amelia about her focus on work, more than once seducing her away from paperwork into their bed. "I'm too busy these days for distractions like that." A reminder of Amelia's own traitorous hand stroking Kai's soft breast flashed to mind. "N-nothing is going on."

Mariam's laugh was full-throated. "Well, I'm very happy to hear that *nothing* is going on. Maybe we could get together next time I'm in London? I'd love you to meet my family. I didn't want to call before in case it would be...awkward." The hesitation was back in her voice, but so was hope.

Do I want this? Amelia picked her emotions apart. She'd keenly felt the loss of Mariam. Perhaps her grief would always remain strong because she hadn't been ready for their relationship to end—the break-up had been forced upon them both.

She also felt regret for what might have been. But amid all that was a swell of happiness for the woman she'd loved. Curiosity, too, to meet the person who'd won her heart, mixed with a little jealousy. But she'd greatly enjoy seeing Mariam with her daughter. A little mini-Mariam? How adorable would that child be?

"Yes," she said sincerely. "I'd like that."

"I am so pleased." Mariam's joy radiated down the phone. "I wanted to call you so many times, but I wasn't sure you were…you know. And when Nedal said you were unattached, I worried I'd make things worse."

It seemed Nedal had been paying closer attention to her life than she'd realized.

"But if you've found someone special," Mariam continued, "I'd love to meet her, too."

Someone special? A pleasing kiss and a fumble with an annoying business rival hardly qualified as that. How odd her mind had even gone there, though. "Should I have someone, I'll introduce you," Amelia said neutrally. "In the meantime, there's something you should know. Someone's in Vegas impersonating Nedal."

"I… What?"

"Grand Millennium Hotels is negotiating for Mayfair Palace with an impostor they think is Nedal."

"Who is this impostor?"

"No idea. I've spoken to him. He doesn't know Arabic, I don't think he's Middle Eastern, and under his fake middle-class English accent, I swear I heard a hint of Essex."

"*Abu reiha*!" Mariam swore.

Amelia blinked. When her ex called someone *the father of stinky smells*— in a nation renowned for perfumed scents, no less—it was especially bad.

"I will tell Father," Mariam said, all business now. "He'll want to investigate. I'll tell Nedal, too, of course, although be aware that he's only interested in our mother now."

"I understand."

"If you find out anything else, let us know."

"Of course."

"And Lia?"

"Yes?"

"Thank you." Mariam sounded heartfelt.

"No problem," Amelia said lightly. "Stay safe, all of you."

"Goodbye, sweet Lia." There was a muffled sound, as if she'd put the phone down but hadn't quite hung up.

Amelia listened and heard the burbles of a baby, and a sudden infusion of joy and amusement in Mariam's voice as she responded in Arabic, "Sweet child, why do you make such a silly face? Come here. If only your father could see this!"

So much happiness. Amelia ended the call and placed Quinn's phone carefully on the table beside her. All her niggling doubts were gone. Wondering whether Mariam was okay. Whether she'd ever change her mind and come back to Amelia. Closure felt a lot like peace—twined with regret and relief.

Kai paced her room, words flying from her mouth in a stream of fury as she told Milly everything. She explained, in vivid detail, all the ways the Duxtons were vile, and Amelia Duxton in particular could drop off the face of the earth, and she'd be cheering.

"Our first meeting in the bar—was that even a coincidence? Was it all planned, to get me to lower my defenses?" Kai demanded. "There are plenty of Duxton middle managers, much lower down the ladder than a *goddamned European vice president*, who could accomplish a simple investigation into staff turnover. There's no reason whatsoever for her to be here, unless she wants Mayfair Palace badly enough to chase Nedal to Vegas. That has to be it!"

She paused and peered at Milly. "And the undercover thing? Well, maybe it was all a way to get into my good graces. To spy on me in ways that wouldn't arouse suspicion—like seeing that fax."

"How did she know you were going to suggest she go undercover?" Milly asked reasonably.

"She didn't—but she seized on the opportunity like the shark she is."

Milly's eyebrows lifted. "She doesn't strike me as particularly shark-like."

"Which shows how clever she is!" Kai glowered, annoyed her profiling of Amelia had been so off. Her spidey senses hadn't tingled once that the woman might be tricky.

"What if she's telling the truth?" Milly asked.

"She can't be. This isn't some two-bit scam. It is impossible to sell something of this magnitude without trained experts picking over any irregularity."

Kai's pacing picked up. "The next step was for Grand Millennium's lawyers to go over the contract, term by term, analyzing all the clauses, and, in the process, they'd confirm which business entity they were dealing with. So what would any conman get out of it? There's nothing to be gained. Isn't that proof Amelia Duxton is full of BS?" Disappointment settled in Kai's stomach. "Amelia just wanted to delay the deal until the Duxtons could leap in with a higher offer. We've been played."

"So why show her hand now?" Milly asked. "Why not pretend to be Lia Hanson until she'd done a deal with Mr. Hamadani? And why would she anger him by dumping water over him?"

Kai stopped as she rewound the disastrous scene. Actually, it was pretty clear the man had never seen Amelia before in his life. Yet hadn't they been in negotiations before he came to Vegas?

This...made no sense whatsoever.

"The mind of a Duxton isn't logical," Kai sputtered to hide her confusion. "They're always up to something. You can bank on that." Kai gave up pacing and sank into the couch.

Milly eyed her. "Do you feel better?"

"Is that all you have to say?"

"I think there's a lot going on and we don't know for sure what's happening."

"Why do you have to be so...argh. Fair! Anger also likes company, you know."

"Is that what you'd like, Ms. Fisher? A pitchfork mob of two?"

"Yes! That's exactly what I'd like."

"Or we could simply ask Mr. Hamadani for proof he is who he says. Actually, our due diligence wasn't the best." A reproachful look entered Milly's eye.

"What do you mean? I went straight to Mr. Stein. Are you saying he's lying?"

"No, of course not. I'm saying he is seventy-four years old. Maybe he misidentified our businessman, maybe he didn't. But because you trust Mr. Stein implicitly, we didn't double-check Mr. Hamadani's identity with anyone else. And I know you never would have entered negotiations with him based on just one person's confirmation if that person hadn't been our boss."

Kai stared at her. *Christ.* Although Benjamin Stein was rock-solid reliable, Milly was right. Kai hadn't dug deep. Or, well, at all. "I can't very well call Hamadani up and say, 'Hey, I know we were about to sign a deal today, but can I see your driver's license or passport first?'"

"So you *do* have doubts?"

"Have you forgotten that Amelia's a *Duxton*? She wants the Mayfair Palace deal and would do anything for it, including pretending to be a friend."

Kai stopped cold. When she'd accused Amelia of playing her, the woman had looked hurt, not to mention genuinely astonished. It was unsettling. "Fine. I'm not entirely sure whether I have doubts or not." She grabbed her phone. "But to be sure, I'll try the old man again."

A moment later, Rebecca picked up. "He's gone to lunch, Kai."

"Can I interrupt him or is it business?" Mr. Stein disliked any intrusions during a working lunch.

"I wouldn't. He's talking to his cousin again."

"Damn. Okay, tell him to call me as soon as he gets back."

"I will. Bye, Kai."

Mr. Stein had had a contentious relationship with his Orthodox family since he'd told them decades earlier that he wouldn't be marrying the woman everyone expected him to. Or *any* woman. Kai had reached her own conclusions long ago as to why that was, but it wasn't something anyone discussed.

Every now and then, Mr. Stein tried to mend things with the only relative who gave him the time of day: his cousin. It usually ended the same way: a furious boss storming back to the office, vowing never to talk to his family again...until the next time.

"Mr. Stein's having lunch with his cousin."

Milly winced. "Not the best day to talk to him then."

"No."

"Why does he always come back from lunch with that man so angry?"

Kai didn't answer. Mr. Stein's secret was his. Privately, she agreed. Why *did* he keep trying? Then again, it had always been so easy for her. Her mom had been immediately accepting of a teenage Kai coming out and had even offered to "make a rainbow '*love is love*' sculpture" to celebrate.

Kai had passed.

"I think you should try him again later," Milly gave her a worried look. "Just in case Rebecca doesn't remember to pass on the message."

"You really think Amelia might be telling the truth?" Kai asked. "Come on! The Duxtons are cold, ruthless, greedy, entitled assholes who treat their staff like slaves."

"Except Ms. Duxton's not like that."

"She used an assumed identity to get close to and commit industrial espionage on her competition! Claimed she was investigating 'staff turnover,' lied to my face, then sneaked her way into my...*business.*"

"*Business.*" Milly couldn't entirely hide her smile.

Kai narrowed her eyes at the innuendo. "My *contract negotiations.*"

"But why would she bother?" Milly asked. "She could have just made a better offer. She doesn't need to creep around. Maybe she really did want to understand the staffing problems, then saw you being scammed and decided to speak up."

Kai stared at her assistant, incredulous that after ten years of working with her, Milly could still be this naive. "She was eliminating the competition."

"She didn't need to do that, either. The Duxtons have deeper pockets than we do. They could have outbid us easily."

That was...annoyingly...true.

"Well, there's only one thing for it," Milly said, straightening.

"Oh?"

"I'm going to ask her." Milly gave a firm nod.

"You're...what?"

"Yes. Perhaps you're too close to the situation."

"You're just going to waltz up to Amelia Duxton and ask what she's been up to?"

"Yes."

"Milly—"

"No, Ms. Fisher, it's fine. I'll be right back."

"Or I could go."

"Didn't you tell her she was a schemer who hurts people?"

"Maybe," Kai muttered. "Well, that was more about the Duxtons in general."

"And didn't she get extremely upset at you?"

Kai paused. Yes, she had indeed caused uptight Amelia Duxton to swear at her. "Possibly," she admitted.

"What room's she in?"

"How would I know?"

"Never mind," Milly said. "I'll ask my contact." She was already texting. Her phone beeped a minute later. "Room eight-thirty-three. May I suggest you ask Mr. Hamadani whether he's ready to sign again while I'm gone? He'd be dry by now, surely?"

"Milly? If she's a con artist, she'll be manipulating you. Be careful."

"Yes, Ms. Fisher." Milly smiled. "Of course, she hasn't taken on me yet. I'm more persuasive than I look."

Kai stared at her in astonishment. Where had this plucky young woman appeared from? "Go. Impress me."

"How are you doing?" Quinn asked when Amelia knocked on the adjoining door and handed Quinn back her phone.

Amelia didn't reply. This emotional upheaval with Mariam felt too much to put into words yet. And it wasn't exactly any of her deputy's business.

"Here. Maybe this'll help." Quinn handed Amelia a full ice bucket she'd clearly just fetched, and a bag of limes.

"Your room has limes?" Amelia took both items and headed back to the prep area next to the minibar, Quinn on her heels.

"Nope. I picked some up on the way from the airport because I know how much you like 'em in your drinks."

"That's thoughtful," Amelia rummaged around drawers, pulling out a knife, then added ice to her high-ball glass. She poured in her best guess of two ounces of gin and squeezed in half a lime's juice, then topped it with fizzing soda water. After slicing the other half of the lime, she added a ring. She sipped. *Much better.*

"Thank you," Amelia said. "You'd make an excellent assistant."

"Not keen on a demotion, thanks. Besides you hate having assistants underfoot—it's just someone disrupting your well-ordered office."

"True."

The silence stretched out. Finally Amelia stood and moved to a chair by the window.

Quinn followed and sat beside her. "How'd the call go?" she asked gently.

"I can't believe I thought the worst of Nedal. All this time, his mother was on her deathbed."

"His mum's been sick?"

"Still is. He did a mercy dash. Hasn't left her side and turned his phone off."

"And that office guard dog of his let us believe we'd been axed? Bastard." Quinn's expression darkened.

"I should have realized Hanif was just stirring up trouble."

"How were you to know?"

"Nedal's always been decent. I should never have doubted him. I never want him to know I did."

"Of course." Quinn regarded Amelia. "Now what happens? Your undercover work's done. You'll write up the report, do the speech on Saturday, and leave. Is that it? I mean, we don't care about Fake Nedal now, right?"

Amelia studied the horizon, the bold, bright hotel names blinking back at her. "No. I've alerted the two parties affected. If Fisher or Nedal's family want to do anything about it, that's up to them."

Her stomach clenched at the way things had been left with Kai. The horror on her face as she decided Amelia had been playing her.

Would I have leapt to the same conclusion if the situation had been reversed?

No! Amelia couldn't fathom the intimacy they'd shared as being anything but genuine. Apparently Kai thought Amelia could just turn that on for a deal.

"So...speaking of this elusive Ms. Fisher," Quinn said, fanning herself. "She's pretty hot. If you're into confident executives with legs up to heaven and a strut to go with it. And her eyes...lord. Molten lava."

"You haven't even met her. How do you know?"

"So you think it, too, huh?" Quinn smiled. "I looked her up and found footage of her at an awards night last year. She scrubs up well. I mean, *mercy.*"

Amelia looked sourly at her glass. "I'm done talking about her."

"Roger that."

Silence fell for a few beats.

"She called me a liar," Amelia suddenly growled. "Me!"

"That's a new one. Your whole undercover, fake-name thing notwithstanding."

"Not relevant." Amelia slammed her empty glass on the small table beside her. The ice cubes bounced. "Anyway, *she's* the one who lied. Claiming she was in hotel marketing and did a *few* deals."

"To be fair, she started out there, got promoted to Acquisitions, but she's still listed at Grand Millennium under Marketing."

"She's the damned Closer. That's not someone who does a *few deals*. That's someone who *exists* for the deals."

"Right."

"So *she's* the liar, not me." Amelia gave an indignant glare.

"I thought we weren't talking about her anymore?"

"We're not."

After a moment, Quinn frowned. "You know…it just occurred to me. Wouldn't it be kind of humiliating for Grand Millennium to be dealing with a conman?"

"Of course. They won't come out of this looking good."

"Doesn't it make you wonder if *that's* not the point? Think about it. If you hadn't spoken up, what would have happened next?"

"The deal would go to the lawyers."

"Yes, but what *else* would happen? What always happens with Stein's deals—prematurely, I might add?"

"Stein would announce it all over Twitter as soon as he had the in-principal agreement. He's a fool, never waiting for deals to be final. No restraint."

"A fool, yes. And so predictable. But this time, there'll be an announcement but no deal. Result: complete humiliation."

Amelia's mind whirred. "So who has the most to gain from Grand Millennium being taken down a peg?"

"Um, what about the obvious? Us. Hotel Duxton."

Amelia drew in a sharp breath. "No. We would never be party to something so tawdry. Even my brother wouldn't dream up a stunt like this. It's way over the line."

"Even if it meant scoring big brownie points with your dad? Conrad would love it if Stein took a hit in the press."

"Oliver isn't completely stupid. Besides, your theory doesn't explain something else: Fisher said her boss had identified Nedal from a photo she sent him. And Stein's met him personally."

"That's weird. Okay then, I'm all out of theories."

"We don't know how many enemies Stein has made over the years. As far as I'm concerned, this is nothing to do with us. It's for Nedal's people to investigate; Fisher's, too, if she ever decides I'm telling the truth."

"Okay." Quinn nodded. "This conversation's tabled for good then."

There was a knock at the door.

"Expecting someone?" Quinn asked.

Amelia shook her head. She strode to the door and opened it.

The eternally sweet face of Milly Valentine peered back.

Amelia sighed.

Chapter 16

Enemies and Allies

AMELIA ALLOWED MILLY INTO THE suite. The petite redhead did a quick scan of the room before her eyes settled on Quinn with curiosity.

Quinn leaped to her feet and virtually galloped over to greet her. "Hey. I'm Quinn. Quinn Hartman. Amelia's deputy."

"Milly Valentine."

Quinn beamed. "That's funny."

"Why?" Milly frowned. "What's wrong with my name?"

Amelia hid a smile. The miffed assistant looked like a cross Disney woodland creature.

"Nothing!" Quinn said hastily. "It's just you're Valentine and I'm Hartman. You know, like heart, and…" She stopped. "Shit, sorry for rambling."

Milly relaxed and offered a small smile. "Oh. Right."

Quinn shrugged then grinned, looking pleased.

What *was* happening here? Quinn's cheeks seemed red under her dark skin.

"If you're quite finished," Amelia swished a hand between their locked gazes, "I'd like to know why The Closer's assistant is gracing us with her presence?"

"Oh shit," Quinn gasped. "That's who you work for? Wow."

Oh, for God's sake! "Yes, fascinating," Amelia said dryly. "Ms. Valentine, why are you here? I'm fairly sure your boss made some denigrating statements about me, my family, and my moral fiber. I did not expect to see or hear from her again."

"She's...stubborn," Milly said. "You've dropped a bomb in her lap and she's processing."

"Drink?" Quinn asked. "We have all sorts. And lime. We have lime."

Amelia stopped and stared at Quinn so hard the woman's cheeks grew even darker.

"I'd love a glass of Sprite. Um, with lime," Milly added.

"Coming right up." Quinn beamed as she busied herself preparing the drink with more enthusiasm than Amelia could recall the woman ever making *her* a drink.

Amelia turned to Milly, who appeared calm, measured, and respectful. It was a shame her boss shared none of those traits.

"Are you saying you believe I was telling the truth?" Amelia asked.

"I'm saying there was nothing to be gained in doing what you did. So I came to seek more information. Ms. Fisher's not really taking in new information right now, so I thought I'd see what I could learn."

"What if I said I was done being involved, and you can just go trotting right back to Ms. Fisher and tell her to sort her own messes out?"

Quinn almost spilled Milly's half-poured drink and gave Amelia an askance look. "Boss!"

"I'd say," Milly said, pausing to toss Quinn an appreciative glance, "that before you throw me out, could you clarify some points for me? If that's okay?"

How on earth did someone so nice cope working with Kaida Fisher? Was she even for real?

Quinn bustled over to Milly, passing her the drink. "I hope it's okay. I put extra ice cubes in. It's a hot day. Oh! You did want ice, didn't you?" Her expression faltered.

"I love ice cubes, thank you."

Amelia sighed and stalked a circuit of the room so she didn't have to witness this perplexing mating ritual any longer than necessary.

The clang of ice cubes told her Milly had taken a sip. She turned to find Quinn still grinning cheerfully at the woman.

"Ms. Valentine, you know who I am, right?" Amelia asked.

"Yes, Ms. Duxton." Milly put down her drink. "You run Europe for the Duxtons."

"I do." Amelia eyed her. "You know I was also doing a deal for Mayfair Palace."

"Yes."

"With the real Nedal al-Hamadani."

"Allegedly real," Milly said quietly. "Until the facts are proven either way." There was steel in her tone, but she remained polite.

Quinn flicked Amelia a worried look, as if afraid she was about to eject the woman on the spot.

Actually, Amelia appreciated her accuracy. From Milly's point of view, nothing was established. "The thing is, I know Nedal's in Dubai for family reasons. He'll sign with me when he returns. He is definitely not here selling me out to a rival. Nor would he, as he's a friend." That word burned on the way out.

"Do you have any proof of your claims?" Milly asked evenly. "Because we also have the CEO of Grand Millennium who swears the man here is the same Nedal al-Hamadani Mr. Stein met in London. He says *we* are dealing with the real developer."

Amelia wondered how you proved a thing like this, before her mind tripped over how Stein could possibly get an ID so wrong. Aside from a beard, the two Nedals didn't look much alike. "I have no proof."

"You could be trying to scare off the competition with talk of impostors," Milly said neutrally. "Ms. Fisher could be right about that."

"Do I strike you as someone who would tell such ridiculous stories? Inventing fakes?"

"I don't know, Ms. *Hanson*," Milly shot back, with a tiny smile. "Are you?"

Quinn snorted.

Touché. "For the record, I did your translations accurately," Amelia said, sinking onto the nearest chair. "I was scrupulous. I want Ms. Fisher to know that. She didn't seem to believe a word I said, but it's true."

"Yes, we know. We got a second translator to check later. Very accurate."

"You verified the translation, but you didn't bother to verify who you were dealing with for Mayfair Palace?" Amelia asked in astonishment. "I don't understand."

"Mr. Stein's say-so was all the verification Ms. Fisher needed."

Based on Milly's strained look, the assistant clearly thought her boss had erred.

"I had a brief conversation with your fake Nedal," Amelia said. "I suspect he's from Essex, not Dubai."

"Perhaps," Milly said placidly. "The question is why anyone would concoct some elaborate hoax? Who does it benefit? Ms. Fisher feels you have the most to gain by scaring off the competition. Is there an alternative theory we could consider?"

"You know, it's not down to me to solve your mystery. As far as I'm concerned, I'll sign my deal with Nedal when he returns from overseas. What your boss does with the conman is up to her and no longer any interest of mine." Amelia leaned back in her chair. "Maybe pass that along to her. When she's...calmer." Her lips curled.

"Why are you even in Vegas, Ms. Duxton, if not to steal back the deal?" Milly asked.

"I'm giving a speech at the conference in my brother's stead. And I'm evaluating the efficiency of Duxton Vegas, examining its turnover issues."

"I'm sure you understand the turnover problem now," Milly said diplomatically.

"I'm aware the points system is problematic. I will report that it is a failure and..." She stopped. Why was she oversharing with the competition? "Now, Ms. Valentine, I think I've been very patient with being interrogated, but it's time..."

A banging on the door sounded.

"Bollocks!" Quinn jumped. "I don't think that's room service, thumping like the bailiff."

Milly sighed so hard that Amelia suddenly realized exactly who was on the other side of her door.

Kai paced her room, wondering if a call or a visit would be the wisest course to tackle Hamadani.

Milly had been right. Kai's due diligence had been flawed. It had simply never entered her head that she might not be dealing with the real developer when she'd met a man calling himself Nedal al-Hamadani at a place where he was supposed to be. Who could predict that?

If she went to his room now and he signed, would that feel like a victory? Would she feel good about that?

No.

Damn it. Amelia had put doubts in her head. If Kai could get confirmation from Mr. Stein, she'd feel a lot better.

Her phone rang.

"It's Graham," said her informant from the front desk. "Your man, Hamadani, just checked out. Blew out of here like a tornado. If you run…"

She didn't wait for the rest.

The elevator took too long to get to the ground floor, the seconds ticking down interminably. *Come on!*

Finally, the doors opened, and she elbowed her way out past an indignant couple and skidded into the foyer. One glance told her Hamadani wasn't here, so she sprinted for the exit.

The doorman was just closing the door on a taxi as she reached the sidewalk. Through the passenger window, she could make out Hamadani. He turned and caught sight of her.

For half a second, she just stared. He lifted a hand in farewell as the taxi accelerated away, his expression turning mocking.

Fuck! Kai's stomach dropped into freefall.

"Are you okay, ma'am?" the doorman asked.

"Of course," she snapped. "Why do you ask?"

He pointed down.

She stared at her stockinged feet.

Oh.

Kai returned to the lobby, fuming and appalled. She'd been suckered.

Heading over to Graham, she said in a low voice, "I need to know what name the guest you called me about has on the credit card you have on file."

"I can't do that." His eyes darted about. "I mean I can't legally tell you that. Whatever name he uses or doesn't is his private—"

"Please just tell me if the names *match*. You don't have to give me a name. Does the name he was using match the one on the card he paid with."

"Mrs. Menzies was the one who checked him out, so I don't kn—"

For fuck's sake, was the man an imbecile? "Graham!" she growled. "It's urgent!"

"Right." He nodded obediently, then tapped on the keyboard. "Uh. Huh. Oh."

"What?" Kai tapped the counter.

"There's no card on file."

"How is that possible?" Every hotel demanded a credit card to charge any guests who sneaked out or trashed rooms.

"He's been comped. All expenses paid by management."

"Why?" she demanded.

"That's outside my pay grade. No clue."

Of course he didn't know. No one knew a damned thing around here, including her. "All right. Thanks for tipping me off he was leaving." She blew out a frustrated breath. "I'll send Milly down later with a bonus for your assistance."

Kai strode back to her room, thoughts frenzied. She grabbed her Mayfair Palace folder, shuffled through the paperwork, and withdrew the Arabic fax. This was the only paperwork with any clues as to Hamadani's true origins on it.

At the bottom of the page, she studied the numbers the fax machine had automatically added. It showed the fax number the document originated from and couldn't be faked. She typed the number into Google. The results were instant.

Oh hell. The first eight numbers matched a hotel's *Contact Us* fax number. The end two digits did not, which meant only that it belonged to a different fax machine within the same company.

Welcome to Hotel Duxton New York. Contact us on....

"Son of a bitch." The Duxtons!

She slapped the fax onto the coffee table. What a game-playing family of assholes!

Kai leapt to her feet. Now she had all the proof to wipe the smug smirks off every last scheming Duxton—starting with the one who'd called her delusional.

She slipped on her heels and snatched up the fax. Even if Amelia wasn't directly involved, she'd be able to find out exactly who in her family was the culprit from this paperwork.

The door to room 833 opened to the long-suffering face of Amelia Duxton. "Not today, Satan."

"Hilarious," Kai growled. "Let me in?" It was only barely a question.

"I suppose I don't have a lot of choice," Amelia drawled. "Between you and your assistant, apparently my room is your room."

Kai pushed her way in as Amelia stepped back, and then she glanced around.

Milly was standing close to a beautiful, dark-skinned woman in a smart purple suit.

"Quinn Hartman," the woman said in a British accent, throwing in a charming smile. "To save you asking. I'm Amelia's second-in-command."

Such an odd mix, this short, friendly, soft-butch woman next to reserved, angular Amelia Duxton.

"Right." Kai turned to Amelia and held up the fax. "I have proof your family did this. The Arabic terms came from Duxton's New York offices."

Quinn flicked a weighted glance at Amelia, who frowned in reply.

"You knew?" Kai asked, shocked. "All this time…"

"No." Amelia held up her hand. "Quinn suggested the possibility. I'm well aware my brother enjoys juvenile games, but I thought even he knew a terrible idea when he saw it." She walked over to Kai and held out her hand.

For a moment, as Amelia's perfume—woody, spicy, evocative—washed over Kai, she faltered. It reminded her of another time they'd been this close, for entirely different reasons. Why was Amelia holding out her hand? Surely she didn't want to clasp Kai's hand in some attempt to soothe her? Another manipulation?

"The fax?" Amelia asked.

Oh. Feeling foolish, Kai handed it over.

Amelia scanned the numbers at the bottom and knitted her brows. "That isn't Oliver's fax machine."

"No?" Kai asked skeptically. "It's definitely from Duxton New York's building."

"Yes. That doesn't mean I know the source. I'd have to look some things up to obtain that information."

"Cover up some things, you mean?" Kai said.

Amelia's lips pressed together. "Might I remind you, if not for me you'd have signed a deal with a con artist."

"You want me to thank you for preventing me from falling for your own family's scam?"

Amelia's expression became frosty. "I am not them. I'm as much in the dark as you are. And you don't get to barge in here, grilling me on something I'm not involved in."

"Not involved in?" Kai's voice rose. "How do I know all of this isn't also part of the scam? You faking innocence. Give me one good reason why—"

"I don't have to give you anything! I informed you that you were dealing with an impostor. Now you insult me and demand answers I don't have."

"Answers you refuse to give."

"I don't lie." Amelia tone was resigned. "We've been through this."

Kai snorted. "No? So who *was* that translator in my room two days ago?"

"I wasn't aware that you—"

"And who also kissed the bejesus out of me after telling me they had no interest? Not to mention what your hands were doing..."

Amelia's expression turned murderous.

"Oh goodness." Milly's skin went so pale that her freckles stood out.

"Sweet Jesus," Quinn mumbled at the same time. She turned. "Um, hey, Milly? Why don't we hide out in my room while our bosses figure out their shit?" She jerked her thumb over her shoulder at the adjoining suite.

"Yes, please." Milly nodded hard.

The pair bolted. The door closed with a loud clunk.

"That was inappropriate." Amelia rounded on Kai, eyes flashing. "How dare you raise our personal business like that? Will you put an announcement on Twitter, too?"

"What was inappropriate was you taking advantage of me when you already knew I hated the Duxtons. Didn't you think to tell me you were *one of them* before kissing me?"

"I had no idea you worked for Grand Millennium then! I thought you were just low-level annoyed with us for some reason."

"No, I'm fucking high-level pissed off! Your family are the most sanctimonious assholes. They lie, cheat, steal wages..."

"Typical Grand Millennium lies."

"Typical Duxton denial. Even when something is proven, no one cares. Under the rug it goes." Kai made a sweeping motion. "The entitlement is breathtaking."

Amelia's eyes tightened. "Quite the list."

"I'll give you a list: chronic underpayment of staff, timed bathroom breaks, forced unpaid overtime, inadequate meal breaks, excessive micromanagement, culture of fear, culture of bullying, culture of—"

"Just because you say it's so, doesn't mean it is, Kaida." Amelia's tone was bored.

"You think I just made it all up?" Kai glared.

"Either that or you swallowed all the BS from Scorched Earth."

"What's that quote about all it taking for evil to flourish is for good men to do nothing?"

"I'm...evil?" Amelia looked truly furious now.

"Your family does evil, and if you do nothing about it, you're not much better."

"For God's sake, don't you think I'd know if my own company was abusing staff? I'm in upper management! If even a tenth of what Scorched Earth claims was happening was going on, there'd be urgent investigations and firings. There haven't been, because it's *not happening*. I would never stand by if any of this was true."

"It is true—and you're doing nothing."

Amelia's jaw ground. "We're never going to agree on this. You've decided you're right and my family is the devil spawn."

"Did you know about the points system?" Kai asked silkily.

Amelia fell silent. Doubt flashed across her face.

"If you didn't know about that," Kai pressed on, "what else don't you know about?"

"One poorly conceived scheme does not mean the whole company is rife with abuse."

"And was the Hamadani scam poorly conceived, too? Or do you admit it was a little evil?"

"It was...illegal."

"That's not what I asked."

"It was wrong, yes." Amelia's lips pursed. "Appalling."

"Tell me something. *Do* you think Oliver did this? Deep down?"

Amelia paused. "I'm aware he's capable, but that doesn't prove a thing." She eyed Kai. "Does that mean he's evil? Just for having the means to do something? You know what? You sound fixated. What is with your obsession with us?"

"You'd be obsessed too if you'd lost your career because of that asshole brother of yours."

"Your career? You're The Closer! You're not exactly suffering from lack of recognition."

"My *former* career. I was a lawyer once, rising fast. Oliver stole that from me."

"Why would he?"

"Because he wanted to silence me."

"Silence you on what?"

"Occasionally my company allowed me to do pro bono work. Some hotel cleaners came to me and told me stories of chronic abuse by management. Hours of unpaid overtime. Forced to buy their own uniforms and cleaning supplies, bullying. That sort of thing."

Amelia squinted. "You're not seriously suggesting these were Duxton staff? And I never heard about it?"

"They were all Duxton workers, yes, and you know, I'm starting to think that you not hearing something about your company does seem to be par for the course."

Whoa. If looks could kill, Kai would be smoking ash right now.

"Anyway," Kai continued, "after I heard their stories, I started to make a big noise to drum up public support. Your brother was furious. One day he approached my law firm and told the partners that he was thinking of giving all Duxton USA's legal work to them. Only catch—they had to let me go. Within days, I found myself out of a job. But that was only the start of it."

"What happened next?"

"Every job I went for, even ones where my prospects were great, suddenly I didn't even get an interview. It turned out my previous employers had been damning me with faint praise in references, at Oliver's suggestion. The sort of faint praise that makes a potential employer wonder what the hell I'd been up to. And while I'd love to share all the fucked-up details of everything that went down—and trust me, that was the sanitized version—I'm bound by a non-disclosure agreement with your brother."

Amelia's disbelief was clear. "Why didn't you sue for wrongful dismissal? What happened to the cleaners? What did Oliver have on you that would force you to sign an NDA?"

Kai eyed her. "That is between Oliver and me. But, bottom line, your brother ruined me and then rubbed in my face how much power he had over me. He's probably still laughing about it."

"Oh, I doubt that. Surely you're a bigger thorn in his side as The Closer than you ever were agitating for a bunch of cleaners?"

"Perhaps. But while that is a satisfying thought, it'd be nice if *I'd* been the one to decide I was due for a career change, not him."

"Mmm," Amelia said. "I'll fact-check this with my brother, of course."

"You don't believe me? Why would I lie?"

"It's called verification. Of all people, you might want to look into it some time."

"Wow. Must be hard being so perfect," Kai shot back. "Tell me: do Duxtons ever admit when they're wrong?"

"Do you?" Amelia arched an eyebrow. "Can you at least admit I'm not the mastermind of the Nedal con? Or even an accessory to it?"

"I'll admit that if you admit your family is at least a little evil since they're behind that hoax."

"Hyperbole much?" Amelia's eyes hardened. "This topic is closed."

"Of course it's closed. Because Duxtons love denial. I don't know why I even bothered trying to convince you. You're always right, aren't you?"

"Well," Amelia mused, "I'm not often wrong."

"Seriously? That's what you're going with?"

"I'm not saying that to boast. I'm simply diligent."

"And I'm not. *Right?*"

"I suggest you don't pin your anger on me at being scammed. You're making this very personal and it isn't at all."

"Not personal? So kissing me was just a business strategy? My God, you people are truly awful."

Amelia's eyes went hard as diamonds. "*Kaida.*"

Kai felt the censure in that admonishing tone right down to her bones. All right, so she wasn't being entirely fair. Amelia *had* warned her about the scam. And she was likely the only Duxton worth a damn, although that wasn't saying much.

On the other hand, did Amelia even believe Kai's story of how Oliver had ruined her? Did denial really run that deep?

Kai had left out a lot. It had been a depressing, soul-destroying time in her life. Yet Amelia had just looked at her as if Kai was mentioning the weather.

Why do I even care if she believes me? Kai sighed. God. She just *did*. But the real question now was whether Kai truly believed there had been a hidden agenda when Amelia kissed her.

If she were being honest, the answer was obvious. Amelia had lowered her guard and made herself vulnerable with Kai against her better judgment, and she likely still hated herself for it. No one could fake unsettled reactions that well.

"Fine," Kai conceded. "I don't think you kissed me for nefarious reasons. But given who you are, who I am, and what someone at Duxton's been up to with this scam? You have to admit, it looks damned suspicious you meeting me when you did. What was I supposed to think?"

"You were supposed to use your brain and conclude that I am not the sort of person to do what you suggest for *business*." Amelia glowered.

"So what we shared *was* personal?" Kai couldn't resist asking.

"No! It's rapidly approaching regret."

"Oh, fuck you." Kai threw Amelia's words from earlier back in her face.

Amelia suddenly looked amused. "No thanks, I think you'd have enjoyed that far too much. We can't have that."

And just like that, the charged air shifted, stirring up that chemistry that always seemed to be swirling around them. Amelia's gently mocking tone sent a shiver through Kai.

"You know," Amelia continued, "I'm starting to think you'd prefer it if our kisses *had* been about business so you could wipe them away as nothing. Now you have to deal with the awful fact you kissed a Duxton—and liked it."

"You liked it, too!" *Of all the...* "You weren't exactly holding back. either."

"A lapse in judgment," Amelia said idly.

"And now you regret it."

"Don't you?" Amelia gave her an exasperated look. "I mean, seriously? We can't seem to work out whether we hate or like each other. Our interactions are fraught. Chaotic. This…rollercoaster ride…is not pleasant."

"I know. Hell, I *know*. Weirdly, I'm not sure I do regret it." Kai threw up her hands. "So sue me."

Amelia snorted. "Well, I suppose that's an improvement on you cursing the ground I walk on."

"Oh, I still want to curse you because of who you're related to." Kai lifted her chin. "But I'm resisting the urge for now. It'd be so much better for everyone if you were running your company." Kai's tone turned challenging. "Actually, why aren't you? That's the million-dollar question, isn't it?"

"Just because I deal in honesty, Kaida, doesn't mean I tell just anyone my family's secrets. But on this, a smart reader of people could surely work it out."

Kai studied her even look. "Oliver's the golden child. And you're a woman. And a lesbian?"

Amelia didn't deny it. She glanced away.

That felt a lot like confirmation. "*Will* you be running Duxton soon, now Oliver's not golden?" Kai pressed.

"That's out of my hands. It's not up to me."

"Even if you don't win the company, at least tell me you're going to fight to fix the rot?"

"*Again* with the evil nonsense?" Amelia sounded exasperated. "My family is not evil."

"How can you say that, even now? Even after working here undercover?"

"How would you like it if I called your mother evil? How can you possibly think I'm okay with such a sweeping judgment? I know they're not perfect, and yes, of course things have to be improved, but this is my family you're trashing."

"So evil *will* flourish then." Kai sagged in disbelief. "And you'll just stand by and watch—because *family*. Shit. I actually forgot for a moment that you're one of them. A *Duxton*."

"Is that really the only way you see me?" Amelia sounded offended.

"How else can I see you? Your family has twice tried to ruin me. The first time, it succeeded. This time, with this scam, remains to be seen."

"That wasn't me—either time."

"Close enough."

There was a long silence, and the air felt like it was closing in.

"I see." Hurt was tight in Amelia's voice. "Why are we even talking if you see me that way?"

"I..." That brought Kai up short. *Why am I?* "I don't know."

"Then I'd say we're done here." Amelia strode over to the adjoining doors, yanked them open, and called out, "Time to go, Ms. Valentine." She paused and added dryly, "Well, after you've extracted yourself from my second-in-command."

Kai's head whipped around to catch sight of Milly disentangling herself from Quinn, and her mouth fell open. "Milly!"

Milly Valentine, the too-busy-to-date, possibly virginal assistant from the gods, had been wrapped in a sensuous kiss with a woman. A woman who was the enemy.

"Ms. Fisher," Milly scrambled to her feet, her cheeks flushing. "It wasn't what it looked like."

"You weren't inspecting the tonsils of Ms. Duxton's deputy with your tongue?" Kai suggested.

"I...uh. Well..."

"Oh, for God's sake," Amelia snapped, shooing them to the door. "Argue semantics outside. I'm done with both of you."

"See ya, Milly," Quinn said, a goofy grin on her face. She mouthed, "Call me."

"Bye, Quinn." Milly's eyes were bright. "Thanks for the drink. And the lime. It was really nice."

Kai peered at them, confounded.

Amelia's foot tapped, eyes narrowing.

Milly exited first. At the door, Kai turned to regard Amelia. "I—"

"Yes, yes, I'm evil, blah-blah-blah. Tell someone who cares." Her voice was sharp, but her eyes were radiating hurt. "You say I'm in denial, but you conveniently ignore that I saved you from this scam when I didn't have to. You're welcome! Don't ever contact me again. Not that you would, of course. Because...*evil*." Amelia slammed the door in her face.

Kai stared at it, then turned to face Milly, who was discovering a sudden interest in her shoes.

"*Et tu,* Milly? I know I said you should live a little, but she *is* the enemy." She sighed in defeat. "I hope she was worth it."

Milly smiled. "Mm." Her cheeks bloomed redder than a tomato.

Great.

Chapter 17

Shifting Boundaries

AMELIA SLAMMED THE DOOR AND then eyed her deputy.

"Really, Quinn? She works for The Closer!"

Quinn still had a big dopey grin on her face. "Have you *seen* her, boss? Anyway, I'm surprised as hell she fancies me back."

Surprised? Their mating dance had been visible from outer space. "We only left you two alone for an hour!"

"Don't forget before that, when Milly turned up to get information for her boss. That was another twenty minutes of quality Milly time, easy."

"Fine...so before you abandoned all reason thanks to eighty minutes with the enemy—"

"Enemy?" Quinn sounded indignant. "Says the woman who snogged the actual Closer!"

Gritting her teeth, Amelia said, "Can you at least try and *pretend* to remember that I'm your boss? I do not want to hear any commentary about my personal life."

Quinn fell silent, and real anger sparked in her brown eyes.

Amelia met her gaze with fury of her own. She'd always allowed Quinn's over-familiarity because she was damned brilliant at her job. But having Amelia's weakness with Kai thrown back in her face was the last straw. It was inappropriate. Okay—humiliating.

"I'm only going to say this once," Amelia said, her tone pitched low and lethal. "There is a line. Do not cross it."

An uncomfortable silence fell. After a moment, Amelia began to prepare another drink. She hated arguing with Quinn. But she hated feeling exposed, too. This was beyond disconcerting.

Amelia threw ice in a glass, anger spiking anew. Quinn had *no* right to judge her for what had happened between her and Kai. She didn't know anything. Amelia sliced half a lime with unnecessary force. Quinn certainly didn't know how it felt to be treated as some brainless villain who ignored staff abuse because it was convenient. That scalded.

Who did Kai think she was, likening Amelia to Oliver? They were nothing alike! And Kai's tale about how he'd ruined her career? Oh, Amelia would be talking to her brother about that, because there were holes in that story wide enough to drive a bus through.

Soda water slopped over the edge of the glass as she poured—not surprising given her hands were shaking. She gave the glass a vicious wiggle as she reclaimed her equilibrium.

Kai Fisher thinks I'm evil. Me!

That hurt even more than Quinn—loyal, faithful Quinn—taunting her as if she had the right to. As if Amelia's kisses with Kai were something shallow to mock. Her jaw ached from tightness.

"Amelia?" Quinn murmured. Her shoulders sagged. "I just really like her. Milly, I mean."

"She is…likable," Amelia conceded. "So?"

"So I think I got really afraid you were going to order me not to see her again or something."

Amelia met her eye. "I'm not your mother, Quinn. See whoever you want. Just don't bring up that *other* topic with me again. Kai Fisher and I are not involved. We were *never* involved. I don't wish to hear any speculation or innuendo about that. Ever."

"Understood. Sorry. Didn't mean to rake over a sore spot, I promise."

"She's *not* a sore spot." Amelia squeezed the other half of the lime with bruising force into her glass. "She's a *dead* spot."

Quinn lifted her hands. "I hear you."

Amelia huffed. "It's not like I'd have any romantic interest in a woman like that. She's all cockiness, manipulation, and arrogance. Give me some credit."

"You know, I learned a few things about Kai from Milly. Stuff that might surprise you."

"Oh?" Amelia took a sip of Gin Rickey. *Ugh. Lime overdose.* "Such as?"

"Such as, wherever they stay, they pay off staff to get the scoop on how the place runs."

"Bribes? Naturally. It does explain how she seems to know everyone around here."

"Not just bribes. Milly found out that her boss often secretly helps out one or two struggling employees as well."

Maria Espinosa's spirited defense of Kai came to mind. Had Kai helped the housekeeper financially? Amelia shook her head. "It's probably one big tax dodge under charitable donations."

"All cash in hand; no tax write-offs, and no one knows she does this, aside from Milly."

Amelia took her drink over to a chair. "So that's why she hates us. She sees herself as a crusader for the underdogs. And the Duxtons are the opposite. We're the embodiment of wealth, power, success, and so on. Is she idealistic? Or does she do it to assuage her guilt at all those rich deals she makes and how much she earns?"

"No, that's not it." Quinn lowered herself into the armchair facing her. "Um, you know that stuff Scorched Earth's been saying about how Hotel Duxton treats its staff? Milly says it's true."

"Nonsense." Amelia waved her hand. "I'd have heard if my family routinely abused staff. Sure, isolated cases might occur, but I don't believe it's systemic, beyond the points-system nonsense here. Those are lies that have gained a life of their own."

"Boss? Not lies."

"And how would you know? Because Milly Valentine whispered it in your ear? I don't think a Grand Millennium employee is a reliable source given their history with us."

Quinn leaned forward. "I know you're smart. Hell, you can think circles around pretty much anyone alive."

Amelia side-eyed her, not liking where this was going.

"So think of this like science. Is it fair to assume that just because *you* haven't heard of something happening, it isn't happening?"

Oh for God's sake. "I see Ms. Valentine sings from the same choir book as her boss."

"Is it so crazy to believe that what you hear might be filtered, especially since you're rarely in the US? But see, that's how Milly and Kai know what's going on. They travel all over and ask workers on the ground what's happening."

"They bribe them, and the staff all play to their audience. They see a social justice warrior coming and make up bleeding-heart stories."

"To what end? Kai doesn't offer cash for sob stories. She just asks around, learns about people's lives. That's how she heard the Duxton stories, too. She heard them firsthand, along with Milly. If you don't believe Kai, do you think Milly seems like a liar?"

"Or Ms. Valentine might simply be too trusting."

"Why is this *so* impossible to believe?"

Amelia sighed. "You want me to accept my whole family—not just Oliver, but Simon, Joe, Dad, *everyone* running our hotels, is in on this and I'm clueless? I'm in some bubble off in Europe while this goes on all around me? Seriously?"

"Why don't we find out? Let's invite Milly to dinner this evening and ask. Grill her on everything. *All* of it. I only got snippets today. Let's hear how widespread this abuse is. Not just in Vegas, but everywhere."

"*Alleged* abuse."

"Right. So we'll gather evidence, compile data, weigh the facts up. Unless...you're afraid of what you might learn?"

Amelia placed her glass on the coffee table, straightening it perfectly. Kai's comment about her turning a blind eye to evil still rankled. She was wrong, though. Amelia wasn't afraid of truth. So what harm could there be in sitting down with the unassuming Milly Valentine and letting her talk? Amelia would easily be able to assess whether she was reliable or had been taken in by shrewd staff looking for a payout.

"Boss?"

"Is this really about business, or are you using me to see Ms. Valentine again?"

"Can't it be both?" Quinn grinned.

Amelia rolled her eyes. "I'm assuming you exchanged details at some point before getting amorous?"

"It wasn't like that! It was one kiss!" Quinn protested. "Well, two, sort of, because we stopped to take a breath." Her eyes became dreamy again. "And yeah, I have her number."

"Arrange it."

"Okay. Wouldn't Ms. Fisher be good to include, too, to—"

"Absolutely not." Amelia's jaw hardened. "She's made her position clear: I'm an evil Duxton."

"I'm sure she didn't mean…"

"She did."

"Okay." Quinn suddenly looked eager to change the topic. "So, about the mess with Fake Nedal—where are we now?"

"Nowhere. It's Ms. Fisher's problem. She's decided I'm the enemy so she can go it alone."

"But the fax showed—"

Amelia gave Quinn a sharp look. "Ms. Fisher can lie in a ditch, dig herself out, or whistle 'Dixie' for all I care."

"Aren't you even a tiny bit curious about how involved your family is? Like, *who* sent the fax?"

Am I curious? Yes. Oh, how Amelia enjoyed unpicking a mystery. Would solving it matter one iota for her? Especially now when she had a report to write and a speech to finalize?

"Not interested in the least."

Quinn's mouth fell open. "Wow. Hold the front page."

"What?"

"Amelia Duxton just straight out lied to my face."

Amelia pursed her lips. "Call Ms. Valentine. Arrange dinner. I have a speech to work on."

The moment Kai and Milly returned to Kai's room, she rounded on her assistant. "Quinn didn't waste much time, did she?"

"Ms. Fisher? What makes you think *she* came onto *me*?"

"She's one of those charming rogue types. I know I warned you off the silver-tongued gentlemen in Vegas. I should have told you to be careful of the gorgeous ladies who let you touch their feathers."

"Feathers?" Milly shook her head. "Ms. Fisher, this really isn't your concern. Quinn and I..." She paused and smiled so brightly it lit her eyes, the room, and most of The Strip. "We really hit it off."

"You hid it so well."

"She's funny. I love her outfit. She's a great listener, too."

"You left out she's the enemy."

"She's not, Ms. Fisher. And I learned a few things."

"Oh, I'll bet you did."

Milly gave a long-suffering sigh. "I found out all sorts of things. Quinn flies kites for fun. Isn't that quirky? At fourteen, she won an academic scholarship to study business at the University of Oxford, the first in her family to go to college. Oh, and she told me what Ms. Duxton's really like."

Kai leaned in. "Well?"

"Amelia threatened to resign when her father opposed Quinn being chosen as her deputy."

"Let me guess—racism wrapped up as traditionalism?"

"Quinn didn't say, but I'm guessing yes. She did tell me Amelia has a soft heart under her icy veneer."

Kai snorted. "Oh, please. She's as warm as frostbite."

"Not entirely. Amelia loves kids."

"You're pulling my leg. Wait, maybe she's harvesting their stem cells."

"Seriously—she apparently has more patience for children than for her whole staff put together."

Kai tried to visualize aloof Amelia deigning to converse with a small child. *Nope.* She could picture kids running screaming from her quite easily, though.

"She even set up a charity that gives poor kids in the UK school uniforms so they don't miss school because they don't have one. She thinks intelligence is a terrible thing to waste."

"Okay, that sounds more like her." Kai thought about that. "Well, good for her, she's not a total asshole, but do we just gloss over the bit where she conveniently doesn't notice the abuse problem at her hotels?"

"Because there isn't one. Her hotels are run beautifully. The peak of efficiency, Quinn says."

Kai snorted. "Well, booyah for Europe. You know I meant the US. You've heard the horror stories, too. Amelia just doesn't care."

"It sounds like you really want to lump her in with the rest of her family," Milly said carefully.

"She's a Duxton! She should be lumped in with them!"

"Why do you want to see her as like them so much?"

Kai glared.

"I apologize, Ms. Fisher. I'm sure you're probably not actively looking for a reason to dislike Ms. Duxton." Milly's tone was oh so perfectly polite.

Kai threw up her arms. "She aids and abets her family's misdeeds by claiming ignorance."

"Maybe she really is ignorant of what they do?"

"How can she not know?" Kai asked, askance. "*We* know and we don't work there."

"Because you are The Dragon and people send you their stories."

Kai paced. "She could have listened to me."

"How did you phrase your mentions of staff abuse? Did you let her know that some disturbing stories had come to your attention and maybe she should investigate?"

"Not...exactly."

"Ms. Fisher, did you by any chance declare she and her family were evil? I ask because of what she said as she slammed the door."

"Well, they are!"

Milly sighed.

"Now you make me sound like *I'm* the villain," Kai grumbled.

"I don't think there are any villains here. But I see two hurt and angry women fighting when they could be teaming up to get to the bottom of things."

"Me teaming up with *her*? When pigs fly!"

"Well...it sounded like you weren't averse to *teaming up* at one point," Milly said delicately.

"Bold's a new look on you, Milly." Kai scowled. "And that was a brief distraction." Her face heated up. "I don't even know why we're discussing this!"

"You're right." Milly arranged her expression to bland. "What would you like to talk about instead? We have to tell Mr. Stein his deal of the decade isn't going to happen."

"Yes. Damn it. Where *is* the real Hamadani, anyway? He could be anywhere!"

"Dubai."

Kai stopped and stared. "How do you know that?"

"Ms. Duxton told me. She said he went to Dubai for family reasons and that he'd sell her Mayfair Palace when he returned to London."

So *that's* why the deal hadn't been signed? Kai stalked to the window and gazed out. "Any idea how long those family reasons will last?"

Milly didn't reply.

"I mean, it would be a simple matter to bribe airport staff for a tip-off the moment his pilot logs the plans for a return flight," Kai murmured. "His executive jet can't be too hard to track down. A smart woman could be waiting to do a deal in the airport lounge in London before Amelia's even realized he's back home."

The room was far too quiet. Kai turned to see her assistant's paling face. "What?"

"Don't," Milly said quietly. "Please. Ms. Duxton didn't tell me that so you could use it to try and steal her deal a second time."

"It's what I do." Kai resumed gazing out the window. Her jaw hardened. "I'm The Closer. I'm good at what I do. What a *Duxton* wants is irrelevant."

"You're also The Dragon. The Dragon cares about people."

Kai felt angry all over again about being humiliated at the Duxtons' hands. "Amelia's not some vulnerable employee. She's part of the power structure. She's in the asshole family who just conned us."

"Someone in her family might have done that, but I'm pretty sure it wasn't Ms. Duxton."

Kai exhaled. "Still defending her?"

"I believe her when she says she didn't know."

Although it pained her, Kai had to admit she believed Amelia, too. Even so, the obstinate woman still seemed to think her family were angels. "Can you track down Mr. Stein for me? I need to know how this clusterfuck happened." Kai stopped. "By the way, who told you Hamadani was going to be in Vegas in the first place?"

"Rebecca."

"Rebecca?" Had the Duxtons paid off Mr. Stein's assistant to set this scam rolling? It seemed inconceivable, but then, nothing surprised her anymore. "Okay, see if she's free for a chat, too. I'm getting a drink."

"Yes, Ms. Fisher."

Kai sighed. Nothing felt right anymore. And somehow, she felt sure it was all Amelia Duxton's fault...even if it wasn't.

Fifteen minutes, and one bourbon and Coke later, Kai didn't feel much better and Milly was looking far too distracted. She kept glancing at her phone.

"You have an update?" Kai finally asked.

"Mr. Stein's out. Rebecca's at her desk now, if you wanted to call. Um... and I have to go out."

"Oh?"

"It's...to dinner." Milly didn't meet her eye. "So, if there's nothing else..."

"Will Quinn be there by any chance?"

"Yes," Milly's eyes darted to the door, as if itching to get ready. "Is it okay? I mean, unless you had other plans for me tonight?"

I do, Kai wanted to say. *Stay clear of the Duxtons. They're all vipers.* But Milly was giving her a look of such hope that she waved her away. "Go. I'll solve our Hamadani mystery; you break your dry spell."

"I'm not sure why you're convinced I have a dry spell."

Kai laughed at her adorably miffed expression. "You told me once you were too busy at work to date. Are you telling me that all this time you've been bouncing on the pillows with someone different every night?"

With a shy smile, Milly said, "We both know that's unlikely. I just don't know why you believe my love life is a topic for so much interest."

Kai regarded her for a long moment and realized her assistant truly meant it. "Sorry. I didn't mean to make you uncomfortable. I thought I was being amusing—or helpful. I'll behave myself."

"I wasn't uncomfortable, Ms. Fisher. More...a tiny bit exasperated. But matchmaking me every now and then seemed to make you happy, so—you know." Milly shrugged. "Occasionally I indulged you and went along with it."

Kai stared in disbelief.

"Now, though, I just think maybe it's time you got a new hobby. Ms. Fisher," Milly added, respectful as ever.

"You are too precious for words. I'll be good in the future," Kai promised, crossing her heart. "Now, Quinn Hartman is obviously quite the charmer, so just make sure you don't spill all our secrets."

"Of course not." Milly looked slightly offended.

"All right then. Out. Have fun."

Kai sobered as Milly left, and reached for her phone. No putting this off.

"Mr. Stein's office."

"Hello, Rebecca," Kai began, then stopped cold. How *does* one politely inquire as to whether someone's a traitor secretly on the Duxton payroll?

"Oh, hi Kai. He's still out—has been since lunch, as I just told Milly. How's Vegas?"

"Glitzy. When's he back?"

"I'm not sure. He's been in a snit since the cousin lunch. Canceled everything and didn't return."

"Ah." Kai really did wonder why the man kept persisting. "This is awkward...but has Mr. Stein been getting forgetful or confusing things lately?"

"What? Heavens, no!"

"No problem recognizing people?"

"Mind like a steel trap, same as ever. Why?"

"I emailed him a photo last weekend. I'm trying to work out why he said that the man in it was Nedal al-Hamadani when he wasn't. They don't look much alike."

"Wait, aren't you doing a deal with Hamadani right now?"

"I thought I was. Turns out I'm dealing with a scammer."

"Hell, Kai." Rebecca's voice was shocked. "So we don't have a deal for Mayfair Palace on the go?"

"Unfortunately not. I do have a new lead, though."

"Well..." Rebecca exhaled, sounding relieved. "That's something. Good."

"Yes. But speaking of leads, where did we get ours? Milly says you gave us the tip-off that Hamadani would be in Vegas."

The assistant inhaled sharply. "What are you asking me, Kai?" The woman was clearly no fool.

"Where your tip came from." Kai tried for a light tone.

"Mr. Stein. He said he'd heard it around and about. You know he speaks to a lot of people."

"That's true." Actually, it would have been quite easy for the Duxtons to make sure a tip landed in Mr. Stein's ear. But that didn't explain one thing.

"So, back to the photo I emailed Mr. Stein. There are only two options: He misidentified the man pictured, which I agree is unlikely. Or someone altered the email that I sent him, removing the fake photo of Nedal and attaching a photo of the real Hamadani. So—who has access to his emails?"

"You think I set you up?" Her voice lifted in outrage. "Me?"

"I only asked who has access to his emails."

"You know damned well I'm the only one who can go through his emails. Christ, Kai, I thought we were friends."

"I thought so, too."

"You really think that I could set you up? That I'm on the take? That I'd hurt my company? Mr. Stein? I've been loyal for twenty years! Screw you, Kai." The line went dead.

It was hard not to notice Rebecca hadn't actually denied anything outright. On the other hand, it did seem greatly out of character to picture Rebecca as a furtive mole who sent Grand Millennium chasing after a conman. However, Kai's list of suspects was exceedingly short, and at the end of the day, you never really knew anyone, did you?

She'd thought she knew the Duxtons, for instance, and then along came Amelia, with her cool eyes, direct gazes, gorgeous body, and an intelligence that still rattled Kai. The woman did not fit any mold the other Duxtons popped out of. So what did Kai know about anything?

Right now, not a damned thing.

Chapter 18

The Anointed One

As much as Amelia tried, she couldn't focus on her speech. At this rate, she'd be taking to the podium tomorrow night and just reading out Oliver's version, crass jokes and all.

Her mind drifted to dinner and what Milly might reveal. No, no focusing on that. It would just ramp up her tension. Amelia stared at the copy of Oliver's speech and the lack of new notes. All it contained was a lot of red pen, crossing things out.

Glancing at the clock, she smiled as she thought of something far preferable she could be doing. Amelia dropped her pen and reached for her computer.

A moment later, the cheerful face of Imogen Duxton smiled back at her.

"Auntie Lia!" Imogen squealed. "You called!"

"As I promised. I'm sorry it's been a few days; work overtook me. Now, you have an important question about owls?"

"I don't care about owls anymore." Imogen pouted. "I want to know about taking my fish with me on a plane."

"Did you decide where you and your fish are vacationing?" Amelia asked, relaxing. "The destination you choose might affect our research."

"I already said: New York."

"You hate the cold, darling."

"I know, but Dad says we have to move there. It sucks. I want to stay here with my friends."

"Move?" As in… Suddenly Amelia took a closer look behind the girl. "Imogen, why are half your room's contents laid out?"

"I'm packing. I can't decide what's a 'has to come with me now' and what's a 'it'll come later.'"

Amelia drew in a tight breath. "Sweetheart, *why* are you going to New York?"

Imogen's eyes welled up. "Dad says he got a big promotion and we have to move. *Forever.* So can you help me with my fish question? Dad says it's silly to want to bring my fish. I don't think it's silly. I love them. Why can't they come?"

A chill slithered down Amelia's spine. The emergency board meeting! Damn it. That had been two days ago; she'd lost track of time. Joe usually called to apprise her of any company developments. Why hadn't he? She should have remembered herself, though, and would have if her brain hadn't been overtaken by the fake deal and Kaida Fisher. She froze. Wait, did this mean *Simon* would be CEO of Hotel Duxton International?

"Imogen, darling, could you put your father on for a moment?" she ground out. "I have a work question. And no, worrying about your fish isn't silly. I'll talk to him."

Imogen nodded and disappeared. Five minutes passed before the sandy-haired Duxton Australasia VP came into view. Tanned, wearing a printed shirt of little pop-culture Sydney Opera Houses, he was as laid-back as he was untroubled with excess intellect. Or, to quote Oliver, he made camel spit seem smart.

"Lia?" Simon frowned at her down the video.

"Anything you want to share, Simon?" Amelia asked, tone silky.

"Didn't my dad tell you?"

"Joe must have forgotten to call, because I'm quite certain I'd remember him telling me that you somehow magically slithered into the top job."

Simon shifted uncomfortably. "It wasn't my idea. I'd be just as happy staying here."

"Oh, I'm sure it wasn't." Her voice dropped to a murmur. "Perhaps you should explain exactly what happened and why Imogen will soon be a New Yorker."

"Um…I think you should talk to Dad. *Really.*" His tone was pleading. "I don't want to fight."

"We're not fighting, we're chatting. Let's discuss the meeting—the one I couldn't attend because I was needed in Vegas."

"Uh, first they voted on whether Oliver should be given another chance. That was almost unanimous against it, but your dad voted yes. Then it was suggested maybe the board should consider a clean skin without any of Oliver's baggage. That's when my name came up."

"You."

He squirmed.

"Why you?"

"It was suggested I was doing an okay job running the Australasian region?" His voice pitched up. Indeed it should be a question, because no one in their company could possibly think Simon was qualified to run the entire global business.

"Simon, who told you to cancel your international ad campaign— Holiday at Duxton Down Under, Home of Sun, Surf, and Sharks—because no one outside of Australia would know the sharks reference was a joke?"

"You?"

"Who noticed the seventeen errors in your last annual report, and pointed out how two of them could get you charged by the Australian Securities and Investment Commission if you didn't pulp it?"

"You." He sighed.

"Who suggested you *not* use Derek Matheson as the face of Duxton Australia for your summer campaign last year?"

"How was I to know he'd be found with a stash of kiddie porn? I'm not a bloody fortune teller! Besides, the man was an Australian icon at the time."

"How many times have I warned you about brand leakage, Simon? *This* is why."

"So I'm not perfect like you. What's your point?"

"My point is, why are *you* now the anointed one?"

Simon squirmed. "Just talk to Dad. He can explain what went down. I thought for sure they'd prefer you."

"And yet here we are. What are you leaving out?"

"That your dad still hates your gay ass? Okay? Now I have to get back and pack. I'll send Immy back in. For God's sake, don't let her obsess over the fish. We're leaving them here. Housekeeper can sell them or flush them, I don't care."

"They're her pets!"

"They're *fish*. I'm her father. End of story."

"Wait." She swallowed back a caustic reply. "If she has a friend who can take them, will you allow that?"

"Fine." He rose abruptly, so Amelia got a screen full of yellow board shorts—probably planning an all-morning surf knowing him. Oh yes, perfect CEO material. "Just get Immy to see reason. The fish she has are a dime a dozen—not worth the shipping fees. And don't offer to pay yourself. I've put my foot down, so don't undermine me. Okay, Lia? Bye."

He didn't wait for an answer and left.

Asshole. Not like he was short of cash.

"Auntie Lia?" Imogen sat down, expression hopeful. "Can we talk about my fish now?"

"Darling, I'm sorry, but I couldn't talk your Dad into taking them…"

Imogen's big, beautiful eyes began filling with tears.

"…But may I make a suggestion?"

"W-what?" She sniffed.

"Your father has agreed to let you give them to a friend. So maybe find someone you trust, and if you ask them nicely, perhaps they can send you photos and updates of how your fish are doing. You'll still know they're happy even if you're not with them."

Imogen bit her lip.

"I know it's a poor substitute, darling, but sometimes we don't always get what we want. That's why a smart young woman like yourself should have a plan B."

"I'll miss them."

"Of course you will. But you'll still get to see them this way. And I'll bet when you're in New York, your father will let you have a new aquarium."

"It won't be the same!"

"I know, sweetheart. But if this plan works, you'll have photos of your fish coming often, and new fish to make friends with. Does this sound like a workable plan to you?"

Imogen sniffed. "It's going to be hard."

"It's okay to miss them."

"Dad's so mean. He can afford to send them to New York. Why won't he?"

"Perhaps he's thinking of the fish? It's a long, long way for them to come in a bumpy plane. Not very pleasant even with the best containers."

"Oh! Do you really think that's why he said no?"

How Amelia wished she could lie. "Even if that's not the reason, maybe it's a sacrifice you can make for the sake of your fish? Your fish will never know what you did for them, but *you* will."

A look of resolve crossed her face. "I'll do it."

"Maybe we can research new fish together. Later, when you're all settled in."

She brightened. "That'd be nice. Thank you, Auntie Lia."

"Anytime, sweetheart."

"You're really good at fixing things." Imogen smiled. "I want to be like you when I grow up."

"Your father will be *so* pleased to hear that," Amelia hid a smirk. "I have to go. We'll talk again soon. And for the record? Owls *do* have knees."

Imogen's awed "wow" filled the speakers as she ended the call.

Amelia exhaled slowly. Her dream to run her father's hotels had not just been ripped away but stomped on. She would have been far less gutted if they'd given Oliver yet another chance. That would have been almost predictable. But to give it to someone so inferior to all other options was beyond the pale.

What on earth had happened at that meeting?

Heart in her mouth, Amelia called Joe to find out. She glanced up as the phone rang, distracted by flashes of color as Quinn whooshed past the small gap in the ajar doors joining their rooms. She'd been doing this for the past half hour, wearing a different outfit every time.

"Amelia," came her uncle's amused tone. "How's Vegas? Getting some relaxation in?"

"Hardly. I'm working, Uncle Joe."

"On that subject, I gotta say I laughed my head off when Quinn told me of your plan to go undercover. I was the one who got the ball rolling on that, by the way. I challenged you to give us thorough, and you sure went boots in."

"I have a lot to report. There are some regressive staff systems in place here."

"You mean the points system Oliver's trialing?"

"You knew about it? Wait, *trialing*?"

"For the past few meetings, the board's been debating rolling it out across the rest of Duxton USA. Next meeting there's a vote on it. Your report will help them evaluate it."

"Are you serious? The points system's the reason for the high turnover."

"I'm aware."

"What? So why did you need me to come all the way over here to look into this if you already knew?"

"Honestly? We just needed a report to present to the board, something to say we've considered all angles, so it looks fairly evaluated. The bottom line is, Oliver's points system is actually clever. It's a legal way to under-pay people, because the employee starts with a good wage, but their own actions are what costs them. See? It's not on us, it's *their* fault. And on balance, we still come out ahead by replacing staff often rather than paying them all the full amount. Okay?"

She gasped. "That's terrible. And that's not what I'll be concluding."

"It's not terrible, it's fiscally smart. And any report you submit will have its conclusions reviewed before I submit it to the board."

"Reviewed? As in…changed?"

"It depends on what you write. Look, at the end of the day, we both agree the business always comes first, yes? You have a reputation for being a straight shooter, so if you recommend a sweeping new system, the board will be favorable toward it. This is just you putting the company ahead of yourself."

"So…my reputation's being used? This whole thing is a waste of time—a way to get my name on a report that will conclude whatever you want it to?"

Joe laughed. "Sometimes I wonder where you sprang from, that you don't have a political bone in your body. Amelia, it's not personal. It's just smart business. Besides, you being in Vegas is hardly a waste of time. You were needed there anyway for the speech. Win-win."

"I won't let you change my report, Joe."

"And how will you stop me?" he asked lightly. "Come on, this isn't the hill to die on. Moving on...I'm glad you've called. I need to know if we have Mayfair Palace."

"We don't. Hamadani had a family emergency. He's in Dubai."

"But the deal was so close! You were signing it within the hour last time we spoke."

"And he left before it could be finalized. I'll sign when he returns."

"I had a big media event in the works. We were going to announce it to the world!"

"So announce it later. What's the problem? The media can wait."

Joe muttered. "No problem, it's just inconvenient. All right, is that everything?"

She cleared her throat. "Isn't there something you forgot to tell me? Something about Simon?"

"Oh, that. Yes, I know how it looks, but don't panic. There's nothing officially announced until the next board meeting. Simon's the interim pick, true, but the vote that matters is in three weeks."

"Joe, what happened at the board meeting? You said you were going to fight for me!"

There was a long, long silence. "I tried, I really did," he said, sounding defeated. "I knew my brother was stubborn, but Conrad really doesn't want you to take over. A few board members expressed concerns that you went to Vegas instead of attending such an important meeting. They suggested it was proof you didn't care about being CEO."

"*You* sent me here!"

"I know. I explained that—all of it, your report and Oliver's speech. I pointed out it was a keynote speech being covered by business reporters. I talked up your CV, mentioned your awards, but they didn't budge. That was when I realized they were using your absence as an excuse to vote against you. I'm sorry. Some people share Conrad's backward views."

This again? Amelia sagged. She'd always assumed when push came to shove, upper management—including her father—preferred making money ahead of everything else. Apparently not.

"And then they picked...*Simon*?"

"Not at first. One or two wished that Douglas was on the table."

"Douglas is an embezzler. An arrested embezzler."

"Amelia," Joe growled, "that's still my boy you're slandering."

"Actually, he's a grown man. And I was being accurate; I even refrained from editorializing."

Joe hissed in a breath. "Anyway," he said forcefully, "that's when Simon's name came up. He was right there, so he gave a presentation. Honestly, I was shocked at how well he came across. I didn't know he had it in him. Anyway, he gave a glowing account of how well he's running things across Australasia."

"Australasia practically runs itself, though. I could do it in my sleep—the way he's doing it."

Joe's voice tightened. "Look, Amelia, I get you're disappointed. And my youngest might not have your head for business, but he's keen to learn and baggage free, without any rainbow skeletons in the closet."

"Joe, Simon thought 'Sun, Surf, and Sharks' was a good slogan for luring international tourists."

"We all have a bad day, Amelia."

"He's having a bad decade. And yet *he's* the one?"

"He's the safe pick. And right now, after so much scandal, the board just wants to steady the ship. You can understand that, surely? Right now, hard as it is, the business must come first."

"I agree. And that's why I should address the board. I want the right to make my case, tell them why I'd do it better. Lay out my plans for the future of Hotel Duxton International."

"I'm afraid that's not possible." Joe sounded regretful. "I wish we could. Schedules are so tight, and they've just had that emergency meeting. The board won't meet again until after Oliver's dealt with by the courts. But you can address them then, right before they formally vote."

"They'll have made up their minds by then."

"You don't know that. You're forgetting you still have that keynote speech to give. Tomorrow night, isn't it? So make them see you as the better choice. The board all know to be watching the live stream. This is your chance. Seize it. Dazzle them."

Dazzle them? She couldn't even write one sentence without nodding off in boredom.

"Right, that's everything," Joe said with finality. "Let me know when you hear Hamadani's back. I'll reschedule our Mayfair Palace announcement for just after that. It's a shame you couldn't have nailed that deal already. That'd have really made your case."

No need to rub it in. "Yes. Bye, Joe."

"Goodbye, Amelia." He hung up.

Amelia looked down at her speech, with its sea of red pen, and sighed. *Dazzle. Them.* She was screwed.

Chapter 19

Just the Facts

THE FUNNY THING ABOUT ATTEMPTING to prove yourself right, Amelia mused as she sipped her red wine and listened to Milly Valentine, was just how often you prove yourself wrong.

When she'd said she'd keep an open mind, she'd thought she meant it. Until Milly began to unravel all the abuses her family's hotels had done over the years in clinical, horrendous detail.

So much detail. Firsthand accounts. Statistics. In-house complaints. Firings. Leaked memos.

By the time they were eating their mains, Amelia felt sick to her stomach. She hadn't spoken much, letting Quinn run the meeting and tease out details from her...what...girlfriend? *That seems awfully sudden, doesn't it?* But the way they looked at each other, the way their shy smiles seemed to somehow match each other as the dinner progressed, made "new acquaintances" feel like the real lie.

Amelia sighed, aware of what she was doing. Distracting herself from the pile of data that even she couldn't sweep away as Grand Millennium lies. Because there was no way Milly could have manufactured all this in two hours. Some of the emails were old. They dated back years; the sender names blacked out.

How did Kai Fisher's assistant even have these?

Milly didn't just have Duxton abuses, either. When Milly flipped folders, Amelia saw names of dozens and dozens of unrelated businesses.

Quinn had been right. Kai really did believe in this. It couldn't be about assuaging guilt. Those older emails were from before Kai was even in hotels.

So she sipped, watched, listened, and grew steadily enraged on behalf of Duxton employees who had endured more than enough. And, for the first time in her life, Amelia wondered if her family were what their critics said about them: entitled, greedy assholes.

I am benefitting from this, a voice whispered in her head. Even if she didn't participate, she was enriched—literally—by the actions of her family.

Amelia set her wine glass on the table. "Thank you, Ms. Valentine. A most thorough presentation." She had cut Milly off mid-sentence, but she'd heard enough and doubted she could stomach more.

"Do you have any questions, Ms. Duxton?" Milly asked.

"No." She exhaled. "Thank you for your time." Amelia now needed alone time alone to think this through.

Quinn took the hint. "Um, Milly, maybe we could continue the conversation in my room?"

Subtle.

Milly, gathering up her folders and notes, blushed. "Yes, sure." She bobbed her head. "I have a lot more information I could make you aware of."

"Well, knowledge is power, right?" Quinn said brightly. She darted a worried look at Amelia. "You'll be okay, boss?"

"I'm sure I can muddle through on my own." She made an impatient shooing gesture. "Feel free to socialize."

Quinn frowned. "Are you sure?"

"Yes," she snapped, before softening. "Relax, have fun. I have my speech to finish, anyway." Amelia headed over to the table where her paperwork lay.

Footsteps retreated, followed by the snick of the door between the two rooms closing.

A moment later a throat cleared. She glanced up to find Quinn hadn't left. "I'm fairly sure I gave you permission to...whatever." She waved in the general direction of Quinn's suite.

"Do you believe her?" Quinn asked.

"Does it matter if I do? I'm based in Europe. I told you before dinner that Simon's now in line for CEO. What I didn't mention was I also called

Oliver. He confirmed, with far too much glee and very little detail, that he'd deliberately ruined Kai's law career—as if that was some achievement." She scowled. "One could argue Oliver's actions gave Kai a strong motive to come after us and she's simply attacking us for a vendetta. So, who knows what to believe? Why does my opinion matter, anyway?"

"It matters. To me. And I think it matters to Kai a whole lot whether or not you believe her."

"Why do I care what matters to her?" Amelia asked, her chin lifting.

"You care." Quinn spoke without judgment, unlike the last time she'd raised this topic.

"She called me evil. She also said that all I'd ever be is a Duxton to her."

"So prove her wrong. Tell her you agree she made some valid points."

"Why should I? She should be apologizing to me!"

"She hurt you," Quinn said gently. "And I know how rarely you open up to people, how rarely you give anyone a chance to get to know you. And you haven't really dated much since Mariam. So this hurt way more."

"I'm *not* dating Kai Fisher." Did the woman suffer a hearing malfunction?

"Would you like to?"

Amelia glowered. "Quinn. Enough."

"I think you two have way more in common than you realize. You both fight for what's right."

"Really?" Amelia arched an eyebrow. "I might do right by my staff, but I didn't even know what was happening elsewhere in my own company! It's grotesque what we heard tonight. I'm ashamed of my family."

"I know. So tell Kai you don't think it's all Grand Millennium lies."

Amelia's jaw tightened. "I think you should clock off now."

"Right." Quinn nodded. "You've got lots to mull over. Talk to you tomorrow." She headed toward her own room.

"Quinn?"

She turned back. "Yeah, boss?"

"Milly *is* lovely."

"Yeah, boss." Quinn smiled from ear to ear.

Amelia sat by the window, gazing sightlessly over a city which seemed to shimmer like a bawdy, seductive barmaid. It was funny how she was starting to get used to all the garish neon. But she doubted she could ever adapt to what she'd heard about Hotel Duxton tonight.

How could she process this? It wasn't even the types of complaints, although some were reprehensible, but the sheer volume of them. Managers were given free passes, and in some cases promotions, to keep on doing their worst.

Kai's comments about the evils of the Duxtons no longer felt like hyperbole.

What can I even do?

Amelia was one woman and had no power over anything that went on stateside.

I'm not just one woman, though, am I? She worked inside the upper echelons of the rotting organization. She was one of them.

Amelia had the power to send a memo to All:Staff in Duxton management—and she would be heard. But would that kiss away any chance of being CEO?

Probably.

But hadn't she already lost that chance?

Not entirely. If she nailed her speech and Nedal returned in time to sign before the next board meeting, she could still be voted CEO. And then, when she was boss, she would change the whole culture of her company. Torpedoing her chances now in some dramatic gesture was just foolish.

Right then. That settled, she leaned back in her chair.

A new thought struck. *But what if I don't win? Then what?*

A knock startled her out of her thoughts. She climbed to her feet and went to answer.

Kai's tight face greeted her. "May I come in?"

"I thought you'd said everything you wanted to say to me earlier."

"I remembered something else."

"I'm really not in the mood for more abuse." Amelia began to close door.

Kai's hand flew out to keep it open. "Wait. Truce?" She sounded sincere.

Amelia sighed. "Truce." She stepped back, letting Kai enter.

Kai shut the door behind her but lingered awkwardly near it.

"Sit," Amelia suggested, waving her to an armchair. "Drink?"

"No thanks." Kai settled into the chair. Her eye fell to the papers on the table. "Working on something?"

"Conference speech." Amelia eased into the armchair opposite.

"Ah," Kai said. "Milly texted that dinner with Quinn was over. She said you'd been there. That was news. I thought it was a date. Knowing Milly, I imagine she spent the evening defending me and arguing Grand Millennium hasn't been spreading lies. Am in the ballpark?"

Amelia dipped her head.

"She's loyal like that." Kai looked thoughtful. "Milly suggested that I talk with you. Perhaps...debrief?"

"Presumptuous." Amelia rose, walked to the minibar, and pulled out a soda water and gin. "Last I checked, you thought I was evil."

Kai looked pained. "It's been pointed out to me recently that that's not the best way to make a case."

"No kidding."

"I know. Occasionally I get a full head of steam and say things without thinking."

Amelia chopped a lime in half with a thunk. "How do you win deals with that bedside manner?"

"I don't. For some reason, I don't feel the need to censor myself around you."

"Yes, I got that part." Amelia paused slicing. "So, with me, you give a *non*-optimum experience. Lucky me."

"I'm trying to say something nice here!" Kai eyed her in exasperation.

Snorting, Amelia said, "Careful you don't sprain something." She resumed slicing.

"Do you know how rare it is for me to be completely *me*? You draw that out in me for some reason. Around you I'm more the unfiltered Kai than I am with anyone, except Milly." Kai shook her head. "It's strange. I can't explain it. Maybe honesty rubs off?"

Amelia met her eye. "You're here to see whether I believe your Duxton stories now. And you're buttering me up by telling me how honest you find yourself when you're with me."

"I wouldn't say buttering you up. I'd say being frank. But yes."

"I see." Amelia finished making her drink. "And if I said I didn't believe your tales of abuse?"

Disappointment flashed across Kai's face. "Then I'd be sad Milly wasn't persuasive."

"Why does it matter to you what I believe? Aren't all Duxtons the same?" She took a sip.

Kai fidgeted. "I used to think that."

"And now?" Amelia moved back to her chair with her drink.

"I think you're nothing like them. Or at least I have a strong need to believe that."

"Why?"

"Two reasons: When we first met, I thought you were intelligent and insightful—someone who looked beyond the surface. I don't like being wrong." She smiled. "And because, as annoying as you are, I possibly like you."

"Possibly?" Amelia lifted an eyebrow.

"Well, the evidence is leaning that way."

"You have an unusual way of showing you like people. I'm usually called names only by sworn enemies."

"You have actual sworn enemies? *You*? What sort?"

"Just the usual, I imagine—ambitious middle managers with more ego than sense, who don't appreciate being pulled into line by a woman. Don't you have enemies, too?"

"That seems a personal question to ask a girl," Kai said, tone teasing. "Like, 'Can I buy you a drink, oh, and tell me about your sworn enemies.'"

"And they say *I* can't do small talk," Amelia deadpanned. "So on that note, let's cut to the chase: why are you here?"

Kai became serious. "I have to know: What do you think is the truth about those Duxton allegations?"

"I believe you didn't lie."

Relief filled Kai's expression.

Amelia hesitated. "What I heard tonight was disturbing and devastating—and sadly, it's only going to get worse."

"Worse?" Kai choked. "How could it possibly get worse?"

"They want to take the points scheme national. I've been sitting here stewing about what to do next if I don't win the power to fix it."

"What about your report on turnover? That's why it's so bad here."

"It appears..." Amelia gave her drink a surly swirl, "that my report is worthless. It's all a set-up. They'll find a way to implement the scheme no matter what I write."

"You have to fight it!"

"How?" Amelia regarded her evenly. "I mean it: how? I'm open to any suggestions, but I can't see what I can do. The main issue is that I'm based in Europe. US operations fall to Oliver. And soon..." She grimaced. "Soon, they'll fall to Simon. *All* of it, will fall to him."

"Simon? Wait...." Kai's mouth widened. "Sun, Surf, and Sharks Simon?"

"You heard about that? I thought we'd stopped it in time."

"Comedy gold always leaks. Scorched Earth posted it."

Amelia's eyes narrowed. "Of course it did."

"So what's next? You roll over and hope Simple Simon fixes this? Or will you write a sternly worded email to dear old dad?"

Actually, that was exactly what she'd been thinking of doing. Something direct to Conrad that could be handled in-house. It would only work, though, if he didn't know. "Well, what would you have me do? Initiate a coup? If you have some genius idea, tell me."

"Isn't it obvious? Fight! Now, while you still can, before they go national with the points system. Fight for your staff. Fight to beat out Simon as CEO. Hell, why is he even in contention next to you?"

"I have baggage and he doesn't."

"Baggage? What, that you're a lesbian? Is that it?"

Amelia didn't answer.

"Shit, those Duxtons are awful. New depths." Kai shook her head. "Listen to you, though: you're snatching defeat from the jaws of victory. You could carve up that lesser Duxton in five minutes."

"Without board backing, that's irrelevant. My expertise, my experience... all irrelevant. Our best bet is that if I deliver a good speech tomorrow, I'll have a chance of beating Simon in the vote."

With a snort, Kai said, "One speech? It all comes down to that?"

"And maybe if I sign Nedal, too. But he may not be back in time."

"So...one speech."

"Yes."

"For a smart woman, you can be pretty naive about how things work. Machiavelli is *not* your middle name."

"Excuse me?" Amelia snapped.

"Can't you see it? They have you accepting that your fate rests on whether you do a nice speech extolling the virtues of Hotel Duxton or not. That is ridiculous. No CEO position is ever decided like that. Name even one CEO who got there because they gave a pretty speech?"

Amelia froze. Actually, it did sound absurd.

"You're being spun a line," Kai continued fiercely. "They're telling you this to sideline you in a way that you won't kick up a fuss about being passed over. And when you don't get the job, you'll assume your speech wasn't good enough—so, your fault. It's the same as their points scheme! Staff tolerate it because they believe any underpayment is *their* fault for a few minor mistakes."

"I hardly think it's the same thing."

Kai glared. "It is exactly the same, and it's total crap! Don't accept it. You're not just ice, are you? Where's your fire? I know it's in there; I've seen it. If it were me, I'd shout from the rooftops that the CEO job deserves to be mine."

"The chaos option?" Amelia shuddered. "I'm not like you. I prefer to reason with facts, and make a case that—"

"Amelia, wake up! You're being set up, railroaded, and ultimately you'll be demolished. And you're accepting it, passive as a lamb."

Passive as a lamb? Indignation shot through her.

Was Kai right? Amelia *was* being asked to accept possibly losing a job she'd earned without making a fuss.

One thing Kai *was* right about: one speech singing Hotel Duxton's praises wouldn't sway a single board member. They'd had years to know whether they wanted her or not. Giving her the suggestion of agency—the idea that winning the CEO position was all in her hands—felt like the lie. Which meant...

I've already lost.

Fuck! Amelia bit back a gasp. How had she lost *again*? It wasn't fair. It hadn't been fair the past two times, either, but she'd let herself have hope this time.

More fool me.

"Be bold." Kai was clearly still on a roll. "Kick some heads in, make some noise, be heard!"

Amelia cut her off with a growl. "Look, in my family, you don't blow things up to get attention. It's counterproductive. We do traditional, dignified, and conservative."

"And you hire conmen."

"Allegedly."

"Have you even looked into the scam? Who did it?"

"That has nothing to do with me anymore. It's your mess to figure out."

"Great, just great." Kai threw her hands up. "So in sum, you're powerless, your stupidest relative will become CEO, while all the abuses continue and, for extra fun, they'll roll out the points system nationally. You'll slide on back to Europe and forget all of this. You don't even care."

"I never said I didn't care. I said I don't have a way to fix it unless I'm CEO. And instead of pointing out all my weaknesses, maybe you should be more worried about your own position. The Closer, taken in by a conman? Imagine if that got out."

"Are you threatening me?" Kai's eyes widened.

"No! I'm pointing out we both have untenable positions now. Why is mine the only one you're fixating on?"

"Because yours has the potential to ruin thousands of lives! Mine will only ruin me. And honestly, I've been there, done that, got the T-shirt." Kai rose. "I can't believe I'm about to say this to a Duxton, but here goes: you're better than this! Okay?

"Kai—"

"No. Start acting like it. Stand up and fight. I don't care how, just do it now. Hold nothing back. Later is too late. If you believe nothing else, trust that."

"I need to fight, but I have no weapons!" Amelia protested. "Apparently I won't be CEO no matter how good my speech is tomorrow. So now what?"

"I don't know! It's *your* family—you know how they work. All I know is it's time to attack. Where's Amelia Duxton, the bold woman who kissed me senseless? Who just grabbed me and went for it!"

"Will you keep your damned voice down!" Amelia hissed at her. "And *that* woman isn't me."

"Sure looked like you." Kai's eyebrow lifted.

"Stop that." Amelia rolled her eyes. "So I had a…rare…moment of…I'm not sure what it was." She glared. "You bring it out in me for some reason."

Kai fell silent. She looked intrigued. "Don't you think it's interesting that we each bring out something in the other person that's out of the ordinary for us? You make me much more direct. And I draw out your spontaneous side. Together? It might even be dangerous."

"It's not dangerous, it's irrelevant!"

"Are you so sure?" Kai asked, a smile curling her lips. "We're good for each other. Think about that when I've left this evening." She rose to leave, then added ruefully, "And for God's sake, fix your damned family."

Amelia watched her go, not sure what to say, and no closer to any solutions.

After an hour more of staring at a wall, with few conclusions, she did what she'd planned to earlier and wrote a sternly worded email to her father. It outlined many of the abuses she'd learned from Milly, the dangers of the points system, and a warning for the future of Hotel Duxton.

She hit send, not even bothering to agonize over it line by line as she usually would. What was the point? He'd probably ignore it the way he had almost every other email she'd sent him for the past twenty years.

At midnight, Amelia sat bolt upright in bed. Suddenly she knew exactly what she could do to fix everything. She gasped at the idea. *What a staggering thought.*

Of course she'd never do it. It was ridiculous. Middle-of-the-night ideas usually were.

Besides, she wouldn't dare. "Daring" and "Amelia Duxton" were never used together in a sentence.

She tried to go back to sleep, but the audacious idea took hold and burrowed into her brain. Amelia sat up again. She might not be the next CEO, but she could prevent any more staff suffering under the points system. She would expose it to the world.

Within minutes, she was banging on the door to Quinn's room.

Together, they sat for the rest of the night and into the dawn, side by side, yawning, brainstorming, and typing up a storm. Quinn didn't complain once.

Amelia had chosen to ignore the Milly-shaped lump in Quinn's bed when she'd first banged on the door. It was for the best.

By five a.m., the Milly-shaped lump turned into an actual Milly who fetched them fresh tea and coffee and croissants and offered her own suggestions. She was shy at first, but when encouraged, the young woman opened up. She had a brilliant mind.

"Final draft," Quinn said, returning from the lobby where she'd used the printer. Her pajama collar stuck out from under a hastily tossed on gray hoodie. "Here." Quinn lay the paperwork in front of Amelia and passed a copy to Milly,

They all looked at the title of the speech Amelia would deliver tonight: *Hard Lessons Learned from Working Undercover in My Own Hotel.*

Five minutes later, Amelia put it down, a little impressed at her own audacity, and found Quinn and Milly gazing at her with a mix of pride and awe.

Amelia winced, unaccustomed to invoking either expression. "You have thoughts?"

"It's amazing," Milly whispered. "You cover it all. The points system. The fines. How some staff live in cars and…wow. All of it. Wow."

"What she said." Quinn smiled.

Amelia shuffled some papers to hide her self-consciousness. "I have a duty to speak for the voiceless. Now the issues will have to be addressed."

"Are you going to get fired?" Milly asked carefully. "I mean, won't your family think you're a traitor? Not to mention how they'll hate you revealing that they plan to spread the points system everywhere."

"They might fire me. But someone recently reminded me that standing by and doing nothing is as complicit as doing the evil myself."

"My boss does occasionally say profound things." Milly smiled.

"How do you know I meant her?" Amelia asked.

"It sounds like her. So will Quinn be all right, if they fire you?"

Quinn shot Milly a soft look that was altogether too mushy for a near-empty stomach.

"I'll make sure she has other prospects," Amelia assured them. "I have excellent contacts across the industry."

Amelia shifted and her back protested painfully. "God, I can't believe we worked through the night."

She glanced down at herself, still in her pale-blue cotton pajamas. Milly was the only one who'd taken the time to properly get dressed. Even so, she looked fairly rumpled.

"It was for a good cause," Quinn said. "The best."

God I hope so, Amelia thought. But what choice did she have? If the scheme spread, it would be disastrous enough. But what if it went global? It would break her heart if all her beautifully managed hotels fell prey to it, hurting staff and destroying all the goodwill she'd built up with her employees. This was her one chance to stop it dead.

"Conrad's gonna go ballistic, isn't he?" Quinn eyed her pensively.

Not just her father. The whole family would. "Yes. But I can't say that I adhere to honesty and transparency and only stick to it when it suits me. That would be hypocritical."

Which reminded her—it was time to do right in another area. She reached over to her paperwork and pulled out the Arabic fax as the other two women got more coffee.

Flattening the fax onto the table so she could see the time, date, and sender's number, Amelia sent an email to Tamara, asking Quinn's assistant to find out whose fax machine the number belonged to. Amelia added a query about which staff who had access to the machine were in the building at that time, according to the building's security logs. Finally, she told her the fax was in Arabic, in case that helped her investigations.

Done, she looked up just as a Skype request came in. Her father? She swallowed.

Conrad Duxton's thin face filled the frame as she hit Accept on the video call.

"Dad?"

"Amelia." His face was pinched. "I got your email. I need you to drop this nonsense investigating staff abuses and raising flags about the points system. God knows what barrel bottom you're scraping it all up from, but it's unseemly."

"I was only making sure that you knew—"

"I know. All of it. I have the situation in hand, and you're not helping. I suspect you are seizing on controversial rumors to agitate for attention to get the CEO position. Enough. The board has chosen, even if neither of us likes the outcome. They'll finalize their choice next meeting, but Simon is the next CEO. You making a fuss now will not alter that." He eyed her for a beat, then added with a faint sneer, "You had to know it was never going to be you."

Amelia's stomach plummeted. *And there it was. The truth.* "This—making a fuss—as you call it, was never about me. You were the one who taught me the principles of Pirkei Avot when I was a girl. *If I am only for myself, who am I?* I took those lessons to heart. This is about looking after our employees. And, as a nice side effect, doing that also prevents any lawsuits and publicity black eyes."

"Nice spin." He looked furious. "And how dare you try to manipulate me with scripture! That's rich, coming from you. Anyway, I won't have your bitterness at being passed over causing us problems. So, I'm telling you, stop. Finalize your work in Vegas, return to London, and focus on your own affairs. The end." He made a cutting motion, then leaned forward, jabbing a button.

The screen went black.

Anger surged. All this time, her father knew and didn't care. He *knew*!

The room felt uncomfortably silent, and she glanced up to see both Quinn and Milly staring. They'd heard every word. Her complete humiliation had witnesses. *Perfect.*

"I need a shower," she said, her voice tight. "And then I have a speech to memorize."

She strode into the bathroom without another word. As her father had pointed out, she needed to focus on what mattered. And what mattered were the vulnerable employees of Hotel Duxton International.

Chapter 20

Common Ground

KAI POKED OVER BREAKFAST IN the hotel's main restaurant, wondering why her assistant had yet to answer her texts. It wasn't like Milly to sleep in.

She still hadn't reached Mr. Stein, either. His cousin lunch funks rarely went for more than a day, but he hadn't yet returned her calls or emails. Maybe Rebecca was screening her?

In the meantime, she supposed she could make arrangements to track down Nedal's jet. Kai's conscience pricked her. Well, more like supplied an elbow to the ribs.

Should she do this? Amelia would be hurt if Kai snatched Mayfair Palace from under her nose. On the other hand, Amelia knew exactly who Kai was and why she was here. It could hardly surprise her if The Closer, when presented with a tip to get a deal she'd been wanting, went after it.

Still, though... This was Amelia's deal.

Kai blinked. What was Amelia to her that she'd even hesitate? She wasn't a friend, a lover, or family. She was a rival, from one of the world's nastiest families.

And yet...

Kai stared at her toast, unwilling to think too deeply about her hesitation. Well, she didn't have to decide now.

After breakfast, Kai went in search of Milly. She knocked on their adjoining doors. On getting no response, she poked her head in. No Milly, and no signs she'd slept in her bed. *Well, well.*

Five minutes later she was knocking on Quinn Hartman's door. Amelia's deputy answered, looking as if she hadn't slept a wink. Not in a delirious, post-coital lack of sleep way, either.

Milly sat at a table, chewing on a bowl of cereal and going through a purple folder. The same folder Kai and Milly used for filing Scorched Earth business.

A cold shudder went through her.

"Milly?" Kai stepped inside, eyes fixed on the folder. "Your phone's off."

Milly looked up in surprise and scrabbled around for her phone. "Oh! I'm so sorry."

"What's this?" Kai inclined her head at the folder, working to keep the accusation from her voice.

Quinn glanced between them. "I'm just going to get a quick shower. Leave you two to talk." She grabbed a handful of clothes and disappeared.

"I needed it for the presentation I gave last night to Ms. Duxton. She wanted proof of everything you've been saying."

"So she really was listening?"

"Yes."

"Did you..." She stared at the folder. Had Milly breached her privacy? Surely not.

"She has no idea you're..." Milly lowered her voice. "The Dragon. Quinn, either. They both think we're a bit obsessed about hotel injustice."

"I...see. So what did Amelia say?" Kai asked.

Milly paused. "Not much. But she had a face like one o'clock."

What? "Is that good or bad?"

"Bad. Very bad. Sorry, it's a thing Brits say. Quinn must be rubbing off on me."

"Mmm..." Kai stared pointedly.

Milly blushed and continued, "It was hard for Ms. Duxton to hear that about her family."

"It's hard for Duxton staff enduring their assholery."

"You know what I meant. Did you visit her last night after my text?"

"I did. The woman seems to have some absurd idea that she should stick to polite Queensberry Rules—as if that'll get her anywhere. Her family is playing her for a fool. I tried to put a rocket up her, but I doubt it worked."

"You might have been way more successful than you realize."

"Oh?" Kai glanced at all the papers strewn about. "Wait, why do you look like you *haven't* been up all night doing the wild thing?"

Milly hesitated. "We were helping Ms. Duxton with her keynote speech."

"I'm fairly sure you work for me, Milly."

"Yes. But it was important. I didn't think you'd mind."

"Important? Making the Duxtons sound good and respectable to the world?"

"The opposite, actually." Milly rummaged through some papers, and then held up a page. "This is her speech."

Hard Lessons Learned from Working Undercover in My Own Hotel.

Kai inhaled. "Are you serious? She's going to dump entrails all over her own company? Doesn't she know that the national media covers the keynote speech?"

"She knows. She said if she can't fix things as CEO, she can at least prevent it all spreading."

Kai stared. "She said what?"

"She said she won't stand by while evil flourishes."

Stunned, Kai muttered, "I don't believe it."

"Ask her yourself." Milly wandered over to the adjoining doors and gave them a nudge. "It doesn't sound like she'll be much longer on her Skype call."

There was a definite twinkle in her assistant's eye, and Kai wondered what joke she was missing.

She peered into the adjoining room. Amelia was in an armchair, her back to Kai and her laptop on her knees as she video-chatted with a little girl. The child looked maybe ten?

"I doubt you'd actually see a coyote in New York," Amelia was saying. Her voice was soft, warm, and gentle, and a shiver went through Kai. "I know you say there was a story about one on a roof in Queens but—"

"Auntie Lia, can I get one as a pet?"

"I thought you wanted fish?"

"Can I have both?" The child's face was so hopeful, Kai almost laughed.

"Coyotes are wild, darling. It wouldn't be good for either of you. It might eat you!" Amelia laughed.

The girl joined in laughing. "It wouldn't eat me! I'm all skin and bones. It might eat Dad!"

"I think he'd be too salty, all the surfing he does. Sorry, we have to rule out coyotes. How's the packing going?"

"Done. And Sally's going to take my fish and send me photos every day!"

"Every day? She sounds like a good friend."

"She is. I'll miss her."

"I know darling. You can call her, though."

"I will."

"All right, I have to go—I have a speech to memorize, and I can't believe how late it is for you. You shouldn't be up all hours."

"I can't sleep because of the move!"

"You certainly can't if you're talking to me. Bye, Imogen. We'll talk soon."

"Love you, Auntie Lia. Night!"

"Love you, too."

The screen went black.

So hard-ass Amelia had a secret soft streak. Kai wouldn't have believed it.

Amelia stood and turned, revealing that she was wearing a simple but flattering navy skirt and a white blouse, unbuttoned three buttons. *Oh Lord.*

Amelia turned, catching sight of them. "Visiting hour at the zoo?" she inquired.

"Sorry." Kai grinned. "And I have to say I'm on the kid's side. Who wouldn't want a pet coyote?"

"Of course *you* would, chaos agent that you are." Amelia glanced over her shoulder to Milly. "Where's Quinn? I need my speech printed in a bigger point size. My eyes are useless."

"Shower," Milly said. "I could get that organized for you." She glanced at Kai. "I mean, if you don't mind, Ms. Fisher?"

"Go on," Kai agreed. "I want to have a chat with Amelia anyway. It seems I slept through some interesting developments."

"You did." Amelia's eyes glittered. "Come on in. We'll talk." She flicked a glance at Milly. "Don't disturb us. I suspect your boss has a lot of apologizing she'd prefer to do in private."

Milly shot them both curious looks.

"I..." Kai began to protest. She gave up, nodded at Milly, and followed Amelia into the suite, closing the door behind them.

Amelia took in Kai's stunned expression. Her amusement built at the self-righteous woman, so sure she knew the Duxtons, lost for words.

"Drink?" she asked. "Snack? Perhaps...humble pie?"

Kai snorted. "Water, please." She sank onto the end of Amelia's bed.

Amelia fished a bottle from the minibar and found a glass. "I'm sure there's something you're dying to say."

"Are you really doing this? The speech?"

"I am."

"When I said fix your family, I didn't think you'd choose the thermonuclear option!"

"I'm exposing bad business practices before they spread—not just to Duxton hotels, but who knows how many other unscrupulous businesses might be inspired and decide it's worth copying?" She poured the water. "It was your idea to fight this. I don't know why you're so shocked now that I am."

"There's no walking this back if you do this."

Amelia handed her the glass. "How else to enact change? How else to be heard? I talked to my father and found out he already knew. Claimed the situation is *in hand*."

"They'll fire you. You, the only decent Duxton, and they'll toss you off a cliff."

"I thought all Duxtons were the same?" Amelia lifted an eyebrow.

"Yes, well." Kai took a sip. "I was wrong."

"I'm sorry, I didn't quite hear that. Surely my ears are failing me..."

With a roll of her eyes, Kai repeated: "I. Was. Wrong."

"And?"

"And what?"

"An apology for misjudging me. Please make it good. I have so little to amuse me these days."

Kai sighed. "You're loving this way too much."

"Perhaps. It's infuriating how you leap to conclusions. Calling me evil, for instance. I particularly resented that."

"I'm sorry. I did make assumptions that you were like the rest of your family."

Amelia winced.

"And I'm sorry they're like that. It must be hard."

Sympathy? Amelia didn't like the taste of that. She paced for a moment until she found herself standing in front of Kai.

Kai peered up at her.

Amelia met her eye. "So...you run Scorched Earth."

Kai gasped. "What? Who told you that?"

"You did. Just now. I wasn't entirely sure. Although it occurred to me earlier that Milly's dossier on abusive work practices reads like a Scorched Earth primer. Then I realized that all Scorched Earth's Duxton horror cases were in the folder, too. Did you think I wouldn't figure it out?"

Kai took a deeper gulp of water.

"I always wondered at The Dragon's hatred toward all things Duxton," Amelia continued. "As if they'd been personally injured by us. Quite slow of me not to join the dots sooner, actually."

Kai looked away.

"A bit unprofessional, isn't it? The Dragon heckling me from the cheap seats? You used my core values quote on Twitter to mock me. My words about guests feeling at home in hotels were heartfelt and you twisted them. And *hashtag Dunceton* is still trending, by the way."

"I'm sorry." Shame filled Kai's expression. "I didn't know you then. I thought you were just another entitled Duxton."

"Well, I'm not! You made me look a fool, then suggested my hotels were second rate. My hotels exude excellence, damn it!" Amelia's hand curled into a fist and she sank down onto the edge of the bed next to Kai.

"I'm so sorry I said that."

"It was *petty*."

"It really was. I was so mad at Oliver."

"So you decided to attack me."

229

"I was really only thinking about getting under Oliver's skin." Kai dipped her head. "I'm sorry I hurt you in the process, Amelia. You are not someone to be mocked." She reached for Amelia's hand. "I respect you. I was a total smart-ass on Twitter, and you didn't deserve it."

Amelia stared at her for a moment, assessing her authenticity. Seeing only sincerity, her shoulders sagged. "God, you're annoying." Amelia's words lacked fire this time. "So annoying."

"I really am," Kai conceded with a grin. She gave Amelia's hand a small squeeze.

Amelia glanced down, suddenly noticing the warmth of fingers around hers. She extracted her hand and said, "Finally, something we agree on."

"Oh, I'd say we agree on a few things."

"Really?" *Since when?*

"Well, we both think what your brother does with hotels is wrong."

Amelia had to concede that.

"We both enjoy each other's company in swanky bars called Prohibition," Kai continued, "Oh, and we hate the way Tim makes a Negroni."

Amelia snorted.

"And, the big one, we both find the other inconveniently attractive."

Amelia froze. "Speak for yourself."

"Come on, we have a spark. It's always there, every time we're in a room together. I loved it when you kissed me, and I know you did, too."

"Why are you so presumptuous?"

Kai smiled. "I'm not saying any of this as a come on. I'm just being honest. I don't know how this happened. God, you're the sister of the man who ruined me!"

Amelia sighed. "I'm sorry about whatever Oliver did," she murmured.

"You believe me now?"

"I asked him about it. He didn't deny it."

"Did he..." Kai paused, "at least sound regretful?"

Amelia pressed her lips together. "No. He sounded glad."

Kai's eyes hardened. "Did he tell you what he did?"

"Not in exact terms. He said there was an NDA..."

"That non-disclosure agreement is between me and Hotel Duxton. He could have told you if he wanted. The fact he didn't means he knows how underhanded he was."

"Will *you* tell me?"

Kai drew in a breath. "If I do, you'll hate him. It's why I didn't tell you before."

"I already hate him. He's the architect of the points system."

"Deeper than that. You'll hate all of him."

What has my little brother been up to? Amelia braced herself. "Tell me."

Kai drew in a steadying breath and began.

"In high school, I had a good friend who spent a few months, on and off, couch surfing with us when his parents kicked him out. When I left for college, Remi called me often, telling me all about his various jobs. He worked all over Manhattan's bars, clubs, restaurants, and hotels. Some of his stories were awful. We talked about what we could do but drew a blank because he didn't want a rep as a troublemaker. But within a few years, suddenly the internet was exploding and he called me up all excited with the idea of a whistleblower website. He had a friend who was good with computers create Scorched Earth for me."

"Did Remi work for Duxton?"

"Not back then, but later he wound up as a cleaner at Duxton New York. He was who convinced his coworkers to approach me about the abuses they experienced."

"You took that as a pro bono case, right?"

"No." Kai paused. "I only said that so you'd think they approached me as a lawyer. They didn't. They wanted *Scorched Earth* to expose their conditions. So The Dragon began naming and shaming Oliver for the abuse, given he was the boss of Duxton USA."

She shook her head. "My two worlds were separate—corporate lawyer and whistleblower. Then to my astonishment, one day Oliver turns up at my office wanting to see me. Just me. In return, as I mentioned before, he told my bosses he was considering them for all his legal work."

Kai's stomach twisted. "When he got his meeting, he pulled out a tape recorder, told me he wanted a personal record of our confidential meeting, then reeled off all the ways he screwed over his staff. Every case he could think of. Awful, cruel, ruthless, illegal crap. Far beyond what I'd ever suspected. I was staggered. I asked whether all his victims were suing. I said I hoped they were."

"What did he say?"

"He said, 'No, I'm destroying Scorched Earth.' I was shocked. Turned out he'd hired an investigator and found out who was behind the site. He said recording our conversation provided proof of what he'd shared with me confidentially. So any story I put on Scorched Earth about Hotel Duxton in the future, he'd say I'd heard it from him. Therefore, I'd disclosed confidential information that should have been protected by attorney-client privilege. He'd get me disbarred and also reveal who The Dragon really was."

Amelia's expression became pinched. "He hadn't even hired you at that point?"

"Ah," Kai said. "You think someone who hasn't officially hired a lawyer can't demand attorney-client privilege? No. The presumption of privilege exists in most US states, whether money has changed hands or not. It's not like on TV."

"I see. So, what was in the NDA you signed?"

"The deal was he'd never out me as The Dragon or as being affiliated with Scorched Earth. He knew that my being unmasked would decimate my career, given the rich and powerful were most often my targets. And they're who regularly need lawyers. I'd be political poison to employers. In return, I agreed to close Scorched Earth's website and never break stories on Hotel Duxton. I put up a Twitter feed, sure, but all it does is respond to news already out there. Essentially, Oliver broke The Dragon's back."

"You were blackmailed."

"Yes. Then he salted the earth so I'd never work in law again, demanding my bosses give out suspiciously unenthusiastic references in exchange for his future legal work. And Oliver did actually move some of his business to them, so they complied."

"I'm so sorry." Amelia sounded appalled. "How did you go from there to hotels?"

"I couldn't find a job, couldn't make rent, and I'd sold everything that wasn't nailed down. Finally, I conceded defeat and moved back in with my mom. The next week, I received an anonymous 'welcome home' parcel filled with homemaker goods, like a Martha Stewart stand mixer. The note said: 'To help with your new career. Cheerfully yours, Oliver.'"

Amelia ground her jaw. "Sounds like him."

"Not long after that, when I was looking at job ads for Bed Bath & Beyond, a hotelier turned up out of the blue."

"Stein?"

"Yes. He'd loved Scorched Earth and when it disappeared, he wanted to know why, and whether it could be resurrected."

"Of course he loved it; all it did was attack the Duxtons twenty-four-seven."

"No argument. Anyway, Mr. Stein had hired a private investigator to determine where The Dragon went. Get this—he hired the same investigator Oliver had. So Mr. Stein was at my door within the day. He sat down and said, 'My investigator says you're an excellent lawyer who wins many cases, yet your former employer warned me off hiring you. I know what that means. So I want to help, Kaida. While I'd love to hire you just to annoy Oliver, I also hear you have people skills and make good deals, and these are things I'm less good at. So, I'm thinking we should start you in Marketing? There's a vacancy there.'"

Kai drew in a breath. "Marketing? I almost threw him out on his ear. I was a trained lawyer, good at what I did."

"A trained lawyer looking at Bed Bath & Beyond ads."

"Well, there was that. But my ego was bruised. Anyway, he told me his hotels were expanding and soon he'd find something better suited to my skills. He kept his word. And that's why he has my loyalty. Mr. Stein rescued me when I was at rock bottom. He is a decent man and a good boss. I love him. I don't like to think where I'd have ended up without him."

Amelia digested that. "What happened to the cleaners? The ones who started your crusade?"

"They were all fired."

"And Remi?"

"He's now a trained masseuse at the Wellness Center at Grand Millennium Fitness."

"Quite a coincidence," Amelia's lips quirked. "Almost like he had a friend in high places. Would I be right that all those cleaners now work at Grand Millennium?"

"Funnily enough, most of them do."

Amelia smiled. "Good. I'm sorry my brother is such a bastard. I knew he had the streak in him. But hearing that…"

"You believe me?"

"Of course." Amelia gave her a startled look. "Aren't we beyond doubting each other by now?"

Kai met her eye. "Yes. We are."

"I…trust you." An uncertain expression washed Amelia's face. "I don't know how you accomplished that. I find myself in awe of how you picked yourself up again after what happened. I'm glad you didn't let my brother crush you under heel. I can see now why you were so angry when I blew in on Twitter, defending the Duxtons."

"Still, you were right: I was being petty."

Amelia's smile widened. "Obviously. But from your point of view, it would have been salt in the wound."

"Look at us…both on the same page." Kai reached for Amelia's fingers and tangled them with her own. "We certainly went places I never imagined."

Amelia shook her head. "No? I got the impression you imagined us extremely close when we first met." Her eyes glittered.

Kai laughed softly. "Well, yes. And I've never been shot down like that before. *Your proposal is lacking.* It hurt, don't get me wrong. But you forced me to consider who I was that night—the games I play, how often I play them, and why I do."

"That's why you're being more honest?" Amelia looked thoughtful. "Self-examination is a difficult thing. It's why most people don't do it. You're impressive."

Kai warmed at the compliment. "I'm impressive? Woman, your speech tonight is going to be incredible. It'll do more good than Scorched Earth ever could. You are putting *everything* on the line. This new spontaneous streak of yours is getting bolder by the minute. I can't even predict what you'll do next."

"Is that so?" Amelia looked pleased. "I've never been called unpredictable before."

"Never?"

"No. I have been called many names, but never that." Her expression darkened. "And I don't just mean by those who dislike me."

"What do you mean?"

"It's nothing... Never mind."

"Hey?" Kai studied the darkness that had seemed to come from nowhere. "Where did your mind just go?"

"A great many places—but it always does. I overthink everything."

"So tell me what you're thinking of? Please?"

Amelia sighed and closed her eyes. "At any given time, I have a dozen thoughts in my head. I'm weighing up scenarios, working out strategy, picking through emotions, hidden meanings I may have missed, determining likely outcomes, then less-likely outcomes, then..."

"Specifics." Kai said quietly. "What are your top thoughts right now?"

"You're beautiful," Amelia murmured. "I want to kiss you. I want, very much, to have you naked in my arms."

Kai drew in a breath as the visual image slammed into her. "Oh." Her voice was breathy.

"But I haven't been with another woman in a long time—at least two years. You certainly have. So I'm also working out..." She paused and licked her lips nervously.

"If I'm safe, health-wise?" Kai frowned. "I understand that would be important for you. So, full disclosure, my last check-up was six weeks ago. All clear. I've only had sex once since then..." She paused, recalling gorgeous Lacy Fox in the gym shower and her wandering hands. "But that didn't involve anything that could...um...limit our activities today."

"That wasn't what I was about to ask. Although, thank you. That was concern number four."

"You've numbered them?"

"Yes." Amelia gave her a rueful smile. "I was about to say, I'm working out how to overcome my nervousness in the face of your experience. People seem to have certain expectations about me. Most of my past lovers seemed to expect because I'm so powerful in my working life, that I'd somehow be legendary in the bedroom. It's a pressure that makes me so uncomfortable I tend to avoid dating much. And the times I've pushed past that discomfort, I've found the women tended to be disappointed I didn't move the entire universe. I'd hate to have that with you."

"I'm sure you didn't really disappoint them."

"Oh no, I did. That's what I meant by names I've been called. 'More uptight than Mother Superior' was my personal favorite." Amelia's face fell. "It's hard for me to disassociate. I get so tightly knotted, and the more I sense a lover's expectations, the tenser I get. With you my fears are worse, because on top of all that, I'm breaking my own rules to be with you."

"Which rules are those?"

"I don't sleep with women I'm not in a relationship with. That's my second highest concern this moment."

Kai asked gently: "What's concern number one for you?"

"What if...I'm so out of practice, I'm terrible?" Her eyes slid closed, and she turned her face away.

Beautiful, intoxicating Amelia Duxton had performance anxiety? Kai's heart clenched and her protective streak surged. "Amelia? I would love to be with you. You are captivating, inside and out, and that incredible mind of yours takes my breath away. But I have no expectations for you at all. None. If all we did is cuddle, I think my poor heart would die happy."

Amelia's dark expression shifted a little. "Really?"

"Yes. Since I've met you, all I've wanted is to be close to you. It was damn annoying when we were fighting, I can tell you." She rolled her eyes. "So right now I only have one question." Kai waited until Amelia's eyes were back on hers. "Do you want this?"

"Yes." Amelia looked conflicted. "Very much." She tangled her fingers. "I know I sound all over the place. Contradictory positions frustrate me more than anyone."

"It's okay. That's pretty human."

"I suppose." Amelia huffed out a breath. "And maybe it sounds as if I'm ambivalent about sex because I've been second-guessing myself so much. But it's not that. I really do enjoy it."

"Yet you don't pursue it."

"Well, I do have a European hotel division to run. That takes some effort." Amelia gave her an icy look, then sighed. "Sorry, a defense mechanism. I get annoyed when I'm questioned as to why I don't date. Quinn's learned only too well over the years to avoid the topic. But honestly, I really do miss sex at times. I miss the moment of orgasm. I love seeing a lover's eyes half close, and the delight in them when she can no longer hold back. Her breath becomes ragged. I love watching women lose control and being the cause of that. I find it exhilarating. That is…powerful."

"It is," Kai murmured.

"But in recent years, now all I see is the expectation. What people want from me. Sometimes it's the power, or the money, or the reputation—bedding the ice bitch. That last one tangles me up most. And now my brain tends to overthink everything to the point I can feel myself pulling away before I even kiss a woman. Protecting myself by being distant. You say you admire my intelligence. This is the downside of it. I don't know what to do to fix this. I'm sorry. This isn't very sexy, is it?" Shame tinged her tone.

"Oh, Amelia." Kai's heart went out to her. "You letting down your walls with me is the sexiest thing I can imagine. Your honesty is breathtaking. And I'd say the solution is simple."

"How so?"

"We just need to find a way for that over-productive brain of yours to short out for a little bit."

"Easier said than done." Amelia shot her a rueful look. "Unfortunately, I'm not easily distracted."

Kai smiled. "Well, your fancy brain hasn't dealt with me yet. *Naked* me."

Amelia's mouth opened, but no words came out. "Oh," she finally said.

"You're thinking about it, aren't you?" Kai smirked.

"I… Maybe." Amelia licked her lips and her eyes became half lidded. "Yes."

"Good." Kai held out her hand. "Now by the time I'm finished, you won't have time to wonder about your talents because I intend for you to be a wet, exhausted, happy puddle. And then, when we've taken the edge off, we'll start again. And we'll keep going, again and again if we have to. Because there is no way we're going to let a stupid thing like expectations, real or imagined, ruin the fabulousness that is *us*. Okay?"

Amelia shook her head "I hope you know it's not that simple."

"It is." Kai smiled. She pulled Amelia's hand until they were standing facing one another. Kai gave her a scorching gaze. "Remember when you were just Lia Hanson, anonymous woman, flirting with me at the bar?"

Amelia frowned. "I don't underst…"

Kai slid her hands around to Amelia's ass. *Lord, that skirt is sinful.* "Shh, no overthinking. We have a lot of sexy gray matter to distract." She kneaded Amelia's soft swells of ass, enjoying the tactile pleasure of linen and muscle.

"Kai," Amelia said a little more breathly. "I wasn't flirting that night."

"You so were." Kai's racing heart began to kick up a gear. "Biting my ear. Sexy minx," she teased.

"That bite was completely unexpected." Amelia tried to look imperious, but Kai could see right through it to the doubt, fear, and...burning need.

"Unexpected on both our parts. Have you considered that Lia Hanson had no fears?" She gave Amelia's ass another squeeze.

"Why do you keep mentioning Lia?"

"Because she never gave a moment's thought to expectations. She was free and unfiltered and fun and quite possibly a CIA operative—who can say?"

Amelia laughed. It was sudden and stark in the quiet of the room, and her shoulders relaxed. "You're ridiculous."

"So you keep telling me." Kai smiled. "Okay, stay right there." She left Amelia to throw the lock on the adjoining doors, then slipped a *Do Not Disturb* sign outside the main door. She returned and gathered Amelia's hand back in hers. "Now then, back to Operation Distraction... Let's cut to the chase." She offered her most sensuous smile. "I believe the burning question was asked: what happens when fire meets ice?"

Amelia's voice was low and throaty when she replied: "I think we both know the answer. It's steam."

"Yes," Kai reached for her, and slipped a hand under Amelia's skirt. "It is."

Chapter 21

Steam

KAI LEANED IN, PRESSING AMELIA against the wall. "Focus on what I'm doing to you. Feel my hand?" she whispered. "I love how soft your thigh is." She inched Amelia's skirt up higher with her wandering fingers. "I plan to touch every bit of you." She kneaded Amelia's skin. "How will that feel? Would you like my fingers on you? My tongue trailing up your body?"

Amelia's nostrils flared, and her pupils darkened. Her lips pursed. "Yes."

Kai's hand slid up higher still. She leaned in and kissed her.

When Amelia moaned softly against her lips, the sound was as arousing as silk dancing against nipples. Kai's breath was ragged as they parted, her eyes searching Amelia's face. All she found was desire and hope.

"You're a superb kisser," Kai murmured, turning to nibble against Amelia's throat. "I could kiss you all day. But then other parts of you might feel neglected." She shifted her hand under Amelia's skirt, savoring the naughtiness of all that bare thigh.

The flesh under her fingers quivered. Kai smiled.

Teasingly slow, Kai let the back of her hand rise until it connected with damp silk. *Ooh. Already wet.*

The flash of embarrassment across Amelia's face told Kai she was only too aware of that fact.

"I'm wet, too," Kai whispered, rubbing against Amelia's sex. "I can barely stand, you have me so turned on."

Amelia's jaw clenched and she said nothing, but her chest rose and fell more quickly.

Kai thumbed a crease into Amelia's panties, the material only becoming more damp under her playful ministrations. "My God, women are incredible. So responsive. I'm dying to be inside you."

Amelia's breath hitched as she swayed in, chasing the friction of Kai's hand. A flush crept up her neck as she found purchase with Kai's fingers and shamelessly rubbed herself against them.

Kai's nipples hardened at the sight of complicated, tightly wound Amelia Duxton straining against her hand. Kai became so wet, she wondered if there was any moisture left in any other part of her body.

Nudging aside Amelia's silken underwear, Kai pushed her finger through slippery flesh. She barely touched, though, just teased, gently around the edges, playing with her.

Amelia whimpered. "Oh," she said, voice strained. "Please."

Please. Kai inhaled sharply. "Please, as in you would like me inside you? Or please you want me on my knees, right now, my tongue against you? Or perhaps you'd prefer to be bent over a table as I grind into you?"

"*Oh.*" The heat in Amelia's cheeks had turned scarlet. She swallowed.

"Or all of the above?" Kai suggested, then slid a finger inside. "We can do that."

Amelia's clenching body pulled Kai's finger deep inside, so Kai added another.

"I don't think I can keep standing," Amelia said, voice tight as a bow string. Her thighs trembled.

Kai pinned her in place against the wall. "You will. I'll be here to catch you if you fall. Put your leg around my waist. I need more of you."

Amelia complied, her thigh slipping over Kai's hip, and Kai leaned in with purpose. "Now, to take the edge off." She slid her thumb over Amelia's clit, then swirled all around it, tapping, teasing, and toying, as her fingers thrust deeper inside.

Amelia's head banged against the wall and she gasped. "Faster."

Kai complied, thrusting, then swirling, thrusting, then…

"Oh. Oh!" Amelia tightened around Kai's fingers, and she trembled all over. Her eyes squeezed shut. "Oh yes."

Kai rubbed harder. "I think I'll do you on my knees next," she said conversationally. "How will that feel? My tongue fucking you instead of my hand."

Amelia gasped. The trembling magnified, and her words became incoherent as she flew apart. A soft cry in the back of her throat signaled she was there. "Oh," she finished, and sagged against the wall. "My God."

Kai leaned into her and examined the rumpled woman with immense satisfaction. So beautiful. She whispered in her ear, "Can't wait to taste you."

Amelia's eyes flew open. "Well," she said, giving a boneless wave. "I can't even think of anything to say to that."

"Then we have success. One fried brain." Kai grinned.

A small smile tugged at Amelia's lips. "Exceptionally fried." Her eyes slid to Kai's body, and her expression became appreciative and heated. "You're wearing far too much."

"I thought you might like to fix that for me." Kai's lips curled.

"Hmm. Or I might just prefer to enjoy the show of you stripping for me, Kaida."

A tremble shot through Kai at the way Amelia said her name. Commanding and cool, this was the woman she was used to seeing in business mode. There was something so arousing about this side of Amelia. The put-together, take-charge woman. The woman she'd first seen in the lobby.

Amelia's eyebrow cocked at her reaction, apparently working out exactly what was making Kai shiver and squirm. Amusement crossed Amelia's face, and with it seemed to come an understanding that she held the power. She straightened.

Oh hell, Amelia with her mojo back would probably kill Kai.

As if reading her mind, Amelia said, "I think I'm ready to test out my talents on you." Her voice was thick and interested.

Kai quivered. Amelia, looking at her like *that*? Kai's whole body seemed lit up, every burning nerve ending suddenly alive. She'd never wanted a woman so much. And seeing Amelia's dark, amused, definitely interested look was sending flares of arousal through her.

"Undress," Amelia ordered, as her fingers fell to her own shirt's buttons.

Bossy. God, that was hot. Kai began to tear off her clothing, eyes fixed on her lover.

Amelia stripped with the speed and efficiency she seemed to do most things in life. Shirt quickly unbuttoned, then pulled from her torso. Black, soft bra, unsnapped, dropped to the floor. Her small breasts swayed into view and bobbed as she leaned over and slid her tailored skirt down, followed by her panties.

Behind those designer executive suits, Amelia hid a beautiful body. Her pale skin was sleek, smooth, and toned. At the sight of Amelia's hard nipples and…her eyes slid south…undeniable wetness, Kai's breath caught. Commanding Amelia Duxton was even more intimidating naked than she was clothed.

Kai hurriedly kicked off the rest of her clothes, then stood naked before her.

Amelia straightened, too, her strong, imposing angles just stunning. Everything about her screamed power and confidence.

Amelia trailed a heated gaze across Kai's body. "Very beautiful. I always imagined you would be."

She imagined me. Kai grinned at that.

Reaching up, Amelia trailed the backs of her fingers down Kai's cheek. They dropped to her neck, then slipped lower to her breast before falling away. "*So* delicious." Her tone became low and authoritative when she said, "Get on the bed, Kaida. I intend to do a lot more than look."

Mouth going dry, Kai obeyed.

Amelia's gaze felt like a touch as it lingered on Kai's exposed position. Her eyes burned.

Kai spread her legs wide, and Amelia's eyes virtually stroked between her legs, her breasts, her arms, and face, finally landing back between her thighs, where her gaze stayed…and sharpened.

Amelia was upon her in seconds, prowling up Kai's body, her expression filled with a desire fierce enough to immolate them both.

Where had *this* woman been hiding?

Leaning down, Amelia kissed her. It was explosive and heady—but naked kisses always were. Amelia lowered her body and molded herself to Kai, tugging her close and digging fingers into her back. She pressed their centers together, raking teeth-grazing kisses down Kai's neck.

Slipping farther down her body, Amelia covered Kai's breasts with slippery kisses. Her tongue teased Kai's nipples, while a hint of teeth threatened to make her pay, indeed.

Kai was barely able to hold back by the time Amelia's hot breath washed her clit. Then her tongue pressed against Kai's flesh, into her, and up again. She flicked and laved all over Kai's most sensitive spots, drawing out helpless moans and trembles.

Oh God. Of course Amelia Duxton would be a goddamned efficiency expert at cunnilingus, too. She was so focused, so clever in her strokes, teasing then hard, withholding then generous. The woman could hold a masterclass in torturing women with pleasure. How she could ever doubt herself was a complete mystery.

Amelia paused her slippery, heated trails and met Kai's gaze, asking a silent question as her fingers circled Kai's entrance.

"Yes," Kai whispered. "Fuck, yes."

Amelia's lips twitched, and she slid inside Kai—one finger at first, then two. She stroked firmly and then lowered her mouth back to its teasing games.

Kai's brain melted. How could a woman as famously cold and tightly wound as Amelia love a woman's body with so much intensity, softness, and feeling?

Amelia had a lot of feelings, it turned out. She murmured them against Kai's swollen flesh, the words vibrating. *You're beautiful, Kai. How delicious you taste. You're making me so aroused. God, I'm soaking. I think I will allow you take me over a desk as you suggested. How will* that *feel?*

Kai bucked and cried out. Raggedly, she combed Amelia's hair with shaking fingers, urging Amelia's talented mouth on, before finally letting go. She didn't so much tumble over the precipice as fly above it and shatter into pieces.

"S-stop now. Oh, Amelia. *You.* Christ."

Amelia's head lifted, lips wet and curling. The devilish glint in her eye revealed how much she'd enjoyed seeing Kai lose control. She stayed above Kai, leaning on her arms, watching her recover. Then she turned to Kai's inner thigh, sliding her lips all the way along it, as if claiming the whole leg as hers.

It was sensuous as hell. Kai trembled anew. "Fuck," she whispered. "That was... You were..." *Fuck.*

A small, pleased smile was playing around Amelia's lips.

"You enjoyed that," Kai said.

"You have no idea how much." Amelia looked decidedly pleased with herself. "Thank you. For reminding me just how much fun it can be. I get too much into my own headspace. You are a tonic."

"We're not done yet." Kai eyed her. "Not even close. I get another turn with you."

"Mmm." Amelia rolled onto her back. Splayed out like this, waiting to be attended to, she looked like a commanding queen. A naughty one.

Kai's mouth went dry.

"Well? I haven't got all day," Amelia drawled.

Kai laughed and gently slapped her stomach. "You'll pay."

"That was the general idea." Amelia's eyes darkened with arousal. "Do you always talk so much when you should be doing? How did you ever seal those deals, *Closer*?"

Kai trembled at the taunting way she said it. There was demand in that question, and *so* much desire.

Without answering, Kai bent down. She started by lavishing every part of Amelia's body with kisses, discovering which places made her squirm, which made her tremble, and most especially, which made her gasp. Kai spent a lot of time on those latter spots.

Amelia loved being teased, Kai discovered. Loved being played with. Loved delicate licks and soft touches over forceful swipes of tongue. For a woman who enjoyed power, she could be turned into a mewling kitten quite easily.

Her breath was ragged, her thighs twitching under Kai's soft touches, but her gaze had not once left Kai's eyes. Her expression said just one thing: *Make me come.*

"Patience," Kai whispered, and bent forward. She waited until Amelia trembled, her eyes filled with need, before she made contact.

Kai slid her tongue gently, sweetly, softly, over Amelia's swelling flesh. She did it over and over, until Amelia's back went taut, her whitened hands fisted the sheets, and her neck snapped back, arching. She cried out. It was only one word, over and over. "*Oh.*"

Her eyes suddenly snapped shut as her body bucked, twisted, then slumped.

Kai nuzzled the flesh before her, enjoying the taste of Amelia's arousal and the tiny, residual twitches of her ecstasy.

Amelia's eyes fluttered open, and she sighed. "My God," she murmured. "It's been ages since I've felt like that."

Kai slid up next to her and hooked a thigh across Amelia's stomach and hips, claiming her. Because there was no way she was letting a woman like this slip out of bed and away. Not after this.

"Me, too."

Amelia cocked an interested eyebrow. "Really?"

"Yes." Kai nodded. "That was…mind blowing. And I have to say, it was off-the-charts thrilling making you lose control. I'd guess this is the only time you do give up control?"

"I suppose." Amelia's eyes drifted closed. "I rarely experience feeling uncontrolled. It's like fear meets ecstasy. It heightens the experience."

"So, can we do it again soon? I mean, I'm going to need a lot more memories like that stored up for after you've gone home to London."

"Storing memories?" Amelia snorted. "There's a line if ever I heard one."

Kai grinned. "Probably. But say yes anyway?"

"I'd like to." Amelia hesitated. "But I'm not sure beyond today where I'll be."

"Why?"

"After my speech, I may be fired."

"So…you're saying you could be open to staying here? In the States?" Kai asked, startled at how much hope was in her own voice.

Surprise darted across Amelia's face. "I thought you didn't do relationships?"

"For every rule, there can be an exception."

Amelia reached out and stroked the bare thigh draped across her hip. "Will you explain what you mean?"

"I don't fully know *what* I mean," Kai admitted. "Just that I don't want you to go."

"From bed?"

"From me."

That had slipped out. Wasn't it too soon to be making plans? Wait, what if Amelia thought they were done now? "I…ah…"

"I think it'd be interesting being in a relationship with you," Amelia said casually.

"Interesting?" Kai asked, trying to hide the rush of relief.

"Yes, in the Chinese proverb sense. Chaotic, unpredictable, fascinating, maddening, and so on. But I was under the impression relationships were off the table. Are they or are they not?"

Trust Amelia to cut to the chase. "Well, we do have the problem that we live in different countries."

"That's true. Although that could change rather soon, given I'm not sure where I'll be living." She searched Kai's face. "Why do you want a relationship with me after so long of not wanting them at all?"

Kai hesitated. The answer felt too big to explain in words. "You're different."

"So I'm often told," Amelia said dryly.

"I mean you're unlike anyone I've ever met. I find your intelligence, your sense of right, so attractive. Then there's your body. *Divine.* I can't even think about letting you get out of bed right now without feeling disappointed." She tightened her leg a little over Amelia's hips.

Amelia smiled and ran her hand appreciatively over that bare thigh. "You make an excellent argument." Her hand stilled. "Kai, this feels like something, doesn't it? Not just...fun?" A hint of vulnerability crept into her face.

"It feels a lot more than fun, which makes it kind of terrifying for me." Kai swallowed.

Amelia smiled softly. "Well, if it helps, I'm out of my depth, too. It's been a long time since I've seriously considered a relationship. On the other hand, aren't we both excellent problem solvers? Did we not just find a way for me to overcome my doubts about taking you to bed? I find it impossible to believe we can't just handle any issues that crop up."

She looked so aggrieved at the idea that anything would dare stand in their way for longer than a minute that Kai laughed.

"God, I love your confidence. It's hot."

"You are breathtaking, Kai. Not just for this"—Amelia's fingers trailed Kai's thigh—"but for your compassion. The way you fight for others. And, most of all, your clever mind. I noticed that most the first time we met, even though you were alternately annoying and intriguing. I never did decide that night whether I liked or disliked you."

With a laugh, Kai suggested, "Both?"

"I suppose." Amelia rolled her eyes. "Yes, fine. Both."

Kai chuckled. "I can't believe I'm contemplating a relationship with a Duxton."

"It could be worse," Amelia said with a huff. "Imagine one with The Closer."

Kai nudged her. "Has anyone ever told you you're hilarious?"

"Not a soul. Maybe you're imagining my hilariousness?"

"That must be it." Kai eyed her. "We could lie here all day, you know," she said hopefully. "I have no plans beyond trying to track down my boss. He's been AWOL since lunch with his cousin yesterday."

"Ah. Well, all I have left to do is call my uncle. Tell Joe that..." She paused for a beat, as if deciding something. "Tell him Nedal phoned me first thing this morning to update his travel plans. When I'm giving my speech tonight, Nedal's jet will be landing at Farnborough Airport in London, at seven a.m. their time."

Kai froze. "Why would you tell me that?"

"Because I want you to know I trust you. If we're to have something together, we need trust. I'm aware you could jet off anytime in the next six hours and be in time to meet Nedal and maybe steal my deal. There's nothing I can do about it. But I don't believe you'd do that." Her eyes held a question.

Guilt filled Kai. Hadn't she once considered doing just that? But that had been before they'd... *before*.

"I won't steal your deal, Amelia."

"Well, that's good," Amelia said lightly. "Because I'd like to go out in style from Hotel Duxton. Between signing Mayfair Palace and tonight's speech, I don't think they'll forget me in a hurry. Although, given how bad I am at public speaking, they might remember me in a whole other way."

"No, you're going to give the speech of your life," Kai said firmly. "Know why? Because this isn't about you or the suits in the crowd. It's about the employees you'll be speaking for. When you're on that stage, just remember why you're doing it. You'll knock it out of the park."

"You're really good at that," Amelia said. "Pep talks."

"I believe in my material—which is you. On that note, can I read your speech?"

Amelia glanced at their naked, entwined bodies. "Now?" Her brows hit her hairline.

"Yes. And may I say, what better proof can I offer that I want more from you than your hot body?" She climbed out of bed. "Where is it?"

"You think I have a hot body?" Amelia pointed. "On the table by the window."

"Hottest ever." She rummaged around and found the speech. Kai turned back to see a reddish tinge on Amelia's cheeks. "What?"

"You're stark naked. I'm distracted."

Kai grinned. "Hmm. It's cold out here. I think you should warm me up somehow while I read your glorious speech." She bounded back to bed.

"I'm sure there's something called a blanket."

"Think harder. Be more creative," Kai said, yanking a sheet over herself.

"I'm not really known for my creativity. That's more your domain."

"No? Who worked out how to have nearly full vacancy rates during the financial crisis?"

"That's different." Amelia's hand slid across Kai's stomach, a sign she apparently did know a few things about warming a girl up.

"How so?"

"It was about hotels. I was playing to my skills."

"You have more than a few skills," Kai murmured appreciatively. "And not all are focused on hotels."

"You and your smooth lines." Amelia smiled.

With some difficulty, Amelia tried not to think about all the ways her body was singing with arousal as Kai lay against her, reading her speech. She traced circles across Kai's bare stomach.

She'd been a revelation when they'd made love. Kai was beautiful and had been so responsive. Her breasts were a delight, with plump nipples that loved being teased. Then there were her long, lean legs. Amelia had mapped the powerful muscles in those for some time. She was quite sure she could feast on Kai Fisher for days and never tire.

Such intense desire felt foreign to her. Perhaps she should be panicking? Except her overactive brain seemed to be switched off, and all she wanted now was to stay right here, with her hand tracing circles over Kai's belly, listening to her soft breathing.

Finally, Kai put the speech down. "It's…not bad."

Oh. Well. What had she expected? High praise? Did it need a rewrite? There was still time. She sat up. "If it's awful, I need to rework it."

"Nope, slide back on down, little lady," Kai pushed Amelia's shoulder to horizontal again. She retrieved Amelia's hand, placing it firmly back on her stomach. "That's not what I meant. What you say about staff exploitation is explosive stuff. Brilliant. It'll pin back the ears of all those executives. The media will eat this up."

"Then what's the problem?"

"You're the problem."

"Excuse me?"

"You're not capitalizing on your speech. It's a list of crap things, with no way forward. There's no bright ending—nothing about the future."

"How can there be a bright ending? Hotel Duxton is abusing their staff."

"Right, and you give no solutions. All you're saying is 'Don't do this.'" Kai grabbed a pen from the nightstand and started scribbling. "I know you're going to fight me on this, but trust me." After a minute, she handed the last page of the speech back. "Say that."

Amelia stared at the words. "Absolutely not. I'll sound self-serving, as if I've only exposed any of this to shout about my bid to be CEO."

Kai met her eye earnestly. "Amelia, I was wrong when I said one speech couldn't get someone a CEO job. This is the exception to that rule. And your audience needs to know two things: that Duxton management is in flux right now, and that you're the answer. They need to know that if you were CEO, you'd fix this. The media will champion you. And that puts Conrad in an awkward position—trying to choose anyone other than you will look like poor judgment."

"It's not *me* to be shouting to the world 'Pick me!' I can't just say that."

"Even if you are the best choice? Come on, how many mediocre managers have you seen who talk themselves up and can't deliver? Those men strut around like they're God's gift to business even if they can't run a bath. You *can* deliver, and all you have to do is say that you're the right leader to fix things."

249

"It's…" Amelia cast around for the right word. "Undignified."

Kai snorted. "It's accurate. Own it."

"I don't feel comfortable—"

"Listen: We both know how this will end if you don't make a public play for CEO. You get fired. Hotel Duxton keeps doing what they're doing since Simon's so weak he'd approve anything put in front of him. That includes making the points system national—hell, global. How would you feel seeing your beloved European hotels forced to use that toxic system even if you no longer work there?"

Horror filled her. "I'd hate it."

"So, stop it. Stand up and be the hero."

"I'm no hero."

"You will be if you succeed. Your employees will cheer."

"My employees hate me. I'm the ice bitch."

"After this, you'll be a god."

Amelia sighed. "I don't want to be a god. I just want our hotels to be efficient and fair."

"You know, 'Option c) All of the above' is possible if you do this."

Silence fell. Finally Amelia stopped frowning and nodded. "All right. Thank you." She offered a wry smile. "Don't hate me for saying this, but in one selfish way I'm glad you left law."

Kai's expression fell. "Why?"

"If you were still a practicing lawyer, you wouldn't be here now."

Kai's eyes widened, and a smile touched her lips. "Amelia Duxton, you romantic."

"Hush. I didn't mean it that way." She hesitated. "Or maybe I did."

Kai chuckled. "*Mushy* Amelia Duxton. It's a miracle."

Amelia poked her in the ribs. "Don't start—I am never mushy."

Kai leaned up and kissed her soundly. "A pity—because *starting* something was exactly what I had in mind."

"Ah…" Amelia gave her an interested once-over. "Well, who am I to argue with The Closer?"

It was late afternoon by the time Kai's eyes fluttered open again. One lovemaking session had turned into several more, broken up by room service, and more of Amelia working on her speech until they'd both declared it as good as it was going to get.

That had led to additional practical celebrations, before exhaustion had overtaken them.

Kai yawned and glanced at the clock. 5:11 p.m. The sinking sun was its usual deep red, settling over Vegas's towering buildings and ever-present billboards as lights were starting to blink on.

She glanced at Amelia, whose breathing was deep and even. Kai wasn't surprised—she'd been up most of the night writing that speech.

Kai let her sleep, knowing Amelia's alarm would go off soon enough, in time for her to get ready to deliver it. Besides, why spoil this rare sight of her lover with her mask down? All warm and naked, tangled up in rumpled sheets, Amelia was so peaceful without her chilled persona that kept the world at bay.

A beep sounded. Again. Kai recalled her phone had rung while she was busy with Amelia. She crept out of bed to retrieve the voicemail.

Ms. Fisher, Todd Burbridge, the New York Times Business and Economics section. Just saw the tweet. Congrats! I'd love a quote to go with a story about the sale. This is huge. I'm assuming you nailed this one, but correct me if I'm wrong. Call me.

Kai swallowed. *What the hell?* With shaking fingers, Kai jumped to Twitter and scanned impatiently. And there it was, in Mr. Stein's feed:

Grand Millennium is delighted to announce it will be buying the world-class Mayfair Palace hotel, London.

Panic surged. *Oh shit, oh shit, oh shit.*

Why had Mr. Stein assumed she'd signed? Why had he tweeted without checking? What a disaster!

Kai flung her clothes on and bolted for the door, shooting Amelia a regretful glance.

Chapter 22

Wake-up Call

KAI BANGED ON THE DOOR to Quinn's room, then glanced around the hallway. No one was about, which was good, because she was fairly sure she looked like a nightmare.

Her calls to Mr. Stein's office and private cell had not been answered. Her email saying to delete the Tweet had been ignored. It still remained online three minutes after she'd first seen it, which was twenty-two minutes after it had first been posted at 4:49 p.m. Vegas time.

Milly opened the door to Quinn's room, tightening the belt on a hotel robe. "Well, you're not room service." She smiled.

"No." Kai frowned. "Get dressed; I need you now."

Milly's smile evaporated. "Everything okay?"

"No. It is very much *not* okay."

"What happened?" Milly walked to a nearby chair, reaching for a pile of clothes.

"Work." Kai couldn't go into this now. She needed her highly efficient assistant to *hurry the hell up*.

Quinn stepped up to the door as Milly disappeared out of sight with her clothes. "Can I help?"

"No." Kai's panic magnified at the thought of this becoming everyone's business. "Thanks."

She most definitely didn't want the Duxtons involved in any part of Mr. Stein's mess. Better yet if they never got wind of this train wreck. "It's Grand Millennium business."

"Ah." Quinn shifted to the side, allowing a now-dressed Milly to pass. "Well, good luck."

Milly offered her a soft smile then followed Kai. "What's up?" she asked, speeding up to keep pace with Kai's stride.

"Not yet. When we're in my room." Not that it was likely anyone would overhear them, but her chaotic brain was throwing up all sorts of dire scenarios.

Finally, when Kai had shouldered her room's door shut behind them, she passed her phone to her assistant, cued up at the text. "We're about to become a public joke."

Milly gasped. "Why would he—"

"I don't know. I can't reach him." Kai paced the suite.

"He sent it at 7:49 New York time," Milly said. "It's already been online for—"

"I'm well aware of when it was sent," Kai snapped. "Half an hour ago." Was Milly suggesting she'd been so busy lost in Amelia that she'd dropped the ball here? Guilt surged. *Had* she dropped the ball?

"If you couldn't reach Mr. Stein, what did Rebecca say?"

Kai paused. In her panic, she hadn't thought to call her boss's PA. She still wasn't sure if Rebecca could be trusted.

At Kai's lack of answer, Milly pulled out her own phone. "I'll ask."

Kai nodded and resumed pacing, ears sharp on Milly's end of the conversation.

"Okay, thanks, Rebecca." She hung up the phone and turned to Kai.

"Well?" Kai stopped.

"She's in the dark. He sent her home early this evening, saying he had to go out. His phone's off now, but he obviously sent the tweet from wherever he is."

"Shit!" This made no sense.

"Rebecca says she'll pass our concerns along when he makes contact again."

Kai shook her head. "That isn't good enough. We don't even know if Rebecca's screwing with us. Contact our pilot. We have to be in New York *now*."

"But aren't we staying for Ms. Duxton's speech?"

"You want to spend more time with your girlfriend, you mean?" Kai said snidely.

Hurt seared across Milly's face before the assistant grabbed her phone and began tapping.

Damn it. She hadn't meant that. Kai had known for days about the fake Nedal, and she should have tried harder to get the information to Mr. Stein instead of waiting to talk to him. All this respecting his space because of his damned cousin lunch! She should have protected him better. Still, she shouldn't take it out on the world's sweetest human. "Sorry, Milly."

"I'm not asking to stay for Quinn," Milly said, a hint of censure in her voice. "But on the topic of girlfriends, wouldn't Ms. Duxton expect you at her speech?"

Girlfriend? Mild panic fluttered through Kai at the word. Although, the title "lovers with tentative relationship plans" didn't exactly roll off the tongue.

Gah! She couldn't think about any of this now. Did she want to be around for Amelia's speech? Of course! But Mr. Stein was being manipulated somehow and she had to save him and Grand Millennium's reputation. That took priority.

"Amelia has the brain of five Mr. Steins," Kai said firmly. "She'll be fine. *He* needs me."

Milly looked ready to argue but then closed her mouth.

"He'll be ruined if I don't get on top of this," Kai continued. "I need to be on the ground at Grand Millennium, doing damage control, working out strategy, fixing this and whatever's about to hit us next. Have you contacted the pilot?"

"I've texted him. He'll be ready."

"Good. Go pack. I'll meet you downstairs in ten."

At the front desk, a young man Kai didn't recognize checked them out. *The turnover problem strikes again.*

"Can I help you with anything else, Ms. Fisher?" He slid her credit card back.

Kai paused. "I'd like to leave a message for someone. Amel...Lia Hanson. Room eight-thirty-three."

"Certainly, ma'am." He slid a notepad and pen over. "I'll see your message gets to her."

She stared at the blank page. What could she say? She'd left the woman after sex. That was not a good look when they'd made certain undertakings. Amelia might take her departure as disrespectful, even though this was an emergency. So she had to explain herself well.

Okay. Um...

She tapped the page.

Christ.

"Ms. Fisher?" Milly appeared. "We have a taxi."

Amelia stared sightlessly at her assistant, trying to understand the young woman's words, her eyes dropping back to the notepad. Panic rose.

Milly glanced at it and comprehension seemed to dawn. "I have Quinn's details. I can ask her for Ms. Duxton's number. You could call her on the way to the airport and explain."

Of course! She was over-complicating everything. "Yes," she said, then glanced at the man. "Never mind." She pushed the notepad back at him.

"No problem. I hope you enjoyed your stay," he said automatically.

Kai's lips twisted. "It was...an experience."

Amelia's rumbling stomach woke her. Not exactly surprising given she'd skipped breakfast, then burned quite a few calories with Kai and had only a small snack for lunch—followed by even more hedonistic delights.

She rolled over to ask Kai about dinner plans for after her speech, only to find hastily flung back sheets and a missing lover.

Amelia sighed. Duty had no doubt called. Kai had a work ethic matched only by her own. She smiled at the reminder of their lovemaking. When was the last time she'd felt so free to be herself? No walls, no games, no expectations. Not since Mariam had she felt like her old self. It was wonderful feeling so normal and desired for who she really was. It had been a long time since she'd felt like any other woman—taking a lover for that simple, honest connection.

But it was more than a connection, wasn't it? Kai seemed to *know* her, even if it was purely instinctual. She had somehow figured out how to push past all Amelia's frustrating blocks that had cursed most of her relationships after Mariam. She'd simply refused to see Amelia's fretful overthinking as an impediment and pulled Amelia out from behind her walls. Astonishing.

She grabbed the hotel phone. "I wish to speak to Kai Fisher, room three-oh-three."

A clatter of keys sounded. "I'm sorry, Ms. Fisher has checked out."

Amelia's throat went dry. *Checked out?* Why would Kai rush off without a word? "Were there any messages left? For Lia Hanson?"

"No, ma'am."

Amelia hung up, dismay flooding her. *She's just gone?*

She had a quick shower, which only worsened her mood, then pulled her clothes on in sharp jerks, trying to prevent her mind from wandering where it was trying to.

You told her about Hamadani returning to London. What if she's flying there right now, about to steal your deal?

Amelia yanked on her jacket. *No!* Kai had looked her right in the eye and said she wouldn't do that. Amelia had believed her. She still did. Did that make her a fool?

Striding to Quinn's door, she knocked sharply.

"Come in."

Her deputy's stunned face spoke volumes.

"You know," Amelia said.

"Yeah. They're gone." Quinn sat slumped on the edge of her disheveled bed.

"Do you know why? I was under the impression they'd stay for the speech."

"Kai came by to get Milly, saying it was a work emergency. She looked freaked. Then Kai tore out of here like the devil was on her tail."

What work emergency? Amelia reached for her phone and scrolled to Grand Millennium's Twitter account. She froze at the top tweet from Stein.

"Oh hell." Amelia turned her phone to face Quinn.

Her face froze in shock. "That is *not* good."

"You know Nedal's call I told you about?" Amelia asked, her throat dry. "I told Kai about his plans. So now I can't help but wondering..." She trailed off, feeling foolish and exposed.

"Why did you tell her that?" Quinn asked, eyes wide.

"I needed to know what she'd do." Amelia swallowed. "Looks like we're seeing her answer with her disappearance."

"No," Quinn said firmly. "Kai wouldn't betray you."

"Maybe she wouldn't if it was just about protecting herself. But what if it was protecting her boss from humiliation?" Amelia suddenly found it difficult to breathe. "Because if she can secure that deal with Nedal, then Stein's tweet becomes the truth. His reputation will be saved."

"We don't know she did that." Quinn snatched up her phone. "I'm calling Milly." She eyed the device. "Damn, battery's dead. Lemme just plug it in for a sec and I'll call her."

"Don't bother. Milly will be forced to lie to you to protect her boss, which will hurt you both. It's better not to put her in that position." Her jaw ground.

"Or, there's no lie to tell because they're not doing what you think."

Amelia moved to stand in front of the window. "Kai's The Closer," she reminded Quinn, trying to harden her heart as she faced the bitter truth. "It's in her nature to be ambitious and bold. However, I also thought she was essentially ethical in her work practices. It seems I have been naive."

Quinn frowned. "I think Kai *is* ethical. She is clever but not devious. She wouldn't throw you over for a deal."

"Even if that's normally true, she has a soft streak for her boss a mile wide. Kai loves him. She might consider things she usually wouldn't, such as seizing on a tactical advantage when she realized what would happen if she didn't."

"No, boss, I don't buy it."

If only confidence could make it so. Amelia slumped. She'd trusted Kai. It had made little sense how quickly she'd decided to do so, but she had so wanted to believe Kai. How…disappointing.

Amelia met Quinn's worried gaze. "Do you really think rolling over and just letting the world humiliate Benjamin Stein would be something The Closer would tolerate? Especially when she has the means to stop it happening?"

"Even if she wanted to, I don't think Milly would let her."

"You think adorable Milly Valentine could stop her boss from doing something when the woman has a full head of steam? *That* sounds likely?"

"I think Milly has her boss wrapped around her pinkie, even if she doesn't realize it."

Unlikely. "Do you think their jet's left yet?"

"Want me to find out?"

"No." Amelia's jaw hardened. "Whatever Kai does or doesn't do now, it's out of our hands." Resignation filled her, mixed with loss. Anger kicked in next.

Damn it! Mariam had chosen family over Amelia. And if Kai was on her way to England, then, in a way, she'd done the same. "She's gone now." The line came out laced with an almost embarrassing ache. *Christ.*

Quinn regarded her for a long moment. "You really like her, don't you?"

"God knows why." Amelia couldn't bring herself to evade the question. "I keep getting caught up with people who aren't as invested in me as I am in them. The equation is eternally lopsided." Well…that was uncharacteristically forthcoming. Her cheeks heated. "Sorry," she said stiffly. "I didn't mean to over-share."

Quinn came up beside her at the window. "You know, I often wished you would. We've worked together for far too long, Amelia, to always be at arm's length. I like you a whole lot. I'd love it if you let me in every now and then. Life's too short, you know?"

"I suppose it is. And you have been consistently loyal." She drew in a breath. "Unlike others I could name."

"We just don't know what's happened yet. And from what I've seen of Kai Fisher when she's around you, she'd never betray you."

"If that were true," Amelia said with a glower, trying desperately to harden the words, "she'd be here."

Chapter 23

Unraveling

IT WAS A FOURTEEN-MILE DRIVE to Henderson Executive Airport. Twenty-five minutes in this traffic, the cab driver had said, but it felt like an eternity.

Kai felt Milly's eyes on her the whole time, but she was in no mood to meet her assistant's reproachful gaze. A decision had been made: fix the clusterfuck now; sort out interpersonal relationships later. It's not like they hadn't tried to contact Amelia, but calls to Quinn's phone had gone straight to voicemail, and the woman hadn't answered Milly's texts, either.

"Who has access to Mr. Stein's Twitter account?" Kai asked.

"Just him."

"Are you sure? Rebecca has access to Mr. Stein's emails and work phone. Knowing him, he'd use the same password on everything. She might even be lying about him being out right now and preventing me from speaking to him."

"I don't think she did this, Ms. Fisher."

"Then who?" Kai asked in exasperation. "Someone told him the deal was done!"

"Yes, but Mr. Stein's a grown man and should have known to check with you directly before posting that tweet."

"How do we know he didn't? What about the IT guy? Could he have sent Mr. Stein an email that looked like it was from me?"

"You mean Phillip? He's devoted to Mr. Stein. He'd never hurt him. But isn't the most urgent issue what we do now?"

"I suppose. Unfortunately, there's only one fix," Kai grumbled. "A shitty one."

"What fix? The media's seen the tweet now. Getting it taken down solves nothing, so what do you have in mind?"

"What if I made it true?"

Milly took a few moments to digest her meaning. "You can't possibly mean what I think you do."

"Hamadani's flying back to London as we speak. I even know when and where his plane's landing—Amelia told me. So if we divert to London instead of New York, I could be waiting to make a pitch." Her stomach turned at the words. "I could fix this."

"And Ms. Duxton could never be there first," Milly joined the dots, "because of her speech."

"Right." Kai tasted bile in her throat.

"And she told you that, knowing she could never be there."

"Yes." Kai swallowed. "So i-if I directed our pilot to take us to L-London..." Why were her eyes so wet and blurry?

"Ms. Fisher?"

This was just business. This was what she did: sealed deals. A week ago, she'd never have hesitated. Hell, she'd have loved snatching the deal out from under a Duxton's nose. Laughed in Amelia's face. But now...

Now I know her. She doesn't deserve this. She's not like them. I don't want to hurt her.

Kai's fingers squirmed into knots. "That way *we'll* be the ones to meet Hamadani first."

"Ms. Fisher?"

"I mean...he m-might be agreeable to..." Kai trembled. *Why am I shaking?* This was absurd.

"*Kai.*"

She was yanked out of her downward spiral by Milly's first-ever use of her given name. Kai darted her a surprised look. "Yes?"

"We're not doing that. You are not going to breach Ms. Duxton's trust—her test, if you want to call it what it is—by stealing her deal."

"It's the only way," Kai pleaded. "You must know that."

"Even if that were true, we're not."

Lifting her chin, Kai said, "I'm fairly sure I'm the boss here."

"Kai," Milly said, voice firm, "you're not going to do it because if you did, I would resign." She looked disappointed. "It's underhanded and wrong."

Oh hell. Kai sagged. "I know," she said in a small voice.

Milly regarded her. "Besides, it would break your heart and Ms. Duxton's heart…and mine, too, while we're at it. You already know that or you wouldn't be sitting here crying and shaking even proposing it."

"But I can't *fix* this, Milly! He saved me and I can't save him!"

"You can't save everyone, Kai."

"I just really wanted to do this. I owe him."

"I know, but the price is too high. You'd be the same as those ruthless bosses you've spent your life exposing, who don't care who they hurt. And that's not you. You do not betray people you care about."

"How do you know?" Kai asked, shame flooding her. "I might be as bad as them. I had the thought, didn't I? I seriously considered it."

Milly laughed. It was soft and light and without mockery. "Oh goodness, you never seriously considered it. Your entire body went into a meltdown at the thought of it. I doubt you'd have even made it to the check-in counter. I suspect you'd have been curled up in the fetal position just inside the airport doors."

Kai narrowed her eyes, unimpressed at how close to the mark Milly probably was. Feeling exposed was far outside her comfort zone. Still, a weight had lifted, too. *I'm not going to do this.* "You really think it would have broken Amelia's heart?"

"I'm sure of it. I don't know if you've noticed, but she looks at you as if you're the most confounding person she's ever met."

"Oh, I've noticed."

"She also looks at you as if you're the most fascinating person, too. You're someone she respects. You and Ms. Duxton do business in completely opposite ways—you with your clever schemes, her with her forthrightness. Yet you're both so similar—driven, focused, honorable, and smart. I think neither of you are quite sure what to do with yourself around each other, because you've both finally met your match."

Kai slumped in her seat. "She certainly is different."

"I can't help but notice you didn't argue when I said she was someone you care for," Milly said gently.

Oh. Kai hadn't even paused on it. Alarm shot through her. *Just how far gone on Amelia Duxton am I?*

"Maybe it's best not to overthink it," Milly suggested, seeming to divine her panic. "Sometimes unexpected things just happen. Trust me, I know."

Kai closed her eyes and sighed. *God, I care for a Duxton.* As in *really* care.

"So...where are we flying today?" Milly asked after a silence. "The pilot will need to know if there's a change to his flight plan."

Kai cracked an eyelid. "New York."

Milly said nothing.

"You have a different opinion." Kai opened both eyes.

"I really thought Ms. Duxton's speech would be important to attend," Milly said. "What can you do in New York that you can't do from Vegas?"

"Look Mr. Stein in the eye and explain how he's been hoodwinked—with no one getting between me and him. I have to get to the bottom of this."

"Can't you just Skype him when he surfaces? And investigate everything else by phone for now? It's only a day's delay, but it would mean a lot to Ms. Duxton if you were there."

Kai was considering that as her phone rang. She glanced at it. *Thank God.* "It's him." She stabbed the phone. "Mr. Stein? At last!"

"Kaida, my dear. Sorry I've been out of reach. I think we should talk."

"He's a fake!" Kai's words tumbled out as she launched into a monologue about Nedal, the bad tweet, and how a deal had never been done. "The Duxtons are behind this," Kai finished, voice rising in anger. "I'm not sure which one, but someone's making a fool out of you."

Mr. Stein cleared his throat. "Those damned Duxtons."

Kai blinked. She'd been around the old man long enough to know how he sounded when he was truly outraged. This was not even close.

"You already knew," she said finally.

"Yes."

"How?"

There was a long pause, and then: "I was at a bar with Joe Duxton when you tried to call before."

What the hell? "Why?" she rasped out.

"Joe wanted to ensure I sent out the tweet." He sniffed. "Typical Duxtons. Even when you do a deal with them, there's no trust. Haven't I always said they were a snake pit?"

"A deal? Why are you in bed with snakes?"

"I'm showing everyone what they're like. It won't be long now."

"Can we start at the beginning?" Kai suddenly felt exhausted. "Because the Benjamin Stein I know would sooner fling himself into a volcano than do a deal with a Duxton."

"Normally," he said, sounding slightly guilty. "But these are unusual circumstances. So, the beginning…" He paused. "A few months ago, Joe Duxton called me, asking to meet to discuss a mutually beneficial arrangement. Over lunch, he tells me that at a recent Duxton party, he'd overheard Oliver telling his girlfriend about a scheme he was putting into play. He was extremely pleased with himself."

"What scheme?"

"His usual stupidity. He wanted to hire an actor, have him play a developer, and convince Grand Millennium that we have the world's biggest deal in the bag. He'd wait for me to boast about it on Twitter before it was official…" Mr. Stein paused. "Did you know I was famous for doing this?" He sounded slightly offended.

"Yes, Mr. Stein. I have warned you *repeatedly*."

"Hmph. Well, I get excited!"

"You do."

"So after I announced we had Mayfair Palace, the Duxtons would announce they already had it. Oliver thought his father would think him a genius for humiliating me in this way."

Kai sighed. Juvenile and cruel. Trademark Oliver Duxton. "Where does Joe fit into this?"

"He thought the idea was so ridiculous and risky that it might finally ruin Oliver's chances for CEO. Exposing Oliver as a fool might convince the board to go with Joe's preferred pick—his son, Simon—as the new CEO. At that point, Oliver hadn't disgraced himself by being arrested yet. Joe asked for my help to sink Oliver by going along with the con, then later revealing it."

Kai sat frozen. "Are you saying Joe would expose his family to worldwide ridicule just to ensure Simon becomes CEO? He hides his viper streak well."

"He is smart like that," Mr. Stein noted with a grunt. "And yes, all he cared about was his boy getting power. So, I was told everything about the Vegas sting, including when and where to send you. I agreed to post a tweet about winning Mayfair Palace, and to later leak to the media information from Joe proving Oliver was behind this fake-developer scam. So instead of Grand Millennium looking foolish, the headlines will be how the Duxtons are underhanded and despicable." He sounded pleased. "Exactly as I've been saying for years."

"But what about Amelia Duxton? Isn't she also Simon's competition? How will Joe eliminate her as a threat?"

"She's already been eliminated. Joe sent her off somewhere so she couldn't be at a board meeting she was supposed to attend to present her case. Apparently the board was furious she snubbed them. And he's making her give some big industry speech. Apparently her speeches are so dreary, it'll bury her."

"One bad speech shouldn't ruin a good CEO candidate, though."

"Well, Joe says she also has personality defects—she's too rule-focused, rigid, and black-and-white. She is also homosexual, so Conrad would never approve her." His voice morphed into disdain at that. "And Joe says she's emotionless—she had her own cousin arrested and didn't even care."

"Maybe he deserved to be arrested."

"Probably. Anyway, she's not a contender. All Joe's energies have been on destroying Oliver."

"I...see," Kai said. "And you're okay with all this?"

"What do I care? Simon is no bully like Oliver. A little stupid, but that's for Joe to worry about."

"There's a small flaw in the plan: the Duxtons don't *have* Mayfair Palace. They can't announce what they don't have."

"Not yet, but Joe says it will happen soon."

Kai's stomach dropped as a depressing thought suddenly occurred. "Did you ever even *want* Mayfair Palace? Was any of this real?"

"It is true I met with Hamadani about it in London. He laughed at me." Mr. Stein's voice became tight. "But then he apologized and explained the price he wanted. I realized his hotel was not in our range. Mayfair Palace was never going to be ours."

So all this had been for nothing? Kai couldn't believe it. And it was hard not to notice that in all Mr. Stein's glee at hurting the Duxtons, he'd forgotten something important.

"Why didn't you tell me it was a setup?" she asked, betrayal flooding her. "You used me."

"My dear, it played much better if you looked like you believed what you were doing. When this comes out, there will be eyewitness accounts to sell it. There's a hotel conference going on over there, and you're well-known among the industry. People will have seen you in discussions with that actor. Joe made sure you were always negotiating in public places."

She'd been played just so some reporter could quote gossipy observers in a blow-by-blow telling of the scam that made her a laughingstock? Did her boss even care?

"So," Mr. Stein concluded, "when it all comes out, the Duxtons will be condemned even more thanks to you playing your role to perfection. You did well, my dear."

Kai's temper rose. "Mr. Stein, I'll be known as the negotiator too stupid to spot a fake developer." The reminder of all the little clues she'd glossed over felt even more galling now.

"A small price to pay—but it was necessary, don't you see?" His tone was cajoling.

"Necessary? The worst part is, I didn't even sign a deal, but I'll be mocked just the same as if I had."

"Meh. I was always going to send out the tweet regardless of the deal's outcome."

Kai fell silent. Her humiliation had been planned from day one.

"As The Dragon, you used to reveal the truth about the Duxtons, and now I'm doing it," Mr. Stein finished. "How is what I've done so different?"

"I don't hurt innocents in the process."

"Innocents? Come now, Kaida, you are many things but not an innocent. You know what that vicious family is like. They act so smug, but they're hypocrites. Every single day I regret we were ever in business together."

Shock rippled through her. "*What?*...You and the Duxtons? When?"

He exhaled. "I will tell you, but I do not want it passed around."

"Tell me what?"

"Grand Millennium was originally founded by both Conrad and me. When we were young, we were closer than brothers. When we fell out, I bought him out and tweaked some details in the company history. Few people know. You'd have to look up the official records to find out."

Kai choked.

Mr. Stein sighed. "I know, I know. Some days I do not believe it, either."

"What went wrong?"

"Our families decided I should marry Conrad's sister. Lilith was a lovely girl, a friend, and they kept at me until I agreed. I knew it was a mistake. I told her just after the engagement that I could not go through with it. My family was angry, but the Duxtons acted as though I had spat on her. I was a boot scraping."

"Was she heartbroken or something?"

"Lilith was fine, and she's been happily married to her husband now for forty-seven years. You see, I told Conrad why I could never marry his sister. How it was impossible. Do you understand?"

"Yes," Kai said quietly. "I've known for years."

After a long pause, he said, "Well. I grew up in a different world. Conrad seemed fine at first, but before long, the lies about me started. The Duxtons mocked me often. It died off for a while, but then Oliver grew up and realized the fastest way to his father's approval was to be cruel to me."

"I'm sorry."

Mr. Stein's voice caught. "All I ever did was save a girl from an empty marriage. I did *not* dishonor her. All I want is the truth told about what the Duxtons are really like. So people *see*."

"It must have been devastating. You thought Conrad was family and he betrayed you."

"Exactly."

"But Mr. Stein, I thought *we* were family," Kai said, her voice strained. "How do you think I feel now?"

"It's not the same at all! I was vilified! You— People will soon forget what happened. This is nothing. Come on now, you *know* this is nothing!"

"I'm not saying it's the same as what you went through, but it's also not nothing." Kai felt sick. "From now on, every major story I'm ever mentioned in, my being scammed in Vegas will be the footnote at the end. I'll be a joke. My reputation is about to be trashed."

"You're being selfish, my dear. Exposing the Duxtons is more important than anything else. I thought you, of all people, understood that."

"Revenge matters more to you than me?" Hurt pierced her.

"You're twisting my words. Listen to an old man: I promise it'll blow over. Come home now and we'll talk some more. We'll put this behind us."

Put it behind us? Like it was some silly argument?

Suddenly she didn't care about his old grudge, or about honor, ego, and power-plays, any more than she did the Duxtons' cruel games. She felt so used.

Kai wanted to be away from here, her boss, this conversation. All she wanted was to be with Amelia and watch her present a groundbreaking speech.

"Actually, Mr. Stein, I'd like to network at this conference before I leave. This is important to me. I'll fly out tomorrow." She suddenly realized she had never asked Mr. Stein for anything before.

"No, Kaida, it's time you were back home, doing actual work. Besides, I've missed you," he added cheerfully. "All right? No more debating. Come to New York immediately."

"Mr. Stein—"

"I will see you soon."

The phone went dead. Kai dropped it in her lap and stared at the ceiling of the car for a moment.

She turned to Milly. "Did you catch any of that?"

"All of it." Milly's expression was guarded. "What are you going to do now?"

Kai didn't answer, aware only that she'd never felt less like obeying an order in her life. And he'd just blown through all her objections as if they were nothing. Had her boss just gaslit her? Or maybe he truly believed that what he'd done to her was nothing?

Meanwhile, she'd always seen her relationship with him as closer than family. Apparently she was the only one. Where was his loyalty? Was she only ever a useful tool to him?

The taxi pulled up at the airport. "We're here, ma'am," the driver announced.

Kai's emotions whirled. At the end of the day, what was clear was that Mr. Stein had no problem sacrificing her if it dealt a blow to the Duxtons.

She'd always known that behind his grandfatherly veneer he could be an uncompromising bastard when crossed.

Funny thing was, so could she.

"Driver." Kai leaned forward. "Take us back to Hotel Duxton." She glanced at the time on her phone. "We need to be back by six-thirty. There's a fat tip in it for you if we make it."

The man nodded and stomped the gas pedal.

Milly grinned.

"Are you going to get cocky now about me doing what you suggested in the first place?" Kai allowed a hint of amusement in her tone.

"Me? Oh *never*, Ms. Fisher."

"We're back to that again? Ms. Fisher?"

"Of course. You're my boss," Milly said agreeably. "Unless…are you planning to quit?"

Kai's stomach clenched. "I'm not sure. I'd always thought I mattered far more to Mr. Stein than I do. Apparently, I'm more a means to an end."

Milly eyed her thoughtfully.

"Would it cause you problems if I did quit?" Kai asked.

"No. I would leave, too."

"Why? There's no need. Mr. Stein would give you your pick of postings. Your experience is invaluable."

"Perhaps." Milly lowered her voice, although it wasn't necessary given the driver was now blaring out Johnny Cash on the radio. "But I was only ever in this for The Dragon, not The Closer. When I found out your secret, I was so proud. I'm not brave enough to do what you do—that's not me. I'm more a puppy than a dragon. But if I can support you behind the scenes? I want that. So wherever you go, I'll be with you." She paused. "I mean, as long as you're okay with it."

"Don't underestimate your abilities," Kai said. "Who else to nudge wayward, thick-headed dragons back on their path than persistent puppies?"

Milly's face brightened. "I'm glad you think so, Ms. Fisher."

Kai turned to gaze outside at the dusk. "I'm torn on whether to resign, because I can see why Mr. Stein's so hurt. Imagine having someone you thought of as a brother shun you because of something you can't change about yourself. He's blinded by pain."

"I know." Milly hesitated. "However, Mr. Stein hasn't even thought about your feelings once. He hasn't acknowledged how much he's hurt you, and until he does, I think you'll find it hard to work for him."

"Well." Kai sighed. "I do feel disposable. Honestly, I don't know what I'll do next."

"I'm sure whatever you choose, it'll work out."

Milly's absolute certainty was calming.

Kai decided she didn't want to think about her boss or the Duxtons or their games. She had bigger priorities. Namely one tall, icy goddess named Amelia. A woman who was brave and decent and, according to Joe Duxton, apparently so bad at speeches she might need some moral support.

Now that was someone worthy of her attention.

Chapter 24

Always Bank on Smarts

AMELIA PACED HER ROOM, TRYING to memorize her speech as her nerves and uneasiness grew. Kai should be here, calming her anxiety in that supremely confident way she always had. Oh, Amelia was good at projecting confidence even if she didn't feel it. But Kai made her *believe* it.

So, where was she right now? Halfway to London?

She still fought the idea. The look in Kai's eyes when she'd said she wouldn't go after Amelia's deal had been sincere. But that had been before Stein's tweet.

Her phone rang, and she pounced on it, then immediately deflated. *Not Kai.*

"Hello, Tamara."

"Ms. Duxton. I have news about the Arabic fax."

"Oh?"

"It was sent from Joe Duxton's office machine."

What? Her uncle would never indulge in such juvenile antics as hiring a fake Nedal. "Joe sent it?"

"No, he was out. His assistant did."

"Pamela?" Never had a more dim-witted soul wandered God's green earth. It was the world's worst-kept secret that Joe had hired his PA for her bra size. "Did you ask Pamela about it?"

"Mm. The conversation went something along the lines of: 'Oh, that, yes, I sent it when I was supposed to. Joe left me a reminder, don't worry, it was sent.' And then: 'Oh! Wait, I was supposed to send it from Oliver's fax machine, wasn't I? Well, I don't suppose that was important. As long as they got it in the end.'"

Silence fell. "Joe wanted the fax sent from Oliver's machine," Amelia said slowly. "The only document with a trail that linked to the Duxtons, something Grand Millennium could seize on, and Joe wanted it blamed on Oliver?"

"Yes."

"So Joe was behind the hoax? Not...Oliver?" Amelia still couldn't quite believe it.

"Oh, no, it was your brother. Joe just capitalized on an existing scam."

Amelia blinked. She hadn't told Tamara anything about Fake Nedal. "You know about the scam?"

"Amazing what you find when you tap into the assistants' network. They know everything. Oliver had the idea of hiring an actor to embarrass Grand Millennium. Oliver's assistant, Eleanor, was told to make all the arrangements. She believed the project was just some elaborate practical joke on a friend of Oliver's in Vegas."

Amelia sighed. "Right."

"Eleanor was also instructed to translate a document into Arabic—fake Heads of Terms that Oliver dashed off. He thought it was a hilarious way to screw with his 'friend.' When Eleanor asked whether she should hire a translator, he told her no, it'd be much funnier if it was barely coherent as it'd drive his friend crazy trying to work out what it meant. He said to use a free online tool."

So messing with Kai's head meant more to Oliver than ensuring his scam was watertight? *Imbecile.*

Tamara continued. "Oliver told his PA to send the fax on a particular day from a *non*-Duxton location so it wasn't traceable back to him. He was insistent on that." There was a rustle of papers. "Eleanor was told to send it on the evening of Wednesday the eleventh—"

The day the fax arrived.

"—but two weeks before the scam was due to start, Joe burst into Oliver's office, saying he'd heard about it, that it was a terrible idea, and ordered it shut down. Eleanor was told to turn over all materials to him. The poor woman was shocked to learn Oliver wasn't pranking some Vegas friend at all."

"Joe didn't do a very good job shutting it down," Amelia noted dryly. "The actor arrived, impersonated Nedal, and the fax appeared on cue on Wednesday."

"Yes, that's the interesting part. See, Eleanor says payment for the actor's accommodation and work was meant to be done in cash in Vegas by Oliver, right before the job began. No paper trail that way."

"Makes sense."

"Instead, Oliver was arrested and couldn't go to Vegas, so the actor should have arrived, found no Oliver or money, and left."

"So someone paid him to go ahead with it?"

"I found that a 'Nedal al-Hamadani' was comped for a free stay in Duxton Vegas under Oliver's staff account. Eleanor says Oliver didn't authorize that."

"Joe did?"

"That's my guess. Few people have the power. He's one."

"So Joe made a big scene of declaring how this was a terrible idea to Oliver's staff," Amelia concluded. "He put it on the record this had nothing to do with him. That's a lot of effort for someone not involved."

"Exactly."

So Joe had been setting Oliver up for weeks. A prickle shot down her spine. *Probably not just Oliver.*

Her brain skidded back over every major conversation she'd had with her uncle in recent times. When the emergency board meeting had chosen Simon instead of her, she'd wondered how Joe had been so ineffectual at championing her. She'd had no reason to doubt his efforts—*then*.

"Tamara, can you get me a copy of the minutes from the emergency board meeting?"

"I already have them, Ms. Duxton. When I realized what happened, I thought about why Joe might have done what he did. And, well…Simon is his son and now in line for CEO."

"So would I be right that he didn't sing my praises in that emergency meeting?"

"The opposite. Every time your name came up, he changed topics. Except for one time when someone asked why you weren't there to give a presentation on your candidacy and Joe said you were in Vegas, preparing for a speech and..." She paused and said delicately, "Probably touching up some showgirls."

Joe, you scheming bastard.

"I see." Amelia gritted her teeth. "I'm sure I can guess how it went from there."

"Well, he dropped a few hints about how Simon was good at giving speeches and closing deals, then he kept mentioning all these big deals that Simon had nothing to do with. I think he was trying to subliminally link them in people's heads."

No wonder Joe had been annoyed Mayfair Palace hadn't been signed. That'd be a dream deal for Simon to take credit for.

Amelia thanked Tamara and ended the call.

Jesus. Joe had played her. Had he been scheming for *years* to get his son made CEO? Talk about a long game. All this time, she'd thought he cared about her. She felt ill.

Everything was kabuki theater—choreographed dramatics. Joe storming into Oliver's office, snatching the paperwork off his secretary, then using the information to coordinate with the actor. Secretly comping the actor's accommodation from Oliver's account. There was probably a payment for the actor's fee, too, from one of Oliver's accounts. Something that'd turn up during an in-house audit. All of it left Joe with clean hands, nothing to lead back to him. Except...

There was that ridiculous fax. A fax Joe had known would provide the perfect trail for Grand Millennium to follow and sink its sender.

And it had been sent from the *wrong* machine.

Amelia snorted softly. Even the cleverest of minds slip up sometimes. Joe's mistake had been hiring a PA for cleavage over brains. Amateur mistake.

Always bank on smarts, Joe, she tsked. *Always.*

Chapter 25

The Speech

AMELIA'S PALMS WERE SLICK. IN ten minutes, she'd be in front of the packed convention room. The conference coordinator had pulled her into this backstage area twenty minutes ago, given her one glance, laughed, and told her not to look so terrified.

Easy for her to say.

Amelia had supplied a mutinous glare. The woman had quailed—so that was something—but, it was true, Amelia was not feeling in the least bit settled.

She could hear a distant introduction spiel, something about the state of the industry, followed by a thunder of applause indicating no small crowd.

Amelia wondered how disappointed they'd be to see her, not Oliver. The name change had gone up on the board outside the conference rooms two days ago, but did anyone even read those things?

Nervously, Amelia smoothed down her dress. It was a L'Wren Scott forest-green sheath, flecked with deep crimson, and a matching long, silken jacket. It was beautiful and always made her feel in control. Usually.

Her mind would not stay focused. How could it when her lover might be on her way to steal the deal of Amelia's career?

What felt worse was her sense of loss that Kai had gone. That seemed so out of proportion. How could she feel bereft given how briefly they'd known each other?

A low, appreciative whistle made her turn.

Amelia spun around.

Kai Fisher was sauntering toward her with a cocky grin, as if she hadn't just caused Amelia's tightly controlled universe to crack.

"*Kai.*" Amelia should probably be embarrassed by how much affection and relief her tone revealed. Kai not only hadn't betrayed her, but she was *right here.*

"If I'd known you'd be wearing that stunning number, I'd have never left your side." Kai's voice was admiring. "I'd have loved to have watched you slide that on an hour ago."

Amelia strode over to her. "You're not gone."

"No," Kai said with a smile. "Not gone."

"You checked out! Rushed off." Hurt warred with relief. "No explanation, you were just gone from my bed. I thought I might not see you again."

"I'm so sorry." Kai's eyes expressed regret. "I tried to call, but Quinn didn't answer her phone."

Amelia winced, remembering telling Quinn not to bother with her phone or reaching out to Milly. She had leaped to the worst conclusions far too quickly. Why? Did she think so little of Kai, or did she think so little of herself, that Kai would betray her without thought?

Christ. Both options were awful. She scowled and looked away.

"But you thought I'd left." Kai regarded her with a troubled expression. "For good? That's a...disappointing reaction."

"I saw your boss's tweet." Amelia exhaled, wishing she didn't have to admit the rest. "I'd told you about Nedal, so I wondered if you were off to London to fix Stein's error." Shame rose up. "I wanted to trust you, but I also know how much you care about your boss. I'm sorry, Kai."

"No—don't." Kai drew in a shaky breath. "You weren't entirely off-base. I wanted so badly to protect Mr. Stein that I considered it."

"For how long?" Dread filled her.

"I think...um....five seconds? Milly claims I never seriously considered it because I was having a meltdown at the time." Kai gave a rueful look. "All I know is, I wasn't thinking straight, but the second that I was, I rushed back here."

"Oh." Amelia's mind was in chaos.

Kai took a step closer. "Suddenly the thought of not being here for your speech seemed the worst thing. I just wanted to be here, supporting you as you blow the hotel world apart." She took another step, right inside

Amelia's space. "All I wanted was to stand in front of you and tell you that you amaze me and say, 'Amelia Duxton, you've got this.'"

Warmth flooded Amelia, along with relief, acceptance, and something else from Kai's nearness, something that tingled. "Thank you."

Applause reached a crescendo. A side door opened, and through it, the conference convener's voice boomed. "Coming up we have our keynote speaker, Amelia Duxton, Vice President of the European division of Hotel Duxton International. She will be speaking in place of her brother—"

Adrenalin flooded Amelia. "I'm up."

Kai leaned up and kissed her, lips lingering. "For luck."

Warmth burned through her. "I feel luckier already."

"Good." Kai stepped back. "Okay, go out there and kick ass. You'll be brilliant."

Amelia's heart felt full and her mind clear. She smiled and stepped out into the brightness.

Applause filled Amelia's ears as she slid her speech onto the lectern. The majority of the crowd were male executives, their expressions ranging from neutral to less-than-interested. They were probably annoyed she wasn't her entertaining brother. Or maybe they were just expecting the worst from her given her track record on speeches.

"Duxton Vegas," Amelia began, waving an arm around the room, "is one of my family's hotels, and it's not somewhere I'd *ever* want to work."

A shocked murmur went through the crowd. Two waiters passing out drinks froze and looked up.

"I say this with authority," Amelia said dryly, "because I've just spent a week working undercover here. And let me tell you what I learned."

She waited for the whispers of anticipation to die down.

"Day one. Learning about the points system. All I can say is: don't try this at home."

Chuckles filled the room, and Amelia glanced over at Kai, to the side, who flashed her a thumbs-up and a wide smile.

Well. Maybe she *did* have this.

Amelia came to the end of her speech, and with it the comments Kai had scrawled for her. Inhaling, she read them.

"In three weeks, Hotel Duxton International chooses a new CEO. If it chooses me, I will make sure none of these repressive practices see the light of day again. The theme of this conference is the future of hotels. What is our future, really? New technology, integrated booking systems, VIP passes, loyalty schemes? They all have their uses in efficiency, of course.

"But what makes a hotel even *have* a future, and what makes or breaks its reputation, is the staff. If management streamlines their duties and improves their working lives, then you have a hotel with a bright future."

She eyed the last paragraph of her speech, hesitating, then pushed the page away. Amelia looked up.

"Ten years ago I said something in an interview with a finance magazine: 'At Duxton Europe, we try to establish a connection with our guests so they feel like they're part of our family, no matter how far away from home they are.'

"I stand by those words. Focusing on warmth, compassion, connection, and valuing the staff who make it happen—*that* is our best investment in the future. Thank you."

She'd thrown the quote out on a whim. Now the words Kai had mocked her with on Twitter were the cornerstone of her CEO bid. *Take that, universe!* Amelia sneaked a glance at Kai.

Shaking her head and laughing, Kai was enthusiastically joining in the applause.

Amelia smiled.

She couldn't help but notice that some of the whistles and whooping that had begun—mixed in with the more sedate claps from the wider crowd—came from dozens of Duxton staff lining the walls.

They hadn't been there at the start. Amelia wondered wryly if anyone anywhere in the hotel was getting service at this moment.

A few familiar faces were among them. Mrs. Espinosa, looking stunned, Mrs. Menzies, not much better, and…Monique Carson? She lifted her eyebrows. Well, even CEO sex mistresses might have an interest in the hotel world, she supposed. Lord knew she spent enough time working in one.

The applause died down. Amelia began the Q&A, wondering when her heart would stop racing.

"Ms. Duxton," said one reporter, "did you do a cost-benefit analysis as to how much your company was saving in Vegas by underpaying staff?"

"No," Amelia said, "but I suppose it's not that hard to work out." She stopped and thought about it. She'd seen the expenses in Duxton Vegas's last annual internal report, and she never forgot a number.

"Average employee wages at Vegas hotels are $35,337 per annum, while Duxton Vegas wages only average $24,220 per employee, due to the points system. Now bear in mind, that amount is an average, so many staff earn a lot less."

Amelia quickly did the math in her head. "So the points system gives Duxton an extra $83.377 million bump in profits due to the lower pay for 7,500 employees, minus costs for recruitment and training because we churn through staff. With those costs factored in, Duxton Vegas's lower wages provide the company about a $57.12 million a year boost. Roughly."

The room fell silent.

"Um…" The journalist gaped at her. "You did all that in your head? Just now?"

"Yes." She glanced around. "Next question."

"Ms. Duxton," a female reporter chimed in, "are you anticipating you'll be branded a traitor by your family for these shocking revelations?"

Amelia eyed her sourly. "I'm sure Hotel Duxton is as keen as I am to weed out harmful practices. They'll want to be on top of this." *Well, they probably will be, now I've shamed them.* "As for my standing in my family, that's not for me to judge. You should ask them, shouldn't you?" She smiled a cool, hard smile.

Mercifully, the questions ended soon enough, and the moderator wound things up. Amelia left the stage only to be swarmed by executives. To a man and woman, they informed her she was *brave*. Most wore "better you than me" expressions.

Well, she'd known from the outset this wasn't a safe move.

"Well, well." Monique Carson slunk up. "So look who has teeth. When half the hotel staff started twittering about some speech you were giving, I had to see it for myself."

"Ms. Carson," Amelia said. "Was there a point?"

"Can't I say 'well done,' one businesswoman to another?"

"I suppose so," Amelia said as her combativeness ebbed away. "Thanks."

Monique held a business card out to her. "It occurred to me you might need employment soon. Call me if you do."

Amelia frowned. She was not about to sell her body to… She glanced at the card. *Carson Investments.* Wait, THE Carson Investments? The corporation was worth hundreds of millions. "This is *you?*"

"Yes, darling. My day job here is more an amusing side endeavor I choose to do now that I'm semi-retired. What can I say? I happen to enjoy helping women discover their own bodies. But that's not to say I don't ever talent scout for possibilities in *all* my businesses."

She tapped the card. "I thought it smart to get in first, because I know a diamond investment when I see one. Call me if you need a new opportunity, because you're about to have a lot of offers. And not just offers. I suspect a worldwide shit-storm will soon rain on your lovely head."

Monique melted back into the crowd, and Amelia stared after her in surprise.

Amelia's phone beeped with an incoming text. *Joe.* Her stomach tightened.

So you DO know how to give an entertaining speech. And on the virtues of embracing humanity, no less. How unexpected! Btw Oliver and Conrad want to tear your head off. Probably best to go to ground for a month…or six. Talk soon, Joe

Amelia pursed her lips. A week ago, she might have assumed Joe was just looking out for her, but she knew better now. The text was a barb designed to slice, not her uncle's attempt at humor.

Putting her phone away, she allowed herself to be pulled aside several more times for executives' questions. After they'd moved on, she tried to find Kai.

A tall glass appeared in her hand from a passing server. "Thanks," she murmured.

"No, thank *you.*"

She glanced up and realized the server was Tim.

"Thanks from all of us. Word spread while you were talking. It's online. It's everywhere. All of us working today sneaked in at least once to hear you. You're a legend, Ms. Duxton."

"I see. Thanks for the drink, Tim."

He grinned. "Yeah, well," he scratched the back of his ear, "Thanks for not firing me for getting your order so wrong that night. I got it perfect this time." He nodded at her glass. "That's my best Negroni."

Amelia took a sip. "So it is."

"Okay, boss. I better get back to work." He was quickly swallowed up in the crowd.

Kai reached her side, sliding an arm around Amelia's waist, and gave her a quick peck. "You were great. And that quote! Cheeky devil!"

"Well, I can't let Scorched Earth win a trolling war."

"I'm sure it's hoisting the white flag now. On that topic, I have it on good authority you're live-streaming on their Twitter feed."

"What?" Amelia glanced about to see Milly, discreetly holding a video camera, panning the room.

It was one thing for the conference's website, with its limited audience, to stream the event. But Scorched Earth had two million followers. Amelia winced. "I don't want to be a social media star."

"Too late," Kai said.

Quinn appeared. "Boss," she said breathlessly, "you're melting my phone. Half a dozen business reporters want to talk, and a few big-name hotels have called with feelers out in case you leave Hotel Duxton."

"I'm not deciding anything now. I need to know how the board will vote, and I have to talk to Dad about Joe and his schemes."

Kai's head snapped up. "You know about Joe?"

"Wait, *you* know?" Amelia asked.

"Know what?" Quinn chimed in.

"I only just found out," Amelia said. "Fake Nedal was originally Oliver's scheme. But Joe's using it secretly to remove Oliver as CEO. He wants Simon to be the next boss."

"That skeezy bastard!" Quinn said. "To think I liked him!"

"Um," Kai looked pained. "There's more. Mr. Stein's been working with Joe to roll Oliver. He played me to do it."

Shock filled Amelia. "Stein? The same man who despises every last Duxton?"

"Bollocks," Quinn muttered. "There's a plot twist."

Amelia frowned. "I have no idea how my father will handle this."

"We should discuss it properly before you talk to him," Kai said. "Let's compare notes. And we should celebrate, too. Your speech was a triumph! You're trending worldwide."

"Lucky me." Amelia met Kai's warm, hypnotic gaze, then got a little lost in it.

Finally, Quinn cleared her throat and said, "I'll leave you two to your eye-sex. I'm going to find Milly."

Amelia turned an indignant glare on her deputy.

Quinn snickered, said, "That look doesn't frighten me, you know," and scampered away.

"We scarred your deputy." Kai's eyes danced.

"She'll survive," Amelia said. "I want to thank you, by the way. If not for…" she lowered her voice, "a certain fire-breathing enterprise you run, I would not have had all those facts and figures at hand on industry abuses."

"And I want to thank you for backing up everything Scorched Earth's been saying for years. With that validation, we can be taken seriously. I know you hated having to do that, though."

Amelia couldn't disagree. "It was the right thing to do."

"Amelia? You showed me who you are today. I'm so damned proud of you." Kai gave her a quick kiss, and her hand tightened on Amelia's waist. "You're amazing as hell."

Amelia's cheeks warmed. "Have dinner with me. It's my last night in Las Vegas. Let's celebrate."

"Ooh. Are we celebrating your magnificence today?"

"No. Us." Amelia hesitated. "I'd say we've earned some downtime after learning that people we loved used us for their own ends."

Kai's face fell. "Mr. Stein's going to leak Oliver's involvement soon with dirt from Joe and shout from the rooftops Grand Millennium was conned. My reputation will be toast, but Mr. Stein doesn't care. He says it's nothing."

"I'm sorry. I know he means a lot to you."

"Yes. Maybe I'm an idiot. It's partly my fault for putting him on a pedestal."

Amelia shook her head. "That doesn't make it right, betraying your trust. I'm sure Oliver feels I did that to him. What a mess. I have no idea what the board will make of all this."

"Surely they'll see you're a much better prospect than Simon? You've got him on the mat. You could highlight Simon's weakness as a candidate."

"No. I want the job because I've earned it, not because I've done an effective smear campaign. Not to mention it would devastate Imogen if I started publicly badmouthing her dad."

"Ah. Is that the girl who wants a pet coyote? She's adorable."

"Yes." Fondness rose up in Amelia. "She'll probably want a giraffe tomorrow."

"Tell me, what is it with you and kids?" Kai asked curiously. "I just can't figure that one out."

"I'd have thought it was obvious." Amelia's eyes crinkled. "They're truthful and blunt and have no agendas. I love it when they're bursting with a need for knowledge. I've always thought a clever young mind is an awful thing to waste."

"It is. And it's why your clever mind shouldn't be overlooked for Simon—what a waste that would be. God, that reporter's face when you did eight-figure mental arithmetic! I laughed my head off. I think you stunned the whole room."

"They must be easily impressed."

Kai smiled. "Well, I know I am. So, dinner? That's a big yes from me."

Chapter 26

A Serve at Dinner

DINNER WAS A ROMANTIC AFFAIR, involving a candle-lit table for two at Duxton Vegas's Mexican restaurant.

"The service here is phenomenal," Amelia said as yet another waiter rushed over to fill her wine glass before she could ask. She'd never seen anything like it.

"I'm sure it has nothing to do with what you did for Duxton staff today." Kai smirked. "They're very grateful. *Superstar.*"

"I'm not a superstar. And I don't think this service is anything about me personally."

A waiter stepped up to the table and offered a low bow. "Ms. Duxton, would you and your guest enjoy a visit from our in-house mariachi band?"

Kai snorted.

"No thanks," Amelia said quickly, pushing down her horror at the thought. "We're fine."

"Of course, ma'am." He made a hurried gesture to shoo away a colorful quartet inching toward them and all five disappeared.

"You were saying?" Kai grinned.

"I'm still a Duxton."

"Same name, very different personality. On the subject of family, has there been any word from your father?"

"No. And I don't think...." Her phone rang, and she glanced at the screen. "Speak of the devil."

"Take it," Kai said. "That way you won't spend all night second-guessing how this will turn out."

True. Tensing her jaw, Amelia answered.

"How could you!" Conrad began. "I can't believe you decided on war because I told you to stop spreading stories! It's so disloyal."

"I wasn't being disloyal," Amelia tried. "We have a duty of care to our staff. The points system is legalized wage theft."

"Well, Nevada's Office of the Labor Commissioner agrees. It just announced it will conduct an audit and investigate us for chronic underpayment of staff, among other things. We've had to put out an urgent statement to the media saying the points system was only ever being trialed in Vegas and has since ended. That's humiliating! You're destroying the family name!"

"Our family's doing a pretty good job at destroying that itself."

"Oliver will probably face charges, too," Conrad continued.

"You say that like he shouldn't be held accountable. He made his own bed."

"As you've made yours. And really, Amelia? Bedding that Stein lackey? Have you no taste?"

Amelia darted a startled glance at Kai. "Who told you that?"

"I saw the Scorched Earth live feed. I know you—you'd never allow the intimacy of someone kissing you even in passing, unless…" His voice became icy. "You're *involved.*"

"Who I date is none of your concern."

"So you *are* in league with Stein? No. I'm taking Europe off you. You're done."

Outrage filled her. "In league? Of course I'm not. And if you fire me, Duxton shares will dive."

"Nonsense. Shareholders don't care about our internal politics."

"They do. Because they know what comes next: an investigation. Every shifty scheme Oliver's ever done will emerge. The shares will dive and dive. That's the start. Would you like to know what's going to happen next?"

She could hear her father's sharp breaths. He was listening at least.

"The media will speculate that someone needs to sweep through Hotel Duxton," Amelia continued. "They'll decide it should be me, because they'll look up my record, qualifications, and awards, and conclude that

I'm in no way involved with the abuse scandal since I am the one who exposed it. They will demand a clean broom, and pressure will be brought on the board to appoint me as CEO to stop the plunging share price. And the board *will* listen."

"Simon's a clean broom, too. So we'll throw *him* to the press. Unlike you, he can turn on the charm when he wants."

"But will he do a good job?"

"That's not the point!" her father barked.

"What?" Amelia recoiled. "Then what is?"

"That I will never let anyone *steal* my company from me!"

"Steal…" She stopped. Her father's harsh breathing filled her ear as she turned over the word.

Wasn't that what she'd been trying to do? Steal his company? And if she fought this tooth and nail in the boardroom, Conrad would make it his mission to destroy her.

Even if she succeeded, the bad blood would forever stain the company. She'd be remembered as the one who wrenched her father's beloved company from him. Even if she could save Hotel Duxton International, that didn't make it okay.

Amelia sagged. "You're right."

"Right about what?"

"Hotel Duxton is yours. I know how hard you worked to create it. So, no, I'm not going to steal it. You have my word I won't undermine you in the media, or campaign to take votes off Simon for CEO. If anyone asks me outright, I'll explain why I believe I'm the better candidate, but I won't chase votes. All right?"

"I don't understand."

"Oh, and you should demand Joe's resignation."

"Joe? What does he have to do with any of this?"

"He's working against Duxton interests. He's playing everyone to ensure Simon's CEO."

"Don't be ridiculous! My brother's as loyal as a man can be."

"Joe is working with Stein to get Simon promoted. In fact, he's arranged for Stein to leak to the media that Oliver was behind the fake Nedal con. Joe doesn't care if he embarrasses us all to get Simon in the top job."

"Lies. He would never—"

"Can you please remember this is me you're talking to?" Amelia said in exasperation. "I don't lie."

"You just did."

"And when the story comes out about Oliver, what will you believe?"

"That you leaked it to set up Joe."

Amelia sighed. "Look, Joe's office sent a fax to The Closer outlining Heads of Terms to be negotiated. Pamela sent it on Joe's orders."

"You bribed Pamela to lie? That's appalling."

"Go to the fax machine. Look at the logs. It's easily proved."

"You'd say anything, wouldn't you? I don't believe a word you've just said."

"And you'd go through any mental tricks to avoid facing the truth. But one thing you can't pretend about for too long is what I said will happen to the share price. Its nosedive will start the moment you overlook me as CEO."

"There's no way I want you working for us after what you've done, and you can't force me to."

"Nor will I. Here's the deal: the only way I will take the CEO position is if you ask me yourself, and you get rid of Joe."

Conrad snorted. "Hell will freeze over first."

"We'll see. Now, I haven't had a vacation in years. So I'm taking three weeks off until the board votes. I have therefore neither resigned nor been fired, should the media ask you. That removes any ammunition that you got rid of the most qualified candidate."

He snorted. "Most qualified?"

"Name a Duxton better qualified."

Her father stuttered. "What's in it for you? Just disappearing without a fuss?"

"Do you really care, as long as I do it?"

"What happens after those three weeks?"

"If you don't want me as CEO, I'll quit Hotel Duxton completely."

"Just like that?" Suspicion filled his voice.

"Yes. Quinn can replace me as VP in Europe."

"That mouthy woman? She's not a Duxton." The disdain told her his disapproval went a lot deeper than Quinn being outside the family.

"You're right," Amelia said, tone biting. "She's highly qualified, experienced, and an Oxford University business school graduate, not to mention ethical, clever, and extremely hard-working. So, no, definitely *not* a Duxton. Do you really want to have to deal with spot fires on multiple fronts by breaking in someone new over there? Promote Quinn and you will never have to worry about Europe."

There was a long silence. "Fine. There's enough on my plate."

"So we're agreed," Amelia murmured.

"Yes." After a sigh, her father said, "You're a strange one. You always had a head for business—but that's all you had a head for. You've disgraced our family's name today and don't even get what you've done. I'll never understand you."

"And I'll never understand why you won't believe me when I tell you who the real villains are. But you're one of those people who know what they believe and believe what they know, no other opinions entered into."

"Mumbo jumbo. Christ, Amelia, you were always such a disappointment. You're not even family to me now."

"I know the feeling."

Conrad grunted and hung up.

Silence fell as Amelia's eyes lifted to Kai, whose face was awash with disbelief.

"You're going to *quit*?"

"I'm hoping it won't come to that. But one way or another, my days of running Europe are over. I'll either be CEO in three weeks or unemployed."

"Why did you tell Conrad you wouldn't fight for the job?"

"Stealing my father's company would cause no end of resentment. I'd spend my days battling management loyal to him. And I realized it wasn't right to wrest control of a company he loves more than anything. This has to come from him."

"Will he come around? I can't see him changing in three weeks."

"That depends on how much he loves his baby. And I don't mean me or Oliver." Amelia's mood sank at the reminder.

"I hope your gamble pays off. Not just for you, but for the sake of Duxton's employees."

"Me, too. At least I've secured Quinn's future. She'll be an excellent VP." Satisfaction filled her.

"She'd stay in London then?"

"Of course. It's her home."

"Milly will miss Quinn a great deal."

Amelia reached for her wine. "It's funny. I used to laugh off the idea of love at first sight. With those two, now I'm not so sure. Do you believe in it?"

"I used to believe in *lust* at first sight. God knows I felt it the day I met you. Of course, looking back, I'm pretty sure I misinterpreted our... tension," Kai smiled.

"Oh, so it was hate at first sight?" Amelia lifted an eyebrow.

"Actually, it was a bit of everything. But for some reason I didn't recognize the signs there might have been something else going on. I assumed it was just simple attraction. Chemistry."

"Kai Fisher bad at analyzing human emotions? Isn't that my domain?"

"I freely admit relationships aren't my strength. Honestly, I didn't know how to process someone like you."

"Someone like me?"

"Girlfriend material." Kai gave her a rueful look. "Back when I used to do relationships, I kept choosing beautiful women I had nothing in common with. I couldn't relate to them, and they thought my work was boring. The break-ups were so inevitable that I gave up. I turned to hook-ups every now and then, with no promises and no broken hearts. I thought I was content...until you."

"I make you not feel content?" Amelia hid her smile. "Not the best pick-up line, just a head's up."

Kai groaned. Her expression became earnest. "The thing is, you make me want *more*."

The hope and fear lacing her gaze were almost too hard to look at. Amelia suddenly felt nervous in the face of all that intensity. "Well, that's good, because I can't shake you, either."

"You tried?"

"Didn't you?" Amelia shot back.

Kai laughed. "Of course. But I think two miracles happened at the same time: I was ready for a relationship. And I've met my match."

"Why, Kaida Fisher, are you *flirting* with me?"

"Heh. I remember when you asked me that at the bar. You came right out and asked." Kai shook her head. "Should have known then you weren't like anyone else."

"I almost left that night. Several times. I'm glad I stayed."

"Me, too." Kai aimlessly prodded her salad with her fork. "So what do we do now? I mean aside from the fact I plan to take you to bed soon, and this time, I'm in charge. You got to be bossy last time. I might even try out that idea with you on the desk." Kai threw her a look so heated, Amelia had to force herself not to squirm.

The idea derailed her entire brain.

"You know, I'm not normally that bossy," Amelia murmured. "In bed, at least. I surprised myself. There's something about you."

"You enjoyed the challenge."

"I really did."

They stared at each other.

Amelia's interest in her meal was forgotten. She wondered if she should suggest abandoning their dinner and…

Kai's phone beeped. "It's Milly." Her playful expression fell away as she read the text. "Mr. Stein has redeployed her to a new position because her current role is now obsolete."

"Obsolete? I don't—"

"He's firing me," Kai said slowly. "That's the only explanation. Milly has handed in her notice. She awaits information about my next post."

Amelia frowned. "Why would your boss fire you? That makes no sen—"

Kai's phone rang. *Mr. Stein.* She met Amelia's eyes. "I'm about to find out. Do you mind if I…?"

"Please, take it."

Kai's stomach was in knots. "Mr. Stein."

"I cannot believe it! You're screwing her!"

Kai gasped. "What? Who?"

"The *Duxton* woman." Mr. Stein's voice sharpened. "I saw the way you were around each other. The hand. The kiss." Her boss's voice was cold. "You slept with her? I cannot allow this!"

"Allow… Mr. Stein, that's not up to you."

"You don't deny it?"

"Do I deny dating a woman who is good, decent, beautiful, and brilliant? No." Her eyes slid to Amelia.

"She's a *Duxton!*"

"Who just exposed all her family's dirty laundry. Aren't you happy about that?"

"That just means she has no loyalty. I suppose she's why you didn't come straight home?"

"She needed my help with her speech and—"

"Oh, her speech. *Sure.* I thought you had standards! I won't tolerate this. We can't just brush this away." His voice shook with anger.

Kai's fingers tightened around her phone. It seemed she'd only ever been on the same page as her boss when they'd both hated all Duxtons. How quickly their bond fell apart when she scratched beneath the surface.

"Let me get this straight: I did *one* thing you don't approve of, and you're done with me?"

"You slept with a *Duxton.*"

"You're a hypocrite. How much have you hated being judged for who you choose to have in your bed? You're doing the same to me."

"Not the same, Kaida! Attraction isn't a choice. But you can choose *who* you screw. I'm done arguing. Dump her and return to New York now, or you're fired."

"Haven't you already fired me? You've redeployed Milly!"

"No. Losing her was your punishment for disloyalty. Choose. Right now."

How had he made Kai's love life about him? "Fine. I pick Amelia."

"*Now* you're fired." The phone went dead.

Shocked, Kai lifted her eyes to Amelia. "It seems we're both at a loose end now."

"I'm so sorry, Kai."

"He's so filled with anger, he can't see straight. He thinks I've lost my mind." She ground her jaw. "I'm not blameless in this. I've been foolish."

"I don't follow."

"One thing I've learned as The Closer is how often people see what they want to see. We project onto others our own feelings and thoughts. I'm good at using that to seal a deal, but it turns out I'm blind to it in myself.

I always thought of Mr. Stein as family. I convinced myself he felt the same way. I should have known that the only family he wanted was his own." Her stomach sank. "And that's on me. He's always been who he is, and I was so thankful he saved me when I was at rock bottom that I built him into someone else. In reality, he's no different from everyone else. Flawed and human."

"It's hard learning who people really are."

Kai studied Amelia. "Not for you. You see us all as we are. You don't add layers to people or indulge in wishful thinking. That's unique." She gave a mirthless laugh.

"I don't know about that. Joe had me fooled." Embarrassment tinged Amelia's voice.

"Only because he manipulated you for years. He did that *to* you."

"I suppose. I doubt I'm unique, though."

"Amelia, as someone who spends her days working out what makes people tick, trust me on this. At the bar that first night, you took my measure so precisely, I felt X-rayed. You called me out on all my BS. And it was my best BS, I'll have you know. Top drawer."

Amelia smiled. "Should I be disturbed you grade your BS?" She paused and became serious. "What did you mean about Stein being judged for who he has in his bed?"

"I—" Kai might be furious and disappointed with her former boss, but she wasn't about to out him.

"Has he met some gentleman we're not supposed to know about?"

"You know about him?"

Amelia frowned. "I know that's why he didn't marry Aunt Lilith. She wasn't bothered. She told me years ago, so I'd know what to expect when I came out to my father. She was right. It wasn't pleasant." Amelia waved a hand at Kai's concerned look. "I dealt with it. What will you do now?"

"I was about to ask you the same thing. I could go anywhere, do anything. With…anyone."

Amelia smiled. "You know, I find myself with three weeks of vacation. I don't want to go back home, face jet lag, only to immediately return to the US if I'm asked to be CEO. And I do have a little business in Las Vegas that I want to sort out. Actual business, I mean, not just you."

Kai laughed. "Just trying to picture *you* willingly lounging around Vegas for three weeks. What will you do? Hit the Elvis or Mob Museum?"

Amelia offered an arch look. "Who can say what I'll do?"

"I know you think you're hilarious, but I'm calling your bluff. I'd pay good money to see uptight Amelia Duxton at some of Vegas's dodgier delights."

"You know, I'm not quite as uptight as you think."

"No, you're really not." Kai softened. "You're about nine-tenths marshmallow inside. And I've seen you talking to Imogen, so don't bother denying it."

Amelia rolled her eyes. "Baseless speculation." She sobered. "What a mess. Everything's falling apart. How did it come to this?"

"I think it's been coming to a head for years in both our companies. Your speech was just a catalyst to kick off the implosions."

"Well, partly my speech, and partly your wandering hands," Amelia said. "Without us becoming intimate, the outcome would have been quite different. Stein wouldn't have fired you, for a start. But you're insatiable, so here we are."

"Me? Need I remind you of when you were working in housekeeping? My God, your hands were inside my robe in two seconds."

"Not quite how I remember it."

"Oh?"

"You were virtually daring me to pin you against a wall and have my way with you. You kept playing with the ties on your robe, widening the cleavage..." Heat rose up Amelia's neck. "I was on the back foot the moment you came on to me."

"Your defense is feeble. *You* leapt on *me*."

Amelia's eyebrows rose. "I was helpless to defend myself from your charms. And *so* much skin. You are breathtaking. What was I to do?"

Kai chuckled. "Why, Ms. Duxton, are you trying to get into my pants?"

Amelia eyed her with interest. "Now that you mention it, yes."

Kai glanced at a passing waiter. "Check, please!"

Amelia's eyes gleamed in amusement.

With a smirk, Kai said, "Oh...I have *such* plans."

Chapter 27

The Bubble

THREE WEEKS LATER

"That dinner was incredible," Kai sighed as they waited for the elevator. "I didn't know it was possible for humans to make so many different types of dumplings. And you! I had no idea you had a dumplings fetish. My God, when you were discussing the balance of finely minced beef infused with garlic and ginger in the chef's gyoza, I thought you were about to come."

Amelia sniffed. "You like tragic dance TV shows, I like steamed dumplings from around the world. Everyone's different."

Kai laughed. "You're so full of surprises. And dance shows aren't tragic. You're sounding delusional. But anyway," Kai said quickly as Amelia looked about to argue, "thanks for taking me out tonight. It was amazing."

"It was my pleasure. Besides, you suggested all our other activities." Amelia's eyes narrowed a little. "Did we have to do *all* those silly museums?"

"You're not still mad about what happened at the erotic museum, are you?" Kai's eyes lit up.

"I was never *mad*," Amelia said as the doors opened with a ding to an empty elevator. "I was unimpressed. There's a difference." She stabbed the button for their floor with force.

"Come on, it was funny. I laughed my ass off when you shredded the guest lecturer for calling vibrators 'penis substitutes.'"

"How that stuffed-shirt could claim to be an expert on women's self-pleasure is beyond me. Also, *vibratorologist* isn't a real job." Amelia glowered. "I simply informed him of that fact."

"That's my girl—causing chaos in a sex museum."

"Did you or did you not tell me not to stand by while evil occurs?" Amelia gave her a playful look. "Don't blame me for following your advice."

"That was *evil* you were defeating? Heckling the vibrator guy?" Kai laughed. "But it was a vacation highlight for me for sure. I loved seeing you so fired up about something. It's fantastic. Very sexy. Oh, and did you hear the round of applause from all the women in the group? They loved you."

"Uh-huh."

The elevator came to a stop and the doors opened. Amelia groaned inwardly. Of all the people to meet when she was out with Kai. She braced herself as a certain nosy sex mistress entered.

"Ms. Carson. We meet again," Amelia said stiffly.

"We definitely do." Monique's gaze ran all over Kai. "So *this* is the one?"

"The one what?" Kai asked.

"Did you know when I first met Amelia, she was wound up tighter than a drum?" Monique asked.

"I'd hardly say—" Amelia began.

"No denials—you were." Monique's eyes sparkled. "Do you have her swinging from the chandeliers, darling?" she asked Kai. "Good for you."

"Not your business," Amelia reminded her.

"I suppose not," Monique said with a wave. "Shame. I'd love to know more about who puts that glint in your eyes. You look a lot less like a rubber band about to snap."

"I *am* on vacation."

"Is that what they call it now? Anyway," Monique added conspiratorially, "you two make a *divine* couple. You could be on a magazine cover: *Gorgeous corporate ladies who love the ladies.*" She winked.

Amelia sighed.

The door opened at the sixth floor, sparing her a reply. Monique left with a wave and a suggestion that Amelia call her to discuss "any other business" that was on her mind.

Kai stared after her curiously. "What was *that* all about?"

"That's Monique. She's best ignored. She loves to bait me for her amusement."

"What did she mean when she said, 'So *this* is the one?'"

"She's been trying to work out whether I've acquired a lover. She's intrusive like that."

"Is she some ex?"

"God, no. Monique's a guest I met when I was undercover. She has a fascinating job and I've been talking to her about it recently. She's the head of Carson Investments." As an afterthought, Amelia added, "Oh, and she's also semi-retired and runs a CEO-sex-fantasy business for female clients out of her suite in her downtime."

Kai blinked, then burst into laughter. "That's *so* you."

"Excuse me?"

"Only you would think her fascinating job is the one involving investments."

"Well, the other one is of little interest to me—even if she did try to recruit me once." Amelia gave the faintest shudder.

"I'll bet."

"You don't..." Amelia paused uncertainly, "think I'm interested in her, do you? Are you jealous?"

"Those are two separate questions." The elevator came to a stop on their floor. They exited. "Am I jealous of the MILF sex-goddess with eyes that roam all over you as if she appreciates the promised land as much as I do?"

Amelia wondered what a MILF was.

"Yes, of course I feel a bit territorial," Kai said. "If she stood any closer to you, I'd have considered my more juvenile options, like sliding my hand around your waist and pulling you hard against me." She laughed. "But do I think you're interested in her? I don't. I trust you. The first time we met you were very clear that cheating for you is like lying."

"It's worse. Why betray people when you can just be open and honest?" Amelia sounded genuinely puzzled.

"I love that I always know where I stand with you."

"Of course. If you ever want to know my true thoughts on anything, all you have to do is ask."

"Anything?" Kai teased, as she flipped her key card against the door panel. "Oh, the possibilities."

Amelia followed her into their suite. "I can't imagine what you're dying to know."

"Nothing major. I was actually wondering about Imogen yesterday. That bond you share. Is it because she's like you? Really smart?"

"Yes, she's gifted," Amelia said with a soft smile. "Simon gave up quite early trying to relate to her and outsourced that side of things to me. It's no hardship engaging with someone so full of curiosity. And I also understand how it feels when you don't have someone who understands you."

"You were a misunderstood kid?"

"We moved around a lot, hotel to hotel, when my father was building up his business. It was impractical for me to be in school. I was educated by tutors and had no friends. I felt like I was bursting out of my skin wanting to know so many things, and my tutors treated my intelligence and interest in everything around me as tedious. When I see that same frustration in other children, my heart goes out to them. I was determined Imogen wouldn't feel that way. I love her very much."

Kai leaned back against the door to their suite. "I just realized you don't talk of love often."

"No." Amelia wandered toward the chairs by the window. "Come enjoy the view with me?"

"Sure. And I mention love *all* the time." Kai joined Amelia. In front of them, brightly lit buildings and billboards fought the night's blackness. "I say I love this outfit or that person or that style. I'm not sure I've ever heard you say it once."

"It's an important word. I only use it when I want to invoke all its power." She held Kai's eye. "So, when I tell someone that I love them, they'll know I've thought about it a great deal and I mean it with every fiber of my being."

Kai's eyes widened. "*When* you say it? Not *if*?"

Amelia's eyes became half-lidded. "When, not if." She willed herself not to add anything more. It was too soon. Even so, her heart was thundering at the thought of what Kai might make of her half-admission.

"That's good to know," Kai said with a fond look. "I'm sure anyone told that would be over the moon."

"Anyone?"

"Well, not anyone. But…" Kai fiddled with her watch. "Anyone who felt the same way would."

Amelia smiled as relief flowed through her. "Well, yes. That *is* good to know."

An awkward silence fell. Because how do you follow up an almost-conversation on love? And they hadn't even discussed what would happen after tonight. Three weeks ago, they'd made an unspoken agreement not to let the outside world—with its looming votes and board meetings—ruin their vacation.

Kai stretched a little. "Damn. We're going to have to leave our bubble soon."

Amelia sighed. "Unfortunately. I never thought I'd actually *not* want to leave Las Vegas. It's been a welcome break these few weeks."

"Aren't you nervous about what the board will do?" Kai glanced at her watch. "I mean, in just under forty minutes, you could be CEO of a multinational company in charge of hundreds of thousands of employees. Me, I couldn't be just lying around after dining out, waiting for the outcome. I'd be reviewing whether I'd done enough, and number-crunching allies."

"You know I couldn't actively campaign with the board because of my deal with Dad. I have, however, been approached by four board members at various times in the past few weeks to inquire about my status. I told them all the same thing: I'd be willing to become CEO and I'm the best option, but I'd only take the job if Dad asked me. I'm not interested in a coup."

"That'd have set the cat among the pigeons."

"They didn't have follow-up questions after that."

"So why aren't you nervous?"

"Because I know I won't get the job. I'd have heard from Dad by now if it was happening."

Kai studied her. "You don't sound bothered. Have you got something else up your sleeve?"

"Could be." It was too soon to tell Kai her possible plans. Everything was still in flux. "I do like to be prepared for anything. Monique has offered me a top management job in her investment company. It's one of several I'm considering. I'm trying not to think about the fact I'm Duxton's best

CEO candidate and I'm being overlooked for the worst. I'm focusing on what's next."

"Sounds smart."

"So when Simon is named, I'll go home, formally resign, and examine my other opportunities. And Kai? I'd love it if you came, too."

Kai froze. "You want me to move to England with you?"

"Do you have any commitments in the US I don't know about?"

"No. It's just…this is big."

"I know. I also don't see this, *us*, as some vacation fling. I hoped you felt the same way." She kept her expression neutral, fearful she was giving too much away.

"I do, but it's one thing to be your lover, curled up in your bed in Vegas, and quite another to get on a plane for London to be with you."

"I realize I'm asking a lot. So why don't we try what Quinn and Milly are doing—just have a vacation together in London to see how it goes? No pressure, no commitments, one day at a time. We could do that, too."

Kai fell silent.

Amelia inhaled. "I'm aware it's daunting, but I just can't imagine looking at my future without you in it."

"What if I said I'd rather you moved here?"

"Is that what you'd like? Us in America? I do have offers over here I can look at if that's your preference. Is it?"

"I'm not sure. What would I even do in London?"

"I've thought about that. You're still The Closer, Kai. No one can take that away. You'll still be brilliant at closing high-octane deals, here or in London.

"It's not that I miss the deals, it's that I miss the problem-solving," Kai said. "And I really miss feeling indispensable. I loved having a boss who thought I could do anything. Mr. Stein made me feel like a conqueror, always expecting me to rise to impossible tasks."

"There are plenty of opportunities in London to feel like that again," Amelia said. "I'll support whatever you decide to do, and I have a few suggestions of my own. But in the short term, I just really want to extend our time together. And if you don't like London or we don't fit, that's fine. Nothing's set in stone. But for now, will you come home with me?"

Amelia injected every ounce of sincerity into her voice, hoping Kai would see what she was offering. She rarely let anyone into her private world.

Kai smiled. "I'm in."

"Are you sure?" Amelia asked, even as relief surged through her.

"Am I sure I want to spend more time with my gorgeous, clever lover, who makes my skin tingle when she touches me? Who makes me feel like I'm the most interesting person in the world? Hmm. Let me think."

"To think you once claimed you never did relationships. You're surprisingly good at making me feel wonderful." Amelia smiled.

"I'm still surprised I'm even *in* a relationship. Maybe it'll be a hot mess, maybe not, but how do I know until I try? I'm ready for a risk. I like London. And I want to spend longer in your orbit, too, and see where this goes." She paused. "I'm a little surprised about you, though. Your overactive brain must have many doubts. We've only known each other a month. You're not the adventurous type, usually, are you?"

"No. Which is why I know this is a good idea."

"How so?"

"Kai, when someone who does nothing but calculate odds on all conceivable problems, issues, and outcomes has *no* doubts, it can mean only one thing."

"What?" Kai whispered.

"That you're the one for me." Her eyes crinkled.

"Wow." Kai drew in a breath. She shook her head in wonder. "Hell, a Duxton and The Closer giving a relationship a real shot? The universe must be laughing hard right now."

"Let it laugh. Because we're right where we're meant to be."

Kai smiled. "You know, we have little bit of time yet till we hear the vote result and our little bubble bursts."

"Barely."

"Just enough."

"My phone will be ringing off the hook when the announcement's made. I'll be doing interviews with media from all over as to my thoughts on the decision, win or lose."

"I know." Kai sagged. "You're right."

"So we'd have to be quick."

Kai sat up straight and beamed. "I really don't think that'll be a problem for me. I've been thinking about you having your wicked way with me for the past hour. I'm so wound up, I might be finished before you get me naked."

"Well." Amelia gave her a dangerous smile. "Never let it be said I don't rise to a challenge."

Chapter 28

A London Luncheon

AMELIA GAZED ACROSS THE RESTAURANT'S garden, waiting for their guest to arrive, while Kai studied the traditional English menu with enthusiasm. Being in London with Kai after three weeks apart, having waited impatiently while Kai tied up loose ends at home, felt surreal. All of it did. Like reconnecting with an urgency Amelia had never experienced in her life, needing Kai's touch, her taste, her warmth. Discovering that her minimalist existence at home was only enhanced by another person in her space, not crowded, as she'd feared.

Today, Amelia had overseen the packing up of her office, only too aware it would be the last time she'd ever set foot in the building, or any Duxton office.

Kai had helped, trying to lift her mood, cracking jokes, poking through her economics books under the guise of packing…and naming her Scorpionfish.

Apparently it was now called Boudica, although only after Amelia had rejected "Karen—for its glassy, judgmental eyes" and instructed Kai to stop defaming Karens. Which had led to an amusing argument, many kisses and, as Kai had no doubt planned, a much-improved mood on Amelia's part.

"What on earth is a Toad in the Hole? Does it involve real toads?" Kai asked grimly, still staring at her menu. "No, I don't want to know."

Amelia's smile was tempered by the emotions that had been warring within since she'd left her office for the last time. She'd conquered the world from that room. Won leadership awards. Worked out how to ride out the European economic crisis.

And what had her drive to be Duxton's best manager gotten her? Not her father's approval, that was clear.

"Christ, Amelia, you were always such a disappointment. You're not even family to me now."

Idly, she took a sip of wine and wondered what being called a traitor by Conrad would mean in practical terms. What was there to miss, except Imogen?

That fear suffocated her. Simon hadn't prevented her talking to Imogen—yet. But what if Conrad insisted? Her father had told everyone else in the family to blacklist her, including her mother.

Amelia's throat tightened.

Well. She'd make her own family then. Amelia flicked an affectionate glance at Kai. Beautiful, amusing, clever Kai Fisher...who was busy mumbling about whether Spotted Dick was a real thing.

Amelia smiled.

Kai glanced over the menu at her. "Do the English *know* how their food names sound?"

Amelia laughed and felt a little better.

A shadow fell over them and she looked up. *At last!*

Rising to greet their lunch guest, Amelia then took enormous pleasure in introducing him to Kai.

"Kai Fisher, please meet the real Nedal al-Hamadani. Nedal, this is Kai."

"So *this* is the lovely Ms. Fisher? Delighted!" His face lit up.

"Kai, please. It's wonderful we're meeting at last."

"I do agree. I wanted very much to know this woman who has turned my good friend's head. I'm quite sure I've never seen Amelia this excited about anyone."

"He exaggerates," Amelia muttered. "I'm not...excited."

"Tell that to your red cheeks." Nedal laughed. "Oh, how pleased my sister will be. Mariam despaired of you ever finding someone who made you happy. And now, here we are."

"Here we are," Kai agreed. "I'm sorry you weren't who I was dealing with in Vegas. You're much nicer."

Nedal reached for a water. "Was 'other me' at least good at negotiating?"

"Sort of. He was cunning and slippery. He never let himself get cornered and was forever telling me that I was asking about finer points his lawyers would sort out in detail later."

"Ah," Nedal said. "My father ordered an investigation. We learned the actor usually works in London playing Middle Eastern businessmen and wealthy sheiks. He has been used many times by tabloids and police to catch politicians in undercover stings. A minor, distant royal was even caught out in a bribery scandal involving him years ago."

"I heard about that," Amelia said. "So he's a high-level scammer at least."

"That doesn't make me feel much better," Kai mumbled. "It should have been obvious to me that he wasn't a real developer."

"My understanding is you signed no deal with him, so you were not hoaxed." Nedal eyed her. "This is what Amelia tells me."

Kai flicked Amelia a surprised look.

Amelia said nothing. So sue her for wanting to protect Kai from further ridicule. It was bad enough everyone knew Kai had been dealing with a con artist, thanks to Stein's many tweets.

"Yes," Kai said. "I didn't sign a thing."

"Then you are far smarter than most," Nedal said. "A number of clever and successful people have been fooled by this man over the years."

"So, will anything come of it?"

Nedal's expression hardened. "That is a matter for my father, but I suspect Oliver will have plenty of regrets about involving our family in his games."

"He'll have regrets, too, about the points system," Kai said. "Did you hear he's being sued over it?"

"The class action involving Duxton Vegas staff?" Nedal said. "Yes. My father's idea. He sent several of his top American lawyers to offer free legal assistance and to unofficially help claimants pursue damages. Oliver is appropriately terrified."

Amelia winced. Nedal's family lawyers were infamous. She hoped Oliver wasn't too fond of his wealthy lifestyle.

"So which company won Mayfair Palace?" Kai broke in. "I'm guessing the Duxtons are out."

"I will never sell another hotel to them again." Nedal scowled. "So much disrespect."

"If not the Duxtons, then who? Grand Millennium?"

"Stein is as bad as the Duxtons, going along with childish schemes. I will never sell to him, either."

"Then who? Is it Sheraton? Aren't they expanding right now?"

"No. I sold to St. Eames Hotels."

"I've never heard of them." Kai looked perplexed.

Nedal smiled gently. "Excuse me, I need to wash my hands. I'll let Amelia explain." He rose and left them.

"Amelia?" Kai asked.

"St. Eames is my new company. And my first acquisition is Mayfair Palace. However, since I have limited resources now after emptying out my savings and trust accounts, divesting all my Duxton shares, and selling a small stake in St. Eames to Carson Investments, at this point Mayfair might be my only acquisition. Well, unless it's a big success."

Kai stared at her in amazement. "Wait, you bought Mayfair Palace? God, *you* clinched the deal the entire hotel world wants?"

"I did."

"And...Carson Investments? As in Monique?"

"Yes. That's the business I was finalizing in Vegas. Carson Investments is now a silent partner and owns six percent of St. Eames."

"I still can't believe you pulled this off. Mayfair Palace is a massive coup."

Amelia took a steadying breath before continuing. "I'm also hoping for another coup. I'd like headlines announcing The Closer is joining the world's hottest new hotel company."

Kai gasped. "Did you...just offer me the hotel industry's most plum job?"

"I'll require someone on the ball to help me manage things—a deputy CEO. Ideally someone clever, who's had hotel, marketing, and negotiating experience. Someone I trust. It's London based, so you'd have to move here."

When Kai didn't reply, Amelia plunged on. "In case you're afraid we'd be in each other's pockets, we wouldn't. I'd deal mainly with the financial aspects of hotel management; you'd be in charge of the practical...especially the people—guests, contractors, and staff. I thought we might complement each other well in that regard. Honestly, we wouldn't see much of each other at work."

Kai still hadn't spoken.

Amelia licked her lips nervously. "You should know your skill set is impeccable, and I would offer you the job whether we were dating or not. So even if we break up, I'd still want you running St. Eames. That's just good business. I always think the best person for the job should get it. You're ideal."

"Amelia?" Kai shook her head. "I'm overwhelmed."

Amelia didn't know how to interpret that. Perhaps now was the time to put it *all* out there. Her nervous stomach quivered. "I couldn't think of a better way of using all your skills and asking you to stay in London permanently."

"You want me to stay...for the job?" Kai asked tentatively.

"Of course. And I mean, because..." Amelia drew in a tight breath. "I love you."

Kai's eyes widened. "You do?"

"I felt I did in Vegas, too, but I needed to see how we were outside of the bubble. It's easy to get caught up in a romance far from home. But now you're here, it feels even more right." Amelia's pulse was thundering. "I love you. And the job is yours even if you don't feel the same way. You've earned it. You're a perfect fit. For the job. And me. Well, both."

"Amelia?" Kai smiled. "You're rambling. And I love you, too."

Oh. Thank God. Amelia's cheeks were on fire. "I don't ramble," she protested.

"Sure you don't."

"But I'm glad you love me."

Kai kissed her. "So am I. Okay, so back to your enormous news. Tell me everything about St. Eames."

"I thought Milly could come on board as a PA. I'd like to share her on occasion, but she'd be primarily your assistant. I've offered her a substantial relocation bonus. It's expensive moving countries."

"Well, since Milly will get to spend more time here with Quinn, I'm sure she'll seriously consider it."

"Actually, she said 'Where Ms. Fisher goes, I go.' So thank you—if you come on board, you'll also be bringing St. Eames an excellent assistant."

Kai smiled. "Well, I'm glad she agreed. She has a ton of skills and is so smart." She suddenly laughed. "Oh, I'd love to be a fly on the wall when the Duxtons find out who's buying Mayfair Palace."

"And who's running it with me. Assuming…" Amelia gave her a guarded look. "Will you take up my offer?"

"Didn't I say yes yet? Yes! Of course I'll help you run *the* best hotel in the world."

"Excellent." Amelia beamed in satisfaction. "I have so many plans."

"Me, too. When we get back to your place, I'm going to celebrate so hard with you." Her expression was so blatant that heat flooded Amelia.

"Do *not* look at me like that in public."

Kai leaned over and kissed her soundly. "Please, you love it."

Nedal rejoined them and chuckled. "So, I think I know the answer. Amelia fretted so about whether you'd want to stay on with her."

"I'm in, boots and all," Kai said.

"Excellent. So now that business is concluded, might I ask for a few more details about my fiendish double? This time it is not for me." Nedal's eyes sparkled. "My wife will wish all the salacious information."

Kai laughed and reached for her phone. "Want to see what he looks like? Don't worry, you're way more handsome."

Nedal chuckled. "Ahh, I see how you have captured Amelia. You have a most charming tongue."

Kai's eyes turned bright, and she appeared half a second from an inappropriate comment.

"She does," Amelia cut in, tone painfully neutral. "She really does."

Their eyes met, and Amelia's heart squeezed. This felt so right.

She marveled at the contentment flooding her. It was odd. Two months ago, happiness had meant a very different thing. Everything had to be in its place, and aside from her affection for Imogen and Quinn, the only thing she'd truly valued was running a tight operation. Now it felt as though someone had opened a window, and her view had shifted to trees, sky, the rich scent of peat and the sound of life all around her. The change was as shocking as it was unexpected.

"Hey," Kai whispered. "Are you okay? You went quiet."

"I just realized I'm happy. I love my life. Work will be amazing. And I love you."

Kai's eyes were bright and warm. "As it turns out, I know the feeling."

Epilogue

AMELIA SLID ONTO A STOOL in Prohibition Bar and ordered a Negroni. How the year had flown. It was surreal to be back where it all began.

Tim laughed as he made up her order. "Old time's sake, huh? Great to see you back, Ms. Duxton. How's Europe treating you? I hear you're doing terrific with that fancy hotel of yours."

"It's doing well, thanks, Tim. And how's the new management team treating you? What's turnover like?"

"Much improved, thanks." The bartender placed a drink on her coaster. "On the house. Having no points system helps us a lot."

"I'm glad." Amelia rested one hand on her tailored pants. It was the same executive suit she'd worn the first time she'd been here. She trusted Kai would notice.

Glancing at her watch, Amelia wondered how long her lover would need to finish networking after her speech. "Securing the Deal—Secrets from The Closer" had seen a packed main convention room at Duxton Vegas, not to mention an enthusiastic reception from the hotel executives.

They'd been far warmer in their applause for Kai than for Amelia a year ago, but then, executives did like to hear how to make money, not how their industry had screwed up.

Not for the first time she was glad to have Kai at her side professionally, too. She had such a talent for promoting St. Eames—and with considerably more ease than Amelia could muster.

"May I join you?"

Amelia turned in surprise at the familiar voice. *Dad?*

Conrad Duxton lowered himself stiffly to the stool beside Amelia.

"What can I get you, Mr. Duxton?" Tim asked smoothly.

"Single-malt scotch and some privacy," he replied.

Amelia studied her father. In the twelve months since he'd retired and Simon had taken over, Conrad had rarely been sighted. Whispers around the family said he was depressed, but Amelia suspected it was something else: her father processed change alone.

The lines in his face were deeper, his hair whiter. In his smart black jacket, buttoned up around his lean frame, he could be any traveler to Vegas, seeking a drink before a show. His stooped shoulders told a different story: he didn't want to be here.

Amelia hadn't seen any family member since the board vote. These days she spoke occasionally to her mother, regularly to Imogen—who hated New York even more than green beans—and once to Oliver, who'd told her she was dead to him.

Tim placed Conrad's drink in front of him and walked away to give them the requested privacy.

They each sipped their drinks.

"How're things?" Amelia asked eventually.

"I think you know. I think you know very well." Defeat laced his voice.

"Ah." Yes, she'd caught the news. Hotel Duxton's share price was near rock bottom. It had taken a pounding over the damning Nevada Labor Commissioner's report on staff conditions in Duxton Vegas.

Oliver was facing six months' prison and a fine of up to $5,000 per employee he'd underpaid. The total would be catastrophic, although Duxton lawyers were working overtime to get the fines reduced.

Simon hadn't been faring much better, lurching from one poor decision to another. One financial magazine had named him as one of the five worst CEOs in the US. At least the photo had been flattering—if you wanted a picture of a man in a Hawaiian shirt on Bondi Beach.

"Are you here for the conference?" Amelia asked.

"I caught some of it. But no, that's not why I came. When I saw Kaida Fisher's name on the speakers' list, I made inquiries and found out you were checked in, too. You're not often back in the States; I thought I'd take advantage."

"So this is a friendly family catch-up?" Amelia asked. "Since when do we do those?"

He grunted in agreement, then sighed. "You *can* say 'I told you so.'"

"No thanks." Amelia didn't need her father to grovel. He was probably in hell enough as it was, watching his dream dying. His hotels were being sold off to pay for shortfalls, climbing expenses, and Oliver's legal fees. "Believe it or not, I don't like seeing what's happening to the family business any more than you do."

"You predicted it. You warned me that overlooking staff abuse and putting Simon in charge would lead to ruin."

She had. "Why are you here, Dad?"

"Your new venture is doing well. St. Eames? A second Mayfair Palace is in the works, I hear? In France? I'd have thought the market had dried up on the extreme-luxury end."

"There's always wealthy people with enough money to pamper themselves. You just have to offer guests the best and they'll choose you. But we won't be calling the French acquisition Mayfair Palace. There's only one, and we want guests to believe that one is unique. You diminish the mystique otherwise."

"You always did know hotels," Conrad conceded.

"You put me through the world's best hotel management school. How could I not pick up a few things?"

"It's more than that. You have a nose for it. Your brother doesn't. I really wanted him to. If wishing for a thing would make it happen, he'd be the one who..." He sighed.

"Succeeded?"

Conrad shook his head ruefully. "Was it too much to hope Oliver would at least stay out of prison?"

"He's always shown signs of who he was. The family excused his bad behavior for too long."

His jaw ground, but he didn't argue. "I'm here because the board fired Simon."

Amelia blinked. "How did he take that?"

Conrad's bark of laughter was mirthless. "He said, 'That's fine. Please can I go back to Sydney now?'"

That was Hotel Duxton International's glorious leader? "Ouch."

"Yes," her father said. "Ex-actly." He took a morose sip of scotch. "He'll get his wish. Meanwhile, the board wants you as CEO."

Amelia stilled. Using every ounce of discipline, she hid her sense of vindication. "And what do you and Joe think about that?"

"Joe suggested we instead replace Simon with Douglas, now Douglas has served his time."

Amelia choked. "Joe wants his oldest son to be CEO at the company he *embezzled* from? You can't be serious."

"As a heart attack." Her father's eyes narrowed. "That was the last straw. Joe was fired, too. Well, *retired*. He consistently chooses his own ambition over what's good for the company."

"I bet you didn't like being overruled on that one."

"Actually," he paused, "I moved the motion."

"What?" *Not possible.*

Her father shifted. "The second he recommended Douglas, I saw how self-serving my brother is. It occurred to me in that moment, for all your faults, you would never have done that—suggested an inferior choice for CEO even if it helped you."

"For all my faults?" Anger stirred. "What are they? Turning hotels into profitable empires?"

"You know what I mean."

"That I love women."

"It's not right. I can't change my view on that." Conrad hesitated. "Your mother begged me not to say anything about it when I came here. But since you've raised the topic, can we just…work around it? The board wants you for CEO. I can admit to the merit in that as well. So, what if we just never discuss my views on your…situation?"

Amelia saw his fear. He was desperate for her to agree. "So you'd rather do a deal with the devil than see the company you love founder."

"I'd rather a Duxton rescue it."

"I'm family now?"

"I regret certain statements said in anger. Last time, I was…intemperate."

"Is that your attempt at an apology?"

Irritation crossed his face. "You act like I'm not giving you what you've always wanted. It's CEO of an international hotel chain. My God, it's your family business."

"It's not what I want anymore." She couldn't believe how right saying that felt. "Dad, I'm happy. I run the world's number one hotel. I live with a woman I love, who feels the same. And I'm not prepared to upset our life to fix a death-spiraling company that treated its staff like trash and then complained it got caught. A company so conservative that it ignored the family's superior CEO candidate in order to appoint the only male who wasn't in prison. Not a high bar there."

He sighed. "No need for the recap, Amelia. I was there."

"Now you want me to bail you out—the person who warned you. The person you exiled. Why should I? I don't need the aggravation."

He sagged.

"The irony is, right now you already have on staff the solution. You don't need me."

"What? Who?"

"Quinn Hartman has done incredible things in Europe for Hotel Duxton. She's shown impressive leadership, and her vacancy rates are the lowest they've ever been. And if this was a company not hidebound by tradition, Quinn would have replaced Simon ten months ago, after his first disaster."

"Hartman's not family. Not to mention she's..." He stopped and eyed her in annoyance. "You know."

"Black? Gay? Even blunter than me? Yes, she's all of those. And she has a fine business mind. If you want to fix Duxton, name *her* CEO. And before you dismiss me, remember: You didn't take my advice last time, and look where it got you. Take it this time. I know I'm right."

Conrad eyed her uncertainly.

"Frankly, you should be grateful she's even available," Amelia added. "I know she's been getting offers from all over the world to run hotels, but she *will* actually consider your offer. Aren't you lucky?"

"You've already discussed this possibility with Hartman? You... predicted this? My visit?"

"Of course." She eyed him impatiently. How could he not know this about her? "I asked Quinn two months ago what she'd do if you offered her the CEO position because I like to consider every eventuality. You didn't raise a stupid kid."

"I don't know about that," he muttered.

At her aggrieved expression, he waved his hand. "Not you."

Amelia started. An actual criticism of Oliver? That was new.

"How long?" Desperation entered his eyes. "I know you'll have done the sums. How long does my company have?"

"It'll be dead in eighteen months at the current expenditure and share price plunges. That class action going to court will be what sinks you in the end. A high-profile court case will crush what's left of investor confidence in the Duxton brand."

His jaw tightened. "I'd hoped we had three years."

"You don't."

"So how could Quinn Hartman fix that?"

"You know Hamadani's family lawyers are the ones behind the scenes pushing the class action, to punish the Duxtons for dragging Nedal's name into a scam? Hundreds of hours of time and resources have been donated to the cause, although it's all unofficial. Their involvement is largely payback. Nedal's father is sensitive about his family name and has a vicious streak."

"I'm aware." Conrad's eyes narrowed. "And?"

"Nedal is fond of Quinn thanks to working with us on deals over the years. If Quinn were named CEO, Nedal would want her to succeed. He might talk his father into calling off the dogs. His lawyers might finally urge the employees settle now instead of dragging the case through the courts for maximum humiliation. If it hits court, only the lawyers win."

"We did make a fair settlement offer but were turned down. All right." Conrad straightened. "I'll consider Hartman on one condition. You oversee her for six months."

"She doesn't need overseeing." Amelia frowned. "Why...? Oh. You want to use my name."

"I think 'Quinn Hartman, mentored by hotel-management genius Amelia Duxton' will have a better ring to investors than, 'We couldn't find one of our own so we're trying an outsider.'"

"You think I'm a genius? Talk about burying the lead."

"Don't let it go to your head." Conrad looked pained. "It'll play well in the press, at least."

"Dad, you can't say I'm mentoring your new CEO. How patronizing does that sound? Look, Quinn's CV speaks for itself, so just put that out. All right? It's a good decision, by the way. You won't be sorry."

"I'm already sorry."

She almost snapped before realizing he hadn't meant it how it sounded. "Sorry for what?"

"That I never understood you."

"I'm sorry you didn't, too."

"I take responsibility for my actions, but I think I should explain some things. The day you told me about your...inclinations...Joe was immediately up in my ear about how much shame you'd bring the family. I heard it day in, day out. Same speech he used to give me about Benjamin, years before."

"Are you saying Joe was involved in your feud with Stein?"

"Involved?" Conrad snorted. "He started it. When Benjamin told me he dated men, well, I was young and hadn't heard of such a thing. I talked to my brother and asked what it meant. Could I just carry on as if he wasn't so different and we'd keep working together?"

Amelia stared in astonishment. "You didn't hate him for being gay?"

He shifted. "I...hadn't thought about it long enough to form an opinion. But Joe told me there wasn't anything worse. Whenever I wavered, Joe would say if I wasn't shouting my objections to Benjamin's perversion, everyone would assume we'd been involved because we were so close." His mouth curled in distaste.

Amelia peered at him. "Funny—Joe always told me he had no issue with me being gay."

Conrad's mouth fell slightly open.

"So why would Joe want to poison you against your best friend?" Amelia asked.

"Jealousy, I think. Benjamin was my business partner and not Joe. I didn't want to work with my brother. I knew he'd be as bossy as he always was and try to take over everything. Turns out I was closer to the truth than I ever knew."

"So Joe drove a wedge between you and Benjamin to get involved in your company?"

"That'd be my guess." Conrad stared at his glass. "Truth is, he's drummed into me the shame of homosexuality for so long that I can't see it any other way. I just can't."

"Oh, Dad."

"But the absurdity of all of this is I've gone my whole life fearing our family would be hurt because of your..." Conrad pursed his lips. "*Shame.*" He stopped. "And it never happened. Instead people only ever talk about how exceptional you are. Same for Benjamin. In fact, the only person who mentions shame is Joe." Anger flickered in his eyes.

"He manipulated you," Amelia said. "And me. He's been playing us off against each other for years."

Conrad gave a grim nod. "I should've worked it out sooner. You have never lied to me. I'm sorry I didn't believe you."

"You believe me now. That's a start."

Conrad regarded her for a beat. "Amelia, this doesn't change a thing. I can't magically make a lifetime of beliefs disappear. It's not happening. It doesn't work that way."

"Maybe. But all progress is progress. Doesn't matter how small."

"No, Amelia. I'm too old for relearning everything, so stop looking so hopeful. It's never going to happen." He glanced away, discomfort clear on his face.

Amelia said nothing.

Her father stood abruptly. "I'm going." He cleared his throat. "I expect you at Rosh Hashanah this year. Besides," he rolled his eyes, "my great-niece, Imogen, has far too many questions for us to handle on our own, and that child pouts something fierce whenever you're not around."

Amelia smiled. "I'll be there. I know she always needs urgent answers."

"Always." He hesitated. "And you can bring your friend. Your mother's dying to meet her—she goes on about it often enough. Just don't expect me to make nice with her."

"She has a name. Kai."

"I know her name." Conrad tilted his head. "Saw her speech earlier. Hell of a spitfire. More charm than's probably safe. She'll keep you on your toes."

"She does."

"Opposite of you."

"Yes...except in all the ways it counts."

He shook his head. "Damn, times are changing. I can't believe I'm about to hand over Hotel Duxton to an outsider."

"Is it really the end of the world? Besides, it'll mean your company won't die, not if Quinn's on the case. Your legacy will live on."

"That *is* why I came." He studied her for a moment, then reached out and clasped her hand. He squeezed. The warmth of his rough skin surprised her almost as much as his touch.

"I'm glad you did well for yourself, Amelia. Getting Mayfair Palace? That was some feat. I was in shock for a whole day. Joe turned white as a sheet. I admit, that made me laugh. Never seen anything unsettle him. Anyway, I'm glad at least one of us got it. That made me proud."

Five minutes after her father had left, with Amelia's head still spinning at the encounter, she recognized a scent she knew intimately. She turned.

Oh. Very nice.

Kai wore little red dresses so well. She slid onto the stool next to Amelia.

"Well, hello, stranger," Kai said. "Don't you look sexy? I recognize this outfit." Her lips quirked. "All for me?"

"I could ask the same. You changed after the speech. It's like you know how much I appreciate that dress."

"I don't deny it." Kai waved to Tim. "I'll have whatever she's having." She pointed at Amelia's glass.

Tim nodded from the other end of the bar.

"There's a Negroni in your future," Amelia said.

"Ah. Re-creating old times, are we?"

"It seemed apt for our first anniversary." Amelia smiled. "By the way, your speech was excellent."

"Thank you. I have a purse full of business cards from people wanting to poach me."

"Naturally. What did you tell them?"

"That they can't match the exceptional benefits my boss offers me in my current position." She gave an innocent smile.

Amelia laughed. "You are incorrigible. Well, speaking of job offers, you just missed my father."

Kai's amusement fell away. "What did he want?"

"Simon's been booted back to Australia—with relief all round. Joe's been fired after suggesting his embezzling son, Douglas, take over, so I'm it as CEO if I want."

"What did you say?"

"That I'm happy with St. Eames, and loving life with you in London, and he should promote Quinn if he ever has a hope of rescuing his company. He agreed."

"Just like that?"

"Well…after a fashion." Amelia said, lips curling. "You need to know which of his buttons to press."

"That's huge. I know Milly wants more time stateside to see her family, so this will work out for her if Quinn moves to the US."

"Yes. I'm glad for her, although you'll need a new PA."

"I know." Kai sagged. "I'll have a word with her in case madness seizes her and she feels obligated to stay with me. I'll miss her like hell, but I want her to be happy. Quinn makes her happy."

"Yes, she does." Amelia trailed a finger through the condensation on her glass. "Dad also told me that Joe had been in his ear for decades about how shameful gay people are. It was Joe who kicked off Dad's feud with Stein."

Kai's eyes narrowed. "That asshole."

"No argument."

"So will your dad be nicer to you from now on?"

"He said that none of this changes anything, but in the next breath he invited you to Rosh Hashanah with me. I almost fell off the bar stool."

Kai blinked. "That's like Jewish New Year, right?"

"It is—but in September. It's a big event in our family. Being invited is no small thing. Coming from Dad, it means a lot."

"I'm so pleased for you—and a little terrified for me." Kai chuckled. "I'll be there."

"They'll love you. Mom, at least. Imogen, definitely."

"This is phenomenal, you being back in the family."

"Baby steps." Amelia shook her head. "It's…well, unexpected, but I'm pleased."

Tim reappeared with Kai's drink, lingering a moment to see it was to her satisfaction. Once he was back at the other end of the bar, Kai laughed softly.

"Oh my God! I'm sure I saw his fear when he asked if I liked it. You've terrified him for ever more."

"Doubtful." Amelia smiled.

"You know, the moment you sent back your drink, and pinned Tim's ears back so hard that he looked like a whipped puppy, I was smitten. I wanted to know everything about you."

"You liked watching me correct employee errors?" Amelia asked archly. "How positively evil."

"No, I liked watching the way you ordered your world to be *exactly* as you like it. You were so in control, so sure of yourself. It was a memorable second impression. My first impression, of course, was when I saw you checking in at the lobby. I think I stopped dead and just gaped. Milly had to nudge me to get me breathing again."

"I was just standing there."

"Yes, but with such *authority*. You do understand I meet powerful people all the time, right? But you have an aura of self-assurance that's beyond everyone else. I was entranced by this woman who acted like she owned the place. Of course, it never occurred to me you might *actually* own the place. Clearly I was slow, given you leak 'hotel boss.'"

Amelia shrugged. "Well, now we're both hotel bosses."

"We are." Kai lifted her glass to Amelia in salute and drank.

"On that note, there's something I've been meaning to tell you."

"Oh?" Kai asked.

"Now it's our anniversary, it's probably safe to confess how I came up with the name St. Eames. I was thinking of you at the time."

"I don't follow."

"Just delete the 'es' off the end. When fire meets ice? It's steam. Kai, I wanted the business to be *our* venture. But I didn't want you to feel pressured, so I thought I'd wait to tell you."

Kai stared in astonishment. "Seriously? That's...incredible..." She stopped. "Not to mention a big gamble. We'd only know each other a few months when you named the company."

"Yes, but it felt right. Besides, I liked the name regardless—although obviously I'm very glad we're still together."

Kai smiled. "Well, I love the name. God, can you believe it's been a whole year since I first charmed the hell out of you?" She smirked at Amelia's incredulous expression.

"Charmed me? You had all the subtlety of a bull in a china shop. You asked me if I liked to take charge in all things, including the bedroom! I was a total stranger!"

"Oh, I remember. And you said I crossed a line." Kai snorted. "You're right. I did."

"You had the worst pick-up lines. It was like being trapped in a bad James Bond film."

"Hey! I was carried away by my enthusiasm. For the record, I totally could have won you over, but I didn't know you well enough then." Kai lifted her eyebrows and added, "I'd nail it now."

"Is that so?" Amelia leaned in. "So let's hear it."

"Hear what?"

"Your winning pick-up line to charm me into bed since you know me so well now."

Kai grinned. "All right." She ran her gaze up and down Amelia, then, in her flirtiest tone, asked, "Would you like to come up and taste my Japanese dumplings some time?"

Amelia laughed. "You *have* been paying attention."

Kai's eyes glinted. "I'm in room fifty-oh-six. You like numbers. Can you remember that?"

Fifty-oh-six was their shared room number. "I'll try," she said, dryly.

"I bet you've already committed it to memory."

Ah, she was recreating their first meeting. Amelia darted a look around to make sure no one was watching because she remembered all too well what Kai had done next.

No one was paying them any attention.

On cue, Kai leaned in and danced a fingertip along Amelia's sleeve. She drifted it over to the vee of Amelia's shirt, suggestively tapping the button holding it together.

"That's very forward," Amelia said.

"Don't worry," Kai leaned in even closer, "I *am* after a relationship. Something hot and steamy and long-term. Possibly involving you, London, and maybe even a goldfish in our future."

"A Scorpionfish," Amelia couldn't resist correcting. "Named Boudica."

"Missing the point much?" Kai snorted. "If you keep this up, I'll suggest we put on *Dancing with the Stars* as foreplay."

"No need for threats," Amelia said, before quoting her own words from a year ago. "There's a line between confident and cocky, and you are lying all over it." She curved her lips into a soft, pleased smile. "Just like I'll be lying all over you very soon."

Kai's eyes warmed and her answering smile was gentle. "Is that a promise, love?"

"It is. Your proposal is far from lacking. I think it's time we improve on history." Amelia brushed her lips against Kai's ear in a kiss that offered all sorts of promises. She followed it up with a tiny nip against her earlobe, for old time's sake. "I love you."

Kai laughed. "You've still got it."

"Oh, I agree," Amelia said with the faintest of smiles as she rose, holding out her hand for Kai, "but let's find out for sure."

Other Books from
Ylva Publishing

www.ylva-publishing.com

The Red Files
Lee Winter

ISBN: 978-3-95533-330-0
Length: 365 pages (103,000 words)

Ambitious journalist Lauren King is stuck reporting on the vapid LA social scene's gala events while sparring with her rival—icy ex-Washington correspondent Catherine Ayers. Then a curious story unfolds before their eyes, involving a business launch, thirty-four prostitutes, and a pallet of missing pink champagne. Can the warring pair join together to unravel an incredible story?

The X Ingredient
Roslyn Sinclair

ISBN: 978-3-96324-271-7
Length: 285 pages (103,000 words)

Top Atlanta lawyer, icy Diana Parker, is driven and ruthless, and stuck in a failing marriage. Her new assistant, Laurie, seems all wrong for the job. Yet something seems to be pulling them into a secret, thrilling dance that's far too dangerous for a boss and employee.

How can they resist the irresistible?

A smart, sexy lesbian romance about daring to face the truth about who you are.

Major Surgery
Lola Keeley

ISBN: 978-3-96324-145-1
Length: 198 pages (69,000 words)

Surgeon and department head Veronica has life perfectly ordered...until the arrival of a new Head of Trauma. Cassie is a brash ex-army surgeon, all action and sharp edges, not interested in rules or playing nice with icy Veronica. However when they're forced to work together to uncover a scandal, things get a little heated in surprising ways.

A lesbian romance about cutting to the heart of matters.

You're Fired
Shaya Crabtree

ISBN: 978-3-95533-754-4
Length: 193 pages (61,000 words)

When poor college student Rose Walsh gives out an inappropriate gag gift at her office Christmas party, it backfires horribly. The gift's recipient is her boss, the esteemed president of Gio Corp., Vivian Tracey, and the only thing that can save Rose now is her smarts.

Instead of firing her, Vivian blackmails math major Rose into joining her on a business trip to New York to investigate an embezzlement. A week out of state with a woman she can barely stand seems like the last thing Rose wants to do with her winter vacation. Only, maybe Vivian is not as bad as she seems. Maybe they can even become friends...or more.

About Lee Winter

Lee Winter is an award-winning veteran newspaper journalist who has lived in almost every Australian state, covering courts, crime, news, features and humour writing. Now a full-time author and part-time editor, Lee is also a 2015 and 2016 Lambda Literary Award finalist and has won several Golden Crown Literary Awards. She lives in Western Australia with her long-time girlfriend, where she spends much time ruminating on her garden, US politics, and shiny, new gadgets.

CONNECT WITH LEE
Website: www.leewinterauthor.com

Hotel Queens
© 2020 by Lee Winter

ISBN: 978-3-96324-457-5

Also available as an e-book.

Published by Ylva Publishing, legal entity of Ylva Verlag, e.Kfr.

Ylva Verlag, e.Kfr.
Owner: Astrid Ohletz
Am Kirschgarten 2
65830 Kriftel
Germany

www.ylva-publishing.com

First edition: 2020

No part of this book may be reproduced, scanned, or distributed in any printed or electronic form without permission. Please do not participate in or encourage piracy of copyrighted materials in violation of the author's rights. Thank you for respecting the hard work of this author.

This is a work of fiction. Names, characters, places, and incidents either are a product of the author's imagination or are used fictitiously, and any resemblance to locales, events, business establishments, or actual persons—living or dead—is entirely coincidental.

Credits
Edited by Alissa McGowan
Cover Design by Adam Llyod
Print Layout by Streetlight Graphics

Printed in the USA
CPSIA information can be obtained
at www.ICGtesting.com
LVHW041548200324
775035LV00006B/54